The Trouble with Temptation

SHILOH WALKER

St. Martin's Paperbacks

This is a work of fiction. All of the characters, organizations, and events portrayed in this novel are either products of the author's imagination or are used fictitiously.

THE TROUBLE WITH TEMPTATION

Copyright © 2016 by Shiloh Walker.
Excerpt from *The Right Kind of Trouble* copyright © 2016 by Shiloh Walker.

For information address St. Martin's Press, 175 Fifth Avenue, New York, NY 10010.

ISBN: 978-1-250-06795-1

Our books may be purchased in bulk for promotional, educational, or business use. Please contact your local bookseller or the Macmillan Corporate and Premium Sales Department at 1-800-221-7945, ext. 5442, or by e-mail at MacmillanSpecialMarkets@macmillan.com.

Printed in the United States of America

St. Martin's Paperbacks edition / May 2016

St. Martin's Paperbacks are published by St. Martin's Press, 175 Fifth Avenue, New York, NY 10010.

10 9 8 7 6 5 4 3 2 1

As always, to my family. You're my world.

*Thanks to Monique for believing in the story and thanks
to Alex for putting up with my nuisance questions.*

ACKNOWLEDGMENTS

Thanks to Jim at Turtle Run Winery in Corydon, Indiana. Another thank you to my son, who we shall call Music Man. I needed help on cars and he's becoming something of a car guru when he isn't learning how to play the guitar.

Before Memory

CHAPTER ONE

William was here.

Brannon fought the terror as he sped down the road.

He's dead. I think.

Moira's words circled through his head over and over in an endless loop. His calm, cool, collected older sister had spoken in a shaking voice and he could hear the panic that had underscored her voice.

Moira was *never* afraid. But she'd been petrified.

William was here. He's dead. I think. Neve killed him.

His hands shook and he tightened them on the wheel.

If William Clyde *wasn't* dead, then Brannon would rectify that.

He'd touched his sisters. The son of a bitch would die for it.

Breathing through his teeth, fighting the urge to pound something, he flicked a look at the clock.

When he looked up, he swore long and loud, slamming on the brakes with a force that all but shoved the pedal through the floor of the car.

Joe Fletcher stumbled toward him.

"She's dead. I think . . . I think she's dead. I didn't . . ."

He sucked in a breath and then went to his knees on the shoulder as Brannon rolled down the window to tell him . . .

"Hannah," Joe croaked out.

Nothing else could have gotten through to him. Nothing but that single name. The words penetrated the fog of rage and fear and his aggravation stuttered, veered immediately into a whole new kind of terror.

Hannah. The woman he wanted more than he'd ever wanted anything—the woman he'd walked away from only hours before. *His* Hannah?

Throwing open the door, Brannon went to haul Joe back to his feet.

"She's dead. Hannah's dead . . ." The man wretched, then started to puke.

"Where's Hannah?" Brannon demanded in between spasms. Joe swayed and then lifted his head.

"Fletcher, talk!"

Something in his voice cut through and Joe raised a hand, waved toward the trees on the right side of the road. "She wrecked. I ran off the road and was walking . . . she . . . she almost hit me and crashed."

Brannon dropped Fletcher and turned, staring at the broken and busted greenery on the side of the road.

The red car was buried in it, all but lost in the kudzu and grass.

That wasn't Hannah's car.

He started to breathe once more as he jogged over. Shayla. That was Shayla Hardee's car.

Okay, it was a bad wreck and as much as Shayla annoyed him, he hated to think of her being hurt. But it wasn't Hannah—

Long, golden brown hair shone through the window. Brannon's world screeched to a grinding halt as his gaze landed on the blooming red of blood that dripped down her still, lifeless face.

Chief Gideon Marshall stood in the waiting room of the small county ER.

Small though it might be, the emergency department was state of the art. Gideon suspected there was a plaque somewhere with the McKay family name imprinted on it.

One of the women he loved was tucked away in one of the exam beds, with Ian Campbell at her side.

The other—the one who owned his heart—Moira, sat on a chair a few feet away, her hands clenched into tight little fists while she stared stonily ahead.

He wanted to go to her.

But he couldn't.

Not yet.

"Dead," he said quietly after the deputy on the other end of the phone finished up a quick oral report. "You're telling me you found Shayla Hardee dead."

"Yeah." There was a pause and then Deputy Clayton Hodges said, "Hannah Parker was in Shayla's car when she wrecked. We . . . look, chief, we don't know if she was trying to get help or what, but she was driving Shayla's car and our witness said she was driving like a bat out of hell, too. I know Hannah runs out on the path by the river a lot. We're . . ." He hesitated and then continued. "We're thinking she saw something, maybe whoever hurt Shayla, and she was running away or found Shayla's keys or something. We don't have an official time of death, but Shayla's been dead a couple of hours. Dispatch had a call at approximately ten thirty-eight. The connection was touch and go, but the call-taker says she thought it was Hannah. Hannah said something about somebody being dead."

"She saw something."

"The sheriff is sending in someone to question her—"

"No point," Gideon said gruffly. "She's . . ." He closed his eyes and forced himself to steady out before he said it. "Hannah's in a coma. Doctors aren't sure if she'll wake up at this point or not."

"She'll wake up."

Hearing the low, determined voice, Gideon opened his eyes and stared at Griffin Parker, Hannah's cousin—her only family.

The other man came out of his seat, staring at Gideon with bulldog stubbornness in his eyes.

"Hey, Hodges. I'll get back to you. I'm going to keep a man on her door. We'll talk once you get up here."

He ended the call without waiting for a response.

Eyes on Gideon, he tucked his phone away. "Officer—"

"She'll wake up!" Griffin shouted.

Okay, so much for hoping to remind him to stay focused. Although Gideon couldn't blame him.

"She'll wake up," Griffin said again.

Gideon supposed it was just as much to convince himself as anything else. Moving closer, he caught the other man's shoulder and squeezed. "Okay, then. Okay."

"Chief."

The two men turned as one to look at the doctor, standing in the doorway of the waiting room, one hand on the wall. His face was grim, his eyes dark.

Griffin said nothing, but the way he tensed had Gideon squeeze his shoulder once more.

"She's still alive," Dr. Howard Briscoe reached up and tugged off his glasses, giving them a cursory wipe with a handkerchief he pulled from his pocket. He barely flicked a glance at Griffin, his gaze intent on Gideon.

Too intent.

"What is it?"

The physician inclined his head and stepped back, holding up a badge to the electronic scanner near the door. It slid open with a hiss. "I think it's best if we speak . . . privately."

"Tests show swelling on the brain. Likely the cause of the coma. As she recovers . . ." Briscoe grimaced as he stood at the glass window, staring in at his patient. "It's entirely likely she'll wake up as the swelling goes down."

"But . . ."

"It's not much of a *but*." Briscoe nudged his glasses up his nose, an absent-minded gesture of a man who did the same thing a dozen times a day or more. Briscoe was a tall man, rail thin, his graying hair buzzed short. He was going bald, but he'd never been the vain type and didn't attempt to camouflage his slowly receding hair-line. His eyes were hazel and studious, and still as grim as they'd been earlier.

"What is it?" Gideon asked when Briscoe tucked his hands into his pockets and continued to contemplate the silent form of Hannah Parker.

"We did some tests. Standard tests for all female pa-tients."

He turned then, staring at Gideon, his gaze briefly flicking to Hannah's cousin, Griffin was her only living relative and he'd authorized Gideon's presence. Having a cop in the family made things easier sometimes.

The younger man looked on, eyes narrowed. He hadn't figured it out yet.

But Gideon had.

"Aw, hell," Gideon whispered. Turning away, he rubbed his hands up and down his face.

"Now wait a minute," Griffin broke in, his voice rough. "Are you telling me . . ." His gaze tripped over to his cousin, slid to her belly. There was no so sign of the baby growing there.

Gideon wasn't surprised. He had suspected something

was going on with . . . well, he was assuming. He was pretty damn sure he was right, too, not that he had evidence—so to speak.

Knowing Hannah was involved explained even more. But this was pretty damn recent—had to be.

"She's pregnant," Gideon said quietly.

Briscoe neither confirmed nor denied. After a moment, he said, "I've heard what happened—or what the police think happened. I know Shayla Hardee was murdered, that Hannah was in the area—or supposedly in the area. Is there . . ."

When he didn't continue, Gideon turned to him. "Is there what?"

Briscoe took a deep breath, as if bracing himself to speak. "Speculation is that she was there, saw what happened to Shayla—in the wrong place at the wrong time. But what if Shayla was the one at the wrong place at the wrong time?"

"What are you getting at, Doctor?"

Briscoe scratched his chin. "Hannah is a runner. I see her down at the path along the river all the time when I'm out on my own run. Anybody who knows her is likely to know she'd be out there running. What if *she* was the target and Shayla was in the wrong place at the wrong time?"

"Doing my job now for me, Doc?" Gideon scowled at the idea of what Briscoe was laying out. He didn't like the idea. At all.

"I'm just explaining that there are . . . interesting circumstances," Briscoe said, shrugging. "She's pregnant. Involved in something unusual and she's the only one who could shed light on what's going on."

Shit.

He looked like a maniac, busting through the doors— and the truth of it was, if everybody in town wasn't aware of who the wild-eyed man was, it was entirely possible that the sober-eyed uniformed officer would have been moving toward him with a weapon in hand.

As it was, Officer Griffin Parker caught sight of Brannon McKay and curled his lip.

He'd just wrapped his brain around the fact that his cousin was in a coma and then he got slammed with the *new* fact that she was pregnant and *now* he had to accept the possibility—slim as it was—that maybe *she* had been the victim all along.

The last thing he needed to deal with was this prick.

It was respect for his boss and his badge that kept him from turning away entirely.

But Chief Marshall had told him to keep an eye out for McKay and to be honest, Griffin had his doubts about whether or not the bastard would show up.

Looks like the chief called it again. Griffin tried not to let his temper show as he cut McKay off. He didn't want to be out here playing nice with some rich, entitled prick. He wanted to be back there with his cousin. But he was still on the clock and that meant the job came first.

Marshall had given him thirty minutes of personal time to sit with Hannah and get his head on straight, and by the time he came back out here, he had to admit—yes, maybe he could see why the doctor and Marshall were concerned. No, it *wasn't* likely that Hannah had been the target, but yeah, everybody knew she was down at the park all the time running. Nobody ever saw Shayla down there. She was even known to say that she preferred to do her sweating *indoors, thank you very much, where there are showers to be had when it's all done.* People could tell the day and time by when her damn red car was parked outside the gym—Mondays, Wednesdays, and Fridays from eight to ten and Thursdays from one to three.

Fuck, Griffin hated himself, but he hoped she'd been the target and not his cousin.

Some weird shit was going on and somebody might be trying to hurt Hannah.

As Brannon McKay came striding toward him, he crossed his arms over his chest and pasted a bland smile on his face.

Nobody was getting back there to talk to Hannah without the chief's okay.

Including Mr. Mega-bucks here.

As far as Griffin was concerned, Mr. Mega-bucks didn't ever need to talk to his cousin again. Unless it was over a child support hearing. Then he could bleed zeroes for being an asshole.

"Hey there, McKay." Griffin gave him an easy smile. Nobody had to know that he felt like punching the bastard. Griffin and Hannah were close. Maybe they didn't sit around and braid each other's hair, but he knew his cousin and the woman was in love with this prick. Brannon McKay probably didn't love anything other than his cars and himself. Maybe his sisters. But Hannah hurt over him.

"Out of my way, Parker," McKay said, the words coming out in a low, nearly soundless whisper.

"Can't do that." He gave a mock grimace. "Hannah's condition is pretty serious." He paused and then added, "I assume you *are* here to see her. I think your sisters are down the other hallway—unless they've already come and gone?"

"Get out of my way," McKay said again.

Griffin just smiled. "Come on, now. Shouldn't you be sitting with Neve, patting her hand? She could have been killed tonight. Her and Moira both."

McKay just stared at him coldly.

"That's what I thought."

Unblinking green eyes simply held his and Griffin suspected this could continue indefinitely. He crossed his arms over his chest and settled himself more comfortably.

McKay did the same thing.

His suspicion on how long this might last wasn't tested, though.

In the next moment, the doors opened with a light *swish* behind him, and he heard a familiar voice. "Brannon. Had a feeling you'd show up."

The affable smile on Griffin Parker's face didn't fool Brannon at all. He had to admit, Gideon's timing was spot-on. If he hadn't shown up, Brannon might have done something stupid. Something like gotten into a fist fight with a cop. He thought he could probably take Parker. He was bigger, and he suspected he was stronger. He had a healthy respect for the skinny, wiry type—he'd seen that sort lay a person out flat quicker than it seemed possible, but he'd tangled with his share of skinny wiry types, plus, he'd seen Griffin taking a go at both Gideon and Ian down at the gym.

It might have landed his ass in jail for a while, but Brannon would have had a chance to see Hannah with his own eyes and know she was alive, breathing.

Gideon had saved him from that particular complication and for a while yet, he could say he still hadn't seen the inside of a jail. As he cut around Griffin Parker, he gave Gideon a hard look. "I'm seeing her," he said flatly.

Gideon inclined his head. "Maybe in a bit. We need to talk first."

That wasn't a *no*. Running his tongue across his teeth, Brannon debated and then he gave a quick nod. "As long as you keep it short. I need to see her."

"You can't be alone," Gideon advised.

"Fine." As long as he got to see her. His gut had been in a tangle ever since he'd heard the news.

He'd gone to Neve first.

It had taken him too long to get to his sister, because he'd stood by helpless, as paramedics cut Hannah out of the mangled car, then loaded her into the ambulance. The doors had swung shut before he even had a chance to try and leap in.

So he'd had to follow, emergency flashers on. Heaven help the person who tried to pull him over or slow him down.

They hadn't let him into the emergency room and nobody had told him shit. He'd gone to see Neve and Moira, his older sister's words still playing in his head. *William was here . . . .*

But for the first time in his life, he'd been torn between the love for his sisters and his need for Hannah. He'd clung to his siblings, breathed out silent prayers of relief over their safety.

And all the while, he'd worried over Hannah.

The calls hadn't stopped coming in on his cellphone, either. Apparently Joe hadn't seen the point in keeping it quiet. Half the town knew that Hannah had been driving like a bat out of hell, in *Shayla's* car and thanks to too many people who didn't have much of anything else to do but listen to a police radio, people also knew Shayla was dead.

Heard Shayla died.

Heard you found Hannah.

You got any idea what's going on?

He just might have smashed the phone into nothingness, but he didn't have the patience to get a new phone.

What in the hell was going on?

Not seeing Hannah was driving him nuts.

"Parker."

Gideon's brusque voice caught Brannon's attention and he looked up just as Gideon gave his officer orders to take over for Ruiz.

Ruiz—an image flashed through Brannon's mind. Petite woman. Hispanic. Short cap of black hair, big dark eyes that should have looked soft, but they were wicked sharp and could go hard as nails in a blink.

Maria Ruiz—cop. She was guarding Hannah. The implication of that hit home, *hard*.

"You've got cops on Hannah's door," he said softly.

Gideon lifted a brow. "Yes, we do."

"Why?"

"That's my concern, Bran."

Brannon dragged his hands down his face. "Let me see her," he said abruptly.

"We discussed this."

"For fuck's sake," he snarled, whirling on Gideon. "Just walk me by her damn door. I need to see that she's . . ." His breath caught in his chest. "I have to know she's okay. That's she . . . she's . . ."

He couldn't even finish it.

He couldn't say the fear that had taken root inside him when he'd seen her in the car, all that golden hair spilled around her, her face so still. And the blood . . .

All of his fears, all of them, had happened in one day.

Neve.

Moira.

Hannah.

Raggedly, he said it again, "You have to let me see her."

CHAPTER TWO

Seven days had passed.

Seven days.

Brannon almost had the art of telling time down to a science, all by the annoying little *beep beep beep* that came from the monitor in Hannah's room.

He had all but moved into this hospital room.

Hannah lay still on the bed. Her hair gleamed—he'd spent twenty minutes brushing it that morning, and before he left, he'd do it again.

Unwittingly, he reached out and laid a hand on her belly.

She was . . .

Clearing his throat, he withdrew his hand. Gideon had been the one to deliver that news, his voice calm and efficient. He'd also been the one to catch Brannon's arm when he staggered under the news, and he'd been the one to force him to sit and listen.

Hannah was pregnant. But did it even matter?

The doctors had all been pretty clear.

They'd been optimistic the first day, even the second.

But the more time that passed, the less likely it was that she'd wake up. The swelling on the brain that had caused the coma was gone, but she still wasn't waking up. It wasn't good.

Did the baby growing inside her have a chance?

"Brannon."

He lifted his head, but didn't bother to look at the doorway.

Neve came in and sat down next to him.

"Why don't you go get something to eat?" she said softly.

"I'm not hungry."

"But you need to eat." She leaned over and nudged her shoulder against his. "You're not going to help her any if you fall over the minute she wakes up. You've already lost weight."

He started to argue, but decided it would be easier to grab a sandwich and bring it up here.

Neve was turning out to be like their mother— unmovable once she set her course. "Okay. I'll be back soon."

A smile flitted across her face. "Wouldn't expect it any other way."

He leaned over the bed and pressed a kiss to Hannah's brow. "Wake up." He held still there a moment. "Come back to me."

In his head, he relived those last few moments on her houseboat.

I'm not looking for any sort of relationship. Sex is all well and good, but I don't want anything else . . . I get the feeling casual sex isn't really your speed.

She just gazed at him. Calm, steady. *I've been in love with you since high school.*

It had floored him, scared him, scarred him . . . or so he'd thought. What he hadn't realized until it was too late was that her love, something she would have so easily given, could have very well saved him.

What had he done? Thrown it away. Walked away.

"I'm sorry," he whispered. "I was so fucking wrong. Hannah, for fuck's sake. Come back to me."

It was all he could say at that moment. There were a thousand other things he needed to say, but he couldn't voice even the first word until she was able to open her eyes and look at him.

He tugged on Neve's hair and then headed out, blinking at the overly bright lights in the hallway. He'd kept the lights off for Hannah—when she woke up, they'd seem too bright. But that meant everything was too bright for him.

Wake up, Hannah. Come back to me. I'm sorry . . . .

Wake up.

Come back to me.

Those words were the only thing that felt real.

Other people would talk, but nobody seemed to talk *to* her.

Wake up.

Come back to me.

She was almost *there*.

Groaning in frustration—or trying to—she listened for him again.

But his voice was gone.

Wake up . . . wake up . . . .

"Visiting hours are over, Mr. McKay."

He didn't look up from the book he was reading.

It was a romance Hannah had been reading—he'd gotten it from her apartment and it had been on her nightstand, so he figured she must be enjoying it. He felt stupid as hell reading it out loud to her, but Brannon had done some serious cramming on coma victims and the general consensus was that it didn't hurt to read to a person in a coma. He took that to mean it helped. And if it helped, he'd read every damned book he could find.

If he'd found *War and Peace* in her room, he would have read that boring tome—and he'd lost a bet in college over that damn book. Somebody had said he'd never be able to finish it and he'd put down five hundred saying he would. He'd coughed up the cash just to *keep* from having to finish it. But if he'd found that book in her place, he would have read it, and happily.

"Mr. McKay." The nurse's voice was louder now, and firmer.

He put in the piece of paper he was using for the bookmark and looked up.

"As much as we're enjoying the escapades of that young couple out here at the nurse's station, it's time for you to go home." She arched her eyebrows. "And . . ." She glanced at the uniformed cop standing just outside the door. "I'm sorry to say this, but I think you're embarrassing Officer Billings."

"Officer Billings has two grown kids," Brannon said sourly. "He has to know what sex is."

The nurse, Ginny, just laughed. "I'm sure he does. He's just never had to listen to a boy like yourself *read* about it." Her voice softened and she came in. "Come on, Bran. Go home. Rest. Be back bright and early . . . and shock the day shift with your reading material, if you must."

After a minute, he just nodded. "Fine."

Then, as Ginny gave him a minute, he bent over Hannah's quiet form.

"Wake up, Hannah. Please come back to me. I'm sorry . . ."

Wake up.
Come back.
I'm sorry . . .

She wanted to shout at him. *Don't! Don't be sorry! Be here!*

He was leaving.

He had to be. He only said the words when he was leaving and once he was gone . . .

Frustration flooded her, filled her until she wanted to shout with fury. The faint light that seemed to edge in was suddenly gone. *No!*

"Huh."

Ginny Rollings pursed her lips and pushed her glasses up her nose as she leaned in to study the monitor. The readings had changed.

"Everything okay in here?"

She looked over her shoulder to smile at Officer Billings. With the dim light it was hard to stay if his color had gone back to normal, but if it had, she'd be sure to take a moment to tease him. Just to get him going again.

She enjoyed seeing the man flustered. It was always fun to let his wife know how easy it was to get that big, gruff man of hers to blush.

"Oh, fine," she said, looking down at her patient.

"Well . . ." She bent closer. *I'll be damned.*

A faint line marred Hannah Parker's brow and as Ginny watched, her mouth parted.

She reached for the call light, but then stopped. Every single day, Chief Marshall had been in to speak with the nurses who'd been assigned to care for Hannah—there were a set four who'd been given the task. His orders had been specific.

Perhaps the man was being overly cautious, but then again, perhaps not.

"Officer Billings," she said quietly.

When he looked back at her, she gestured to him. "Would you step in here please?"

*   *   *

Brannon was tired.

He was sore.

His head hurt and he figured he hadn't had a decent night's sleep since . . . well, hell. The night he'd been with Hannah. He was pretty sure he wasn't going to get another decent night's sleep for a good long time. Maybe never.

He was existing on caffeine and donuts and anything he could get from the vending machine at the hospital, and that stuff was pure crap, as evidenced by the fact that his jeans were too damn loose. It was only a week and he had already lost weight.

Since his place was farther out, he'd been crashing at McKay's Ferry, the sprawling estate where he'd lived for the first eighteen years of his life. In many ways, Ferry was still home.

Try as he might, he hadn't been able to slip past Ella Sue, the woman who had taken over the job of raising him and his sisters after his parents' unexpected death twenty years earlier.

Brannon didn't know why he'd even tried. There was no slipping past Ella Sue.

If Santa Claus had been real, he would have been like Ella Sue—she saw when a person was sleeping, awake, in the damn bathroom taking a piss, and everything else.

He'd no sooner taken a step out of his bedroom than he heard her smooth, rich voice drifting up the stairs. "Brannon, honey . . . is that you, boy? Get on down here and have some breakfast with me before you disappear."

And there was no such thing as telling the woman you weren't hungry. You might as well try to tell her there was no sun in the sky, or no stars at night.

So he'd eaten.

She hadn't even had the decency to fry him up something fattening that would have turned his stomach.

No, she'd had oatmeal, creamy scrambled eggs, and toast and if he could have just had a little bit of sleep, he might have felt like a new man. Not that he *deserved* to feel like any kind of man.

Mentally kicking his own ass was getting old, but Brannon had no problem falling into a rut if that was where he felt like he belonged, and he was pretty sure he belonged in this one. As he made the drive to the hospital, he dug the rut a little deeper and worried himself sick all over again.

When are you going to wake up, baby?
What happened out there? What did you see?
Come back to me . . . .

Hannah had gotten hurt only hours after he'd left her at her houseboat.

He had hurt her—not physically, never that. But emotionally, yeah. He'd put scars on her soul. He knew that well enough.

And she was pregnant with his baby.

Right now, it was a closely guarded secret, one known only by him, her cousin, and a few needed medical personnel. Oh, and of course, Gideon. The cop who'd taken the time to interrogate Brannon.

She was pregnant.

Guilt choked him.

He'd hurt her. Then, during the hours when he'd left her and when Joe had stumbled toward him, something awful had happened. Had she seen something? Was she running? Had somebody tried to hurt her? Joe?

Hell, the guy was a stupid piece of shit, but he was more of a nuisance than anything else. Could he have hurt . . . But Brannon pushed the idea out of his head. It didn't make sense. None at all.

Nothing made sense. He didn't know what to think about any of this.

The one thing he *did* know was that Hannah lay helpless in a coma, his baby inside her.

The elevator dinged and he stepped out, caught up in the familiar misery for a moment. So caught up, it took a moment for the low hum of voices to penetrate.

Coming to a stop, he looked up.

The voices came to an abrupt halt at about the same time he did.

He looked from the nurses gathered around the station to the two cops standing vigil outside Hannah's door.

Something that might have been hope tried to grow, but he locked it down tight.

Ginny, a familiar face at the hospital, was still here. She'd been working here as a nurse back when he'd had his appendix out. He couldn't think of another nurse he'd rather have taking care of Hannah. He caught her eye and arched a brow. "You're usually long gone by now, Miss Ginny."

"It was a busy night." The smile on her face made that hope he'd hidden expand.

He didn't remember crossing the rest of the hall, didn't remember rushing into the room, but he must have because he was suddenly being shoved back by an irate nurse. "Do you mind, Mr. McKay!" She smacked a hand against his chest as she shoved him back, and he was so stunned, he let her.

Dazed, he wobbled and he would have collapsed if it hadn't been for the solid, sturdy form of Officer Billings. A hand that was almost the size of a dinner plate patted him on the shoulder. "Let them finish up in there, Brannon," Billings said, giving him a steadying smile. "Then you can go in and . . . uh . . . maybe finish up that book."

Brannon found himself looking down at the book he clutched in his hands.

"Yeah. Um." He nodded. "Yeah."

She was awake.

Hannah had been half-sitting, half-lying on the bed, her gown hanging off one shoulder as the doctor listened to her back. Her hair hung in a tangle around her face. And she had stared blankly ahead toward the door, her eyes open and fogged.

Awake.

Hannah was *awake*.

She was awake.

That fact had been pointed out to her in grand detail several times in the past few minutes.

If she heard one more comment along the lines of . . . *Welcome back to the land of the living*! or *Decided you'd had enough rest, Sleeping Beauty?* she thought she just might scream.

As the doctor shone the bright light in her eyes once more, she winced and tried to push it away.

"I know it's not pleasant," he said, an understanding smile on his face.

Then quit doing it! She managed not to say it, but the words leaped to the tip of her tongue and it was a struggle to bite them back.

"Think you can sit up for a few minutes?"

Instead of telling him she didn't want to, she sighed and wrapped her hand around the bed railing. She already knew she was ridiculously weak. Things had been explained to her and she was trying to wrap her head around everything. She'd been in a wreck. She'd hit her head. She'd been in a comatose state for seven days and sometime during the night, she'd started showing signs of reviving. She'd been awake for . . . how long? She didn't know.

She wanted to get up.

She wanted to walk.

She wanted something more than the ice chips they'd given her, but anytime she asked for water, they said they needed to finish their assessment first. If she heard that *A* word one more time, she had an *A* word for them . . . as in *kiss my A-S-S*.

She sat up—or tried—and her body protested the movement. The nurse, a kind, older woman came to help steady her until she had her balance. Once she was mostly upright, the doctor studied her for a moment and then nodded, pleased. "Your motor skills are coming along nicely, almost like you napped for the week."

"It feels like longer," she rasped.

"You'll get your strength back."

She wanted to ask if everything *else* would come back. But she was afraid.

"Let's finish up here so you can—"

"Hey!"

She lifted her head up at the sharp sound of the nurse's voice. Her heart started to pound at the sight of the man in the door. Tall and broad, his face brushed with stubble and a mouth that fell slightly open at the sight of her. That was fine, because she also seemed to have trouble closing hers just then.

He was . . . wow.

He had a powerful face, framed by vivid red hair. That hair was disheveled, making her wonder if he knew what the idea of a *comb* was. But even as she thought it, she had the image of him driving a big, long-fingered hand through that hair.

Green eyes. Such brilliant green eyes. He stared at her and she felt the punch of his gaze, like he'd reached out and touched her. Images swam through her head.

Then the nurse was standing between them.

"Do you mind, Mr. McKay!" she snapped, shoving

him back out into the hall and slamming the door. "That boy, I swear. Ms. Parker, I'm so sorry."

"Brannon," she said softly.

The doctor's head whipped up to hers and the stethoscope he'd had on her back fell away. "You remember him?"

Hannah swayed on the edge of the bed and the doctor had to steady her.

"His name." She laughed weakly. "I don't remember *mine*, but I remember his. Can you explain that to me?"

CHAPTER THREE

The fine, outstanding officers of McKay's Treasure Police Department thought there might be something besides the car that connected Hannah Parker's accident and Shayla Hardee's murder.

It could have something to do with the fact that Hannah had been driving Shayla's car. Shayla, now deceased.

Never let it be said that the local law enforcement goons were complete idiots. Nobody came outright and said anything about the two incidents, but then again, it wasn't necessary.

He was no fool. Reading between the lines was rather easy, considering the fact that a day didn't go by without a cop standing guard at Hannah's door.

Word of it ripped through the little town like wildfire and people talked about it with near-savage glee. The death of Shayla was almost offhand news compared to what people had to say about Hannah.

Why do think they've got cops sitting with her?

What do you think is going on?

Speculation gave way to rumor, but there was little concrete information.

It was odd, because more often than not, there was always *something*.

But very little was being said about Hannah Parker and her odd accident.

It was a problem—a *big* one. He couldn't visit her without raising concerns. Rumor had it that the only people allowed in to visit her as she lay in the coma were those who'd been already screened and approved by the police, namely the McKay family.

Brannon McKay, the bastard, had rarely left her side.

It made a big problem even more complicated.

Nothing had gone as it should lately.

Of course, if things had gone *as they should*, he wouldn't be here now, would he?

Grimacing, he turned away from the river to stare up toward the town.

He hated this place.

He hated the people.

He hated the town.

He hated the heat.

Somebody ambled by, carrying a soft-sided lunchbox and he nodded. "Heading in to work?"

"Yep." Walt Stephenson wasn't one to move around with a spring in his step, but he definitely had a smile on his face.

Since he had a part to play, he cocked his head and gave the foreman a concerned smile. "How is your wife doing?"

"She's doing just fine." Walt's grizzled face softened as the smile on his face went misty. "She's doing just fine. Doc says she'll be good as new, as long we make some changes in how we eat and she starts exercising and stuff." Walt patted at the belly that strained his shirt. "Won't hurt me to make some changes, either. Yep, she'll be just fine. Things didn't get held up too much here, did they?"

He shrugged. "They don't tell me anything."

Walt squinted his faded blue eyes and then chuckled. "Ain't that the truth? Well, I better get on up there and make sure nothing got messed up while I was gone. I'll see you around."

Once he was alone, he went back to studying the town.

It was still the same, quiet small town it had always been. A few more businesses here and there and a few more people.

The same place he'd hated with a passion for as long as he'd known it.

He counted down the days until he was ready to leave.

But yet again, that prospect had to be put by the wayside. He hadn't found what he was looking for and he couldn't resume his search until he had solved this new problem.

Another problem.

It wasn't enough that Neve had come home and was living back at McKay's Ferry. The more people he had to deal with while he searched, the more it would slow him down. Fortunately she spent most of her time with that bartender, but still, she was another nuisance. Another problem.

Just like Hannah.

What had she seen? Did she know anything?

He couldn't eliminate her unless he had to, because the more he mucked around the mud, the more people would start to ask questions.

Of course, all of this would have been easier if the stupid bitch had simply been courteous enough to just *die*.

How long had he been cooling his heels out here? Twenty minutes, thirty? An *hour*? Brannon didn't know. But *finally*, the door opened and Brannon all but pounced on the doctor standing there.

Before he had a chance to slip past the shorter man, Dr. Briscoe caught his arm.

"Not so fast." Dr. Briscoe caught his arm.

The mild-mannered internal physician was stronger than he looked and his hazel eyes studied Brannon closely. "You need to slow it down a bit, Brannon."

"No," Brannon said slowly, as though he was speaking to an idiot. He knew damn well he wasn't but as far as he was concerned, anybody who tried to get between him and Hannah needed to get their head examined. "What I need to do is get in there to see Hannah."

Briscoe reached up and tugged off his glasses, polishing the round spectacles with a handkerchief he unearthed from inside his lab coat. "Brannon, would you step over to the lounge with me? We can get a cup of coffee and have a moment to talk."

"I'm good, thanks." Brannon gave him a tight smile and tried to go around him.

"I'm going to have to insist." Briscoe's voice went hard and the mild-mannered doctor disappeared, replaced by a man more than willing to go head-to-head with Brannon McKay.

The doctor may or may not win, but Brannon knew if he pushed, he'd have his ass thrown out of the hospital.

The cop standing at the door leaned back up against the wall, and it was clear from the carefully blank look on her face that she was trying not to smirk.

Brannon took a slow breath and then backed up a step. "Five minutes."

"I'm going to be terribly personal here, although it's pretty clear what the answer is."

Brannon felt the blood creeping up the back of his neck. It was the bane of most redheads. He might not be as pale as he'd been as a kid, thanks to spending untold hours out working on the winery he was still busting his ass to make happen, and maybe he wasn't as prone to blushing at thirty-two as he'd been when he was . . . oh, say, twelve, but certain people could still make it happen. Ella Sue. His sisters. And apparently, the good doctor.

As Howard Briscoe turned to look at him, his eyes intense over the steaming cup of coffee, Brannon played dumb.

"Answer to what?"

Briscoe snorted and blew on his coffee. "Don't waste our time, Brannon. I know Griffin and you tried to kill each other the night after Hannah was brought in. He practically spits on the floor when your name is mentioned now. It doesn't take much to figure out why you're hovering at her side non-stop either. You know she's pregnant." He paused and added, "I *do* know you're aware of that fact. This isn't violating patient confidentiality. It's just . . ." He cocked his head. "Make this easy on me and tell me what you know I already know. I'm skating the line as it is."

Brannon didn't know why it mattered, but it seemed to. Dr. Briscoe was a damn good doctor and straight as an arrow, so if he was skating a thin line, there was a reason. Rubbing at the back of his neck, he jerked his head in a nod. "Yeah. It's . . . the baby is mine."

Briscoe tugged off his glasses and pinched the bridge of his nose.

Brannon didn't think he was imagining the troubled expression in the doctor's eyes. "What's going on, Doc?" he asked softly.

But the older man shook his head. "I'm afraid that's not my place to say." He hesitated and then reached into his pocket, pulling out a phone. Brannon stood there as he punched in a number, stood there as he spoke quietly—to his office, it sounded like. Then he gestured to Brannon. "Come on. I need to speak with Hannah. You'll have to wait in the hall a moment. You'll . . . understand why in a moment."

Hannah stared outside.

Fat, shiny green leaves blocked her view of the sky.

They were magnolia leaves.

She knew that.

She also knew she loved magnolia trees and strawberries. She knew she hated raspberries and she knew her mother was dead.

She could remember the son of a bitch who had been her stepfather and knew he'd died—choking on a mouthful of BBQ ribs as he had a massive heart attack, but he hadn't suffered badly enough considering the hell he'd put her mother through.

She also had a shameful secret, because she'd been there at the time.

She could remember standing over him, frozen—not out of fear, but because as he struggled to breathe, she kept seeing the way he'd closed his fat fingers over his mother's neck. Hannah had seen how her mother had struggled for air, time after time after time.

It was odd how she could remember all of those things *and* the fact that she knew that she could have saved her stepfather. She had the knowledge. But she had done nothing. Not for the longest time. She'd just . . . frozen as she remembered how he'd used those big, meaty hands to hurt her mom and she couldn't move.

When she'd finally forced herself to *do* something, it had been too late.

She could remember all of that.

But she couldn't remember where she lived. She couldn't remember what she did for a living.

She knew her name was Hannah—they'd told her. But she couldn't *remember* it.

She couldn't remember if she had a car, she couldn't remember what she'd been doing the night of the wreck—they had told her about that. She didn't remember, although she could sure as hell believe it, because her body *hurt*.

It was like her memory was a giant piece of Swiss cheese and there were entire chunks there—and entire chunks that *weren't* there.

One piece that was there . . . the man.

The red-haired, sexy, god-like creature who'd stood in the door, staring at her as though the entire world had revolved around him seeing her.

To her, it had felt like her heart had been waiting for just that moment to start beating again. Like it had been waiting for *him*. Like she'd had to see him before she could really function.

Brannon.

His name was Brannon.

But she didn't know how she knew that and she didn't know how she knew him.

The door swung open and she turned her head. That simple movement exhausted her, but when she saw who it was, she forced herself to roll over onto her side—facing *away* from the door.

It was the doctor.

She was fed up with doctors and she knew she wasn't even close to done with them.

"Hannah."

"What?" she asked wearily.

Dr. Briscoe chuckled wryly. "You sound like you're tired of me already, Hannah."

She flushed. "I'm sorry. I just . . ."

"No, it's alright. Trust me, I understand. Very few

people get as fed up with doctors as those in the medical profession, I assure you." He sat down on the chair near the bed and braced his elbows on his knees. As he leaned forward, he pressed the tips of his fingers together. He had a pensive look on his face, as though he was giving something a great deal of thought.

"I . . ." She frowned. "In the medical profession. Does that mean—?"

She stopped abruptly, going to lift her hands to her face, but she stopped. An image—a *memory*—superimposed over the hands she found herself staring at. Her own hands, wearing a pair of blood-streaked gloves, while the man next to her patted her shoulder. *Hannah, there was nothing you or J.C. could have done. Nothing anybody could have done . . .*

"I know you," she said quietly. "We—do we work together?"

"In a manner of speaking. What are you remembering?"

Looking up at him, she shook her head. "I'm not sure. Blood on my hands—no. There were gloves. A uniform. I wore a uniform. A stethoscope." She blinked and a piece fell into place. "I drive an ambulance."

"Indeed." He patted her shoulder again, a gentle smile on his long, bony face. It matched his long, bony hands. He had the face of a thinker. A serious thinker.

Hannah abruptly realized he had things he needed to tell her.

"What is it?" she asked warily.

He cocked his head.

"What do you mean?"

"You have this look—like you need to tell me something." She sat up and gingerly swung her legs over the edge of the bed. The nurse and she had fought it out for twenty minutes. They insisted she have the bed rail up because she was considered a patient at high risk for falling. Hannah had said she'd keep her ass in bed, but she didn't want the damn bedrail up.

In the end, she'd let them put it up but as soon as they'd left, she'd exhausted herself by lowering it. It had taken forever and for a few minutes there, she'd thought she might end up taking a header out of the bed, but she wasn't going to be penned up like a child.

She'd lost half of her memories—not her brain entirely.

"It would seem you haven't lost your perception, Hannah." Dr. Briscoe continued to watch her. "I do indeed need to tell you something. I've already talked with several other members of the team, but . . . well." He grimaced. "We're a small staff. We are an excellent hospital, but the bottom line is, we don't tend to handle patients with head trauma like yours. We were going to discuss transferring you out to Baton Rouge if you didn't show improvement within another week."

Nerves started to twitch and jump inside like she had crickets dancing around in her belly.

"Since I'm not still in a coma, I don't see what the issue is."

Briscoe pursed his lips. "There is another concern. The other physicians decided it would be best if I was the one to tell you."

"Oh, shit." The bottom of her stomach dropped out. "I'm dying, aren't I? Is it a tumor? Do I have some sort of slow brain bleed?"

For a moment, Dr. Briscoe just started at her and then he just shook his head, a bemused smile on his face. "No, no, no . . . it's nothing like that, Hannah."

Abruptly, he stood up and came over, sitting on the

foot of the bed next to her. "You know, if your nurse sees that you've got that railing down—and if she knows that I'm leaving it down—she'll have both our hides."

Hannah's stomach pitched and rolled. It had been doing that a lot today. They'd come in to talk to her about a dietary plan and she knew she needed to eat, had thought maybe she was hungry, but the later it got, the more nauseated she became.

"Would you please just tell me whatever it is, Dr. Briscoe? I already feel like I'm going to get sick."

His features softened. "Hannah . . . don't look so terrified. You're not sick, I promise you."

"Then what is it?" she half-shouted.

"You're . . ." He paused and then finally, he said, voice flat, "Hannah, you're pregnant."

Dr. Briscoe quietly closed the door behind him.

Brannan stood close to it, feeling more than a little lost.

Thirty minutes ago, he'd been willing to mow down the Mississippi National Guard to get to Hannah, and now he would have done anything to have just a few more minutes to level off and figure out just what he was supposed to say, what he was supposed to do.

A nurse had helped her into the chair.

She was looking at her knees.

He stood there looking at her.

His hands felt all big and awkward and stupid—why the hell were they so big anyway? He glanced down at them and wondered if he should go over there and hug her. Or at least offer to hold her hand. Maybe brush her hair. He'd liked doing that.

"Are you just going to stand there and stare at me like I'm on exhibit?" she asked.

He swallowed.

She was still looking at her knees.

"I wasn't . . ."

Now she lifted her head, pinning him with a level stare. Okay, Hannah was still in there. Maybe she didn't remember him—or at least remember much about him—but everything that made Hannah who she was? All of that was still buried inside her. It made him feel a little better.

Since he still didn't know what to do with his giant hands, he shoved them in his pockets and inched a little closer. Hesitancy, tentativeness were just not things he was familiar with so it made it that much more awkward for him to ease closer. *Like a bull in a china shop* pretty much summed up how he was feeling just then.

Hannah looked at him, her expression curious.

He opened his mouth, again, to say something.

But she beat him to it. "Were we dating?"

"What?" The question threw him even more off balance than he already felt.

"Dating. You know, romantically involved." She eyed the distance between them and then shrugged. "You're not exactly . . . acting like we're involved."

Blood rushed to his face and he finally gave into the urge he'd been fighting and moved closer. Snagging a chair, he swung it around and sat as close as he could. He'd pull her onto his lap, cradle her close if he thought she'd let him. But she had her guard up. "We're involved," he said gruffly as he reached out and touched her knee. He didn't even see it as a lie, because they were—she was carrying his baby, they'd had sex—the best damn sex he'd ever had and she had feelings for him. *Yeah, like it's one-sided,* his conscience jeered.

It wasn't. It really, really wasn't and for him to realize it while she lay in a coma was a kick in the balls. Now as he tried to figure out what to do and where to go, she sat there staring at him with so much apprehension in her gaze. Apprehension, he realized, that she was probably picking up from him.

You're not exactly acting like we're involved.

No, he wasn't. He knew why, too. He was scared shit-less and Brannon didn't handle that well. This wasn't the time for soul-searching, though.

If he searched his soul, he'd just find her anyway.

There was doubt in her eyes and it dug holes into him. Chances were, some part of her even remembered some-thing. Maybe not the fight, but the hurt, because he knew he had hurt her. The memory of pain was one of those things that lingered long after the actual wound was gone. Even emotional wounds—or maybe most *especially* emotional wounds.

He took her hand, slowly, waiting to see what she'd do. She didn't do anything. She neither gripped his nor tried to take hers away. "We had a fight, Hannah." Clear-ing his throat, he forced himself to speak, staying as close to the truth as he could without saying what had driven her to push him away.

He had to fix that—all of that.

"You were angry at me." With a jerky shrug, he looked away. "We've . . ."

He sucked in a breath and then said, "We've just recently gotten involved. Then we had the fight. You were angry. I left. Neither of us knew about the . . ." His eyes fell to her belly. There was no sign of the life that lay hidden deep inside her, but he wanted to go to his knees and press his mouth to the soft swell, prom-ise that he'd take care of her, and the baby. "We didn't know."

Hannah's face flushed. "How did you find out then?" Her brows drew down low over her eyes. "The doctor shouldn't have told you—that violates my right to confi-dentiality."

"He didn't." Brannon looked away. "Somebody else . . . let it slip."

"How did you feel?" The analytical, probing question made him uncomfortable and he realized he hadn't taken much time to *think* about how he felt, knowing about the baby.

He stroked his thumb across the inside of her wrist, lifted it to his lips. Then he let her hand go, watching as she slowly drew away, fingers curling up into a fist.

"How did I . . ." Rising, he moved over to the window and looked out over the streets of Treasure.

"I don't know." He thought of a hundred little lies he could have said that would have sounded *better* than that. *I don't know.* "At first, I just didn't know what to think. It was like I'd been punched in the head. Now I . . ."

He turned and looked at her, his gaze sliding down to her belly. "I can't describe how I feel. I don't know if I've ever felt that kind of fear, that kind of nerves, that kind of excitement . . . ."

"Kind of like how I'm feeling," she whispered, her voice weak.

Kneeling in front of her, he palmed her cheek. "There are a hundred kinds of fear, Hannah. This one . . . well, I wouldn't give it up."

She searched his face. She thought of the way he'd looked, standing by the window, driving a hand through his hair. The sight had sparked something in her mind, a series of flashes, scraps of memory, really, as he did that same motion, long fingers plowing through his dark red hair.

Now he was looking at her, green eyes stroking over her face like a caress. She felt it all the way down to her toes. Her heart skipped a few beats.

"Okay." Her breath stuttered out of her and she wanted

to reach for him. She wanted to smile at him and she tried to make her mouth form the familiar gesture. Part of her wanted to ask him about the fight, but she was so tired and she wasn't certain she could handle having anything else thrown at her. Awkwardly, she smoothed down the generic hospital gown, wishing she had something else to wear. She felt all but naked, stripped bare and vulnerable as she looked away. "I just . . . well. You don't have to be here. Unless you . . ."

She shot him a quick look and shrugged. "I mean, unless you want to be."

Brannon's brows furrowed and he lifted a hand to rub at the back of his neck. "Excuse me?"

"Well, I mean . . . I guess this was kind of a shock, unplanned and all. Since we just got together." She pressed a hand to her belly, still stunned by what the doctor had told her. "We probably haven't talked about this kind of thing. I don't think we planned it, did we?"

Brannon ran his tongue across his teeth and she had the uncomfortable urge to squirm. Unable to hold his gaze as he watched her so closely, she focused on smoothing out the wrinkles in the gown she wore, one by one.

"I don't plan things."

His voice was closer and she found herself mesmerized by the low, rhythmic sound of it. He could make a killing singing, she'd bet. Dragging her eyes up, she stared at him as he once more came to crouch in front of her, balancing on the balls of his booted feet. "I don't plan. Plans and me . . . well, we don't always work out. I just do."

Her breath hitched as he pushed her hair back. "So . . . if that was a subtle way of kicking me out, it won't work. If you want me gone, Hannah Parker, you'll have to outright say it."

That light touch made her heart slam hard against her ribs. "Should I want you gone?"

"Probably." Green eyes moved to her mouth. "There are probably even a dozen, or a hundred reasons, at least. But I'm not going to help you out by telling you what they are."

Brannon watched as her mouth pulled to the side in a lopsided frown. He wanted to kiss it away, wanting to stroke away all the nerves he could feel burning inside her.

"I feel like I should push that," she said, her voice thick with exhaustion. "I have this feeling I'm mad at you."

He braced himself, but as she continued to look at him, the frown was replaced by a smile. An exhausted, vulnerable one. "But I'm just too worn out to care. How can I still be so tired? I slept for a damn week."

"Being in a coma isn't really the same as sleeping." Guilt started to burn in his gut and he knew he needed to tell her something. But was now *really* the time?

When her lashes started to flutter low, that made up his mind.

It wasn't the time. He'd wait until she was stronger, steadier. Less worn out.

Then they'd talk. Maybe he could use that time to fix the damage he'd caused. Maybe he could undo the hurt he'd caused her.

"Do you want to go back to bed?" He reached out a hand and brushed her hair back. It was lank and dull, evidence of the past week. Her eyes were huge, her cheeks looking oddly hollow. She'd lost weight.

She looked fragile, but her voice was steady when she said, "No. I'm tired of the damn bed."

The idea of *anything* making Hannah Parker look fragile was enough to enrage him. His heart twisted.

He'd do anything if he could just undo the past few weeks.

If he'd been smart, the first time she'd caught his eye, he would have made a move. He'd wanted her for a long time. If he was honest with himself, he'd felt a tug of interest back when she'd been way too young for him. He'd been right to stay away from her then.

She'd been Neve's friend and unlike most of the people Neve normally hung out with, she'd stood out from the pack in so many ways. Most of his little sister's friends back then had clearly been out to use her or just out to hang in odd sort of bubbling, chaotic trouble that had followed along behind Neve McKay like a shadow.

That hadn't been Hannah. She was quiet, though not shy. Serious and brooding as a kid, as though she'd already lived a couple of lifetimes.

Most people in town knew about Hannah's stepdad and when he'd died from a heart attack, the only person who'd really mourned for him had been his wife, Hannah's mom. She'd died a year later, leaving Hannah alone.

No, he couldn't have done anything the first time he'd really noticed Hannah. She'd been fifteen and he'd been twenty, already in college. Maybe she'd acted older than most high school kids, but that didn't change a damn thing.

When he'd come home, she'd been gone herself, off to school in Florida, although she'd ended up leaving early and transferring to a smaller, local school and when he'd seen her again, he'd felt it. That hard, demanding tug of attraction.

She'd felt it, too. Their eyes had met while she was out on a date and both of them had felt it—he'd seen it in her warm, dark eyes, but he'd shoved it aside. Not just because she'd been with another guy, either.

Brennan avoided anything but the most superficial of relationships and he always had.

Then there had come a time when she hadn't been with some guy and he'd run into her. Her glances would linger and he had still ignored that tug between them. He'd ignored the attraction—and her.

Why?

The answer, though, was ridiculously simple.

Brannon McKay was a coward.

He knew too much about losing people.

He'd been down that road before and it had all but destroyed his family.

It had all but destroyed *him*.

He could look back at all the things he'd done wrong, all the mistakes both he and Moira had made, the shit they'd done that had screwed Neve up. Everything they'd done wrong. They'd almost lost Neve because of it. Just days ago, he'd almost lost *both* of them and he was still sick about that.

Now, standing there staring at Hannah, he realized that it hadn't done any good—the so-called limits he'd tried to impose on himself. He still wanted her. He still cared. Too much.

Her gaze skittered to his, lingered and then moved away. "I don't understand this. Why . . ."

She stopped. Just stopped.

He knelt in front of her again, covering her hand with his.

"What?" he asked. He'd spent too much time ignoring everything about her and it hadn't done a damn bit of good. He was already lost in her and he'd come so close to her being gone. Now he wanted to know all the things he'd pretended weren't there, weren't real. He wanted to know what she was thinking, feeling, doing. He wanted to know what she was hiding.

Her jaw went tight when she swung her head back around to look at him. "It's just . . ." She closed her eyes and rested her head back against the chair. "It's everything. Not remembering the most basic things. Being so tired. Part of me feels like I need to be angry with you and the other part wants to just grab you and hold on."

"I like the idea of you grabbing me and holding on."

Her lashes flew open and her gaze bounced to his.

Shrugging, he sat back down in front of her and slowly took her hands in his. "Go ahead and hold on, Hannah. I'm not going anywhere."

Her gaze softened.

"I might have to do that." She squeezed his hands back and again, her lashes drifted down.

Again, he was struck by how vulnerable she looked and guilt began to chew a hole in him. He hated feeling guilty, hated the weight of it, but what was he supposed to do? Throw another burden on her when she was clearly struggling to deal with this one?

Brooding, he focused on her hands. She said she just might hold on to him. He wanted to get on his knees and convince her to do just that—and to let him hold onto her. He didn't know how to handle any of this, relationships, the need, the want . . . it was all new territory for him and he hated feeling so uncertain.

Her hands tightened on his and he slowly lifted his head to meet the soft, dark brown of her eyes. "What?" he asked softly.

"I just . . . I can't explain it. I look at you and feel all these crazy emotions inside, but I can't *remember* us." She paused for a moment before continuing. "There's this thing inside me. I don't know what it is. I don't understand it. But it's big and it makes me ache and wish and want and when I look at you, it only gets worse. But it's like there's something unfinished. Then I think about this baby . . ."

She stopped and laughed. "A baby. How in the world can I be pregnant? I don't remember *anything*!"

Abruptly, she jerked her hands back and shoved them through her hair, frustration turning the air tense.

"Hannah." He used the same voice he used when he was playing mediator or peacekeeper with half the damn town or on the rare board meetings he was forced to attend. It didn't quite have the same effect on her that it had with others, but then again, Hannah was always being contrary. "It's going to be okay. I know it's hard to trust that right now, but baby, it's going to be fine."

Her mouth flattened out into a tight, straight line and she shook her head. "How?"

He took her hands back in his, lifting one to his mouth and kissing it.

Hannah's breath caught and her gaze lowered to their joined hands.

The instinct to lean in and kiss her was strong—damn strong. Instead of giving into it, he rubbed small circles over the backs of her hands. "Because you're alive. Because you're here. Because we are together . . . and that's all that matters to me."

"Chief."

Gideon Marshall bit back a stream of curses and withdrew his hand from the door.

His small police force ran like a well-oiled machine most days. There was one detective—soon to be two—and one lieutenant, and then the men and women he had in uniform. A team of twelve people, all in all. Not a big police department, but McKay's Treasure wasn't a big town.

With it being such a small town, Gideon was often directly involved in investigations, although mostly in supervisory capacity. Not this time, though.

Griffin had left word that Gideon had to get to the hospital and speak with Hannah Parker. Amnesia, didn't that just beat all?

Still, he had to talk to her and he'd made it clear he wasn't to be disturbed over unnecessary bullshit. Even the necessary bullshit could wait. Until it was urgent, he didn't want to be contacted.

Since the detective bothering him was a genius at reading between the lines, Gideon had to assume this was important.

Sighing, he turned and looked at Deatrick Outridge. He'd been on his way out the front door of the station house—seconds away.

Deatrick had a small black fire safe in his long, skinny hands and behind the lenses of his glasses, his eyes were gleaming.

"You aren't going to believe this, sir. I know you need to get to the hospital, but this is crazy."

Gideon braced his hands on his hips and waited.

But the detective shook his head. "Not out here, sir."

Gideon sighed and nodded toward his office. "Let's see what you got."

A few minutes later, he was still gaping in disbelief at what he had on his computer.

"How far does this go back?" he asked softly.

"Years, man," Deatrick said, his excitement becoming more and more apparent. Like Gideon, Deatrick was a Treasure native and like Gideon, Deatrick had gone on to serve in the military. He'd done his one term though, gotten out, and had gone on to college. He'd done a few years on the force in Huntsville before returning to Treasure with his wife, once they had found out she was expecting. He was one of the best cops Gideon had ever worked with—and sharp as a blade.

Both of them knew what they were looking at.

Shayla Hardee hadn't just been a mean-spirited gossip. Judging by what they were looking at, she'd most likely been involved in blackmail.

Now they had the possibility of what looked like a serious motive behind her death.

A motive, and a damn long list of possible suspects. More than fifteen names—and one of them was a damn cop.

"Why the hell didn't he come to me?" Gideon muttered, staring at the broad, shiny face of Officer Theodore Billings. Theodore wasn't in uniform. Matter of fact, he wasn't in *anything*—well, unless you counted the man who was on his knees in front of him.

It seemed Teddy had some secrets, and one of them included a lover who looked about half his age.

"He wouldn't risk it," Deatrick said, shaking his head. There was some sympathy in his voice when he glanced away from the screen to meet Gideon's gaze. "You know how people are about this shit."

The video came to an end and the next one popped up. Both of them went silent as they waited to see what sort of dirt Shayla had on this one—it would be about Teddy. Shayla was nothing if not organized. Gideon had already . . .

"Son of a bitch," Deatrick whispered.

Gideon closed his eyes.

Then he rubbed them, blinked hard twice, and looked again.

"Well, the good news is we can't say this would catch Teddy's wife by surprise," Deatrick said, craning his head as if to get a better look.

It was possible he needed to—the images on the screen

now included more limbs. Three heads. Six limbs. Two of the bodies were male. One was Teddy and the other was the man from the earlier videos. The woman was, without a doubt, LaToya, Teddy's wife of almost twenty years.

"And now we have another suspect," Gideon muttered.

Deatrick looked down at the fire safe. So far, he'd managed to go through maybe a quarter of the contents.

"I'm going to have a long day, aren't I?"

CHAPTER FOUR

"I bet you're ready for tomorrow!"

Hannah managed to smile at the nurse. Her name was Jill. Jill had graduated a year behind Hannah, attended a technical nursing program and then gone on to get her bachelor's degree.

Hannah knew all of this because she'd asked.

Jill had seemed to know her and when prompted, Jill had been more than happy to chatter on easily.

Yet none of the knowledge seemed to do anything to pry loose those memories. They remained stubbornly stuck behind a wall.

Four days had passed and that wall hadn't yielded.

Dr. Briscoe had wanted to keep her in the hospital for a few days to make sure she put some weight on and keep an eye on her—and the baby—but finally, tomorrow, she could go home.

Maybe seeing her own place would knock something loose.

One brick could send that wall tumbling down, or so she wanted to think.

"Stop pushing yourself."

At the sound of Jill's voice, Hannah looked up. "Am I that transparent?"

Jill shrugged. "A little. Not that I don't understand. I'd probably be doing the same thing." She patted Hannah on the shoulder and said, "But pushing isn't going to help. Just remember what Dr. Briscoe told you—it will take time."

A few minutes later, Hannah was by herself, staring out the window.

She'd given it time.

Plenty of time.

How much *more* time was it going to take?

Feeling like the walls were trying to close in around her, she moved to the window and stared out. At least she could walk more than two or three feet without feeling like she was going to collapse. As she neared the plate of glass, she felt the sun's warmth on her and she sighed. She *hated* being stuck inside.

She wanted to be out in the sun.

On her boat—

Houseboat.

She had a vague impression of water. A deep voice giving her instructions, steady and easy, hands guiding her as they showed her how to tie off—

"You ready to eat?"

The memory fell to shreds. Stifling the urge to groan, she looked over her shoulder to see a woman there.

The ubiquitous cop was at her shoulder, a trim, petite woman, and Hannah knew from experience the uniformed officer wouldn't leave until the hospital staff had left the room. The only time the cops didn't escort people in and out of the room was when it was the doctor, another cop, a handful of the nurses and one or two other visitors. Including Brannon. Everybody else had the cop standing at their back. That ranged from people from dietary delivering her food to therapy to housecleaning to the lab techs to the visitors that seemed to come in an unending stream.

Nobody would explain to her *why* she needed the police watch dogs, either, and that was getting damned old.

Once she got out of here, she was going to dig up all the information she could about her car wreck.

"We've got meatloaf—"

Tomato-flavored sponge, Hannah translated.

"Mashed potatoes—" *Starchy, potato-flavored mush.*

"Green beans." *Mushy green slime.*

"And Jello!"

I can eat the Jello. There's always room.

The young woman smiled brightly as though she was delivering an elegant, four-course meal. "I'll be back later!"

As she walked out, Hannah made her way over to the tray and eyed it, revulsion twitching in her gut. Morning sickness didn't come at any certain time, but she'd already started with it and unpleasant smells definitely triggered it. The tomato-flavored sponge entrée definitely wasn't doing her any favors.

"Miss Ella Sue!"

At the sound of her bodyguard's warm voice, Hannah looked up.

Ella Sue. She knew that name.

"Well, child. Look at you."

A black woman stood in the doorway, a basket over one arm while she propped the other hand on her hip.

"Hello," Hannah said. Since she was already tired of the awkwardness, she asked, "Do I know you?"

Ella Sue chuckled. "Honey, you most definitely know me. And don't go worrying about not remembering me, either. We'll just have the pleasure of getting reacquainted all over again."

"Okay." Hannah covered the tray of unappetizing sponge, mush, and slime back up. "How do we know each other?"

Ella Sue came in and she paused by the table, lifting up the lid that covered Hannah's dinner. She wrinkled her nose and covered it right back up. "How can they expect anybody to get well if they have to eat *that*?" she asked, shaking her head. Then she picked up the tray, carried it over to the dresser and put it down. "Have a seat, Hannah. I've got some good food for you. We'll eat and we'll talk."

"You always had a soft spot for my boy." Ella Sue sighed as she watched Hannah scrape her spoon over the bottom of the shallow bowl. Hannah had all but devoured the chicken and dumplings Ella Sue had brought in. It wasn't the dish she'd normally make in the summer, but Hannah was pregnant. She needed something simple and filling in that belly of hers. It looked like it had hit the spot, too.

Hannah slid Ella Sue a look from under her lashes. "Did I?"

"Oh, did you ever. You'd watch him. Not when he could see it, mind you. He was used to girls watching him and he liked it. He wasn't cruel with it, but you could tell he enjoyed the attention. Brannon . . . well, sometimes . . ." She sighed and looked away. "It's terrible to say, but if he hadn't lost his parents, he might have turned out to be a shallow, stupid bastard. Too pretty, too smart, rich to boot. Life came too easy for him and then he up and loses his mama and daddy. That was when he realized life wasn't meant to be easy. He stopped enjoying it so much, but he still took things for granted."

"He lost his parents?" Hannah lowered the bowl, her gaze averted.

"Yes." Ella Sue took the bowl and went to go rinse it out as Hannah stared outside.

"What happened to them?"

The question was casually delivered, but Ella Sue knew it was most definitely *not* casual.

"They were in a wreck. They'd taken Neve to the bookstore." Ella Sue paused and studied the younger woman. "You don't remember Neve, do you?"

"I know she's Brannon's sister." Hannah shrugged and looked away. "She's come by, once or twice. Her face is familiar, but I don't have those memories yet."

"It will come." Ella Sue patted Hannah's hand. "Anyway. They'd taken her to the bookstore. They always did that. It used to be a family thing, and they all went, but this was a special trip, just the three of them. There weren't any witnesses so the exact specifics are unknown—Neve was in the car, but she's blocked most of the night out. But the car crashed. Mr. McKay died instantly but Mrs. McKay . . . she . . ." Ella Sue paused and cleared her throat. "She had internal hemorrhaging, other injuries. It took her well over an hour to die. Neve was trapped in the car, forced to watch the whole thing."

Hannah curled her hands into fists.

"It was a terrible time for them."

"And you."

Ella Sue looked at the younger woman, saw the compassion in Hannah's dark eyes. "Yes," she murmured. "And me. They were my family, too. Those kids, I love them like they were my own. It was one of the worst days in my entire life."

Unable to sit on the bed any longer, Hannah got up.

Neve wasn't just some faceless stranger to her. The woman had come by, bringing pajamas and jeans and tops and toiletries with her. She'd also hugged Hannah so hard it hurt, and when Brannon had tried to make her stop, Hannah had hugged her back.

No, she didn't *remember* Neve.

But she knew her.

Now, she wore the pajamas Neve had brought and paced, her head full of the images Ella Sue's words had conjured. Somehow, without even asking, she knew the wreck the older woman had mentioned had been a long time ago. Neve would have been young. Brannon, as well. A teenager maybe.

"Neve and I . . . we were friends then?" she asked.

"No," Ella Sue said. "That took a while. You ended up in a class in middle school. If I recall correctly, some children were giving you a hard time. You . . ." Ella Sue paused, pursing her lips. "Well, you were a heavy child, Hannah. You lost weight when you got out of high school, but kids weren't always nice to you when you were younger. Neve was something of a devil—she saw some girls picking on you and she dove right in. You told her to butt out and mind your own business. You could take care of yourself. So she told you to do it, then. I think you two almost came to blows. Somehow or other, you ended up as friends."

Hannah smiled as she thought of the redhead who'd come by twice in the past few days. First, she'd been with Brannon, then by herself. She hadn't let Hannah's lack of memories affect her.

Yeah, Hannah could see the girl wading in like that.

She went to turn away from the window, a question on her lips. Her gaze landed on the magnolia tree.

And she froze.

Somebody was standing there.

Staring right at her.

She froze under the impact of that stare, her breath trapped inside her lungs.

"Hannah?"

Backing away a couple of steps, she shook her head.

"Hannah, what's wrong?"

Something moved in the corner of her eye and she turned her head, saw Ella Sue coming closer.

She whipped her head back around, lifting a hand to point.

But there was nobody there.

"Your name is on the list."

Gideon and Deatrick had been forced to take special measures for this particular interview. Sadly, certain people thought they were entitled to special treatment—like senators, for one.

Senator Henry Roberts might try to pass himself off as *one of the people*, but he sure as hell hadn't been interested in coming in for an interview. The only thing that had gotten Gideon and Deatrick through the door was the fact that Gideon had made several not-so-subtle insinuations about the reasons he had to talk to the senator.

He didn't live in Treasure but he was known around here. The last time he'd run for office, he'd tried damn hard to get the McKay family to come on board and support him.

Moira had coolly dismissed him.

Brannon had flipped him off with a smile.

That hadn't exactly made them friends.

Sadly, he'd ended up in office anyway.

The senator was practically a caricature of a politician. Perfect suit, neatly knotted red tie with blue stripes, his snow-white hair immaculately groomed. He had a neat white beard as well, and Gideon couldn't help but think that if he was in a white suit instead of that black one, he'd look like Colonel Sanders.

"We have absolutely no idea why my client's name appeared on this list." The lawyer, a slick-haired, suited-up cretin with the unfortunate name of Lewis Crooks, gave them a smarmy smile. "As the woman is dead, we can't really ask her, either."

"As the woman is dead, we have to ask you about the connection between your client and her," Deatrick replied.

The senator made a show of studying his nails while Crooks chuckled. "You can't really believe my client killed her. Please." Crooks leaned in, hands linked in front of him. "Senator Roberts is a good man, a dedicated family man with a long history of working for this county and this state. He is known for his philanthropy and his kindness and his—"

"He's known for enjoying his cocaine habit and his prostitutes," Deatrick said, reaching into the folder and pulling out the photo stills lifted from the video.

Roberts suddenly lost interest in his manicure.

As the color drained from his face, his eyes bounced from one picture to another. Him snorting coke from a woman's overly-ripe breasts. The same woman licking it from his cock. In the final still, the two of them were frozen in a position that left no room for imagination.

Gideon didn't look at the images. They'd been burned on his brain and despite his distaste for the man, he had to give the man credit. He was in sixties and could party like a damn rock star.

As Crooks started to sputter and voice protests, Roberts reached out and picked up one of the pictures.

After a few seconds, the senator placed it face down and reached over, putting a hand on the lawyer's arm.

"I didn't kill Shayla Hardee," he said, his voice flat.

"Senator, don't say anything."

"Please, spare me. You and I both know how this looks." He shot the lawyer a dark look, then he focused a withering smile on Deatrick and Gideon. "She gave me the video. She claimed it was the only one, but I'm no fool. So I paid her."

"Never thought about . . . eliminating the problem?" Gideon asked when Deatrick flicked him a look.

"There was no problem." The senator smiled glibly. "We had a workable arrangement. I paid her and she was satisfied. She never pushed for more and I never missed a payment. She was a vindictive, greedy woman, but she wasn't completely stupid."

Again, the lawyer tried to silence the senator. "I need a moment with my client."

"Shove it, Crooks. I've got a motive and we all know it." Then he smiled thinly. "But the good news I have an alibi—and it's ironclad. I ended up in the hospital the night Ms. Hardee died. I was at a private dinner party—I'll give you a list of names, if you'll keep it quiet as to why you're asking. Somehow, it wasn't made clear that I have a deadly allergy to shrimp. They had to call an ambulance. I'm told I even stopped breathing for a few seconds en route to the hospital due to the swelling in my throat."

Well, shit.

That pretty much knocked the senator off the list.

They had only a good thirty people left to go now.

Who to call next . . . the sweet lady who ran the B&B? One of the several doctors? Or the county judge?

Outside the large windows, there was a lovely view of the sun setting over the Mississippi. The grounds beyond that sparkling pane of glass were elegantly manicured, and the grass was a stunning shade of green. Flowers chosen for their color and resistance to disease and drought dotted the landscape.

The stunning scene made little difference to the man inside the house.

He'd worked damn hard to get where he was and he enjoyed showing off the fruits of his labor, but he rarely took time to enjoy them for himself.

They were trophies and marks of stature.

Nothing else.

Just then, the very walls with the stunning and carefully chosen pieces of art felt like they were closing in around him, threatening to choke him.

He paced the gleaming hardwood floors, going from hardwood to designer rug and back, his Italian leather shoes striking down with—*click, click, click, click, thud, thud, click, click, thud, thud—repeat.*

He'd been pacing for nearly twenty minutes and he had yet to come up with any sort of solution, had yet to burn off the nerves and fear jumbling inside him.

His wife was on her way to a dinner party, sulking because he'd canceled at the last minute, claiming a work emergency.

He wasn't lying, either.

This was an emergency and he could think of a thousand ways to tie it into his job.

He wanted to hit something.

Hurt somebody. But the source of his rage was already dead.

Shayla Hardee was dead, and with her, his problems should have died. Sadly, he couldn't count on that as a certainty.

The one remaining complication was Hannah Parker. Why had she been in Shayla's car? What had happened? Did she *know* something? Had she been some sort of partner with Shayla?

He smoothed a shaking hand down his tie and fought the urge to go to the phone. A few carefully placed phone calls could get him some of the answers he needed. But those phone calls could be tracked. And if anybody realized he was asking questions . . .

No.

It was better to just *be careful*.

What little Shayla had on him wasn't much, paltry in comparison some of the dirt she had on others—and he knew that for a fact, because in order to get her off his back, he'd given her that dirt.

But he needed *information*.

The entire world turned on information and he'd made it this far by dealing in it. People only *thought* they knew how he'd pulled himself up out of the gutter and gone on to establish himself as a presence—as a *force* in this part of the state.

He hadn't lucked into his position, either, being born into it the way the McKay family had. That had been one thing he'd worked damn hard on, trying to dig up information on them, but unless numerous speeding tickets or frequent business trips out of the country were really fascinating, there wasn't much to be said about them.

They might as well be a family of saints. They donated to charity, they paid their taxes. Fucking McKays. They owned half that town, bits and pieces of the state, and had their fingers in all sorts of different pies. Of course, it all looked nice and legal, but could *anybody* be that clean?

He didn't think so. Not that he could prove it.

But they weren't the problem. Shayla Hardee was the problem.

A dead one, he reminded himself.

It would be fine. Everything would work out.

For the first time since he'd heard, he felt some of the tension drain away.

He'd been struggling with the problem of Shayla Hardee for too long and now she was gone. Now all the senator had to worry about was Hannah Parker and whether or not *she* knew anything.

CHAPTER FIVE

"Home sweet home."

Hannah gave Griffin a wan smile.

He was the one person she could completely relax around. She had real memories of him.

They were old and distant, murky even, like she was looking at them through a film or a veil, but they were real and solid.

He been one of her first visitors, and next to Brannon, he was the one at her side the most while she was in the hospital.

One thing had become crystal clear during those days and it hadn't been her memories.

The two men didn't like each other.

Hannah was too tired to deal with it and she hadn't wanted to put up with the testosterone overload, either. Both of them had been in the room as the nurse went over discharge instructions and she'd braced herself for the argument to come when she was asked who'd be taking her home.

It had come as a surprise when Brannon had ended up coming to her side and brushing a kiss against her brow. "How about I bring you lunch? I can keep you company for a while."

She didn't know who had been more surprised—her or Griffin.

But she'd appreciated it.

So Griffin had brought her home, although Brannon had stayed with her right up until he shut the car door, pausing just long enough to brush his fingers down her cheek.

Now she stood in the middle of her apartment and tried to remember *something*. Drawn to the small balcony, she moved outside, her gaze straying to one of the buildings across the street. Images rolled through her mind and she could see herself sitting out here. "I liked this spot, didn't I?"

She looked over just in time to see Griffin shrug. "Yeah, I think so." He crooked up a brow at her.

She had another flash—a man, his face not too dissimilar from Griffin's, but older, more lined. More tired.

"You read out here a lot," Griffin continued, unaware of her distraction.

"Do you look like my dad?" she asked softly.

He came up short, the question catching him by surprise. Rocking back on his heels, he tucked his hands into his pockets and studied her for a minute. "Yeah. Yeah, I guess I do. He looked a lot like my dad, I know that, and my mom always told me I was the spitting image of him."

"They . . ." She hesitated, almost afraid to ask. "What happened? I mean, they're both gone, aren't they?"

"Yeah." Griffin looked away. "They're both gone. They died the same day. It was . . . they were out in the gulf. Had taken the day to go do some deep-sea fishing. Came across a stranded vessel." He paused, looking back at her. "None of this is ringing a bell, is it?"

"No." She flipped at the latch and slipped outside into the heat of the day. Griffin followed. "If you don't want to talk about it . . ."

"It's fine. It was a long time ago. Your dad . . . well, you should know what happened." Hannah sat while he leaned against the railing, his gaze on his feet. "It's been almost twenty years. We were both in third grade. I lived over in Baton Rouge with Mama. You lived here . . . we saw each other a couple times a month. Our dads, they were close. It didn't surprise me, really. I mean, not now."

He lifted his face up to the sky. "They were good people, both of them. I requested a copy of the report, when I was older. It's why I became a cop. The FBI never solved it."

"FBI?" Her heart lurched to a slow, grinding halt.

"Yeah." He cleared his throat. "It happened out on open waters, in the gulf. The Coast Guard was the first to respond, but they don't handle investigations or anything. The FBI did all that."

He turned away and braced his hands on the railing, the muscles in his back tense. "Not like they had a lot to go on—dead ends everywhere from what I could tell. Only one person to question, unless they missed a shark or two."

The grim stab at humor didn't do anything to lighten to mood.

After a moment, he looked back at her and the expression on his face was bleak. "That stranded vessel—investigating officers were pretty sure it wasn't stranded at all. The most concrete info they had was from my dad's call to the Coast Guard. When they saw the boat, my dad put in a call for assistance—according to that information, he said he thought somebody had been hurt. He saw somebody lying, half over the railing, blood dripping into the water. There were sharks circling. That was what caught their attention. Our dads thought maybe they'd gotten into a fight with some drug runners or something . . . and they stopped to help."

Hannah felt cold.

Griffin lapsed into another bout of silence, his eyes seeing something off in the distance. She was seeing something, too. That flicker of a man's face—the one who looked like Griffin—it was solidifying, becoming more than a flicker now. Almost a memory and she had flashes of him smiling down at her. Music playing—*Brown Eyed Girl*—and they were dancing.

"The FBI agent I talked to, he's retired now, but he suspects the guys were dealers. The deal went south and then our dads showed up—they were dead from the moment that other vessel saw them," Griffin said. One hand clenched into a fist, while his eyes turned hard and flat. "There was only one guy alive at the end of it all and he wasn't about to come clean."

Griffin skimmed a hand back over his short hair, his expression grim. "That's probably the only reason we even know anything at all about what happened. The Coast Guard was pretty close—got there fast. Your dad . . . Uncle Sean held on for a few minutes, but they couldn't save him."

Hannah buried her face in her hands. Then, while the grief dug holes into her heart, she pushed upright and moved to the wrought-iron railing. "And they don't know what happened?"

"They know the basics. There were two people on board—well, two people and a corpse. One of the guys shot our dads—yours first, then mine. They were pulling up alongside the other boat when it happened. My father was soaking wet according to the report. They speculated that he saw enough of what was happening to know there was trouble, so he dove into the water.

Stupid bastard—there were sharks in the water, but if your dad was in trouble . . . anyway, he swam around and came up behind, grabbed one of them as they came aboard Uncle Sean's boat. Most likely, my dad hamstrung him with the knife, but the other guy shot him. The Coast Guard was right on top of them by that time, but my dad was already dead. The stupid fucks tried to shoot it out with the Coast Guard, but that didn't go over well. One guy died right away, the other surrendered, was taken in for questioning, but he was killed in jail within a week. All that much more reason to think it was drug-related."

Hannah closed her eyes and wrapped her hands around the metal railing. Too much. It was all too much to process.

She couldn't think about a man she barely remembered lying dead on the deck of a boat.

All because he and his brother tried to help some strangers.

She squeezed her eyes shut, tried to pull up some memory of him.

You're my . . . brown eyed girl. Do you remember when . . . we used to say . . . .

That bit of song spun around and around in her head and she sucked in a breath, grabbing at her skull as though it was going to fly apart. One sliver, one tiny fraction fell free.

A woman.

Hannah gasped.

Mom.

Smiling.

Her round face—*Hannah's* face—smiling at her from across a darkened yard, lit by the smile and the dancing flames of a fire. She was watching them, Hannah realized.

Watching Hannah dancing with her dad.

"We were happy." Slowly, she looked up at Griffin. "Mama, Daddy and me. We were happy, weren't we? Before he died?"

He pushed off the railing and knelt down in front of her. "Yeah," he said, a smile crooking up the corners of his mouth. He caught her hand and squeezed. "You were. All of us were. Mom . . . she . . . um, well. She tried to get you and your mama to move to Baton Rouge and stay with us, but Aunt Lily didn't want to leave Treasure. Said she'd grown up here, wanted you to grow up here. Didn't want to leave the house that she and your dad had bought."

Hannah nodded and then looked away, tucking that scrap of memory away. She'd write it down, she decided. These bits and pieces that were *real*, that were solid, she'd buy a journal and write *everything* down. Sooner or later, she'd have enough to believe that she really did have a life—something more than the Swiss cheese experiment that was her brain these days.

But that one, bittersweet memory of her mother led to another one.

One of her mother crying. *Begging.*

"She was happy. *Here.*" She looked back at the apartment where she lived but shook her head. "Not in this apartment, I know that. I didn't grow up here. I don't know where that place is, or what it looks like, but it was here. But instead of moving to Baton Rouge, she let that miserable fuck move in and knock her around for the rest of her life instead," Hannah said, frustration bubbling inside her.

"You remember him."

"Some." She managed not to flinch at one particularly clear memory. She didn't want to think about that, or the guilt. Rage threatened to steal the air from her lungs and she sucked in a deep breath. "His name. What was his name, Griffin?"

"Omar." Griffin's lip curled as he said it, as though the very mention of the man left a bad taste in his mouth. "Omar Lovett."

"Omar." She clenched both of her hands into fists and wished she had something in front of her that she could hit. "I remember his face. He was this big, ugly, lazy pig of a man. I wasn't a skinny girl, I know that, but he would sit there at the table, stuffing his face and then he'd take half the food my mother gave me and throw it away, telling me that I was too fat already and I had to quit being such a lazy pig—he sure as hell wasn't going to let me hang around his house forever."

A low noise escaped Griffin, but she didn't look at him. "It was *our* house, mine and Mama's. Insurance . . . I can remember that. Mama paid it all off with my dad's life insurance policy, put some in the bank for me for college."

It was weird the way those memories were just there, as if all she had to do was reach for them.

"I remember him hurting her—I can't remember all of it, but there are these . . . flashes." She waved a hand back and forth in front of her head. She reached for another memory but there was nothing else.

"What else do you remember?"

She laughed sourly and glanced over at him. "It would be better to explain what I *don't* remember. Almost everything is vague impressions. Him hurting my mom, but I don't remember her name." Her voice broke and she had to press a hand to her mouth to keep from sobbing. "Griffin . . ."

He caught her in a tight embrace. "Lily. Your mama's name was Lily."

"Lily." She clung tight to her cousin and tried not to cry.

She tried not to scream, too, because she was angry.

"It's okay, Hannah."

She let him tell her that and she let him think it helped.

But it wasn't okay. Had she been this angry before? She didn't know.

Moments passed as she calmed herself and when she thought she could look at him without him seeing the storm that still raged inside, she broke away.

He made her look at him for a moment and she was able to give him a tight smile.

She couldn't tell if he bought it or not, but it didn't matter.

She had herself back under control and that was what counted.

"Lily," she murmured, nodding. That felt . . . right. Yet another thing that fit.

"I can remember some foods I like and I know I love magnolia trees."

"You hate eggs and you can't stand tuna fish," Griffin offered.

She could believe it because even the mention of either made her want to gag. "You should make me a list."

He smiled.

Turning her head, she found herself staring down the road toward the river. She could see it from here, the way it rolled lazily along and the sun reflected off it, sending a sliver of diamond bright light dancing across its surface. "I love the river, too. That's why I got this place, isn't it?"

"Yeah. That's why you won't sell me your houseboat, either."

"My . . ." She stopped, a smile forming on her face. "A houseboat. I have to see it."

"You remember that?"

"No." She shook her head. "But I don't have to."

Absently, she glanced around and found her gaze lingering on the balcony across from her.

Her heart tugged. *Ached.*

A knot settled in her throat.

"What else do you remember?" Griffin asked, unaware of the quicksilver change in her emotions.

Softly, she murmured, "Brannon." She opened her eyes and went back to staring at the balcony opposite hers. It was connected to a stately brick building, one that looked elegant and old, yet somehow, she suspected it hadn't always looked that way. And she knew without a doubt who lived there.

"I remember Brannon. Not a lot . . . but he's up here," she said, touching her brow.

And in here. She had to fight the urge to rub the heel of her hand over her heart.

"He treated you like shit," Griffin said, sounding disgusted. "Do you remember that?"

Lifting her head up, she met her cousin's eyes. A muscle pulsed in his jaw as he stared at her and she saw the anger he couldn't seem to hide. "Well?" he demanded when she didn't answer.

"I know," she said quietly. "He told me we'd fought— that we had just recently gotten involved. We'd had a fight and then . . . well, that day. He came to see me the day I wrecked. We were going to try and make things work out."

"He *what*?"

Griffin gaped at her, the expression on his face as baffled as if she'd told him that she'd woken up from the coma and discovered that she had turned into a man overnight.

She turned back to the street. "You heard me. We're

involved." Then she slid a hand down to cup her belly. "We're having a baby, Griffin. I don't think we can get much *more* involved anyway."

"Having a baby with some prick doesn't mean you have to . . . hell. Look, the guy is loaded. He can uphold his end of the bargain without you getting trapped up in him."

For the first few seconds, the insult didn't register. Then she spun on him and stalked up to him, driving her index finger into his chest. "You jackass. I'm not about to dog some guy for money—I can take care of a baby *on my own*. I'm getting *trapped up* by him because . . ."

Hannah floundered then. Because . . . because *why*?

"Why?" Griffin stared at her.

The anger drained away. She felt so very tired in that moment. Sinking down onto the edge of the chair, she crossed her arms over her middle and leaned forward, staring down at the cars that rolled by on the street below them. "I looked at him in the hospital, Griffin. He barged in and I *knew* him. I knew his name and more . . . some part of me *knew* him. I can't explain it but there's something big inside me, something that's all his."

It was a hot, windy summer morning, creeping up on noon and had it been just a few short weeks ago, Brannon would have been quite happy to be out there in the fields, talking with the crew, or hassling his manager, or even just taking a moment to stare out over what he was building.

Treasure Winery—nothing fancy—just a nice little southern winery that had been ten years in the making, and she was almost ready.

This place was his baby.

Nobody knew how much this place meant. Nobody

knew how much time and effort and heart he'd poured into it.

They didn't know how much work he'd put into it, how many hours—weeks—months, *years* of his life he'd dedicated to this.

He'd buried himself in research, had visited hundreds of wineries—if not more—across the country and beyond. There had been years devoted to scouting for the perfect piece of land. It had to be in the area. He wasn't leaving home and when luck had smiled on him and given him the ideal spot just fifteen miles from the home where he'd lived for half of his life . . . well, Brannon had been one smug, pleased bastard.

That had been nine years ago and he'd been working to *this* point ever since.

As time got closer and closer and as the wines he was trying to develop got better and better, he'd lost time in his life for anything else that wasn't crucial.

He'd been working on other projects in town—like the bookstore and the hardware store, a few other places that not too many knew about—but he didn't have as much hands-on work there. Most of that was all about him investing money in return for learning more about the business of *running* of a business.

Then there was the pub. Treasure Island. That had come about because the owner had wanted to retire and Brannon had heard the man talking about just closing the bar. Beyond the diner, Treasure didn't have any place decent to get a meal and while there were a few places to get a drink, there had been a decided gap.

Brannon had just made the decision to fill it.

Then he'd acted on impulse and called an old friend, Ian. Ian had been managing a pub over in Edinburgh—or was it Glasgow—for years, but Brannon had offered him something he knew the other man wanted; a chance to have a place of his own. Right now, Brannon owned it, but in a few years, he'd make Ian an offer. They'd already discussed it and Ian, being a smart, cagey bastard, was likely already setting aside money to pay for the place.

So now the Island was Ian's baby.

All of that had given Brannon more insight into the business aspect of things. Now with experience under his belt and his wine list all but ready, he should be dying to open the door to his winery.

If anybody really knew how much this place meant to him, they'd . . . well, they wouldn't believe it, because Brannon McKay was known for not caring about much of anything that didn't involve his sisters or cars.

It probably shouldn't be such a surprise that this place was about ready to get shoved to the back burner, too. Because instead of dealing with the myriad of things that needed to be done—the emails, the marketing plan, one of a dozen meetings he knew he had to take of—he was heading toward his car and he had absolutely no plans to be back for the rest of the day.

He was taking his laptop, though. He needed to look at the resumes that had come in.

"Brannon. *Brannon!*"

He looked up as Marc Norton came running down the path toward him, dust flying up from his shoes, his face flushed, and a hole in the knee of his jeans.

Marc Norton was the vintner he'd hired a couple of years ago to help him with Treasure Winery. Eight years ago, five years ago, two years ago . . . hell, *two months* ago, this place had been the thing that dominated his thoughts, morning, noon, and night and if Marc had been hollering for him in that tone, then he would have been dropping just about everything to see what the problem was.

But he had other thoughts dominating his mind. Hannah.

He checked the time as Marc came stumbling to a halt in front of him.

It was just now eleven. He had a few minutes.

"We need to talk about the marketing for the muscadine. You're still wanting to call it Riverboat Queen, right? We need to get moving on this." Marc held up a hand, panted for a few seconds, gulped in air and then carried on. "We have a meeting with the tourism board in three days and we haven't prepared *anything*. We're supposed to be opening in six weeks. We need to make sure everything is order and we need—"

"You," Brannon cut in.

Marc frowned, clearly not following.

"You and Tag need to do it. You're the vintner, he's the manager. This is up to the two of you. Find him and get to it." He checked his laptop bag, made sure the charging cord was in there. He had to get somebody else out here—yesterday would have been good. Probably a couple of somebodys and an assistant for Marc.

"But . . . I . . . Brannon, this is your deal. You've got your fingerprints all over it. We need you on board with it."

Brannon opened the door of the Bugatti and put his laptop bag inside it. It struck him then how damned cramped the thing was. Hannah would be miserable riding around in it in a few months. And the baby—

His mouth went dry thinking of *that*.

The baby.

"Shit," he muttered as he straightened and stared down at the custom-built car. The Bugatti was literally a work of art. Yet another thing that had his hands all over it. Driving it was like driving a dream—it handled like nothing he could even describe. It was almost better than sex. Well, unless he was talking sex with Hannah and then it didn't even compare. But *aside* from Hannah, there had been plenty of times when he would have much rather had been behind the wheel of the car, wind whipping through his air, music blasting, and nothing around him but the road. No women, no worries, nothing.

And now he was brooding because his pregnant . . .

"Brannon!"

Turning away from the car, he stared at Marc's red face. He looked like a pissed-off ferret, shifting restlessly from one foot to another, his eyes shining behind the lenses of his glasses and his hands moving restlessly as though it was impossible for him to be still.

"You'll have to manage without me," Brannon said levelly.

"We've been doing that for almost two weeks." Frustrated, Marc shoved his hands through his hair, adding to the irate ferret image. "I get that life is exploding around you, but do you want this to happen or not? For the past six months or more, it's been like the winery doesn't even matter."

Brannon stared him down.

Marc glared at him. "I gave up a career in California and a chance to buy into my own place to come out here. You told me you'd make it worth my while. And now . . ." Marc shook his head. "You're leaving me hanging. Do you *want* this place to succeed or not?"

"Yeah." *That* much, at least, hadn't changed. Planting his hands on his hips, Brannon pinned a hard stare on Marc.

The man's nerves jacked up to the next level.

Marc was a great winemaker. Despite the fact that Brannon had been working for this for the past ten years, he still didn't know a quarter of what Marc knew—the man was brilliant and finding him had been a gift from winemaker heaven. Brannon knew that.

But his twitches and jerks and the way he couldn't be still for five seconds sometimes drove Brannon up a wall. He felt like grabbing Marc and just holding him still.

"I want this place to succeed, but right now, I'm needed somewhere else."

"What, the chick?" Marc made disbelieving sound in his throat. Not quite a laugh, not quite a snort. "Look, I get that you've been worried about her but—"

Marc sometimes didn't operate on planet Earth.

Brannon had spent a great deal of time around people who didn't operate on planet Earth. He'd grown up with Neve, after all. Maybe she was more focused now, but he could still remember the hyper drive that seemed to be the one and only speed setting she'd had as a kid.

It wasn't really a surprise that it took Marc about twenty seconds of rambling on to realize he'd shoved his foot in his mouth.

Brannon just stood there and waited.

When Marc finally came to a stumbling halt in mid-sentence, Brannon took a step forward.

Marc took one back.

Brannon let it go. He wasn't going to do the two-step with the idiot all across the winery just to tell him to shut his damn mouth. People in Treasure hadn't yet realized that things had changed—Brannon had an all-new set of priorities.

But people would figure that out, and soon.

Brannon wanted to grab Marc and shake him—*that* chick *has a name. Her name is Hannah and she's carrying my baby, you prick*. But things were still dicey with him and Hannah, so maybe that wasn't the way to handle it.

Voice level, he stared at Marc. "You need to focus a minute, Marc, and focus on me."

Marc made an attempt at what he thought was a charming smile. "Look, Bran, I didn't mean anything by it. I just—"

"Focus," Brannon said, like Marc hadn't said anything. "I won't have this conversation with you again. I don't care that you're one of the best guys for the job out there. I'll fire your ass and have you out of this county so fast, your own shadow won't be able to catch up with you. You won't get another warning. So make sure you remember what I'm about to say—are you with me?"

"Sure, Brannon. Sure." Marc nodded and some of the endless energy drained out of him. He stood there, staring listlessly off into the distance.

"You're not going to bring Hannah Parker up in business discussions again, you got me? If you see her, you're going to be polite—and you probably will see her. If things go as I'm hoping, the two of us will be spending a lot of time together—and the bottom line is, I'll be spending less time here."

"But—"

"I'm not done," Brannon said gently. "Now, I know we're at a crucial time and I'll still give this place what I can, but you two are going to pick up the slack—you'll be compensated accordingly and I am already looking for extra staff, including an assistant manager to help Tag out and more help for you. But priorities *have* changed for me and that means *I* have to change how I'll be doing things."

A vein started to pulse in Marc's right cheek and he opened his mouth, only to snap it closed.

Brannon lifted a brow. "Say what you need to say."

"If I'd known you were going to flake out on me right before the big day, I'd have thought long and hard before I left my job in California, Brannon. I'm serious about what I do—I thought you were, too." Marc said those sentences in a rush, folding his arms over his chest and glaring at the sky overhead as though the heavens were to blame for everything going on.

Brannon rubbed the back of his neck. "Look . . . I . . ."

The need to explain then hit hard, and fast. He had promised Marc—and Tag—a big opportunity. And he was letting them down.

But there were business responsibilities and personal ones.

Brannon could get somebody else to help hold up his business obligations. "Things have changed," he said again. "I'll explain it when I can, but there are circumstances, Marc. Things I didn't plan on, but they have changed. Nothing can be done about it."

As Marc's eyes came back to his, Brannon said, "I'll get you more help out here. This place is *going* to be a success. I want that, you know I do."

He paused and turned, staring out over the fields.

A hundred years ago, this place had belonged to the McKays. It had eventually been sold off, but now it was theirs again. It was only right, Brannon thought, that it had been the right place for the winery. When it came to wine making, location was everything. The soil a few miles south was worthless. A few miles north? The same. This spot here? It was prime.

"I know you're aggravated. You've got a right to be," he said, glancing back at Marc. "I had every intention of being right here with you and Tag, and I promise, once Hannah is feeling stronger, I'll be back out here as often as I can. And I *will* make sure you've got what you need to make this place a success."

"You are what we need," Marc said sourly. He skimmed a hand back over his thinning hair, but the aggravation was fading from his voice.

"No." Brannon cocked a brow at him. "My land, my

money—that is huge chunk of what you need, and you'll still get that. I'm sorry, Marc, but I can't live and breathe this place anymore. I can't."

"Fine," Marc said after a long, tense moment of silence. "Just . . . get some help out here, okay? I can't do the creative shit, Brannon. I need you for that."

"I will," Brannon said. "I'm already looking at resumes. There's a woman who worked at one of the big wineries over in Georgia—I think she'd make a great fit."

Marc gave him a hangdog look. "Okay."

Brannon slid inside the Bugatti. "Chin up, Marc. We'll be celebrating opening day before you know it."

CHAPTER SIX

He was too big.

He was too beautiful.

Even after the past few days, Hannah was hard-pressed to come up with any other summation of Brannon McKay.

She wasn't talking about his physical appearance, either, although he sure as hell didn't lack for that either.

Everything about him was larger than life.

He was the kind of guy you'd read about in some torrid romance book. She had more than a few of them in her house. Apparently, Hannah was big on her romances, even if she couldn't remember a single one of them.

With those wide shoulders and gleaming red hair and blue-green eyes, he just didn't seem real. She knew he was loaded and she wasn't relying on faulty memory for that. She'd done what any rational person would do—she'd Googled him.

The *net worth* figure next to his name had almost tangled her tongue into a knot and now, as she watched him moving around in her kitchen, she tried to wrap her mind around the fact that the man who had fathered her child was worth *millions*—as in *multi-millions*.

"You don't have anything here to eat except ramen noodles," Brannon said and he turned to look at her, bracing his hands on the counter behind him.

The action pulled a faded gray shirt tight across a well-muscled chest and her mouth went a little dry. Had she run her hands across that chest? Did he have any hair on him or was he smooth? She had a sensory memory in the next moment—light hair, just a little, running down the middle of his chest, down his naval . . .

She tore her gaze away and glared out the window. "Look, Mr. Mega-bucks, I'll have you know I probably *like* ramen noodles."

"Look, Ms. Parker," Brannon said, his voice mild. "I love ramen noodles. But you're pregnant and you've lost weight. You need some healthy food in you."

She wasn't in the mood for logic. She was antsy and edgy and in the mood for something that was probably very *illogical*, considering how much of a mess her life was. She wanted to go to him and pull him to her, touch her mouth to his. She thought she remembered how he tasted, thought she remembered the hard press of his body against hers.

No, she wasn't in the mood for logic or food or anything that didn't involve kissing him. But there was a wariness inside her, a caution that confused her and kept her from moving toward him the way she wanted.

Since she wasn't going to let herself close the distance between them, touch him, she busied herself picking at one of her cuticles.

"How about we go across the street and get something from the pub?"

Damn but he wanted to kiss her.

Hannah's gaze had slid to his mouth, lingering for a long moment before she looked away again. Heated, heavy currents passed between them and he'd half-held his breath for a moment, but then she'd looked away, focusing on her hands.

I've been in love with you since I was in high school.

Her voice, those softly spoken words, were like fresh gouges in his heart. She couldn't remember telling him that, or the fight, or anything else but there was still caution in her eyes when she looked at him.

She'd dropped it for a moment when she'd been looking at his mouth and he wondered what she'd do if he went to her, touched her, kissed her.

Would she still love him if—no, *when* she remembered?

He didn't know and the only thing he could think to do was make sure she understood that he wanted her, needed her. That he had messed up. He wanted her with him in so many ways, in *all* ways.

She hadn't answered him about grabbing some food, so he pushed off the counter and moved closer to her.

"Come on," he said, smiling easily. "We can grab a burger or some soup, or whatever. If that doesn't sound good, you can tell me what does and I'll have them figure something out."

"Just like that, Mr. McKay?" Something fired in her eyes.

She wanted to pick a fight for some reason.

He wasn't going to rise to the bait. "I figure if a pregnant woman can't make a special request, then who can?"

"The man who owns half the town?"

"I don't own half the town," he said. "And whatever I *do* own—it's not just me. My sisters own equal parts. And what does that have to do with anything anyway? Are you hungry or not?"

On cue, her belly grumbled. Brannon lifted a brow. She flushed.

"Well, I guess that answers that."

"Fine," she said, a flush crawling up her cheeks. "I'm hungry. We can go eat."

She glanced at him and again, her gaze dropped to his mouth.

Heat gathered inside him, a storm raging to be loosed.

Then, slowly, her eyes lifted and their gazes locked.

For a few seconds, heat and need threatened to drive him insane.

She was the one who broke the eye contact and when she pushed her hair back, he saw the faint tremor in her hands.

Maybe it wasn't a fight she was in the mood for.

He was tempted, so damn tempted, to touch her, see if he couldn't do something about the energy he could all but feel burning through her.

Patience, Brannon.

"Well, well, well . . ."

The voice sent a whisper of warning down her spine.

Hannah had been studying pictures on her phone, hoping something would remind her, but it was proving to be an exercise in futility. Brannon had gone to the restroom and in an effort to dissuade anybody from talking to her, she'd fixated on the phone.

As a shadow fell across her table, she slowly lifted her gaze to see a tall, rail-thin man studying her, a cruel smile twisting his mouth. Nothing about him jogged her memory, although he stared at her as though he knew all sorts of secrets.

He also stared at her as though he wanted to cause her all sorts of hurt.

Hannah casually reached up and put her hands on the table, one of them covering the napkin—and the knife tucked inside it. "Hello. Can I help you?"

"I heard you was out of the hospital." Opaque brown eyes ran over her. "Looks like you're healing up good enough."

"I heard you *were* out of the hospital," she corrected. "And yes . . . I am healing up fairly well, thank you. Mr . . . ?"

He snorted. "You're a jumped-up bitch, Hannah." Then he leaned down, bracing his hands on the edge of the table.

She surged upward, her hand closing around the knife.

But it wasn't necessary.

Brannon appeared at her back even as a tall, bearded man came up to grip the man's elbow. "Mr. Hansen, it seems you've gotten lost on the way to your table."

The hot guy with the beard was Ian. Brannon had reminded her of his name. Ian ran the pub and he was dating Brannon's sister, Neve. He was big, bearded, and Scottish. Although he was smiling, the grin on his face had a hard edge as he moved to put his body between the skinny man and Hannah.

"I'm not lost, you stupid foreign fuck."

"Then you're not hungry," Ian said, his voice going hard.

"Are you okay?" Brannon asked, the words low and soft in her ear. He cupped a hand over her shoulder as he eased in closer.

That light, casual touch sent heat sliding through her and she turned her head, staring at his face, his mouth. Just a breath away.

He was so close, she could have kissed him. The idea of it sent a wash of heat rushing through her and her nipples went tight just thinking of it. "I . . . um." She looked down at the roll of silverware she still clutched.

The knife was still wrapped up in the napkin and abruptly, she felt foolish.

What had she been planning to do? Beat the guy with a set of silverware?

Brannon took it away and she watched as he put it down.

Behind them, Ian was still speaking although the man—Hansen—was no longer exactly *talking*. Yelling was more like it.

"I just wanted to have a word with that high-and-mighty bitch—thinks she can go around poking her nose in other people's business!" he snapped.

Hannah looked back at him.

Voices emerged from the gray fog of her memory.

"You need to keep your nose out of my fucking business, you crazy bitch!"

"Femi-Nazi."

She looked past him and saw the woman who was all but cringing in the background. His wife.

Joanie. The name popped into her head, just like that.

Hannah said, "When are you going to leave him, Joanie? When Lloyd kills you?"

The words shocked the hell out of her.

They infuriated the man—*Lloyd*.

She remembered that and pieces of a puzzle fell into place.

His name was Lloyd and he beat his wife.

As if she'd pulled out a crucial support, a stream of memory tumbled free.

She could see this skinny, evil bastard bent over his wife, holding her down with his hands hooked and cruel, biting into soft flesh. Like Hannah's stepfather had done to her mama.

Lloyd went to lunge to for her—Brannon protectively blocked her even as Ian caught the miserable little man, but Hannah dodged to the side.

Her body—still weak, still tired, didn't want to

cooperate, but she forced it to move. "Leave him alone," she said, sneering at Lloyd. "The coward wouldn't put his hands on me anyway—not here. He might come after me in the dark or when I'm not looking. That's his idea of *real* fight. His targets are always women anyway."

"No man goes after a woman in my place," Ian said.

"Lloyd, please, don't," the woman with him whispered.

And abruptly, Hannah felt ashamed.

This woman, Joanie, she'd pay the price.

Because they always did—the victim always paid. Shaking her head, she looked at Joanie again. "I helped you *leave* him, didn't I?" She rubbed her temple, shaken by the memory she could *almost* see. "I did . . . I know I did."

Ian was dragging Lloyd to the door—it wasn't much of fight. Lloyd was snarling and tearing at Ian's hands and arms, but he might as well have been a gnat butting up against a stone wall.

"Joanie! You stupid bitch, get out here!" Lloyd yelled.

She flinched, unable to look at Hannah. "I have . . . I have to go," she whispered.

"Why?"

The question came from a slim redhead.

Hannah blinked in surprise as Neve McKay moved in to block Joanie's view of Lloyd Hansen and then, as Ian wrested him outside, the man's furious bellows were muted as well.

"He's my . . ." Joanie frowned. "We're married."

"The man beats you," Brannon said, shaking his head. "You didn't sign up for that when you said your vows, did you?"

"I made a promise."

"So did he," Neve said, speaking before anybody else could. "It looks to me like he breaks that promise all the time. Are you going to stay until he puts you in the ground?"

"Eat."

Hannah stared at the shrimp po'boy on her plate.

"I've kind of lost my appetite."

"If anybody can talk sense into Joanie right now, it's Neve," Brannon said quietly.

"I tried to, I think." Dispirited, Hannah picked up a French fry and popped it into her mouth. It was hot and salty and without thinking about it, she reached for another. "If she wouldn't listen to me a few weeks ago . . ."

She stopped and just shook her head.

When Brannon remained silent, she cast him a look.

He was staring out the window.

"Neve . . ." He hesitated for a moment and then looked back at her. "She left home for a while. You know this— or you did. Maybe you'll remember. Maybe you won't. But she met this guy. He hurt her. Bad."

Instinctively, Hannah felt her gaze wander to the windows where she'd last seen Neve, leading Joanie away, one arm wrapped around the smaller woman's waist.

Neither of them were in sight now.

Brannon kept looking toward the street, as though he was thinking about her as well.

"What happened?" Hannah asked softly.

"It's a long story," Brannon said, his voice brusque. "And it's hers. If you want to know all of it, you'd need to ask her. But she got away from him—he came after her. Came here. She knows what it's like to have that hanging over her. You . . ."

He looked back at her, his eyes searching her face for a long moment. "You lived with it, I know. Your stepdad. There's nobody in town who doesn't know what a roach he was. But there's a difference between living with it the way you did and living with it the way Neve and Joanie have."

Hannah chewed on that for a moment and then nodded. "You're probably right." Then, because she could see the shadows in his eyes, she reached over and touched his hand. "Whoever this guy is, I bet he won't try anything again—not with you and Ian watching over her."

"Well." A slow smile curled his hips. "You're right . . . sort of. He won't be trying anything again. But that's because Neve handled him herself."

He nudged her plate closer. "Now eat something, would you? Ella Sue keeps threatening to have my ass if I don't look after you better."

There were few things in life that equaled an unopened bottle of Jack Daniels and some peace and quiet.

Granted, Clive didn't always get the peace and quiet he wanted at home.

Especially not since he'd hooked up with Stella.

Stella Coltrane had a mouth like a damn Hoover and he appreciated that aspect of her personality. But when she wasn't sucking him off, she was either snoring or talking way too much.

Clive didn't always mind the talking.

Sometimes, he even liked listening to her talk. She had a cute little lisp that he thought was kind of sexy, really.

But he'd had a long-ass day and he still needed to get into Baton Rouge and pawn off a bag of his finds. Soon, too, because he had to make rent. Having Stella there made it easier, because she was paying an extra hundred toward the rent, plus buying groceries. Still, he needed to get this shit off his hands.

He settled with his back up against a heavy chunk of stone, his bottle of Jack wedged between his thighs and his duffel bag of loot next to him. The first order of business was to make sure none of the stuff could be traced back to an owner.

If it could, he'd either see if there was a reward or just leave it here so nobody could trace it back to him. He sure as hell wasn't going to keep anything that would land his ass in trouble with the cops. He figured he was smart enough to stay a step or two ahead, but he wasn't going to risk it.

He kept his ear to the ground. A few times, he'd found something that had a reward attached and although the reward usually wasn't as much as he'd like, it was easy money.

Of course, the money usually wasn't as much as he could get by selling his goods, because people were cheap bastards, but it was worth the effort to try. Mostly because he didn't want to get his ass arrested.

Gideon Marshall was enough of a jerk to haul him into jail, all because Clive was lucky enough to find shit people lost.

All a bunch of bullshit, really.

With the rock still carrying the sun's heat, Clive found himself relaxing and fairly happy with the haul he'd be taking into Baton Rouge tomorrow. He might even take Stella. They could hit a club, have a drink and maybe even a steak dinner.

The watch . . . it was a nice one.

He didn't know who'd lost it down at the running path but he knew it was expensive.

He'd developed an eye for the watches. He could tell what was worth five bucks and the ones that were worth fifty—and five hundred and fifty . . . or more.

Granted, he had to be careful about where he tried to sell them, but in his line of work, it was worth it to have contacts.

This one would bring him a few hundred easy. If he could sell it on the level, it would probably bring him a couple of thousand, but he'd take what he could get.

He carefully examined it but there was no inscription or anything else. The guys he usually worked with avoided stuff that was inscribed. Too easy to get in trouble that way.

He should be good with this one.

Putting it down, he picked up the next good find.

It was a ring.

He doubted it would bring him more than a hundred or so. He might be good at gauging watches and electronics, but he sucked when it came to rocks. He thought this one was real and it was a nice size, but it wasn't anything to write home about.

The next few things weren't going to get him much more than thirty or forty bucks a piece—a few lost phones, a silver money clip.

Then the camera.

He went to turn it on, but stopped when he heard voices.

"—tell me there's nothing to worry about!"

Clive hurriedly scrabbled to get all of his loot back into the bag, shooting a look around the bulk of the rock. He couldn't see much of anything, though. The sun had finally dipped down below the horizon and the piss-poor street lamp wasn't doing much to light his bit of landscape.

"Toya, baby . . ."

"Don't you *baby* me!"

Clive slapped the lid on his bottle of Jack and jammed it into his tote, zipping it shut as silently as he could.

Toya.

It had to be LaToya and Teddy Billings. Teddy—Dudley DoGooder. Clive practically hugged the rock to keep them from seeing him. Just his fucking luck, getting trapped here with a cop and his nosy bitch of a wife.

"You got any *idea* what this will do to us if people find out about us, Teddy?" LaToya said, her voice rising. "I swear, boy, if I didn't love you so much . . ."

Clive shifted uncomfortably as her voice broke, although he breathed a little easier. They were so caught up in each other, they probably wouldn't notice him.

"Toya, I'm sorry. That's why I was paying her . . ."

"You should have *told* me what she was doing! I would have snatched that stupid bitch bald, I'll tell you that." LaToya sobbed then and her voice grew muffled.

Curious, Clive craned his head around the stone, peering out into the darkness.

Teddy patted the back of his wife's head with a hand the size of a plate and Clive shrank back as the big man looked around. "Come on, Toya, let's sit down, okay? And don't go letting people hear you talking like that, okay?"

"Why *not*? It was evil, what she did!"

"I know, I know."

A few mutters passed, things Clive couldn't hear.

Then he tensed.

"Why the hell did Shayla have to go meddling like that? It's no wonder she got herself dead," LaToya said.

"Toya, now you gotta stop it."

"I didn't say she *deserved* it," LaToya snapped.

Clive kept still, but he could see, just barely, the way LaToya started to pace. "Blackmailing people, Teddy! Taking videos . . ." She stopped then and Clive didn't dare move, because she was staring toward the river. "How many did she have of us, do you know? How did she find out? Man, it makes me *sick* to think of her spying on us like that."

"I know, baby, I know." Teddy sighed, the sound big and hard as the man himself. "Hell, if I'd known . . ."

"Shh, now." LaToya's voice went soft. "It's not your fault that she went and did what she did. Oh, it's your fault for *paying* her—you shouldn't have done that and don't think I don't want to thump you for it."

"I know. I knew even when I was—"

"Hey, guys!"

A bright, happy voice interrupted them and Clive winced, jerking back into his space, back against the stone as the newcomer interrupted what had to be the best damn shit Clive had heard in a long, long time.

He thought it might be Morgan Wade, but he wasn't sure, and it didn't matter anyway.

A few moments later, the voices were gone, and he found himself rooting through his bag and pulling out the camera.

Curious, he rubbed a finger across the surface of it.

It was scratched up some and the battery was dead.

But now, he had to wonder.

He'd found it out at the park, the same place where he'd found the watch.

Scratching at his chin, he shot another look back where he'd seen Teddy and LaToya.

Then he got up.

He was going to play around with that camera some.

See what he could see on it.

CHAPTER SEVEN

Gideon wasn't a perfect man.

He knew this.

He could be an asshole when he wanted.

He was stubborn and he had an ornery streak and although he hid it, he had a splash of mean in him that he just hadn't been able to completely expunge, no matter what he'd done.

But he liked to think he was a decent man. He liked to think he'd made up for some of the wrongs his own father had done. Thomas Marshall, Jr. had been the town drunk and an abuser. He'd come from a long line of abusers, thieves, and criminals. His dad's brother was serving time over in federal lockup for multiple murders.

The best thing to ever happen to Gideon had probably been his father's death . . . at the hands of his brother. The two of them had gone joyriding, leaving a trail a mile wide behind them.

Theft was only the start of it.

They'd stolen money, drugs, guns. A couple of guys had gotten in their way and they'd stolen two human lives as well. Then a woman hadn't opened up a door and they'd busted down the door and busted her up. The more time that passed without them being caught, the crazier they got.

By the time they wound down at the end of a ten-day crime spree, Tommy and Billy Marshall had stolen well over eighty-five thousand dollars, had caused nearly double that in property damage, and they'd killed three people and put two more in the hospital—one of them had been the woman who'd dared to say no.

Holed up in a hotel room, they'd been counting up their spoils when they'd started fighting. Billy never did say why. He'd pulled his gun and killed Tommy when the other man turned to go into the bathroom. That had driven somebody in another room to call the police.

Billy had been sitting on the bed with the gun in his hands when the cops came.

Gideon heard about it two days later, while he collected cans out of the garbage to sell to help his mother out. He'd read the news in a paper somebody had thrown out. His mother had to have known, but she'd kept it from him.

As he had stood there reading about his father's death, two uniformed cops came strolling out of the café. The topic of the hour had been the downfall of Billy and Tommy Marshall.

At least we're free of them.

Good riddance . . . although you know that boy of his is going to be just as bad. His poor mama. She didn't do nothing to deserve that kind of shit.

A bright, glittering ball of hate had lodged in Gideon's heart that day.

He hadn't done anything to deserve it, either.

It had taken the town a long time, but they finally looked at him and saw *Gideon Marshall*, not Tommy Marshall's kid.

He'd done some decent things in the service and here he was, wearing a badge of all things.

Yeah, he liked to think he wasn't a bad sort of guy.

Sometimes, though, he thought God was out to break him. Either that, or the man upstairs had one twisted sense of humor.

Dragging his hands down his face, he studied his detective in the dim light of the bullpen and saw the same weariness he felt.

The past week had been nothing but endless, meandering circles. They'd questioned more than forty people—and *those* were just people from Shayla's little blackmail ring.

Word was getting out, too.

Earlier that day, Gideon had gone to the diner to grab a burger and Patricia Mouton—and her ever-present, pudgy little pug of a dog—had stopped him in the middle of the sidewalk. This time, Mrs. Mouton hadn't bent his ear about a ticket she'd received because her sweet little Samwise had been crapping all up and down the sidewalk—no, sir. Mrs. Mouton had been pale and tight-lipped and she'd asked him to take a walk with her and Samwise.

While Samwise panted and puffed his way up and down Main, Mrs. Mouton had talked about a time when her and Mr. Mouton hadn't gotten along so well, a time when Mr. Mouton had actually gotten along better with Karen White—the lady who owned Bygone Treasure—you know, the B&B just down the way from the museum?

She'd danced around the subject while Samwise danced around their feet before she'd finally leaned in to whisper in his ear, "I heard there was a *tape*."

A tape.

He'd just stared at her blankly.

"A tape . . . of Mr. Mouton with Mrs. White."

He could have ripped out his hair.

He'd wasted more than a little time telling her that no such tape had been found. Now he had to worry about maybe one turning up. He sure as hell didn't want to watch Mr. Mouton and Mrs. White going at it. But now he'd have to talk to them both. All because Patricia Mouton found something else to obsess over besides her dog's right to shit on the sidewalk.

The whole thing was a fucking mess. Grumbling under his breath, he tried to clear up the chaos of his brain.

"Sir?"

Deatrick cocked a straight brow up, a puzzled look on his thin, aesthetic face. Deatrick looked like he belonged behind a podium, teaching in-depth lectures on chemistry or physics—or maybe in a robe, with a wand in hand. He looked . . . scholarly, with his narrow face and big dark eyes set under those slashing brows. He was tall and thin and the man had been born a cop.

Now he was back in McKay's Treasure and he had the case of a lifetime on his hands.

It was, Gideon knew, the kind of puzzle that would keep a cop like Deatrick working and working until he'd solved it.

Gideon understood that because he was the same way.

But the case was getting more complicated by the minute and they barely had the manpower to take care of the small town as it was. Now they had a murder to solve and the list of suspects was getting longer and longer.

"It's a mess," he said, clarifying his thoughts for Deatrick. "I realize that Shayla didn't go and get herself murdered to complicate my life, but she went and complicated it nonetheless."

A sardonic smile lit Deatrick's dark face. "I'm sure that will give her soul some pause, chief."

Gideon snorted. Then he looked up at the clock. "We're going to have to call it a night."

Deatrick frowned, but nodded. They'd already decided they were going to have to keep this between themselves for as long as they could, although realistically, they were probably at the point now to where they'd be bringing in at least one or two others soon.

People knew something was going on. Specifics? Nah, they didn't have those, but while Treasure had its share of idiots, most of the people in town weren't stupid and they had put two and two together.

Something wasn't right.

That Gideon and Deatrick had kept things quiet as long as they had was saying something.

But people were getting restless, curious *and* scared and once that happened, it would be harder—and more dangerous—to hide shit.

"I heard Hannah Parker's name go out on the radio." Deatrick eyed him across the table.

Gideon grimaced. Reason *numero uno* why he was calling it quits. He had to check on her, check with his officer, check on . . . hell, every damn thing that could possibly be related to Hannah Parker.

Out of habit, he looked out his window, able to see the front of Treasure Island and nearby, the front of Brannon McKay's loft. Across the street, but out of his sight, was Hannah's place. She'd been discharged that morning and although it had burned his gut, he'd been forced to let her leave the hospital.

Her cousin had taken the day off and Gideon knew for a fact that Griffin had been watching her throughout the day. At least when Brannon wasn't with her.

But night was rolling around and she'd be alone soon. Unless she gave into Griffin nagging her. That could go either way, Gideon knew, because the Parkers were stubborn people.

Aware that Deatrick was still watching him, he nodded. "It was handled, but apparently she butted heads with that asshole Hansen again." He blew out a breath and studied his notes. "We need to figure out where he was the night Hannah wrecked."

"You think he might have had something to do with it?" Deatrick's lip curled. "That boy doesn't have the brains God gave a goat."

"Oh, I'm aware. But we don't get the job done unless we investigate everything." He took his time and looked around the quiet station. The small town of McKay's Treasure didn't need a heavy police force and nights were almost always peaceful. Weekends changed things up some and summers changed it up even more.

But nothing felt peaceful right now and Gideon had already advised all of his officers that if anything felt unusual, if anything was out of the ordinary, nobody was to wait—he was to be called *immediately*. He wished he had it in the budget to hire some more people. Even one more person, but that wasn't going to happen.

"But you think Doc Briscoe's idea . . . you're thinking it's maybe on the money." Deatrick watched him narrowly.

"I'm thinking that there's too much we don't know." He looked up then and met the younger cop's eyes. "Now you and I both know what we're looking at here—Shayla Hardee was just plain stupid and that likely led to her death. I can only hope we can find who it was that did her. But . . ." The grim reality of the past few weeks set in and it showed in his voice, showed on his face and in his eyes. "You saw her body. So did I. What he did was cold. Whoever did that is a thinker. He didn't let emotion get in the way and he didn't hurry. He had a job to do and he did it."

Gideon riffled through his files and found the list of Shayla Hardee's personal effects. Clothes, make-up, jewelry. No phone. No camera. "Then he cleaned up. Most of the video was shot on a fairly recent Sony model. I'm going to reach out to the state, see if they can't narrow it down more for me." So far, they hadn't been able to locate the camera. Her husband had told them they'd bought one a couple of years ago, right before an anniversary trip, but he couldn't remember the last time he'd seen it. And it was a Sony.

That camera wasn't in the house.

It hadn't been in her car.

It hadn't been found during the search.

"It wasn't her husband. We've already ruled him out and we've got no leads. So we're dealing with somebody cool enough, collected enough, *cold* enough to kill a woman and then clean up and leave next to no evidence behind. There were a few fibers on her body, but they were cotton. There was no DNA, nothing to actually tie our killer to our vic. Cold. Smart."

"Not her husband, that's for damn sure," Deatrick muttered. Roger Hardee had been a fucking mess ever since his wife's death. Usually the husband—spouse— was the most likely suspect, but they hadn't had to look at him long to know he wasn't the man they were looking for, even aside from the alibi he'd provided.

"Roger can't clean his own ass without help," Gideon said, aggravation chewing at him. Again, he looked out the window, to the apartment he couldn't see.

"You think our perp might be waiting to do that now— clean up again?"

Gideon lifted a shoulder. "I don't want to take that chance."

They both shared another quiet look.

People had come throughout the course of the day.

Most of them had since gone, although she'd had to all but throw a few of her visitors out the door.

It was down to two now, her cousin Griffin and Brannon. She could almost have forgotten Brannon. Okay, well maybe *forgotten* wasn't the right word, but he wasn't a harsh, abrasive rub against her senses the way everybody else was right now.

Including her cousin.

If Griffin didn't leave soon, she thought she just might rip her hair out. Although she suspected she'd feel better if she ripped out *his*.

"I'm tired," she announced to the room in general.

Neither of the men said much of anything.

She started to beat out a tattoo on the arm of her chair, staring at the screen of the television without really seeing anything. As the beat of her fingers got harder and louder, she could feel their attention shift her way, linger, then move away. Every few minutes, their gazes would return.

Finally, she shot a look at Griffin and tried again. "I am *tired*."

"You can go to bed, honey." He smiled at her.

That made her feel bad—and *that* pissed her off.

"I'll lock up for you," Griffin said. He shoved upright and gave Brannon a smile that would have looked more at home on a caged hyena—teeth all bared and his hackles raised.

Man, these two didn't like each other.

"You have a good night now, Brannon." Griffin made a show of being overly polite with the words. Southern women weren't the *only* ones who knew how to kill with kindness.

"Brannon doesn't have to go," Hannah said, the words escaping her before she knew what she was going to say.

Griffin whipped his head around, staring at her.

Brannon was surprised, too, but she barely noticed that.

She stared at her cousin for a long moment and then looked down at her feet. Sometime earlier in the day, Brannon had painted her toenails. Brannon McKay had painted her toenails, all because she'd said she couldn't remember if she'd liked pedicures and he'd told her he knew she did. Then he'd painted her toenails a bright, cherry red.

The sight of the cheerful color now made a knot settle in her throat and she looked at her cousin. "I need him to stay. We . . ." There was hurt in Griffin's eyes. She hadn't meant to do that. She didn't want to hurt anybody, but most especially him. Although her memories were still vague, somehow she knew the two of them had been there for each other when nobody else had been.

"You two really did decide to try and work things out, didn't you?" Griffin said. He looked over at Brannon.

Brannon jerked a shoulder in a shrug. "She's stuck up in my head all the time. I couldn't keep fighting it."

His eyes strayed to Hannah's and lingered and she felt her heart skip a few beats in that moment.

"Hell. That's romantic," Griffin said. Then he blew out a breath. His eyes narrowed on Brannon and he studied the other man for a long moment.

When he held out a hand, Hannah felt something in her chest knot up.

Watching the two men make some move toward friendship had her feeling all stupid and sappy and weepy.

She was going to claim pregnancy hormones.

She was right at one month.

She could do that, right?

It took just a few more minutes for them to be alone and Hannah found herself more self-conscious than she could ever remember feeling. Of course, there was still plenty she didn't remember, so that wasn't saying much. Still, as Brannon finished locking up the door, she busied herself in the kitchen with stupid little things that didn't need doing—like washing her hands, again, and wiping down a counter that didn't need to be wiped down.

Her head was a muzzy, hazy mess and her body ached with fatigue. She was worn out.

Of course, that could have something to do with the fact that she was still struggling to recover from the crash, the coma . . . coming to grips with the baby, the amnesia. All of the above.

The reality of it all crashed into her and she turned, leaning back against the counter. Covering her belly with her hands, she lifted her gaze to Brannon's and just stared at him.

"I don't even know what's going on with my life right now," she said bluntly. "My head is spinning so fast, I don't know what to make of anything."

He came to her.

She held still as he cupped her face in his long-fingered hands.

His touch made her want to shiver.

His touch made her want to sigh.

Then he brushed his lips across her forehead and she wanted to curl herself around him, cling tight and never, ever let him go.

"Six days ago, you were in a coma. A few weeks ago, you were in a wreck that could have killed you. I think you just need to tell your head to slow down so the rest of you can catch up."

She laughed and the half-manic edge in it had her cringing. "You think that will work?"

Instead of answering, Brannon brought her in closer. "Just slow down," he murmured against her brow. "Let yourself catch up."

"I think . . ." She held onto his waist. "I'll just stay right here."

"That sounds good."

Brannon closed his eyes and rested his head against the soft silk of her hair.

She relaxed against him and he was able to push the guilt away. She wanted him there. She'd said as much.

She seemed less . . . haunted.

Yeah.

That word fit.

She'd hidden it well, but during the day, as people came and went, she had been tense and on edge. But now, as the quiet wrapped around the two of them, that tension began to drain away. Smoothing a hand up and down her back, he closed his eyes and turned his face into the softness of her hair.

How had he thought he didn't want this?

He must have been crazy. Or stupid. Both.

Her lips brushed against his neck as she sighed and it sent a rush of heat through him, but he shoved it down. He thought maybe he'd ask her if she wanted him to spend the night. On the couch, that was all. But she might feel better if he was there, right? Yeah, maybe—

Her lips brushed against his neck again and he couldn't stop the low, unsteady breath that escaped him.

Hannah eased away, looking at him from under her lashes.

Her tongue slid out, wet her lips and he had to clench his jaw, remind himself of just how fragile she was right now—not just physically, either. He could still see fading bruises on her face, the fading pink marks on her hands from where she'd been cut when the car wrecked.

It got so much harder to remember that when she reached up and touched his mouth.

"I know we've kissed," she said, her voice low and husky. "Sometimes, I almost think I remember it. But then it's gone. And it's driving me crazy."

"Hannah . . ."

Her gaze dropped to his mouth, lingered there a moment, and then she looked back at him.

Her eyes were huge and dark, a heat burning there that threatened to consume him—and damn if he'd mind.

"I want that memory back, Brannon. I want to know how you taste, how your mouth feels on mine. Will you kiss me?"

Well, hell. It would take a stronger man than him to walk away from that.

Cupping her face in his hands, he arched her head back. Their first kiss had been a mix of fury and frustrated passion. This one wouldn't be like that. He'd kiss her the way he should have kissed her to begin with.

Slowly, he lowered his head, brushing his mouth against hers, once, twice.

Her lips parted on a sigh.

But he didn't take that offering just yet.

Instead, he caught her lower lip between his and sucked lightly, listening as her breathing hitched. Her hands came up to grasp his waist and he moved in closer, letting his body rest against the powerhouse curves of hers.

She made a hungry noise in her throat and opened her mouth under his.

Still, he didn't deepen the kiss—much.

He traced the line of her lips with his tongue, learning the curves as if this was the first time he'd ever had the chance. For her, it was. Maybe it was for him, too. They'd start over. Completely over. And he'd make sure that this time, she knew she mattered.

Hannah grew impatient and tried to take control, her tongue coming out to curl and stroke against his. He eased back, whispering against her lips, "You wanted me to kiss you, baby."

"Then do it." She bit his lower lip.

That demanding nip set his blood to boiling but he kept an iron grip on his control, teasing the entrance of her mouth with quick, light strokes. She caught his tongue and sucked on him and the blood began to drain southward, his cock thickening.

Just a kiss, he told himself. *Just a kiss.*

Her hands slid down to grab his hips, pulling him more firmly against her and he had to keep reminding himself that this was *just* a kiss. Nothing more.

Her breathing sped up.

His heart pounded harder, faster.

The taste of her flooded him as he sought out the hidden depths of her mouth, learning her in a way he'd never taken the time to do before.

She began to move against him, her hips circling impatiently. But he was still in control. He thought. Right up until she slid a hand between them. A shudder wracked him as she stroked him through his jeans.

Aw, fuck . . .

A fist pounded against the door.

They broke apart, panting and staring at each other.

There was another knock.

Hannah licked her lips and he moved to pull her back against him.

"Hannah? I know you're probably worn out, but I'd like to talk to you." There was a pause and then, "It's Chief Gideon Marshall with the Treasure Police Department."

"Damn," Brannon muttered.

"Send him away." Then she frowned. "No, it's my home. I'll send him away."

"You can't." Brannon had a feeling he knew why the cop was here. "You probably need to talk to him, Hannah."

He skimmed the back of his knuckles down her cheek.

Her skin was soft. Soft and warm, her cheeks flushed with more color than he'd seen on her in some time. "I'd rather go back to what we were doing."

"Hannah!" Gideon's voice was harder now, implacable.

"I'll be right there, chief," she said.

As she moved past him, Brannon braced his hands against the counter. The need that had twisted through him was already dying. All it had taken was hearing Gideon's voice, realizing why the man was here.

Nobody had really explained just what all had happened the night of the wreck.

Dr. Briscoe had wanted to give her a few days, to see if she'd remember on her own. She hadn't and they couldn't wait any longer. Gideon had told them that once she was discharged, he'd be talking to her. There wasn't much choice, he'd said. They had to make sure she was safe.

Over his shoulder, he slid a look at her as she opened the door.

She didn't look as worn and tired as she had, but that was about to change.

She was getting ready to have a whole new set of problems dumped on her.

Hannah recognized him.

It wasn't just because he'd been in to see her at the hospital several times, either.

She just . . . knew him.

It wasn't the same familiarity she'd felt when she'd seen Brannon, but the chief was a man she'd known. And he was a man she trusted, even now.

Something about the competent set of his shoulders and the way he studied everything around him, even the grooves around his mouth that showed that he smiled a lot—all of that told her that back before her memory had turned into a black hole, she'd trusted him.

But her instincts told her he wasn't here just for a Friday night chat.

She sank into a fat, round chair that felt more familiar to her than her own name and she drew her knees up, curling into the arm as she studied Gideon. Brannon shifted in the doorway that separated the small, eat-in kitchen from the living room, but all he did was turn and brace his shoulder against the arched entrance, his gaze flicking from her to Gideon and then back.

He said nothing.

Gideon just nodded at him, clearly not surprised by his presence.

"Why are you here, Chief?" she asked softly. "You frequently go around and check on patients who've been discharged from the hospital?"

"Part of the service, ma'am." Gideon smiled at her. "And it's Gideon, Hannah. We're friends. If you don't remember that, then we can just start over from scratch."

"Okay." She waited a beat. "Gideon, why don't you spare me the bullshit and tell me why you're here."

He rubbed at his jaw and glanced over Brannon.

"I'd hoped you'd remember more. This is going to come as a shock, Hannah," Gideon said softly.

"Yeah, well, I'm *not* remembering more," she snapped. Kicking her legs off the seat, she surged upright and started to pace. "I can't remember my middle name.

Somebody had to tell me. I can only remember half the food I like. I don't know what I like to eat when I go to the movies or if I even *like* to go to the movies or whether I hate my job or why I was speeding down the highway . . ."

"You remembered you were speeding."

She stopped and looked at Gideon, her heart starting to pound.

Sweat pooled at the base of her spine and blood roared in her ears.

"Was I?" she asked.

Neither of them said anything.

Anger started to bleed through her and she spun away from Gideon, storming over to Brannon. Grabbing his arms, she half-shook him. "Is that why I had the wreck? Was I speeding? Hell, was I . . . was I *drunk*?" She spoke the final words in a whisper. "Did I hurt somebody? Oh . . . oh, *shit* . . ."

"No." Brannon twisted, shifting around until he held her instead of the other way around. "You were on the road heading up from the boat dock. Down by where you keep your houseboat. Something . . ."

He hesitated.

She watched as his gaze moved over to Gideon.

"Tell me!" she half shouted. "What is it? What did I do, damn it?"

But still Brannon was silent.

There was a quiet, heavy sigh and then, from behind her, she heard Gideon say, "Go on, Brannon. Tell her."

After Memory

CHAPTER EIGHT

TEN WEEKS LATER

"So . . . what's new?"

"I'll tell you something that isn't—that question." Hannah narrowed her eyes at her partner as she slid into the truck next to him. "As a matter of fact, that question is getting decidedly *old*."

J.P. gave her an innocent smile. "Hey, I'm just asking how you're doing."

She made a face at him. "Sure you are." But she relented and smiled. If it wasn't for J.P. and some of her other friends, she might not be sitting here in the ambulance, *finally* cleared to go back to work.

"Look, I'm sorry," she said, punching him lightly in the arm. "I'm just . . . fed up. I can't go anywhere, do anything without people asking me if I've remembered anything yet."

He nodded. "They don't mean nothing by it, kid. You know that."

"I know. I just . . ." She grimaced. "I feel like putting a notice in the paper. *Hannah Parker promises to tell everybody as soon as she remembers anything useful*."

"Well, fat lot of good *that* would do ya." J.P. started the truck. The radio was buzzing, the chatter a familiar background music that Hannah hadn't realized she'd missed. "Ya see, people would actually have to pay attention to what you were telling them in order for it to do them any good."

She rolled her eyes.

But he wasn't kidding.

She'd been telling people just that for months.

Noooooo . . . she didn't remember anything from the night she'd wrecked.

And no, as much as she hated it, she didn't remember anything that might help find whoever had killed Shayla Hardee. Her mind was no longer the block of Swiss cheese it had been when she'd first woken up. Her life unfolded in bits and pieces, small ones at first, and then bigger ones.

But there was a week of time that was gone.

The last thing she remembered really well?

Brannon.

She'd been staring at him. Again.

She could remember how he'd looked, stripped naked, that body that defied description bared for all the world— or at least *her*—to see. The scowl that tightened his features when he met her gaze, as if he couldn't understand why she was able to see him.

Because you don't close your damn curtains, moron.

And then he had—he'd yanked them shut as if doing so would completely shut her out of his world.

She remembered that.

Beyond that? Nada.

The first real, *solid* memory she had after he shot her that dark, fulminating glare was when he'd barged into her hospital room. Even waking up, the bright lights that had all but blinded her, the overly loud voices of the nurses, the doctor talking to her, his voice hardly connecting in her brain—all of it had seemed surreal, more like a dream than anything else.

It had taken Brannon McKay's appearance in her room to snap her out of it.

Even after that . . .

She sighed and rested her head on the miserably uncomfortable seat and waited for J.P. to pull the truck out of the bay.

Movies and books had amnesia wrong. Technically, she'd known that. She was a paramedic. She knew the basics, but knowing the basics from a theoretical standpoint and actually *knowing* it from firsthand experience were two different things.

Man, did people get amnesia wrong.

Those first few weeks after the coma had been the worst and once friends had started working with her, prodding at her buried memories, bits and pieces had started coming back.

But she felt different.

It was like she was sometimes a stranger in her own skin.

She couldn't remember things as easily as she used to—she used to think the movie *Fifty First Dates* was the stupidest thing ever, even though medically she understood that people *could* have problems developing short-term memories. A few weeks ago, she'd watched it and bawled like a baby because she understood.

She'd once had a mind like a steel trap. Now she couldn't go anywhere without notebooks because she had to write down *everything*. She'd gone into the grocery store with one thing in mind. One thing. One thing *only*—she'd even written it down on her hand because she'd lost her notebook. What had she needed? More notebooks.

What had she left the store with?

Tampons. She'd completely forgotten that she'd written herself a note on her hand.

"How's the little guy?"

Hannah was *pregnant*—she wasn't going to need tampons for quite a while. Brushing the annoyances of her messed-up memory, her shattered focus aside, she looked down at her belly with a rueful smile.

The slight bulge of her belly concealed yet one more thing she didn't remember. She rubbed a hand over the hard mound of her belly. She was three and a half months pregnant and although she knew without a doubt who the father was, she didn't remember anything about it.

"*She* or *he* is doing fine," she said loftily.

"Brannon ain't talked you into finding out if it's a boy or girl, huh?"

She slid J.P. a look. "Since when have you ever known me to be talked into anything?"

J.P. laughed. "True, true." They merged into traffic. "We have to take Mrs. Leery in for some tests. She fell a little while ago and they're worried she might have broken her hip."

"Mrs. Leery." Hannah closed her eyes, trying to bring a face to mind.

J.P. handed her a high school yearbook. They'd taken to keeping several things like that on hand, yearbooks, photo albums. When it came to people she hadn't seen since before the wreck, she still needed the occasional jog.

She opened it to the place that was marked by a napkin.

Her heart twisted at the sight of the birdlike face peering up at her and at the rush of emotion, a few memories worked free, followed immediately by more. "I had her for music," she murmured.

"All of us did. She plays piano at the assisted living center." J.P. checked the mirror and then cut over, turning left toward the center. "I sure as hell hope she didn't break that hip."

"What do you think?"

Brannon rolled the wine around in his mouth, swallowed, and then because he knew it would annoy Marc if he didn't answer right away, he took another sip.

Marc's hands tightened on the edge of the counter.

Next to him, Marc's new assistant Alison pressed her lips together to keep from laughing. If Brannon wasn't mistaken, and he didn't think he was, he suspected Alison would be open to being a lot more than just Marc's assistant. Brannon had no problem with it as long as they could work together if it fell apart, and he suspected they could. But Marc was oblivious. As always.

Alison held her own wine glass in her hand. Her t-shirt read: *My boss lets me drink on the job.*

Marc had told her a hundred times not to wear it.

Brannon told her he loved it, and he had asked her to design some for the shop in town.

It was an endless game between them.

Finally, he lowered the glass and put it on the softly gleaming wood of the bar. "Marc . . ." He sighed heavily and shook his head.

Marc's shoulders slumped and he looked crestfallen already.

Brannon smiled. "You're a genius. It's fantastic."

The vintner had wanted to start blending two wines together and Brannon had told him to go for it—he liked the end result and he enjoyed the science of it, but that was Marc's specialty. If he could be around more, he would have been more hands on.

Sighing inwardly, he looked around. Summer was

already gone and he'd missed too much around this place, but there wasn't anything he could have done.

Between Neve coming home, that son of a bitch who'd followed her and tried to hurt not just *one* of his sisters but both of them, and then . . .

His gut clenched.

Hannah.

"Are you okay?" Alison reached out and touched his hand, her purple-tinted eyes concerned.

His new employee couldn't have been more different from Marc if she tried. She was as outlandish as Marc was conservative. Marc was buttoned-up and buttoned-down and uptight. Alison Maxwell was band T's and faded blue jeans and everything laid back and relaxed. Marc's head was lost in his wine vats half the time and Alison noticed everything.

They were a perfect fit. Marc should really open his eyes to the looks Alison made no attempt to hide.

But Brannon wasn't exactly the best person to be lecturing anybody about romance, now was he?

He'd almost lost the woman who all but owned him, all because the idea of caring about somebody again terrified him.

I love you . . .

She'd said those words to him. But it hadn't been a happy confession. She'd told him because she wanted him to know what he was losing.

"Brannon?"

He made himself focus on Alison's face. "I'm fine," he said.

"You're supposed to be going to the doctor with Hannah today, right?" Alison asked, moving out from behind the bar. The winery was slow today. They had been open for a few weeks and had fallen into something of a pattern. Weekends were surprisingly steady and Wednesdays, too, thanks to the specials they offered. They were closed on Mondays, but Tuesdays and Thursdays were pretty dead.

Today was a Tuesday and only a few people had trickled in.

When Alison hopped onto the stool next to him, he managed to hide a wince. He really wasn't up to a heart to heart.

"Yeah," he said, giving her a vague smile and not once looking her in the eyes. He knew all the tricks when it came to this. He *did* have sisters after all. If he looked her in the eyes, he was a goner. The idea was to make a quick getaway and—

The bell over the door chimed.

Saved by the—

He turned.

Son of a bitch.

"Senator." Folding his arms over his chest, he stared at Henry Roberts, a man who had managed to become a thorn not just in his side, but in Moira's, too. Last week, he'd shown up at the pub and had dinner there, and had taken the time to speak to Ian.

It seemed the good senator was *very* interested in Treasure these days, and in the McKays especially. It didn't matter that they'd told him to fuck off.

They had never kissed political ass—their many-times great-grandfather Paddy McKay had gotten his neck stretched all because he hadn't played that game. It was pretty much a point of pride now.

Brannon wasn't about to change that and he knew his sisters wouldn't either.

Henry gave him that wide, affable smile that was part and parcel for a politician. "Brannon." He nodded and looked around. "It sure is a beautiful place you got here. Fine place, fine place."

His staff moved in, flocking around him like crows. Although Brannon thought maybe *vultures* was a more apt term. Despite the heat of the day, they all wore black. Discreet but expensive sunglasses hid their faces and they all fanned out through the public area of the winery, from the counter to the shop. Two of them took up purchase at the window—just like a couple of scavengers, looking for their next meal.

"Is there something I can do for you?" he asked, not moving forward to meet the man.

Clearly, the senator was expecting it.

But Brannon hadn't asked him here. If the son of a bitch wanted something, he could come to Brannon.

A thoughtful expression crossed Senator Henry Roberts' face.

"I had a free morning and I've wanted to come out and see your place," Henry said, smiling. "You and your family do a great deal for McKay's Treasure, for the county. Indeed, for the entire state. This little project of yours intrigues me."

"This isn't exactly a little project," Brannon said, refusing to rise to the bait. "I've invested millions in it. The property alone is worth . . ." He paused and then asked, "How much money did you want to raise at that fundraiser you'd hoped to host here in town again?"

An odd noise escaped one of the muscled goons standing off in the corner. Brannon flicked him a look, let his smile widen a fraction before he looked back at the senator. "Just what exactly were you wanting today, Senator? If you're in the mood for a wine tasting, my staff will hook you up. Otherwise, I've got work to do and an appointment later on."

"Would that be your . . . girlfriend?"

The pause was so slight, Brannon might have imagined it.

But Brannon wasn't the type to imagine things.

He pushed away from the counter.

Fine. The senator wanted him to make a move?

He'd make a fucking move.

"You want to be careful here," Brannon said softly. "I'm not the courteous one in the family, Roberts."

One of the senator's bodyguards cut in front of Brannon. "Oh, chill the fuck out," Brannon said, biting each word off. "Your boss came here to pick a fight."

"It's okay, Aiden," the senator said softly. As the muscle-bound moron stepped aside, Henry Roberts moved toward Brannon. He kept his voice low and his smile firmly in place, no doubt in deference to the security cameras that were out in clear view.

"Now, Brannon. I didn't come here to pick a fight. I reached out to you and your family in friendship. A man in my position could use the support of a prominent family like yours." Henry smiled. "Your parents, your grandparents, both of them were staunch believers in supporting the economic growth of this fine state. I'd hoped they'd passed those values onto their children."

"Oh, they did." Brannon leaned forward, using his greater height to its full advantage. "The thing is—my parents *and* my grandparents believed in supporting the state. They didn't believe in supporting bottom-feeding pissants like you who make promises right up until D-Day and then break them the very next. I don't like politicians, Senator. Period."

Then he stepped back and hooked his thumbs in his pockets. "I especially don't like politicians like yourself— you know, the kind that talk about family values, talk about living life on the straight and narrow, being hard on thugs and drug dealers . . ." Brannon paused, smirking, "Yet you have a bit of problem with hookers and drugs yourself."

The senator's face went red. Brannon's smile took on an evil cast. "Then there's the way some of you preach against abortion and then force your daughter to get one after getting knocked up."

Roberts sucked in a harsh breath and Brannon had to fight the urge to laugh. No, he didn't play the political game at all, but he knew all about how powerful information was. He was a McKay. When Roberts had started making noises around his family, Brannon had done the wise thing and put his ear to the ground. As the older man began to snarl, Brannon cocked a brow. "What . . . did you think you could pay off *everybody*?"

"You . . ." Roberts went red in the face.

An aide rushed to his side.

He waved him away and stormed over to Brannon. "Who in the *fuck* have you been talking to? You . . . did you . . . that Hardee—"

Immediately, Roberts clamped his mouth shut.

"Hardee?" He started to laugh. "Well, shit, Senator. Were *you* one of her marks?" Shayla Hardee's murder was still unsolved but most people in town knew *why* she was dead. Or why she was most likely dead. It had come as no surprise to learn that Shayla had been involved in blackmail.

"I've no idea what you're talking about, Brannon," the senator said, recovering smoothly.

Damn smoothly, Brannon had to admit.

"Who on earth have you been hearing all these crazy rumors from?" Roberts asked, his face now taking on the set of a man heavily burdened. "A man in my position . . . well, you must know what it's like to have enemies."

"Nah. I'm a friendly guy. I don't do enemies." Brannon bared his teeth in a mockery of a smile. "I can't much claim to listen to gossip, but I certainly know people willing to . . . talk."

Roberts' jaw clenched.

"Look, Brannon . . ."

The senator was interrupted by a strident demand. "You better get your fucking hands off me!"

Brannon whipped his head around at the furious sound of his manager's voice.

Tag was built like a mountain man and looked the part, too. When pushed, he also had the temper of a mountain *lion*—a hungry one.

As one of the bodyguards tried to hustle him back out the rear entrance, Tag drew back his fist.

"Tag!" Brannon shouted.

Tag shot him a look.

The bodyguard used that moment to grab him, or try to.

It went straight to hell from there.

"You want to explain this all to me again?"

Brannon stood with his arms folded over his chest while the state troopers and Tag spoke.

Tag had a black eye, a bloody lip and his nose had been busted. The state boys had given him given him some wipes to clean up.

The senator's team was trying to whitewash everything, but that wasn't going over very well.

The two who had been standing unobtrusively by the windows had actually been jamming Brannon's security cameras.

But he could kiss Alison for what she had done.

One of the reasons he'd hired her was because she was a fucking genius. She'd seen one of them watching the cameras so she'd casually slipped back behind the counter and checked the set-up back there. Once she'd seen what was going on, she'd started recording them with her phone camera. How she'd done that without them noticing, he didn't know. Apparently, she had her phone set to simultaneously upload, so the whole damn thing was live from the get-go. It had started live streaming immediately and she sent it to YouTube as well.

The senator might not be able to press enough flesh to fix this PR nightmare.

"Brannon?"

Dragging his eyes away from Tag's battered face, he looked back at Sheriff Tank Granger. He had showed up only minutes after Marc had quietly pushed the panic button on the security system. Seriously, he owed Marc, Tag, and Alison a bonus—and a case of wine. Maybe five cases.

The door opened and he swore at the sound of the jangling bell. "I'm going to rip that damn bell and shove it up somebody's ass," Brannon said, spinning away and bracing his hands on the counter.

The senator's duplicitous face caught his eyes and he curled one hand into a fist.

Gideon blocked his view in the next moment.

"You need to take a deep breath, Bran," Gideon said. He glanced over his shoulder and then back at Brannon. "A real deep breath. Your sister won't be happy if you end up in jail over that one."

"Please tell me you've seen the video."

"I have. Twice." Gideon looked like he was trying not to smile. He settled on the seat next to Brannon.

Brannon wasn't fooled by his friend's relaxed posture, though. He had no doubt if he made even the slightest move, Gideon would be all over him. "Moira called you, didn't she?"

"Moira." Gideon nodded. "Neve. Then Ian. Thanks to Alison's little YouTube exploits, most of the town knows. She tagged some of the people she knew on Facebook as she did it, and they tagged people and they tagged people. You've gone viral, Brannon."

"Shit." Brannon lifted his face to the ceiling. "You'd think I end up in trouble all the time the way they act."

"Nah." Gideon shrugged. "They just know you. When you lose your temper, Brannon, you go nuclear."

"Nuclear, huh?" Running his tongue along his teeth, he stared at the solid form of the senator. Yeah, he thought maybe he'd like to go nuclear on that son of a bitch's ass. Then he turned back to Granger. "Let's get this done. Now's a good enough time, since he's here. I'm sure he's going to want to hear it, too."

Tank ran a hand back over his smooth scalp and shot Gideon a look. Both he and Gideon shared a friendly enough relationship, but they were slightly territorial—as any number of law enforcement officers could be. "You do realize you don't have to tell the chief of police anything. This is outside the city limits."

Brannon snorted. "I don't *have* to. But he'll nag me until I do—and I'm not telling the *chief* shit. I'm telling a friend."

He moved behind the bar and grabbed the bottle of wine Marc and Alison had opened for him to try. He didn't bother offering any to anybody else. Alison and Marc had cracked open a bottle earlier and were talking quietly in the corner. Surprisingly, Marc was the calm one right now and he had his arm protectively curled around her.

Neither the senator nor his people had realized her video was up for all the world to see until the sheriff's men had shown up. Now it was too late for damage control, but the looks they were giving were enough that even Brannon was uneasy.

"The senator wanted to host a party at the museum a

while back," Brannon said, not bothering to keep his voice quiet.

One of the aides came rushing up, her face drawn tight. "*Mr.* McKay, I would advise you to—"

Brannon cut her off with a look. "You do *not* want to fuck with me right now. You think your boss is the only one with reach in this fucking state?" He leaned in and warned, "Try *me*."

Tank whistled under his breath as the woman went white. "Gotta be nice to be one of the most powerful men in the state, McKay."

Brannon gave him a withering stare, ignoring the woman who continued to stand there, a few feet away, all but frozen. "Do you want to hear this or just watch it on social media?"

Tank waved a hand.

"He wanted to host a party there and we assume—or at least Moira assumed—make it seem as though we supported his platform. *We* don't," Brannon said, emphasizing the *we*. Then, deliberately raising his voice, he continued. "As a matter of fact, we hate the pompous fuck's platform in general and don't care for the man."

Gideon reached up and pinched the bridge of his nose.

Brannon continued. "Since then, we've had . . ." He ran his tongue across his teeth as he considered his words. "Well, you could call them interesting little issues. First, even though I'd already received the go-ahead here at the winery, I get a call that I might not be able to open as planned and I need to have another, more in-depth inspection."

"I hadn't heard about that." Tank lifted a brow.

"I made a few phone calls . . . including one to the governor." Brannon shot a thin-lipped smile toward the senator. "The governor was very confused. It was resolved within a few days. Then Moira starts getting calls about items in her museum—she had to verify the authenticity *and* prove that the family owns them, even though they've been in the family for years. Her building permits were inspected—three times. The pub's liquor license keeps getting tagged. I'm getting calls from the food inspectors. Oh, and Ian is getting hassled about his green card."

The senator was studiously not looking at them.

The aide seemed to find her tongue. Jabbing a finger at Brannon, she said, "If you are trying to claim that the senator is responsible for *any* of this, you will find yourself—"

"Save it." Brannon braced his hands on the surface of the bar and leaned forward. "We all *know* he's responsible . . . don't we?"

She sucked in a breath.

"I don't have to claim shit, because we know the truth." He smiled then and said, "He fucked up, though. He picked the wrong family to try and take on, ma'am. If any of you were worth jack shit, you would have warned him he was wasting his time."

He checked his watch and looked up. "Hannah's got a doctor's appointment, soon. Can we speed this up?"

"I'm not going to ask you how your day went." Hannah met Brannon on the sidewalk.

He had his hands jammed into his pockets and his shoulders were tight, braced as though he was ready to carry the weight of the world.

Impulsively, she reached up and cupped his face in her hands.

He looked startled as she rose onto her toes and pressed her lips to his mouth.

It was a quick kiss, light and soft.

She wanted more already. She wanted a whole hell of

a lot more, but things between them were still . . . strange. Not on *her* part. If she had her way, she would have jumped him five times over. Okay, five times a week. Five times a day. But Brannon seemed content to take things slow, like they were in a courting relationship from a time long gone.

They went on *dates*.

They had lunch.

He took his time kissing her each time he saw her.

But when she pushed for more . . . well. She thought he was trying to drive her crazy, and if that was his goal, he was succeeding. Still, there was something about the way he was . . . courting her that made her heart melt. And courting her was the only word to describe it. He brought her flowers he picked from the gardens out at Ferry and once or twice a week, there was a wildflower tucked under the windshield wiper of the ambulance she drove with J.P. He sent her sweet, silly little texts and called just to say hello.

Even if she didn't remember loving him, she'd would have fallen for him all over again.

She sighed against his lips and whispered his name.

He cupped her cheek as she eased back and rubbed his thumb over her lower lip.

Then he caught her hand and they started to walk. "I guess you saw," he said, voice grim. He automatically adjusted his long strides to match hers.

"Is there anybody who hasn't?" She pursed her lips thoughtfully. "Hmmm. Maybe people on the other side of the globe who aren't awake yet and those who don't believe in technology. If they don't believe in technology, they'll know by tomorrow, when it hits the newspapers."

His heavy sigh had her shooting him a look. "You sound glum. I wouldn't think you'd worry so much about a YouTube video."

"It's not the video. It's the prick on the video and the grief he's going to give Tag, Alison, Marc, Ian . . ." He stopped then and jammed his hands into his pockets. "This time, the prick even mentioned you."

"Me?" She jerked her head around and stared at him. Brannon was staring straight ahead, his jaw tight.

"Yeah. He mentioned you. I wanted to rip him apart." He shrugged restlessly. "The prick has messed with every *fucking* body, Hannah. He's already jerking Moira and me around. Neve, too, to some extent, but not as much since she wasn't the one who pissed him off. That was Moira and me. But he's going there. Ian's being hassled about his green card. Now Tag and Alison and Marc are involved. He mentioned you for a reason. Maybe just to piss me off, but who the hell knows?"

"He's going to be pretty busy juggling everything that's come up today. Maybe he'll leave you alone."

"Yeah." Brannon's voice was thick with derision. "Maybe . . ."

He went silent, his steps coming to a halt. Hannah's did as well and they watched as three cars came cruising down the street.

They stopped in front of the municipal building. Hannah squeezed Brannon's hand. He rubbed his thumb across the inside of her wrist.

The senator was a distinguished looking man. Even now, after the debacle that had happened, he looked like the sort of man who could command the attention of an entire room—or all of Main Street. As he climbed out of his car, he smoothed a hand down his tie and looked around. He had a look on his face. It was cleverly hidden, but Hannah recognized that look.

Ruler of all I survey.

Her stepdad had looked around his house like that.

Some men had rule of only a small piece of territory.

Others claimed a larger slice.

The senator looked like he wanted to claim everything his eyes touched and when he slid a look toward Brannon, there was clearly the look of a pissed-off monarch.

Brannon let go of Hannah's hand and took a small step forward.

"Apparently he hasn't figured out Treasure already has a monarchy," she murmured.

The silent standoff lasted long enough that Hannah wouldn't have been surprised to see a tumbleweed roll between them. "Okay, Wyatt Earp. I think this showdown's lasted long enough." She caught his hand and tugged. "Besides, Doc Holiday and your brothers aren't showing."

A smile cracked Brannon's face as he glanced at her.

The staredown broken, Senator Henry Roberts turned and moved toward the municipal offices, his aides, assistants, and bodyguards trailing along behind him like a cloud.

"I guess you're right."

"Yeah?" Brannon crooked a brow. "About what?"

"He's not a man who's going to forget this." She tried to brush aside the uneasiness that gripped her gut. "He's also a man who hates your guts, Bran. You can feel it."

"Let him hate me." Brannon shrugged. "If he's focusing on me, then I'm not worried."

She glanced at him. "He can't really cause problems for Ian, could he?"

"Probably not. I've already got a lawyer handling things." Brannon shoved a hand through his hair and turned back to her. "But he's doing it just to prove he can get under my skin."

"Then don't let him." She moved in and hugged him.

"Come on. Let's get to the doctor. We get to hear the heartbeat today."

"Hear that?"

Brannon stood to the side, hands fisted in his pockets, a knot in his throat as he listened to the rapid-fire beat of his baby's heart.

Try as he might, he couldn't quit staring at Hannah's face.

I love you . . .

His head was a mess.

It wasn't just because of the senator, although that wasn't helping.

It wasn't even because Hannah had given him the soft kiss or that quick hug she'd given him on the street earlier.

I love you . . .

"Brannon, do you hear?" she asked again.

He stroked her hair back. The sight of her bright eyes and the smile on her lips added to the funny little ache in his chest.

Why hadn't he . . .

Can't think about that right now. No way could he think about it now. Hannah held out her hand and he reached out, folding his fingers tight around hers before she could change her mind.

"Do you hear it?" she whispered.

"Yeah." He smiled, although what he wanted to do was go to his knees and pull her to him. Beg her . . . beg her to what? He didn't even know. But he wanted to beg her for something. Anything. Everything. "Hard not to hear. Boy's got a heart like a racecar."

"Boy?" She sniffed. "I bet it's a girl."

He cocked a brow. "Easy enough to find out."

"No." She made a face at him. "I like surprises."

"Then you can let me find out and I won't tell you," he offered.

Dr. Ellison Shaw laughed. "That never works out." She glanced up at them. "The heartbeat is good and strong. Sounds like you two have a healthy baby in there, Hannah."

Hannah's hand tightened on his. Judging by the way his heart constricted, Brannon would have thought she'd been squeezing it, not his hand. He kept waiting for her to pull away, but she kept their fingers linked up until the doctor pulled the tool away that let her listen to the heartbeat. "You can sit up now," she said.

Hannah smoothed her shirt down and Brannon moved in, taking the opportunity to help her—and keep touching her.

She shot him a look, her cheeks flushing pink.

The scent of her flooded his head.

The feel of her so close went straight to his cock.

Memory stirred.

Hannah gasped at the feel of his hand on her lower back.

"I'll be right back," Dr. Shaw said.

Hannah barely heard her over the sound of blood roaring in her ears.

"Hannah?"

Slowly, she lifted her head and met Brannon's eyes.

"Are you okay?" he asked. The soft, gentle note in his voice was so unlike him.

He brushed his fingers down her neck and she looked away. A shiver raced down her spine and she had to fight the urge to lean into his touch, lean into him.

His lips slid across her temple and she caught her breath, need stirring inside her. Need, love . . . so many emotions.

In the back of her mind, she heard the echo of his voice . . . *wake up, come back to me . . . I'm sorry.*

She knew he'd come to see her in the hospital. People told her that he'd been there. Every day. One of the nurses, Ginny, said he'd read to her. He'd read Jude Deveraux's *Velvet Song* to her. The first romance Hannah had ever read and she was on her third copy of it. He'd found her dog-eared copy and brought it to her, read it to her while a cop stood on duty outside her room.

A crazy urge drove her and before he could pull back, she turned her face toward his, lifting her mouth before he moved away. Twisting her head around, she reached for him, fisting her hand in the collar of his shirt and dragging him closer. He didn't move as she pressed her mouth to his.

"You're going to drive me crazy, Brannon," she said against his lips.

When she kissed him again, a harsh sigh escaped him. He stood there, his hands braced on the table, one near her hip, the other precariously perched between her knees. She wondered what he'd do if she wiggled closer and rubbed against him.

Then she stopped thinking at all, because he'd broken the kiss.

The interruption might have lasted mere seconds. He moved from his position at the foot of the table to standing in front of her. One hand went to either of her knees and she sucked in a breath as he pushed them wide and moved to stand between splayed thighs.

Then he reached up, tangling his hands in her hair. "Open your mouth," he said, his voice a low rasp, scraping against her senses like raw silk over bare flesh.

She parted her lips and his tongue swept in.

The taste.

She shuddered and reached up, grasping at his arms, her nails sinking into his biceps.

She whimpered when he cupped her breast, the heat of his hand apparent even through her bra and shirt.

I've probably fantasized about getting my hands on your tits about a hundred times now.

Hannah tore her mouth away, shoving him back.

"Hannah?"

Panting, she stared at him.

Cool air kissed her flesh and she looked down, dismayed to find her shirt open.

How had he managed that? He'd had his hands on her maybe thirty seconds.

"Hannah, what's wrong?" Brannon asked, taking a step toward her.

She shook her head and hopped off the table, moving to stare outside.

I've probably fantasized about getting my hands on your tits about a hundred times now.

It was Brannon's voice she heard in the back of her head, clear as day. She knew what was happening. It was another one of those memories, trying to slip free from whatever held it trapped. It had started like that at first— Brannon had been the one to make all those blocks come down to begin with. He'd sat with her in the room in the hospital, along with Neve. Neve had been talking about school and Hannah had listened, but with despair.

"You hit me in the head with a rock once," he'd told her.

Those words, so easily delivered, had startled her out of her misery. He hadn't even been looking at her as he said it. He'd been busy staring at his phone, tapping away at it, like there was nothing going on outside that screen that interested him.

He'd paused for a moment and looked up at her. In an almost bored tone, he said, *"There I was thinking I'd need stitches and bleeding all over the place and you told me to stop being a baby so you could clean it up.*"

"*Head wounds bleed, Brannon, now stop whining and let me see it.*"

She hadn't meant to hit him.

She'd been over to see Neve, upset about her stepfather and she'd been throwing rocks into one of the elegantly landscaped ponds. Brannon came around from behind a tree at the exact wrong minute.

Now, from behind her, he quietly said, "You remembered something, didn't you?"

"Yeah." With awkward, stiff fingers, she finished buttoning her shirt and then looked back at him. "You . . . um. You were touching me. You said something about touching me."

A hot, hungry look lit his eyes.

It was gone just as quickly as it had appeared, but his voice was rougher than normal as he said, "If I recall correctly, I said a great many things about touching you, Hannah."

She was saved from having to respond to that by the doctor. Dr. Shaw came in, but her normally cheerful smile faltered as she looked between them. "Is everything okay?"

"Yeah." Hannah managed a taut smile. She waved a hand in front of her face. "I'm just . . ."

Brannon cut her off. "Tired. I guess you hear that a lot."

Hannah narrowed her eyes at him, but Dr. Shaw was already talking. "Oh, yes. It will get better, Hannah." Then she laughed. "In maybe twenty years. Assuming you don't have any other kids."

He was ready for it.

The spark of temper in her eyes had flared in the

office, but Hannah seemed to prefer having her battles in private.

As they left, she jerked her head down the road. "You got a few minutes?"

"Sure."

She didn't say anything else, she turned on one foot and started down the road toward her apartment.

He was left to catch up with her and it was a good thing he wasn't any kind of slouch, because the way she was moving, anybody who didn't have long legs and a fast gait would have a hard time keeping up.

She didn't say a single word on the five-minute walk to her place.

Brannon spent those minutes deliberating on the best approach to take.

In the end, though, he didn't have to take one.

Hannah barely waited until he'd shut the door behind them before she took the bull by horns. She whirled on him and drove a finger into his shirt. "You don't get to speak for me, Brannon McKay. If somebody asks me how I'm doing, I can answer just fine on my own." She enunciated her words by driving the tip of her finger into his chest.

He felt like she was trying to skewer him on her short, neatly rounded nail. But he still let her poke him a few more times before he caught her wrist. "Enough," he said. "I know you can answer just fine on your own. I just didn't want you doing it."

She twisted her hand away. "Obviously." She curled her nose at him in prissy little sneer. It made him want to bite her.

Bite later. Talk now.

"Hannah, think about it," he said softly. He went to reach for her, but she pulled away and moved into the small kitchen of her apartment. She'd been left alone for the past couple of months. She'd had a few prank calls—and he knew the source of almost every single one. The town itself couldn't afford to trace her calls, but he could. Gideon had tap-danced his way around it, but the end result was the same. Hannah had consented to letting her phone calls be traced and it had resulted in a whole lot of jack shit.

As a matter of fact, a whole lot of jack shit pretty much summed up *exactly* what had happened since her release. Gideon and Brannon believed it was because she didn't remember anything.

If there was reason to believe that had changed . . .

"Whatever happened to Shayla, whatever you might have seen, you've been safe because you don't remember," he said. "If somebody thinks you're starting to remember, then what happens?"

"But . . ." Hannah stopped abruptly, blowing out a sharp breath of air through her nostrils. "Don't go making sense, Brannon. It will just piss me off."

"Okay." He waited until she lifted her gaze heavenward, watched as she took a couple of deep breaths. Seeing that the tension was draining out of her, he took a chance. "How about you tell *me* what you remembered, though? Maybe I can help . . . stir some memories."

She turned on her heel and strode into the kitchen. Over her shoulder, she said, "No, thanks."

But he caught sight of the flush on her cheeks.

He thought of the way she'd whispered, *You're driving me crazy . . . .*

The kitchen of her apartment was neat and efficient—not too dissimilar from the kitchen where he'd hassled Ella Sue off and on for almost half of his life. But it was small, so small that with both him and Hannah in it, it was a tight squeeze. Brannon decided the word *intimate* suited.

As she opened a cabinet, he came up behind her and put his hands on the counter, effectively caging her in.

She tensed.

"What are you doing?"

He turned his face into her hair.

The scent of it was something that haunted him. That delicate fragrance had lingered on his pillow for days and out of desperation, he'd washed everything on his bed, determined to forget about the woman who'd been driving him crazy. Only days later, she was in a wreck and he would have given anything—*anything*—to have her back in his bed, that long, golden brown hair spilled out over his pillow again.

"I'm just standing here," he said easily. "I love the way you smell, Hannah. I think it's become my drug."

A soft, shaky little breath escaped her.

Since he was already there, he decided to go for broke and he slid a hand around her, curving his palm around the hard mound where his baby rested.

"If it's a girl, what do you want to name her?" he asked softly.

Her breath hitched. He watched as her fingers tightened convulsively on the edge of the cabinet and then slowly, she closed it. "My mother's name was Lily. I know it's old-fashioned, but . . ."

He rubbed his cheek against her hair. "My mom's name was Sandra. Some people think that's old-fashioned now." Then he laughed. "Her middle name was Rose. That's really old, I guess. But it suited her. Dad called her his Rose. She smelled like roses, too. Was always out working in the gardens."

"Rose."

He thought he heard a smile in her voice. "Lily Rose."

She couldn't have had a deeper effect on him if she'd

just reached right inside his chest and wrenched his heart out, squeezed it. His arm tightened on her waist and he buried his face in her hair, all but knocked to his knees by the emotion that swamped him. "I like it."

"I think I do, too." She turned around in his arms slowly and looked up at him. "I think maybe I could tell you what I remembered. In exchange for something."

"Really." The blood in his veins started to pump hotter and he had a feeling it was all going to drain south in about two seconds. Her gaze had dropped to his mouth. "Just what kind of favor are you thinking about, Hannah? Need some work done around here? Want a ride into Baton Rouge or something?"

"No." A smile teased her lips. "I'm perfectly capable of moving things around, taking care of my own work . . . driving myself into Baton Rouge."

She smoothed a hand up his chest and he felt his heart kick against her palm when she pressed it flat against him. Clearing his throat, he moved in a little closer. "Okay, then. Just what is this favor?"

Hannah's mouth pressed to his. "A kiss."

"A kiss?" Fisting his hand in the hair at her nape, he held her steady, staring into her dark eyes, so close to his. "Just whose favor is this? Yours or mine?"

"Maybe it's a mutual sort of thing. We were interrupted earlier after all."

"Hmmm." He rubbed his mouth against hers.

She opened for him on a sigh and he took the invitation. He'd been holding back for so long, even when he could feel her growing frustration, but maybe he'd been holding back *too* much. She wanted him. He wanted her.

Hannah's hands slid up his chest, her arms curling around his neck.

Her breasts went flat against his chest.

She was fuller there already and he slid one hand up, rested it just below the lush curve.

She immediately covered his hand with hers. He stopped, going to pull away. "I'm sorry . . . ."

But all she did was guide his hand higher, staring into his eyes. "You've been treating me like glass for the past two months," Hannah said softly. "I won't break, Brannon."

"No." He circled his thumb around her nipple. Even through the material of her shirt and bra, he could feel how hard it was and he wanted to peel away the clothing, catch that pebbled flesh between his teeth and tug and tug, then suck on her until she made that strangled little noise deep in her throat.

She arched closer and said again, "I won't break."

She wouldn't. But he was starting to think he might. There was still so much unsaid, so much undone between them and the more time that passed without her remembering, the harder it was for him to figure out how to fix any of it.

Swearing, he dragged her head toward his and kissed her, losing himself in the taste of her mouth and the feel of her body against his, so soft and strong.

Her hand moved between them, curved around his cock, stroking him through the faded denim of his jeans.

"Naked," she muttered, pulling away just enough to nip at his lower lip. "I want you naked."

He was just fine with that idea.

But when he pulled back to fumble her out of her shirt, her phone rang.

Hannah groaned.

"Ignore it."

"I can't." She turned her head away when he tried to kiss her again. "I'm on call today. That's the ringtone for work."

As she wiggled out from in between him and the counter, Brannon's mind tried to catch up to what was happening. "But . . ."

Hannah didn't answer. She was already on the phone and judging by the look on her face, they wouldn't be able to pick this back up.

Not even twenty seconds later, he had his answer.

She gave him a quick, hard kiss. "Sorry. I'm needed."

"But . . ."

She winked at him. "Now that you're done treating me like I'm fragile, we'll have to finish this. Soon." She spun around and moved out of the kitchen, all legs and speed and grace. She paused just before she would have moved out of his sight and looked back at him. "By the way . . . what I remembered?"

She glanced at his hands, her tongue coming out to touch her lips. "It was you saying how you fantasized about having your hands on me." She lifted one of her own, grazed it across the curve of one breast. "Here. Now that's about all I'm going to be able to think about until we finish this."

CHAPTER NINE

The good doctor was a cheap drunk and a good fuck.

That wasn't a bad combination for a late-night companion and seeing as how she was very careful about hiding her affairs from her husband and discreet about her liaisons, it made her the perfect woman, as far as he was concerned.

She was also a sexual tigress—one of the reasons she and her husband were having problems.

Her husband adored her and wanted nothing more than to keep her happy, but between her crazy work schedule and his, sometimes . . . well, she was often craving sex when he wasn't there to provide it.

She'd apologized and told him she'd never do it again.

The stupid sap believed her.

Since then, she'd kept her affairs remarkably quiet, which was impressive in a town the size of Treasure. However, to her credit, she'd wised up and started having most of her interludes with colleagues outside of McKay's Treasure.

He was the first lover she'd had in her home town in years. While neither of them were anxious to be discovered, he was relatively confident they could be circumspect.

There were no romantic feelings on either side.

They both had a need the other could fill.

She needed a hard dick, as she'd told him more than once—and she needed it more often than her husband's—or her work schedule—could allow.

The man lying next to Ellison was more than happy to provide such a service. He was careful when taking a woman to his bed. It had been years since his last lover of any note. If and when he had any assignations, they were brief and to the point—and never here. He'd learned his lesson on that.

He was breaking a personal rule with Ellison, but it was for reasons aside from sex. Sex was just a bonus. She was providing him with something he needed, something only she could provide.

Now, cradling a snifter in one hand, she lifted it up and breathed in. "Baby," she said, her voice low and throaty. "This is . . . nirvana. Where did you get this?"

"On a business trip in New Orleans," he said casually. He stared at her, pretending to study her mouth, but he was more interested in the cognac. Or rather, what was *in* the cognac.

Ellison had a taste for expensive alcohol.

Once she was drunk, she tended to talk.

Thanks to the fine powder he'd added to her drink, she'd talk . . . and she wouldn't remember a thing. He'd make sure to give her plenty of water before he left and he'd give her a good hard fuck as well. If she was good and sore in the morning, she could pass off any lingering headache to a night of sheer debauchery. He'd dump half of the cognac and tell her that she really did need to lighten up on the booze. He'd had to tell her that more than once anyway, as had a number of other people.

One would think that a doctor would recognize that she was self-medicating for her depression, along with other issues. But people were strangely blind when it came to their own problems.

She hummed as she took a sip, one hand sliding down his stomach to wrap around his cock. "This is the *shit*," she said, a giggle escaping her a moment later.

He smiled, not bothering to respond. Instead, he folded a hand around hers and tightened her grasp.

She laughed again and he knew by the overly bright sound of it that the alcohol—and the drugs—were already hitting her system. She must not have eaten much today. She didn't take particularly good care of herself. It was a pity. He hated it when she didn't at least take time for a meal. She worked so hard.

She was a means to an end, but she was also entertaining. No reason for her to abuse herself the way she did.

She stroked her thumb across the crown of his dick and he hissed out a breath. "You like that," she said, her voice a low, husky purr.

"I like just about everything you do, darling," he said.

"Sweet talker." She tossed the rest of the cognac back and then, with the lazy grace of a cat, she climbed on top of him.

The wet heat of her cunt closed around him and he grunted in pleasure as she leaned forward. He caught one small nipple in his mouth, but had to release it when she sat back down. "Something for you . . ." She wiggled astride him and then held up the cognac and splashed more into her snifter. "And something for me."

He arched up, driving into her as she splashed a healthy pour into the glass. She gasped and he said, "I've already got something for you, love."

"Don't you just? I'm greedy, though. I want it all."

He took the cognac and sat up, wrapping one arm

around her hips and tucking her in tight against him. She clamped around him, whimpering a little. Her eyes were already glassy. He took the bottle, taking a long, heavy drag from it.

"Don' . . ." She shuddered, then tried again. "Don't you go . . . drinkin' it all, you . . . sexy son of a bitch."

He put it down on the table, just enough off center that he could hit it and send it to the floor when he stood. He wasn't about to drink any more, but he didn't want her having more alcohol in her system either. This would kill two birds with one stone. The lingering stink of alcohol in the air when she woke up would only add to her disorientation.

Then, smiling at her, he caught her hips and lifted her up. "Shut up already."

She laughed and drank the rest of her cognac before tossing the snifter onto the bed. "Make me."

He did.

She was trying to slide into unconsciousness when he sat her up.

Her pupils were wide and heavily dilated.

"Ellie," he said, tapping her cheek.

She gave him a sweet smile. "Hi. You're . . ." she sighed and reached for him, missing him by a mile. "You're boo . . . beautiful. Beautiful. Why can't my husband want me like you do?"

"I'm sure he does, Ellie," he told her. "He just isn't as good in the sack as some men are. You'll just have to be patient and teach him."

She pursed her lips and then nodded. "I can teach him. I'm smart, you know." She hiccupped. "I'm a doctor. I gotsa . . . I gotta be smart. I'll teach him."

"Yes, love." He leaned in and kissed her forehead. "Hannah saw you today."

"Hannah . . ." Her forehead crumpled and then cleared. "She's pregnant. Silly girl. Doesn't remember. How can you forget fucking a man like Brannon? *I* wouldn't."

"Amnesia, right? She has amnesia?"

"My patient." She twisted, trying to pull. Her lashes drooped and he had to cup her chin, guide her face back to his. Tears flooded her gaze. "I have to protect my patients, baby. I don't talk . . ."

"No, no." He leaned in and shushed her, pressed a soft kiss to her lips. "You are protecting her. I'm worried about her, too. I'm scared for her. What if she saw somebody that night? If she did, she could be in trouble. We need to make sure she's safe. If she's remembering anything, we have to make sure she tells the cops, right?"

"But she's not." The troubled expression on Ellison's face cleared. "She can't remember." With the blind sincerity of a naïve child, the drugged doctor nodded. "She's not remembering. It makes her so mad but she can't member—*re*member."

"Do you think she will?" he asked patiently.

Ellison's head slumped.

He shook her slightly. "Ellie, don't sleep yet. This is important."

She blinked and looked around blearily. "I'm sleepy," she said. Then she sighed. "The mind is silly, honey. Nobody knows. She don't know. I doesn't—" She giggled and clapped a hand over her mouth as though amused by her drunken, drugged speech. "*I doesn't!*"

Hooting with laughter, she collapsed on her side.

He watched for a moment, amused.

Then he rose and shook his head.

She was still laughing when he left to get her some water from the fridge. He checked the time. He should

have time to make her eat something before he left. He
had other matters to attend to.

"I was thinking maybe you could spend the night." Hannah kept her gaze locked ahead as she said the words,
told herself that it was more than past time and it wasn't
like they hadn't already gotten involved in a sexual relationship. She *was* past her first trimester after all.

Brannon didn't say anything for the longest time and
she told herself to wait, just wait.

The music of the crickets chirping, the call of birds,
everything else faded away in a rush of heat when he
tugged her to a stop and pulled her up against him.
"Spend the night, huh?" He curled an arm around her
waist and studied her. "You mean like a slumber party,
Hannah?"

"Sure. The naked kind." Hannah suddenly had a
hard time pulling in enough oxygen, her tank top
clinging to her, although it wasn't particularly hot out.
It was mid-September and fall was finally coming to
Mississippi, bringing moderately cooler days and
softer nights. Still, she felt like she'd been plunged into
a steam bath.

"What do you think?" she asked. "Are you interested?"

"Hmmm." He caught a lock of her hair between his
thumb and forefinger, rubbing at it.

They'd gone on a walk. It had been her idea. Brannon
had developed a habit of showing up on her doorstep in
the evenings and today, after her unexpected half-shift,
she'd come home to find him waiting on the front steps
with a clutch of wildflowers and a box of pizza.

They'd eaten the pizza right there and then he'd waited
for her to change before they'd left to take their walk.

Hannah tried to pretend just being this close wasn't

making her come out of her skin. She wanted him until she was blind to everything else, deaf to everything else.

Parts of her body burned, as though those places he'd touched seemed have the sensory memory of their times together. That missing week caused a void in her mind, but she didn't let herself think about it too often. She understood one thing and as far as she was concerned, that was all that mattered.

Hannah loved Brannon McKay.

She'd loved him for half of her life and suddenly he was there.

But the light, easy kisses weren't enough. She wanted so much more. Now, in the small grove filled with picnic tables, the river sparkling under the moon, she stared at him and made up her mind. It was well past the time they stop dancing around each other.

Brannon might not know it yet, but that was fine.

She'd just clue him in along the way.

There was still enough light for her to see his face, though, and the saturnine smile that curved his lips. "A naked kind of party, huh?"

She slid her gaze to his mouth, licked her own. "That's the plan. What do you think?"

As he continued to watch her, she backed up and rested her hips against the edge of the nearest table. Brannon echoed her steps. She ended up with her hips on the surface of the picnic table, her feet propped up on the bench and him leaning into her, a pleased smile curling his lips.

"You got any entertainment in mind for this . . . party?" he asked.

"Oh, lots." She reached up and curled her hand in the placket of his button down shirt. "I was thinking I could take a long, lazy ride. Followed by a nice hot shower.

Since you're my guest, you'd have to join me. I don't want to be rude."

His green eyes seemed to glow for a moment, brilliant with hunger.

"Damn," he said, his voice low and raw. "That sounds like a fine idea."

He leaned in and nuzzled her neck.

She fought the urge to close her eyes.

When his mouth slid up higher along the curve of her neck, she sighed in pleasure. "Is this a yes?"

"Hmm. I don't know. What else did you have in mind? I like to know in advance."

She laughed. The sound ended in a moan as he caught her ear between his teeth and tugged. "You never like to know anything in advance, pal."

"Sure I do. Like . . . what are you wearing under these jeans?"

He straightened up and stared at her.

"I'll tell you . . . in exchange for a favor," she said, grinning at him.

He kissed her, hard and deep, the hunger firing her own. She moved against him, liquid heat spreading through her. His name was an endless chant in her mind and when he pulled away, she reached for him. He caught her wrists and kissed her hands, first one, then the other. "If I keep this up, I'll forget where we are, Hannah."

She panted, staring at him. Then she nodded, swallowing down a groan when she squirmed on the table. She was wet, so wet for him she could feel it, and it had her panties sliding against her when she moved around.

"So?"

She blinked up at him. "So . . . what?"

"What are you wearing under these jeans?"

Now she smiled at him. "Well, you still owe me a

favor. I wasn't going to ask for a kiss. You see, I need an answer about that party invite."

"Is that a fact?" Brannon stood there, hovering so close she could feel his breath against her lips.

She breathed in and it seemed to draw him in. Maybe she swayed forward. She didn't know. But he was just *there* and his mouth was . . .

She groaned and then they were kissing and *this* . . . *this* was familiar.

His tongue slid along her lips and she opened. Moving in closer, she curled an arm around his neck. He was tall, but Hannah wasn't a small woman and she was glad of it. She only had to stretch a little to meet him and he made it easy by curving an arm around her waist and pulling her flush against him.

His mouth slanted over hers and he tugged her lower body closer even as he leaned in, pressing against hers. They fit. They fit *so* well . . . she knew that though, didn't she?

Maybe I don't like being your morning entertainment—

The words bounced around in her head, disjointed and not making sense. She shoved them away, curling her fingers into Brannon's shirt almost desperately.

One big hand plunged into her hair and he nipped at her lower lip then sucked it into his mouth, running his tongue along the curve.

It was an intimate, rough sort of kiss and it sent hungry little shivers racing through her.

Her belly went tight and then hunger pulsed in her as she felt his cock throbbing against her.

"I'd love to spend the night, Hannah," Brannon said against her ear.

Her head fell to the side and she clung to him, the strength in her legs dissolving.

He slid one hand under her shirt. She gasped, the contact shocking. His skin was hot. It wasn't exactly cool out, but the feel of his skin on hers was something that went beyond heat. It went beyond intimacy.

It went beyond *everything.*

She wanted more, needed more—

Opening her mouth, she sucked in the breath to tell him they needed to get the hell out of there.

Tires squealed.

Drunk on the taste of her, it took Brannon a few seconds to process the fact that things weren't as they should be.

Now he liked to think he was a quick thinker and he was pretty certain his survival instincts were as good as anybody else's. He liked breathing.

The hair on the back of his neck stood on end and he jerked his head up as the squeal of rubber grew louder and instinct kicked in. Grabbing Hannah, he wrenched her toward him and threw her to the ground. They rolled and she screamed and he swore.

The one thing he knew for certain was that somebody had deliberately pointed a car toward them.

Sucking air in as fast as he could, he shoved his weight up off Hannah and stared at the bumper of the car as it whipped a right onto Market—already two blocks away and too far for him to make out the license plate. He knew the make. One thing Brannon knew was his cars.

It was a Crown Victoria, black, tinted windows.

About as run of the mill as they came.

Hannah made a low noise. He tore his gaze away from the road and focused on her.

"Are you okay?"

She grumbled. That sound alone reassured him.

"I think so," she said. She pushed up onto her elbows and looked around. "I—"

Before she could finish, a shout interrupted them, followed by the slam of a car door. "Hey! Are y'all okay? I just called 9-1-1 . . . shit, Brannon, is that you? Hannah?"

She closed her eyes and lay back on the ground.

Brannon resisted the urge to stroke her hair as he levered onto his knees and met the eyes of the Good Samaritan.

"No pizza?"

Alison grinned at Marc. "I'm not hungry."

"What about a drink down at the pub then? They got a pretty decent wine list." Marc wagged his eyebrows. "Soon, it will be even better."

"No." She huffed out a breath that sent her bangs drifting up, before they came back down to hang in her eyes again. "Honestly, I would, but today . . ."

Marc looked away. "Yeah. Today." He tipped his head up to the starry sky that stretched out over them like a blanket. "What can we possibly say about today?"

"It was interesting." Alison delivered those words with complete and utter sincerity.

"Interesting." He snorted.

"And it sucked." She wrapped her arms around herself and shivered, trying not to think about the look the senator had given her on his way out the door. All she wanted to do was lock herself up inside her cute little house out on the river and grab a pint of Häagen-Dazs, curl up on her couch, and forget today had happened.

She'd deal with all the emails and phone calls tomorrow. Or maybe Sunday. She was off for the whole weekend. She could have one day to totally veg out and pretend the world didn't exist, right?

Marc looked so crestfallen, though. Pushing off her car, she acted on the impulse that had been living inside her for the past two months. Grabbing him by the collar, she tugged him down.

He stiffened in surprise.

And then, as she kissed him, he made a funny little *hmmmm* under his breath.

Alison had sworn off men six months ago after her ex had emptied her bank account and taken off with her ex-best friend. But she'd known within a few weeks that Marc was worth breaking the rules for. She just had to make *him* see that, make him realize they had something going on between them besides this . . . friendship.

She laughed to herself. He thought it was a friendship, although after that kiss she'd given him, maybe he'd realize it was something more. He was so adorably oblivious. What they had was smoking hot tension. She just had to make him see that.

Soon, she told herself. Very soon. If she wasn't so on edge about the senator and everything that had happened, she would have said yes to the pizza and probably pushed for a lot more, too.

But she was a mess, she was stressed, and she needed to decompress . . . *alone*.

Pulling back, she turned back to her car. As she slid inside, she shot him a wide grin. "Ask me again next week. You'll probably get a much different answer, Marc."

A fast drive down a dark country road could do wonders for the brain. Alison had always loved taking a drive when she was moody and tonight was no different. Her mind had settled more and she realized that while today *had* sucked, it could have gone much worse.

The bottom line—Senator Henry Roberts was nothing more than a well-dressed thug and he'd finally been exposed. He came off as the typical, well-to-do businessman. He pressed the flesh well and made white-bread types feel real secure when he told him he was pushing for *them* when he was in office. *Fighting for your way of life*—that was his motto.

Sneering at the idea of it, Alison parked her car. Out of habit, she looked around. Everything looked as it should. The porch light was on and she didn't see anything out of place.

"Fighting for your way of life—as in anything that didn't disrupt you. Never mind all the others out there who suffer, never mind all the others out there who don't have the *rights* you have." Her despondency had given way to anger and she was just fine with that. She functioned better when she was angry.

House key already in hand, she climbed out of the car and started for the front door. She skimmed the area as she walked. She'd been jumped once in college. She wasn't going to be a victim again.

Once she was inside, she locked up and took a minute to rearm her alarm system.

Then, she headed into the bathroom.

First things first.

After a shitty day, the one thing guaranteed to make all things better was a nice, hot bath.

The typical security system would deter the typical thief.

Joseph Smith wasn't a typical thief.

He wasn't a thief at all—and his name wasn't Joseph Smith, either.

He was what some people called a troubleshooter. Others were more upfront about it. They called him what he was. A hitman.

He was quick, he was clean, and he didn't play with his targets. Such actions had been the downfall of many people in his line of work.

He hadn't been surprised when he'd received the call earlier.

He did have to say he was disappointed.

The senator really should have waited, but Henry Roberts was a rash and foolish man. The video that had now been viewed upwards of a million times was evidence of that. Most people in the country—and plenty of people *outside* of it—knew of the McKay family. Anybody with half a lick of sense would have known they weren't the sort you could push around, threaten, or bribe.

But the senator was used to throwing his weight around. Too many people had given way to him. He was good at finding out secrets and wielding them as a club. He wouldn't have found much on the McKays. Joseph Smith knew this, because out of curiosity, he'd looked. He was, after all, the curious type. The biggest secrets the McKays had were that the youngest had dated a crackhead in her college days and had then gone on to get involved with a man who'd beaten her.

She was a stupid sort of girl—or she had been.

He doubted any of them would cower and hide over those pitiful bits of information.

Roberts should have just let whatever the imagined slight was go.

He hadn't. Now he could just sit back and watch as the dregs of his career passed him merrily by.

It made no difference to Joseph.

The man had asked—no—*demanded* this one final job. He'd ignored Joseph's subtle suggestions that he give it some time. That was fine, just fine. Joseph would do as he was told. But the job would come at a cost.

Joseph would have to disappear after this.

It would get hot fast.

Too many eyes would look to the senator, and he had

no doubt the senator had been gathering up information on him. Joseph would do the same in his shoes. Actually, Joseph *had* done the same and he'd wager he'd done a better job of it.

He'd put the finishing touches on that tonight and then he'd fade away into obscurity.

He enjoyed his job, but he enjoyed his freedom more.

He might resurface under a new name sometime down the road. But then again, he might not.

From under the bed, he listened to the sound of running water.

He'd had most of the evening to plan. Getting inside hadn't taken much effort. He'd simply walked around the perimeter of the house and found a bedroom window. Of course, the signs of the security company were prominent, but while he'd anticipated she'd have a motion sensor, those were typically placed in a public area—one with high traffic.

He'd come in through the bedroom and he'd stayed there. He'd been prepared for her to walk through the house. Many women were becoming more safety conscious, and wise of them, too. But while she'd done a quick walk through, she hadn't checked every room. If she had, she might have noticed the curtains rippling in the breeze caused by the hole he'd created when he cut through the glass.

Now he just waited.

The sound of water running made him smile.

She'd take a bath.

That would have her nice and relaxed. Off-guard, too. Once she was in the tub, he'd make his move.

He decided he'd even be quick about it.

He rather admired what she'd done.

The senator was an idiot and he'd been brought low by a smart woman with a smartphone.

Sadly, though, Joseph Smith was a businessman and he always saw his jobs through.

But he didn't think he'd take the senator up on the bonus.

Roberts had offered an extra ten grand if Joseph made the Maxwell woman suffer for the humiliation she'd caused him today.

Personally, Joseph thought she deserved a gold star.

After a few more moments, the water stopped running. Then he heard sloshing and a long, heavy sigh.

Slowly, he slid out from under the bed and hovered there on his hands and knees, waiting.

When all he heard was more sloshing coming from the tub, he rose and stood.

His feet were soundless as he moved out of the spare bedroom and down the hall. He hadn't had a chance to learn the layout of the house, but he'd spent too much of his life doing this and he'd discovered that most houses were cut from one of a few basic designs. He was already oriented to where the front and back doors were from his outdoor perimeter check, as well as windows for potential quick exits.

The light slanting through the narrow crack in the door was one of the interior rooms that had no window, but it was the bathroom.

The splashing sounds of water grew louder as he drew closer.

Pressing his back to the wall, he edged up to the slit of an entrance and peered inside.

He couldn't see much thanks to the angle so he shifted to the other side of the door and tried again.

Perfect.

The mirror was positioned so he could see in without obstruction and he studied Alison Maxwell's profile. While he'd watched the video that had been uploaded, he had gone out of his way to avoid learning anything personal about her. He knew the things he needed to know—where she lived, if she lived alone, if there was a hulking brute of a dog he'd have to deal with. He refused to kill animals.

But he hadn't known anything about *her*.

And this was his first time seeing her.

She lifted a glass of wine to her lips and sipped.

As she lowered the glass back down to the rim of the tub, he eased the door open, slipping a hand into his pocket.

Poor girl.

She'd done the world a service really.

"It was the senator's men."

Gideon grimaced. Shooting Brannon a look, he said, "I'll be sure to talk to him, but you know it's going to be hard to prove anything."

"I don't care what you prove. I don't even care if you talk to him." Brannon stood out in the hall of the emergency room. One of the doctors from Hannah's OB office had come in—she was in there with the ER doctor now. They'd already done an ultrasound and Hannah seemed to be handling this better than Brannon was.

Brannon wanted to put his fist through something—preferably the senator's head.

"So . . . you don't want me to investigate?" Gideon said slowly.

Brannon angled a look toward his friend. "Oh, no. Please investigate."

Recognizing the tone in Brannon's voice, Gideon put his notepad down and then turned away, pacing for a few seconds before he came back to stand in front of the other man. "Brannon, you need to stay away from the senator. He's put himself in a hole and he'll have to dig himself out. He might try to cause you all some trouble, but he can only do so much. Let me handle this."

"He tried to run us *over*," Brannon said. He jabbed his finger toward the room where Hannah was waiting. "She's pregnant. God knows what that could have done. And you want me to let you *handle* this?"

"I'm saying I don't want you to lose that temper of yours," Gideon said. His eyes narrowed slightly. "I know what happens when you do and you look like you're close to the boiling point."

Brannon wisely said nothing.

Taking a step closer, Gideon gestured toward the closed door. "She's got enough going on. She may never get that week of her life back. She's pregnant. And even though she doesn't let on, things aren't as easy for her. She needs you and it seems like for the first time in your life, you're ready to actually commit to something—to *somebody*. Don't let that pompous prick pull you away from what's important, Brannon."

The door opened and Hannah appeared. She looked pale and wan.

Brannon wanted to cuddle her close and destroy anything that threatened her.

"Hannah." Gideon nodded at her.

She gave him a tired smile.

"You need to talk to me again?" she asked.

"No." Gideon nodded at her. "You get some rest and if I need anything, I'll be in touch."

He gave Brannon a telling look and then left.

"Rest."

Brannon stared at the images on the screen while the OB on call continued to tell Hannah what he wanted from her.

The odd, smooshed-up little thing was his baby.

According to the doctor taking calls for that weekend, the baby was fine. Dr. LaRoche wanted Hannah to follow up with her regular OB/GYN on Monday, but she wasn't anticipating problems.

Wasn't anticipating problems . . . just the words pissed Brannon off and he still felt like he was going to puke.

It hadn't hit him until the doctor had done the ultrasound but he'd kept it together.

Now he had these images and he was a sweaty, shaking mess.

"You're sure everything is fine?" he demanded, interrupting the doctor in the middle of his explanation of when he wanted to Hannah to call. "Maybe we should have her go into Baton Rouge for more tests. A specialist . . . something."

The doctor paused and then turned, looking over at Brannon.

"Mr. McKay," she said, giving him a polite smile. "Absolutely, we *could* do that. But I am a specialist. The equipment here is top-notch. The baby's heartbeat is steady and I see nothing that should concern either of you."

Dr. LaRoche was newer to the practice and lived in the next county over. It had taken her twenty minutes to get there and as far as Brannon was concerned, that was eighteen minutes too long.

"But . . ."

"Brannon." Hannah touched his arm. "I'm fine. The baby is fine."

She gave the doctor a smile and said, "New dads. They get like this, right?"

Dr. LaRoche chuckled as she moved the wand around on her belly. "New dads, second-time dads, third-time dads . . . even doctor dads." She gave Brannon an understanding smile. "Trust me, I understand."

Brannon forced himself to smile back. The woman seemed competent and Hannah was comfortable with her. Brannon tried to make himself accept that and he nodded, looked down at the images he held in his sweaty, shaking hands.

"Okay, Ms. Parker, if you—"

"Bleeding," Brannon said, cutting in a second time. "You said there could be bleeding."

His head started to swim at the thought of it.

"What if she starts bleeding and nobody is there?"

The doctor looked over at Hannah.

Hannah looked almost amused.

She cleared her throat. "Doctor, can you give me and Brannon a moment, please?"

He smiled and nodded.

A moment later, Brannon was alone with Hannah and he stood up, carefully putting the images inside the front pocket of his shirt. "Hannah, I think I should hire a nurse to come stay with you. I can—"

"Not necessary." She gave him a calm smile. "After all, you're spending the night . . . remember?"

"I . . ." He sucked in a breath and spun away. "Well, yeah. I can. Sure, but a nurse . . ."

"I don't need a nurse, Brannon."

He turned back, glaring at her while panic started to choke him. "He said you could start *bleeding*."

"It's just a *remote* possibility," she said. "He wants me to be prepared and FYI, it's a *slim* possibility, if that. I am *fine*, Brannon. You took the impact of the fall. You hit the ground and then you rolled on top of me. I wasn't hurt."

"You could have been!" he shouted.

And that was the problem.

Just *saying* it made him sick and he wanted to puke. Spinning away from her, he braced his hands on the counter and closed his eyes. The room was twisting and turning around him like he'd just gotten off the craziest tilt-a-whirl. "Oh, fuck. Oh, fuck."

"You could have been hurt, too," Hannah said quietly.

He tensed as he heard her approaching.

Her hand smoothed up his back and he turned, grabbing her and hauling her close.

She came willingly and he shuddered as she slid her arms around his waist.

"I was doing fine until they did the ultrasound," he said, his voice squeezing past the knot in his throat. "Then I saw that little guy moving around in there and I got to thinking . . . what if I hadn't been fast enough?"

"I'm fine, Brannon." She turned her face toward his neck and he shuddered as she kissed his neck.

"I don't want you alone tonight."

She pulled back and studied his face. "I'm not going to be. You're coming with me, remember?" She kissed his cheek. "Brannon . . . I can handle this, even if you can't. But there's no way I'm letting you hire a nurse. I've had it with doctors, nurses . . . all of it."

CHAPTER TEN

I can handle this. Hannah could still hear herself saying those words.

Now she was thinking . . . *yeah, right.*

They'd spent a couple of hours in the ER and Brannon had called his sisters and Ella Sue, to let them know what had happened. She had dozed and worried and brooded and tried to pretend she wasn't freaked the hell out.

Now that she was home, she was having a harder time of it.

She knew she ought to be exhausted, too exhausted to do anything but sleep, but as she locked the door behind them, she knew she wouldn't sleep for hours.

"I'll just bunk on the couch," Brannon said, completely unaware of her thoughts.

She turned to see him dumping his bag on the floor next to the long, low couch she'd bought a few years back. The cushions were deep and flat and the couch itself was long enough to hold him. Yet . . .

"No," she whispered.

He'd been in the process of tugging his wallet out of his pocket and froze.

For some reason, the sight of his wallet held her mesmerized.

She stared at it. Hard.

Slowly, she moved toward him.

"Hannah?"

Lifting out a hand, she waited.

He glanced down and then, slowly, he put his wallet
into her hand.

She stroked a finger down the worn, faded edges. It
looked like he'd carried it for ages.

Tightening her hand around it, she closed her eyes.

Slap, slap, slap—

*Her shoes made a rhythmic sound on the pavement
and she ground her teeth together as she rounded the
corner.* I will not go up to my apartment yet. I will not
go up to my apartment yet. I will not—

*Her toe bumped something and she stumbled. She
flailed her arms and caught herself, then she looked
down.*

A wallet, faded and worn, lay on the sidewalk.

Sighing, she stooped and picked it up.

Once she flipped it open, she grimaced.

Should have left it.

*If anybody could afford to lose a wallet around here,
it was him.*

*And if there was anybody she couldn't afford to be
around, it was him.*

*Brannon McKay—the beginning and end of all of her
fantasies.*

"Hannah?"

The sound of her name on his lips made the memory
shatter.

If it were possible, Hannah would have grabbed at it,

tried to clutch it to her, but it fell apart, melting like sticky threads of cotton candy under a heavy summer deluge.

"Hannah."

The memory lodged itself in her brain, but nothing else came. Clearing her throat, she forced herself to smile at him. "Sorry . . . I . . . uh . . ." she pushed the wallet back into his hands. "I remembered something else. Sort of. Your wallet?"

"You . . ." He studied the wallet as if he'd never seen it. "You remember that?"

"Just finding it on the street. It must have been some-time during that week."

"Yeah." His voice was tight, strange.

She looked up to see him staring out the window toward his place. "What's wrong?"

"Nothing." Then he glanced back at her. "It's just . . . you brought it to me. That was the day . . ."

His gaze dropped to her belly.

She blushed.

"Oh. We—um. We slept together that night, didn't we?"

"That night." He dropped the wallet down on top of his bag. He looked like he was going to say something else, but in the end, he just lapsed into silence.

"So . . ." Hannah frowned. "Just that one time? I thought we were . . ." She stopped and blew out a breath.

He came to her, one hand going to her waist, his fingers spreading out to curve over her back. She felt the imprint of his touch and couldn't stop the slight shiver that went through her.

"I've spent half my life avoiding what I felt for you, Hannah. That night, amazing as it was . . . hell, all it did was scare me. And you were smart. You knew it, so you ignored me. That got to me, got under my skin." He dipped his head and rubbed his mouth against hers.

That caress made her breath catch and for a moment,

she forgot what they were talking about. "If I was ignoring you, then how did we end up together?"

"Because I never did like being ignored. I went out looking for you." He rubbed his thumb along the underside of her breast, kissed the sensitive skin behind her ear.

She curled closer to him, a hundred questions burning inside her, but in the end, she didn't ask any of them. She'd spent months trying to uncover those lost days and all it had done was frustrate and infuriate her. She wasn't going to go down that road again. Maybe that memory fragment would lead to more. She hoped it would.

She went to ask him a question, but a yawn interrupted her, one that left her feeling like it would split her head in two. Grimacing at him, she stepped back. "I'm more tired than I thought."

"I'm worn out myself. You've got to be exhausted. I'm going to use the bathroom then you can show me where I can grab some blankets or something to make up the couch."

She didn't say anything as he turned away and her gaze slid down his back, lingered on the narrow waist, his butt. He was almost completely down the hall when she spoke. Hannah barely recognized the rough whisper that came from her.

But Brannon stopped.

"I don't want you sleeping on the couch, Brannon. I'm tired of the two of us dancing around the fact that we want each other, tired of dancing around the fact that you remember what happened and I don't."

Her voice was husky, smooth as aged whiskey, and twice as potent. Standing in the hall, he reached out and braced a hand on the smooth surface of the wall, closing his eyes as he told himself to be smart, to stay in control.

"I think we both know we want each other, Hannah. Neither of us have tried to pretend otherwise."

"Maybe not."

He slid a look at her. She stared at him, cheeks flushed and eyes glassy, bright with a hunger that made him want to grab her and kiss her until they were both breathless. Not that it would take much on his account.

There was a world of emotion on her face. Not just the hunger, either. There was need and lust and longing and . . . love. Emotions he recognized easily enough because they mirrored what he felt for her.

"Maybe we're not pretending, but you sure as hell seemed determined to dance around it and act like nothing ever happened." She lifted her chin, staring him down.

He thought he just might grab that stubborn chin and do exactly what he was tempted to do—kiss her until they were both too drunk on each other to care about anything else. As she continued to watch him with a challenge in her eyes, he reversed direction and moved back to her, his battered tennis shoes all but soundless on the scuffed hardwood floor.

Hannah's chest rose and fell erratically but when he came to a halt in front of her, she seemed to stop breathing. Reaching up, he fisted a hand in her hair and tugged on her ponytail until she was looking up at him. Her mouth parted and a gasping little puff of air fell from her lips.

"You think I'm acting like nothing happened, sugar?" he asked, leaning in until nothing more than a memory separated them—the memory that he was trying to do the right thing, to treat her better.

"I think you're dancing on eggshells, Brannon McKay." She lifted a brow at him, an amused smile on her lips. "And that's so not you. Why don't you just stop?"

"Just stop," he murmured. "And do what?"

Her tongue slid out and he could have groaned as the pink tip touched her lips.

Judging by the glint in her eyes, she seemed to know exactly what she was doing to him, too. That knowing, female look made him want to bite her—bite her pretty lips, her pretty breasts, bite her anywhere and everywhere.

But he just stood there and waited.

"What do you think you should do?"

"That, sugar," he said, lowering his head to murmur in her ear. "Is a loaded question."

She turned her head so that their lips ended up brushing. He didn't move and when she spoke, her reply was spoken directly against his mouth. "No, it's not. It's a very simple question . . . sugar. What do you think you should do? What do you *want* to do?"

At some point, they'd left the living room.

Hannah was on her bed, naked with Brannon McKay sprawled between her thighs.

If she'd had the presence of mind, she might have been more than a little pleased with herself.

As it was, she was too busy whimpering out his name as he twisted two fingers and screwed them inside her. Then he flicked his tongue against her clit and she choked on a scream as she came.

Again.

She wasn't certain, but she thought that might have been the third time he'd made her climax.

And he was still dressed.

Or at least half-dressed.

He went to nuzzle her clit with his tongue. The sensation jolted through her over-sensitized flesh like lightning. She attempted to smack him. Her hand bounced off one sweat-slicked shoulder. Snorting with laughter, she said, "No more."

He lifted his head. "Why not?"

"I gotta catch my breath."

Stroking one hand up her thigh, he skimmed his lips across her belly. "Breathing is overrated, baby."

"*Noooo* . . ." She groaned. She wiggled and went to twist away. "I need . . ."

She blinked, the words she'd been about to say fading from her mind.

They'd been right there.

Brannon, unaware, went to rub his cheek against her thigh.

The words continued to elude her and she twisted away. "Stop, Brannon."

"What's going on?" he asked.

She sat up and he drew up next to her, one leg lifted up. "What's wrong, Hannah?"

"I wanted something. I can't remember . . ." She shook her head, misery in her voice. Then she sighed, stopped, and focused. "Tired. I wanted . . . I'm tired. That's what I wanted to tell you."

Her voice cracked.

"Okay." He stretched out next to her, but he moved slowly with it, as though asking permission. She turned into his body and curled up against him. Some of the tension drained out of him and he draped an arm around her. "You're tired."

"This pisses me off," she said. "I didn't ask you in here so you could go down on me and then have me fall asleep on you."

"Hannah . . ." He chuckled and then pressed a kiss to her brow. "You're pregnant. I think getting tired is part of it. And FYI, even if you *did* ask me in here just to go down on you? Well . . . I'm not complaining."

She made a noise that was half laugh, half sob.

Sighing, she snuggled in closer. After a minute, she said, "This pisses me off."

"Being tired? Why?"

"No." With her head buried against his chest, she mumbled, "No. It's not being *tired* that pisses me off. It's . . ."

The exhaustion drained away under the aggravation and she sat up. "It's not being able to think of the things I need to say. Forgetting. The other day, I was almost late to work because I couldn't find my shirt and it was hanging right on the bathroom door where I've always put it."

Brannon stroked a hand up her back. "You've got to give it time."

"Time." She bowed her head. She could feel him toying with the ends of her hair and it made her smile. "How much time do I wait, Brannon? What . . . damn it, what if I end up having this baby and have to write her name just to remember it?"

"That's not going to happen."

She looked at him. "How do you know?"

"Because you haven't forgotten anything important." As he sat up, the muscles in his belly worked.

It was a beautiful sight and she had to fight the urge to stroke her fingers across that heavy, washboard display. She could have slid her hands across his body for ages and not gotten bored. Giving into the urge, she put her hand on his thigh. The light growth of hair tickled her palm. His muscles jumped under her touch and she smoothed her hand up and down. "I forgot us."

A rough noise escaped him and he covered her hand with his, holding it in place. "I meant the new things. As for us . . . you might get that week back, you might not. You're moving on anyway. But you're not going to forget your baby's name, Hannah. Even the things you have trouble remembering, you get it back within a few seconds, a few minutes most of the time. When you don't?" He shrugged. "That's why you make notes and keep lists. You're making it work."

"I'm tired of making it work, though." Glumly, she looked past him out the window. The sheer curtains were enough to offer some privacy, but not enough to keep the light out. She could hear the noise coming from the town. This late at night, it was muted. Rising, she moved to the window and braced a hand on the wall next to it, staring down into the street. "I just want my life back, Brannon."

He came up behind her.

When he slid his arms around her, she rested against him. One big hand curved over her belly and she shivered at the intimacy of it—at the tenderness of it.

"You've got your life, Hannah. You're missing one week of it," he said softly. "And now things are harder, but think about how much worse it could be. Shayla Hardee is dead and you could have been killed in that wreck."

He rubbed his cheek against hers. "Your life is still your life . . . it's gotten harder, but nobody ever promised life would be easy."

"Yeah, well, if they had, I'd want my money back." She laughed wearily and then, as a yawn cracked her jaw, she stretched.

Brannon groaned, his fingers tightening on her hip. "Do that again."

"Do what?" Then she shivered. His cock was a firm, heavy brand against her hip. Closing her eyes, she rolled her hips and said, "You don't mean that, do you?"

Brannon leaned his weight against hers. "You're tired, remember? Maybe you shouldn't be teasing me."

"Maybe I'm not as tired as I thought."

His knee pushed between hers, slowly.

She spread her legs to accommodate him.

"Do you remember how I told you that I'd fantasized about putting my hands on you?" he asked, the hand on her belly gliding up to cup one breast. "Here?"

Her breath hitched as he tweaked her nipple. She felt the touch arrow straight down, twisting through her sex as though he'd cupped her between her thighs. "Yes," she said softly.

"I still fantasize about it. It's worse now because I can remember how you felt . . . how you taste. I want to taste you again. All the time, every day . . ." He muttered the words in her ear, low and soft. "I want to stretch you out on my bed and fuck you until every time you breathe in, you taste me, you feel me on your skin. Just like I taste you, just like I feel you."

Slowly, she turned and faced him. She curled her arms around him and pressed close. His body was hot and heavy and it felt so good. "I feel you now." Hannah rubbed her mouth against his and hummed under her breath as his taste flooded her system. "I taste you, too."

He caught her up in his arms and boosted her up. "Tell me you're ready for this."

"I've been ready since the moment I saw you standing in the doorway of my hospital room." She fisted her hands in his hair. "I've been ready since the moment I first drew air. I was born wanting you."

They said nothing else.

Hannah gasped as he moved between her legs.

He groaned as she curled her legs around him.

And when he sank inside, they both shuddered.

Her eyes were dark and blind on his, her pulse hammering in her throat. Brannon pressed his mouth to that mad, fluttering beat and slid his tongue over it.

She groaned and jerked her hips. Her pussy contracted around him, sending shivers straight up his spine.

It was enough to make his eyes cross from the pure, silken pleasure of it and he withdrew, drove in again, hard and fast. She tightened her legs and arched against him, swiveling her hips in time with his.

His name fell from her lips.

It was the sweetest thing he'd ever heard—almost.

Tangling his hand in her hair, he hauled her head back. "Open," he muttered against her lips. Then he took her mouth. One kiss wasn't enough. One taste wasn't enough. One night, one week . . . one lifetime.

She yielded to him and when he slid his tongue into her mouth, she bit him.

It made him burn hotter.

Made him need her that much more. He *always* needed more. How had he'd ever managed to pretend otherwise?

Her nails scraped into his shoulders.

Her teeth sank into his lip.

His climaxed roared ever closer and he slid a hand between them, circled his thumb around her clit. She shivered and he did it again, harder, faster.

Hannah climaxed only moments before he did.

The strength drained out of him and for a moment, when it ended, all he could do was bury his face in her hair and struggle to hold himself together.

CHAPTER ELEVEN

He had the best damn shoulders.

Hannah tried not to be so obvious, but her eyes kept straying to him.

He had a great ass on him, too. And really, that man's hair, did a guy need hair like that? She was too lazy to go and dedicate a few hours every six weeks to keep her hair up the way some women did, but even if she spent a few hundred every *week*, her hair would never be as pretty as Brannon McKay's. Really, it just wasn't fair.

When he caught her staring at him, he sent her a slow, lazy smile that sent heat rushing all the way through her. A man's smile had never made her feel quite like that.

She loved it.

She was still picking at her meal when he disappeared into the back of the pub with Ian.

Blowing out a sigh, she looked down at her burger, now mostly cold. She really shouldn't have come here to eat. At least not if she'd wanted to eat.

Ever since he'd spent the night in her bed, she'd found herself so obsessed with him, it was almost insane. Maybe *she* was insane. She went out of her way to find time to hunt him down, to be with him. Not that he seemed to mind.

The chair across from her scraped over wood as it was pulled out.

Hannah flinched at the sound, unable to suppress it in time.

The tired, drawn face of Roger Hardee chilled the warm, comfortable heat that had pooled inside her as she watched Brannon and it chased away whatever appetite she had left.

"Roger," she said quietly.

He nodded at her, his Adam's apple bobbing as he swallowed. He smiled, or tried to. It wobbled and fell away before it really formed. "Looks like you have about as much trouble eating these days as I do."

"Um." She looked down at her half-eaten meal and shrugged. "I was thinking about . . . stuff." She couldn't really go and say she was distracted by the sight of the sexy beast that was Brannon McKay, now could she? "My appetite kind of comes and goes these days still."

He jerked his head in an erratic nod. "I guess the baby?" He didn't even give her a chance to answer before he continued. "I guess . . . well, you haven't remembered anything new."

Hannah shook her head, aching for him.

"You will, though." Roger leaned forward, his eyes dark, almost fanatical. "You're going to remember, Hannah. You have to."

Guilt was an ugly, nasty monster. "I hope I will, Roger. I do, but I . . ." She looked away, tears burning her eyes. "I don't want to give you false hope."

"I need that hope."

His hand shot across the table, and she gasped when he closed his fingers around her wrist. Roger was a big man. Older than her by ten years, he'd played football in high school. That big, heavy layer of muscle had mostly gone to fat, but the strength was still there. His fingers dug in—not in an attempt to hurt. She knew that. She could see it in his eyes, the desperation written there was plain to see.

"I need that hope. Don't you get it?" he said, his voice growing louder. "It's all I've got."

"Oi!" Ian's voice cut through the noise in the air.

Hannah flushed, tugging on her hand. "Let me go," she said, keeping her voice calm. From the corner of her eye, she could see Ian coming out from behind the bar.

"Why can't you remember?" he demanded, as though he hadn't heard her. "It's been months. You were able to go back to work and you've remembered other things. Why can't you remember *that*, Hannah? Why—"

"That's enough, mate."

Roger flinched as a hand clamped down on his shoulder. He let go in the next instant.

"Are you alright, Ms. Parker?"

She looked up and met the cool eyes of Charles Hurst. "I'm fine," she said, forcing a smile.

Moira McKay stood next to him, her moss green eyes firing as she looked at Roger. Charles spoke softly to the man as Moira moved in closer to Hannah. "Sure you're okay?"

"I'm fine," Hannah said again, feeling her cheeks heat. A hundred people—or it felt that way—were staring at her.

She resisted the urge to rub her wrist—and was doubly glad of that when Brannon appeared like a living, breathing storm cloud in the doorway at the back of the pub.

"Damn it," Moira said.

"This will be pleasant," Charles murmured.

Moira cocked a brow and nodded toward her brother.

"Wanna see if you can handle him Hannah? Charles and I will take care of this."

Hannah glanced at Roger. He was staring despondently at the table now. There didn't seem to be much left to handle. "Yeah. Um . . . yeah. Thanks."

She slid out of her chair, just as much to get away and catch her breath as anything else.

Brannon went to go around her.

She caught him around the waist.

"Move, Hannah," he said, biting each word off.

"Stay, Brannon." She pressed a kiss to his chin.

"He had his hands on you."

"He had my wrist and trust me, if I had needed to, *I* could have handled it. You know that."

Her words had no impact so she moved in closer, tightening her arms. He finally looked down at her and the blaze in his eyes sent a shiver down her spine. "Brannon . . . he's just hurting."

"That doesn't give him a right to hurt you."

"He didn't." And he hadn't, not really. The guilt got to her more than anything. "He's hurting, Bran. He lost his wife and they're not having any luck finding who killed her. And I'm . . ."

The tension in Brannon's body drained away and she watched as his face softened.

"Baby, it's not your fault."

Hannah had never thought she'd be one to care for endearments. But there she was, melting because he'd called her *baby*. Then there were the times he'd called her *sugar* in that low, rough raspy voice as he touched her . . . .

Not the time, she told herself. Really not the time. All Brannon had to do was *look* at her and she melted. He cupped her cheek in his hand, his thumb stroking along her lower lip.

The gentleness in his eyes undid her.

"Look, I know it's not my fault," she said, managing a smile. Then, to her horror, a knot tightened her throat and tears stung her eyes.

Stupid hormones.

Brannon went to shift away but she didn't let go. "Come on," he said, sighing. "I'm not going to hurt him. We're just going up to the office."

He shot Roger one last look but the fury had drained from his features.

She let go of his waist and he caught her hand in his.

A few minutes later, sitting on the couch, she watched as he poured her some water.

"You can tell this isn't your office," she said absently, looking around the almost ruthlessly organized space.

"Yeah?" He crossed over to crouch in front of her. After he'd pushed the water into her hands, he brushed her hair back from her face. "How can you tell?"

"It's too organized. Too neat."

"I'll have you know I'm very neat." He tapped the water. "Drink."

She made a face at him. "I don't need you mothering me." But she took a drink, mostly because her throat was dry and the knot still lodged there made it hard to talk. "You're only neat because you worry Ella Sue will come by and do spot-checks on you."

"I'm thirty-four years old," he said mildly. "Do you really think I'm afraid of Ella Sue?"

She pursed her lips and thought it over. Then she said simply, "Yes."

"Damn straight." But he shrugged. "No, it's not my office . . . anymore. It's Ian's and he's freakish about staying organized. That's not me. You saw my . . ."

He trailed off and looked away.

"I saw your apartment," she finished for him. She had, although the only memories she had of it were recent ones. It was clean, yes. But not neat. Clothes were put away and dishes were washed, but there was clutter in odd places, the kind of clutter a person would have if he didn't know exactly where or how he wanted things— or maybe he just didn't care.

"We slept there, didn't we?" She took another drink and then reached over, putting the glass of water down on the table. Studying him, she added, "That first night."

He nodded and reached up, rubbing at the back of his neck. It was a gesture she was familiar with, something he did when he was upset or nervous. "Turn around," she said.

Brannon cocked a brow.

She nudged at his shoulder and said it again.

He relented and sat with his back to her. She settled her hands on his shoulders, her thumbs at his neck. His muscles were tense, taut under her touch and he groaned as she started to dig in. "You're stiff as a board," she said softly.

"That hurts."

"That's because you're stiff as a board," she said. "Give me a few minutes."

He lapsed into silence and after maybe two minutes, she felt the muscles give. He made a grumbling noise deep in his chest. "Now I don't ever want you to stop."

Hannah laughed. "You ought to start getting deep tissue massages. Every week for a while, then maybe once a month. It would do wonders for you, I bet." She hesitated and then said, "I want to . . . ah . . . I need you to tell me what happened. With us, I mean. I'm tired of not knowing and it's not coming back on its own."

For the longest time, he didn't speak and then finally, he reached up, stilled her hands. He shifted on his knees, turning to face her. "You sure that's a good idea?"

"How is it going to hurt me to know what happened when we slept together?"

Brannon cupped her face in his hands and pressed his brow to hers. "It's not that that's got me worried. It's . . . everything else."

"You mean the night Shayla died." Even saying the words made a cold shiver of fear burst through her and she squirmed closer. Brannon responded by wrapping his arms around her and she tucked her head into the crook of his neck. Here, she felt safe and warm. Here, she didn't worry about the darkness of her memories or whatever happened that night.

But she couldn't stay here forever and more importantly, she knew she *shouldn't*.

Those memories shouldn't stay buried.

"Brannon, Roger was right. If I know something . . ."

"Fuck Roger."

Brannon knew the minute he said it, he'd regret it.

But he couldn't stop it, couldn't pull back the words.

He couldn't even regret it, because while he felt bad for both Shayla and Roger, his concern was Hannah . . . and their baby.

But Hannah stiffened against him, and bit by bit, he felt her curling away from him.

Swearing, he let her go and rose to pace. After a minute, he stopped by the window and stared outside.

"It's not that I don't feel bad for the guy, Hannah," he said.

"You sure as hell can't tell by the way you act."

He turned and stared at her.

She glared at him.

Exasperated and pissed off, he reached for her, but the look she shot at him had him lowering his hands. "You think I don't understand that he's hurting? You think I don't have some idea of what he's going through?"

When she said nothing, he took another step toward her.

"I lost both my mom *and* my dad," he said. The years that had passed since that loss made it possible for him to keep his voice steady, but the pain was still there. "It's a miracle Neve didn't die in the wreck as well. We *still* don't know who ran them off the road, so don't think I don't understand that the pain he's got is just eating him up."

"Then why . . ." She looked up at him only to suck in a breath.

He didn't know what she saw on his face.

Slowly, he crossed the floor toward her. The heels of his boots thudded hollowly on the glossy, bare hardwood floors. He went to his knees in front of her and reached up, closing his hands around her ankles and tugging them down. "Answers won't help," he said. "I finally figured that out. Yeah, there's always closure and I'd like to have it, but closure won't bring my parents back. Maybe they weren't hunted down and killed like Shayla was, but they were killed, all the same. Knowing who is responsible won't change the fact that I grew up without them, the same as Neve did. It won't change the fact that Moira had to grow up too soon and finish raising us. Yeah, I'd like closure, but closure won't give them back to me."

He moved into the space between her thighs and lifted a hand to cradle her face. "Now I want him to have answers. I don't want him wondering for years and years. It's agony, Hannah. It really is . . . but I don't want him having it at the cost of *your* suffering. You've been through *enough*."

"I don't need you protecting me," she said. Her heart clenched at the look in his eyes.

"You don't need it, no. But I want to do it." He leaned and pressed a kiss to her lips. "You want to remember, and I can understand that. But when it happens—and it probably will—you'll be in danger."

It infuriated him to think of it.

It terrified him to think of it.

He'd do whatever he had to if it meant keeping her safe.

Then Hannah shattered the very ground beneath him.

Covering the hand he'd placed on her cheek, she leaned in and kissed him gently. With her mouth still against his, she whispered, "Brannon, haven't you realized it yet? I'm in just as much danger, if not *more*, by *not* remembering anything. I don't know what happened, what I saw, *who* I saw. It could have been anybody."

He pulled away, stiffening.

Tugging his hand from her cheek, she watched him solemnly.

"You've got this idea that as long as I don't remember, as long as the town believes I don't remember, that I *won't* remember, whoever killed Shayla will leave me alone. But that's a stupid way to think. Sooner or later, he'll get scared. Sooner or later, I'll remember something, or do something, or say something that will make him nervous and without having those memories, I'm *blind*."

Her eyes were dark and although she hid it, he realized that the idea terrified her. Brannon pulled her against him, fighting the urge to make promises, to tell her that he'd keep her safe.

What was he supposed to protect her from? A nameless, faceless monster?

Swearing, he surged up but his ceaseless pacing offered no respite from the fury this time. He paced to the window and back, to the window again and when he spun around a second time, he almost plowed into Hannah. Catching her arms, he stared into her dark eyes.

"Tell me," she said.

He tangled his hands in her hair.

"Tell me."

He hauled her to him and slanted his mouth over hers instead.

It was a desperate, hungry kiss and it did nothing to ease the raw, ragged ache inside him.

There were more than a few reasons why he hoped she wouldn't remember.

His stupidity included.

But he couldn't put her safety at risk, just to protect himself.

Slowly, he drew away, using his tongue to trace the soft lines of her mouth, the arched bow of her upper lip. She sighed softly against him when he broke the kiss. With his brow to hers, he twined their fingers together. "Come on. Let's go to my place. We'll talk there."

"Well." Moira slid her tongue across her teeth as Charles settled in the seat across from her. Dumbfounded wasn't *exactly* the word she needed right then. *Shocked* . . . closer. "That was . . . unexpected."

"He's suffered a horrible loss," Charles said softly. "It's out of character for him, but he's not a bad sort, Moira. You know that."

"I'm not talking about him." She pinned her ex-husband with a level look. "I'm talking about you. Since when were you anybody's knight?"

Charles had been in the process of picking up his menu, but he stopped. Lowering it slowly to the table, he looked up. He held her gaze only for a moment, but the flash in his eyes made an uneasy feeling twist through her.

It was guilt, she decided. His next words confirmed that.

"It wasn't that long ago that I almost lost you, Moira," Charles said quietly. He leaned forward, his dark blue eyes intent on her face.

"Charles, I—"

He held up a long-fingered, elegant hand.

He'd always had beautiful hands.

Okay, *everything* about Charles was beautiful. Elegant, beautiful, and refined.

They'd made a stunning couple and she knew that. But there had been no heat between them, no true passion, the love they'd shared had been just a shadow of what she knew it should have been.

"Please, don't." He shook his head and shifted his gaze to stare outside. "I know we're over. You've made that more than clear. But there's a difference between us being *over* and you being . . . *gone*."

His voice went rough and he looked back at her.

The expression on his face was enough to bring an ache to her throat.

He'd never looked at her like that.

Not once, in their entire marriage.

She didn't know what to say.

"I can understand, to some extent, the agony he must be feeling," Charles said, picking up his menu and opening it. "It doesn't give him the right to bully others, though. And it would make me a poor man indeed if I'd just stood there while he manhandled Hannah, now wouldn't it?"

Moira looked down at her menu.

Taking a deep breath, she reached up and tugged on the top of his menu, forcing him to lower it. "Thank you."

He quirked an eyebrow. "For what?"

"For stepping up. You know she's . . ." She shrugged.

"Well, you know she's pregnant and Brannon's the father. She's family now."

He reached out and patted her hand. "She is. But I'd have done it regardless. Come now. Let's order. I'm feeling a bit peckish. We've got business to discuss as well and I'd sooner get it done here rather than try to do it at the museum." He winked. "We can't have two minutes for business there without being interrupted, now can we?"

"No." She laughed. "That's the truth. I'm heading out at the end of the week, too. I can't put this trip off any longer."

CHAPTER TWELVE

Brannon let her inside the condo, but he didn't move any deeper.

She stood there next to him, just a foot away from the door. She felt crowded by him and it was a sensation that was both intense and intimidating. He was so big, it was like he sucked all the air out of the room and all the light, too. Even the color. Or maybe it was because he was so vibrant, everything just seemed paler, lesser in comparison.

He turned to face her, moving in.

Reflexively, Hannah took a step back, then another.

Brannon kept moving in and she found herself penned up against the door.

"You found my wallet," he said, his voice gruff.

He reached up and trailed a finger down her cheek.

"You'd been out running and you showed up in just a tank top and a bra, those tight pants you wear. I could see the sweat on you and I wanted to lick it away and peel your clothes off. Just looking at you made me hard."

She gulped in air. It did no good. She felt a little light-headed and locked her legs to keep from sliding to the floor.

The finger he'd trailed down her cheek moved to her neck, the callouses rough, rasping along her skin.

"I was in a bitch of a mood and it always got worse when I saw you."

"I'd noticed," she said, clearing her throat. Then she scowled. "What changed?"

Brannon lowered his lids until all she could see was a sliver of green.

Then he reached out and placed his hand on her belly. "Isn't it obvious?"

She sucked in a breath at the feel of his hand on her, fingers protectively spread over the swell of the baby lying within her. She covered his hand with hers, but even as she did it, she shook her head. "The baby's not enough of a reason, Brannon. You acted like you couldn't stand me for years. Then I wake up and who is it there with me at the hospital every day? *You*. I mean, yeah, I know we got together that week, but . . ."

"Stop." Brannon moved closer, his hand moving from her belly to her hip. "My problems had nothing to do with not being able to stand you."

Then he tugged her up against him and she felt his cock pressing flat against her as he slid his knee between her thighs.

The contact had her groaning.

"It had to do with wanting you and knowing I should keep my distance." He rubbed his mouth against her neck. "Relationships aren't my thing, Hannah. But I . . . you twisted me up, Hannah. After that week, I couldn't fight it anymore."

She wanted to ask him something else, but his teeth closed around her earlobe and tugged.

Thought melted away on a wash of heat.

"You had my wallet," he said a moment later. "And you snapped at me. Asked me why I was such an asshole.

I couldn't stop myself. I put my hands on you and you put yours on me."

"I . . ."

Brannon lifted his head to look down at her.

Hannah licked her lips and his eyes went hot. He pressed his mouth to hers, tracing the path her tongue had taken with his own.

"I want to put my hands on you now." He said the words against her mouth. "Can I?"

"Oh, hell. Please."

Hannah leaned against the door as he straightened away from her. Brannon reached for the buttons that ran down the front of her shirt. He wondered if she'd noticed that her breasts were getting fuller. He had. They weren't quite straining the front of this blouse, but they would soon. He freed the top button, the one below it and then the next, taking his time with each and watching as the pink flush spread up from her chest to her neck and higher.

"You always watched me," he said, surprised he could even talk.

Her gaze flew to his. There was a glassy glint to her eyes. "Yes."

"It drove me crazy."

A smile teased her lips. "You could have closed the curtains."

"Then you wouldn't watch."

She laughed softly. The sound tripped across his skin like a caress and he thought he'd go mad if he didn't get his cock inside her soon. But he didn't want this to end.

So he drew it out, teasing them both as he freed her from her shirt and then draped it over the arm of the couch a couple of feet away. Her bra was pale pink, even paler than the blush still staining her cheeks and her breasts strained it to overflowing. "You're getting bigger," he said, tracing his fingers along the lacy, scalloped edge.

"I know." She bit her lip and glanced down. "Half my bras already don't fit."

Bracing his hands on the wall, he dipped his head and pressed his face to the valley created by her breasts. He breathed in the scent of her as he nuzzled her and relished the sound of her erratic breathing. A sound that was both a whimper and a sigh escaped her when he reached behind her and freed the catch on her bra.

He had to bite back a scowl when he saw the faint red mark left by the bra's band. He kissed it softly before cupping her swollen, heavy breasts in his hands. "Fuck, Hannah . . ."

She cried out when he caught one plump nipple in his mouth.

The sound shot straight down to his cock.

He wondered if maybe he could come just by getting her off—and he thought he wouldn't at all mind putting the idea to the test. She strained against him, shoving her breast against his mouth as she cupped the back of his head.

He suckled on her deeper, sliding one hand down her back and dragging her closer.

Hannah whimpered and brought her knee up against him.

She started to rock, wordless moans escaping her as she moved against him. He could feel how hot she already was and he wanted to rip her pants away, sink inside her. But she clutched at him and moaned and moved. He recognized what was coming just by the tension gathering in her body, although he didn't entirely process it. Not right away.

She sobbed his name, twisted her hips.

He drew harder on her nipple.

Her nails tore into his biceps and she came.

Just like that.

Her hips jerked and rolled against him and even though his brain was struggling to take in what was going on, his body was already at work. His right hand cupping her breast, he used his left arm to bring her in closer, rolling his hips to drive his cock against the cleft between her thighs. She sobbed and shuddered, riding the orgasm that continued to ripple through her.

She was wet, so wet he could feel her through her jeans and his own.

A drop of pre-come leaked from the head of his cock and he thought maybe he'd just keep on moving . . . .

She whispered his name.

The soft, dazed sound wrapped a fist around his heart and squeezed.

Curling his arms around her, he tucked her head under his chin.

She sagged against him and he could feel the ragged rhythm of her heart, pounding in time with his own. His cock seemed to echo that mad beat, pulsing with a vicious ache, but he was content to ignore that—for now.

Or he might have been.

Hannah wasn't.

She wiggled against him and worked a hand between them. She palmed him through his jeans and the rigid flesh jerked. Brannon clenched his jaw.

"I want you," she said, the words spoken against his neck.

He wasn't going to wait for an engraved invitation.

Hannah's head was still spinning.

She'd said those words maybe twenty seconds ago and now she was naked.

Brannon boosted her hips up and she stared up at him in shock as he hooked her knees over his elbows.

He was still dressed.

"Here . . . ?" she whispered.

"You wanted to know what happened." He leaned in and pressed a bruising kiss to her mouth.

"You came here, ran that smart mouth of yours, and I lost it. Kind of like I'm doing now." He crooked a grin at her and everything female in her clenched at the sight of it. "You just have to be around me and I lose it, Hannah."

Then he slid against her.

She gasped and arched her hips.

He didn't enter her yet, though.

"I fucked you right here the first time. And then I took you into my bedroom and I fucked you again."

She whimpered.

He leaned in and bit her lower lip. She bucked against him and shuddered, then almost screamed because the head of his cock passed over her clit. "When I'm done here, I plan on taking you into my room and fucking you again there."

He lifted his head and studied her.

Since he seemed to waiting for an answer, she gulped and nodded. "Oh . . . okay . . . ?"

He shifted the angle of his hips and she groaned as the head of his cock breached her entrance. He watched her, eyes rapt on her face. She braced herself, expecting the hot, heavy drive.

But he slid just a few inches in.

She clutched at him when he withdrew. The head of his cock seemed wedged right at her entrance and it made her shiver. His eyes held her captive as he slowly surged back in. A little deeper, but not all the way.

He kept up that pattern and by the time he was seated

completely within her, Hannah was mindless, sweat dripping from her body as she clutched at him. Begging him
hoarsely, she strained against him, rising to meet each
slow, tormenting thrust.

She clenched around him as he drove inside, squeezing him tight and hoping to keep him within her just a
second longer, a heartbeat longer. He growled against her
lips and she bit his tongue.

He tensed against her and she speared her fingers into
his hair, taking control of the kiss since he wouldn't let
her have anything else.

His body shuddered.

She felt the shift happen in his body and took advantage, sucking on his tongue—*when* she allowed him entrance. When she bit him, he slammed one hand on the
wall. Then, tearing her mouth from his, she sank her
teeth into his lower lip.

Brannon swore.

And she laughed because she'd finally shoved him
past the edge of his control.

He let go of her other knee and she twined her legs
around his hips, rising to meet his thrusts and delight-
ing in the feel of him inside, the width and length of his
cock a brand.

He savaged her mouth, one hand gripping her ass, his
fingers digging into the flesh as he drove into her, harder
and deeper with every thrust.

He tore the climax out of her just as she demanded his.

It was . . . exhilarating.

Hannah woke up crying.

The dregs of a dream clung to her and she couldn't
remember anything but the ache and it was awful.

She swiped at the tears and smacked Brannon's hands
away when he tried to comfort her.

Finally, he gave up and just lay there, watching her. She couldn't look at him.

It hurt.

Even the silence hurt and she withdrew inside her own head.

There was something she was remembering—or almost remembering.

It was right there, like a song where she could remember the tune, but the lyrics or the title escaped her.

And it was something that hurt.

Unable to lie there any longer, she struggled free of the tangle they'd made of the sheets and sat on the side of the bed, staring at the window. Through the narrow slit in the curtains, she could see her own balcony and she sucked in a breath. Swiping at her tears, she shot him a look. "You started closing your curtains," she said. The accusing note in her voice couldn't be missed, not even by her. She didn't know where it came from or why.

Just as she couldn't explain the hot bubble of anger that started to well up inside her.

Brannon sat up slowly, eying her warily.

"Ah . . . yeah. You sort of snapped at me to do it."

She sniffed, her nose congested from her crying jag. Getting to her feet, she looked around for her clothes but they were nowhere to be found. In desperation, she moved to his closet and opened it up. Her jaw fell open and she gaped at what lay behind the doors.

That wasn't a *closet*.

It was a whole fricking *room*.

She'd been happy when she found out she actually had a walk-in closet, but *her* walk-in closet was just that. She could walk in, and if she lifted her arms, they'd brush up against the shirts and what pitiful few dresses she owned.

Brannon's closet was . . .

She reached up and rubbed her eyes.

"I don't know why I'm shocked," she muttered.

He wasn't a braggart about it, but everything about the man screamed money. His car was worth more than her entire apartment building, she'd bet. Shit, the McKay family had paid for the four new ambulances the county had received last year.

Shaking her head, she crossed the smoothly polished wooden floors—she actually had to take five steps to reach the shirts she could see hanging across the room. Reaching out, she snagged the closest one. She shrugged into the shirt as she turned around. Brannon stood in the doorway. He'd already pulled a pair of jeans up over his lean hips and he was still watching her with wary eyes. She ignored him for another moment, taking in the neat stacks of shoes she now faced and the suits that took up the far side of the wall.

"So is this *all* of your clothes or do you have more at the house?"

He jerked a shoulder in a shrug. "I've got stuff back at the house. Some stuff at Ferry, too, although I'm not there too often these days."

"You're a clothes horse, Brannon." She buttoned up the shirt and tried not to think about the way his eyes kept straying to her fingers. She'd get all hot and bothered again if she did and she was trying to stay out of the zone.

Once she was dressed, she shouldered past him.

His fingers trailed down her back.

"Hannah . . ."

She shot another look at the curtains, bothered for reasons she couldn't explain.

Maybe I don't like being your morning entertainment—

Coming to a sudden halt, she stood there, shaking.

The floorboards shifted behind her and she spun around.

"My morning *entertainment*?"

The dread that had lived inside him for months threatened to consume him.

Feeling too big, too out of place inside his own skin, Brannon shifted on his feet.

She was remembering. More and more.

Tell her what happened.

Tell her you're sorry.

Do it now.

The voice of reason shrieked at him from deep inside.

He opened his mouth to do just that.

She took a step toward him and he found himself wanting to take a step back. That just made him feel even more foolish and he stood his ground. She lifted a hand and jabbed him the chest with her finger. "My morning entertainment? You're the one who never bothers to close his damn curtains!"

He caught her wrist and stared into her furious eyes.

Tell her.

Yeah. Yeah, he'd do that.

Clearing his throat, he went to speak.

But the words that came out weren't the words he needed to say.

Oh, they were true. But not the ones he needed to say.

"I liked having you staring at me," he said.

She glared at him.

Stroking his thumb over her wrist, he gave her a piece of the truth because he couldn't find the words for the rest of it. "I'd been staring at you for years and every time you looked at me, it made it easier for me to look back. Even if it did piss me off."

Her lips parted.

A shaky sigh escaped her.

He went to tug her closer.

But she twisted her wrist out of his grasp and stepped away.

"Brannon . . ."

When she turned away, he dragged his hands over his face. *What's the matter with you, you stupid fuck*?

But he knew.

He was afraid. Over the past few months, he'd finally admitted to himself what she meant to him. She meant *everything* and losing her would shatter him in ways he didn't know if he could handle.

He had to make her understand she mattered.

Once she knew that, once she realized he was serious about her, once *he* knew things wasn't going to fall apart after one bad storm, then he could tell her.

A soft sigh drifted through the room and he dropped his hands, staring at her. Her hair, that rich, lush brown, was still mussed from bed and from his hands. It shielded her face from him even as she half-turned back toward him. He wanted to twine it around his hands and tug her head back, stare into her eyes and tell her . . . everything.

Tell her that he'd been half-stupid about her even when it was the worst thing he could do. She'd still been in high school when he'd first really noticed her and he'd been in college. But even before that, he'd liked her. Not in that kind of way, but he thought she was a sweet kid, a tough one. He knew what she put up with, knew what had been done to her mother.

More than once, he'd talked to Moira and the two of them had gotten together with Ella Sue to make sure that Hannah's mother had steady work—she'd worked at a dozen jobs, a waitress, an office assistant, a secretary, cleaning houses, doing laundry, whatever it took to make sure there was money to put food on her table.

More than once, he'd wished he could have dealt with the son of a bitch the law called her stepfather. But fate dealt with him instead.

Hannah hadn't cried at the funeral.

Brannon had hugged her there, touched her for the first and last time up until the day she showed up at his door holding his wallet. His body had come alive with that one touch—something that had been given in comfort and all he'd wanted to do was take big, greedy bites out of her.

Slowly, uncertain of the reception he'd get, he closed the distance between them.

She met him, more than halfway, and the vicious ache that ripped at him whenever he saw her started to ease as she curled into him. Her arms were soft and strong as she wrapped them around him. "One of these days," she said against his chest. "One of these days, we need to have a talk about whatever it is we have going on here, Brannon."

"Yeah." He closed his eyes and rested his cheek against her hair. "Listen, I—"

The sudden, hard pounding on the door interrupted him and he swore.

"Ella Sue would wash your mouth out with soap," Hannah said. Her eyes were shadowed, but the smile on her lips was a real one.

It didn't make it any easier to let her go when she pulled away.

"Brannon, you sod, it's Ian and Neve," a deep voice came from beyond the door. "Open up. It's important."

Hannah looked down at her bare legs and grimaced. "Let me go grab my clothes before you open that door."

CHAPTER THIRTEEN

Hannah stood off to the sidelines, her arms wrapped around her midsection.

Neve and Ian were a few feet away, but none of them spoke.

Brannon's face was tight, the five o'clock shadow darkening his jaw adding to his overall menacing appearance. "What else do you need to know?" he asked, his eyes glittering as he stared at the deputy. After Brannon had talked to Ian, he'd called the county sheriff. They'd met at the winery and both Tank and one of his deputies were there.

Ian had been supposed to meet Alison at the pub—trying a few wines, and when she hadn't shown, he'd called her, then the winery. Then he'd called Marc. Marc had called her house, her cell . . . she wasn't answering.

"She pissed off the senator and all of you have seen how well he's doing with the damage control. He's screwed. And now Alison is missing."

"We don't know that she's missing," Tank said.

Brannon's stream of curses turned the air blue.

Hannah was mildly impressed. She heard quite a bit of swearing in her line of work, and quite a bit of it was directed at her. Some of it, of course, was just directed at the situation. Nothing like having a bone poking out of your skin or seeing your toddler with his head stuck between the top and bottom of your chair to learn just how inventively you could swear—or how ardently you could pray.

Brannon was very inventive. She'd learned that over the past few days, but this was a whole other side.

He'd always been the more laid back of the McKays, but the temper was something people hinted at.

Moira was serene, elegance personified. Once a person got to know her, Moira was also a wonderful friend and warm and funny, with a wicked sense of humor. But one could never consider the eldest McKay to be *laid back*.

Neve was, plain and simple, a hellion. Trouble, just like her nickname said. She seemed to have settled down some, but her temper was just as sharp as ever. Hannah adored her.

Other than the fact that he'd always been prone to snapping at her, Brannon had been the easy-going one of the bunch. If you needed something and were afraid to approach Neve—or too intimidated by Moira—then Brannon was your guy. If Neve had been edging too close to the point of no return, then Brannon had been the one Hannah would reach out to back in school—when he was home.

Now, though, she could see that temper, hot enough to burn.

As he advanced on the sheriff, Neve groaned under her breath. "He's going to get his ass thrown in jail. Ian . . ."

"I can try to talk him down, love, but chances are it will end with both of us getting our arses tossed in." Ian looked grim.

Hannah gave them both a withering look. "The last thing we need is *more* testosterone out there."

She braced herself, because this was so not going to be pleasant.

Neve reached for her hand, but she sidestepped. "He'll listen to me or I'll just punch him," she said. And she was almost certain she meant it.

"I've tried that," Ian said, stroking his beard. Then he winked at her. "Never worked well for me, but I've an idea it will work differently for you."

She could feel a smile tugging at the corners of her mouth and she resisted the urge to let it show. It was so not the time to smile. When she turned, she caught sight of Marc, sitting on the steps that led up to the winery and she wanted to go to him, hug him, tell him . . . tell him what?

That everything would be okay?

She'd be lying and she knew it.

She had a bad, bad feeling in her gut.

Instead of making empty promises and offering comfort that might not be welcome, she focused on the problem she could fix. Brannon was now in the sheriff's face and his voice was at a bellow now, full of pure fury.

She reached out and tapped his shoulder.

He jerked his head around, words already trembling on his lips.

Cocking a brow, she said, "Yes?"

He snapped his jaw shut.

"This isn't helping," she said quietly. Nodding toward Marc, she added, "You think he needs to hear this right now?"

"What he needs is to know where Alison is," Brannon said. He jerked his thumb toward the sheriff. "But the enterprising sheriff here seems to think we should wait until . . . oh, I don't know . . . hell freezes over?"

Tank opened his mouth, his face bleeding to red.

Hannah cut him off. "Brannon, you dumbass. He's got a job to do—there are lines he can't cross."

"So what am I supposed to do?" he demanded, spreading his arms out. "Just wait until the good sheriff thinks he can safely investigate?"

"Brannon," Tank said, his voice stiff. "I'm going to send a car out to her place and have somebody check on her. I already told you that. I—"

But Brannon was already walking away.

Hannah gritted her teeth and then jogged over to where he was talking to Neve.

"Yeah, I can hang a while," Neve was saying, lifting a shoulder. She glanced up at Ian.

Ian nodded.

"Good. I don't want Marc alone for a while, but I need to do something." Brannon turned back and caught Hannah's gaze. "Stay here."

"Can't." She gave him a brilliant smile. "I've got a job to do. I've got a shift at three. You were supposed to take me back to town, remember?"

"I . . ." He stopped, shoving a hand through his hair. "Hannah, just stay here!"

"No." She crossed her arms over her chest. "Either take me with you or I'll call around until I get a ride, but I'm not hanging out here and twiddling my thumbs. Which one is it going to be?"

If there had ever been a woman as stubborn as Hannah Parker, Brannon didn't want to meet her. But just as quickly as he had that thought, he was mentally shaking his head. He knew two women that stubborn—his sisters. They drove him crazy with it, too. And here he was, half-stupid over a woman who did the same thing.

"You realize the sheriff is going to have your ass for

being out here." Hannah climbed out of the car and looked around, shivering a little as the breeze blew in off the river. It was overcast and under the trees that surrounded Alison's house, it was chillier than it had been for a while.

"He can't really stop me, now can he?" Brannon bared his teeth in a smile. "He hasn't declared her missing or done anything official yet. Right now, I'm just checking up on my employee. She hasn't clocked in today. I'm not happy about that."

He made an exaggerated show of checking his watch. "And she's like three hours late now. Nope, not happy."

Hannah just shook her head.

As he moved to the door, she fell in with him.

"It's quiet out here," she said softly.

"Yeah." He glanced around, trying to pretend he didn't feel uneasy. "Part of her job package was that I'd help her find a place. I'm covering her payments for a year. She saw this place and fell in love with it."

Hannah made a *tsking* sound under her breath. "You McKays are just up for sainthood, aren't you?"

"I wanted her to come and work for me. I called it a wise investment in my winery. She's a great employee." Brannon shrugged it away, a scowl on his face. He lifted a hand and started to bang on the door. The knock was loud, echoing through the silence. There was no answer. After a minute, he knocked again.

As they waited, he turned and stared at the car.

It sat in the driveway.

Narrowing his eyes, he studied the sunroof. It was partially open. "It rained last night, didn't it?"

"Yeah. Why?"

He just shook his head. He took the steps on the porch in a leap. Hannah followed him and he could feel the weight of her curious stare as he moved toward the car.

He didn't try to open the doors—knowing his luck, Alison would have an alarm system. But he didn't need to open the doors.

He peered inside the window and his gut went tight as he saw the water puddled on the console.

"She hasn't been out since it rained." Straightening, he looked back at the house.

"What are you . . ."

As he started back, he heard Hannah's frustrated sigh. "Where are you going?"

"Taking a look around." He debated telling Hannah to wait inside the car, but in the end, he decided he'd rather have her with him. Besides, she wouldn't listen anyway, and they'd fight and waste time.

Together, they circled around, looking at the windows, the grounds. Brannon had no idea what he was looking for.

It was Hannah who saw it first.

She grabbed his arm, her nails biting into his arm. "Brannon. The window."

He went still.

Dread, and a sick knowledge, twisted in him as he stared at the perfectly round hole in the window.

There was nothing else out of place.

But that hole . . .

"Come on," he said, grabbing Hannah's hand. He half-dragged her up to the back door and once they were there, he let go. "For the record, I'm pretty sure I've got a legit case for breaking down this door, but if you don't want to come inside, then don't."

Hannah said nothing. She wrapped her arms around herself and stood there white-faced, but after a second, she gave a single, short nod.

He stared at the door for a moment and then took a few steps back.

It was surprisingly easy, but then again, Brannon was a big guy and he knew how to use the strength he had in his body. If he'd been a foot shorter and hundred pounds lighter, he probably would have bounced off the door.

It crashed open and immediately an alarm started to echo.

Hannah grimaced at the sound.

"Well, that's going to get the cops out here," she said sourly.

"Grab the phone," Brannon said, nodding to it. "That's the same people who handle our security. They'll call. Tell them we found signs of forced entry. Tank is probably already heading here anyway. Alison!"

The phone started to ring.

Hannah answered it.

He barely heard what she said over the noise of the alarm and the sound of his own racing heart.

The kitchen was empty, neat as a pin.

The same for the living room, the hall, the bedroom.

The door to the bathroom was open, the light on. It was the only light on in the whole house.

He saw her right away.

He lunged forward, grabbing her out of the water.

Later, much later, he'd think about how cold the water had been.

Later, much later, he'd recall that Alison's body had been just as cold.

Later, much later, he'd realize that she'd already been gone.

But all he could think at that moment was that she was laying in the water, her eyes open, her body still.

Distantly, he heard Hannah's voice, sharp and clear, as he dragged Alison out of the water, as he put that cold, cold body on the ground.

"Move *back*!" Hannah shouted. Then she shoved him.

He went to snarl at her and then he stopped, remembering. "Help her," he said. "You can help her."

Oh, baby . . .

Hannah's heart broke for him.

Brannon, he wanted to be everybody's hero, wanted to save everybody, take care of everybody.

There was no helping Alison Maxwell, though.

Reaching up, she laid a hand on his cheek. "She's gone, Brannon."

"No." He shook his head. "Get back. If . . ." He swallowed, like he was suddenly having a hard time speaking. "If you won't do it, I will."

She closed her eyes. "We'll both try."

Sometimes, you just had to try. Just so you knew you'd done something.

Aware that she had people shouting at her through the receiver, she lifted it to her ear. "We need the police, EMS, immediately. Ms. Maxwell is . . ." *dead* . . . "There's a medical emergency here. There were signs of forced entry and nobody answered so we broke in through the back door."

As Brannon bent over Alison's lifeless body, Hannah gave her name and assured them she'd keep the line open.

Then she went to her knees and tapped Brannon.

He was doing chest compressions.

Water bubbled out of Alison's mouth.

"I'll do the chest compressions," Hannah said. "We'll try."

Brannon only nodded.

It was a relief that the county deputies weren't far away.

It took only a few more minutes for the fire department to arrive. Brannon stepped aside only when the EMTs told them they'd take over. They shared a grim look with Hannah. She just gave a small shake of her head.

They knelt by Alison and checked her over while Hannah moved to block Brannon.

"Why aren't they . . ."

She caught his arms. "Brannon, she's gone."

"No." But the stubborn note was fading from his voice, replaced by something rough.

Lifting a hand, she laid it on his cheek. "Brannon, she's been dead for hours, maybe longer. There's nothing anybody can do for her now."

Then a man came into the room.

Gideon Marshall, moving side by side with Tank.

The chief of police glanced her way, his eyes lingering on her before he looked back to the sheriff.

Well, no.

That wasn't exactly true.

They could find who'd killed Alison.

They could make the son of a bitch pay.

CHAPTER FOURTEEN

McKay's Treasure wasn't a town unknown to tragedy.

If one looked back far enough, they'd find that Treasure had been borne of it, was steeped in it, and like a phoenix, had risen from those ashes.

The man who'd bought a piece of land to build a home for his young Quaker wife hadn't known he'd started what would become an empire. He also hadn't known that when he'd agreed to patrol the Mississippi for river pirates that one day, the very men who'd hired him would turn on him and he'd end up hanging from the end of a rope.

Patrick McKay had founded McKay's Treasure. He'd bought the property that would eventually become McKay's Ferry, the jewel of his family's crown, and the land around it would eventually become McKay's Treasure, a tribute to the man who'd sacrificed all for love and for honor.

Save for a few poor farmers, not many had lived in this area.

He'd fallen in love with the river—next to his beloved Madeleine and the children she'd given him, the river was the great love of his life.

He'd made his fortune on that river, but as his family grew, his wife had wanted him home. Unable to deny her, he'd done as she'd asked.

McKay's Ferry, still called that to this day, had been an anomaly almost from the beginning. Madeleine Garrett had shocked her family when she'd fallen in love with a swaggering Scot. She'd told him she'd follow him anywhere and he'd promised he'd make her happy. He'd done just that, too. They'd gone south, and she'd told him that he'd never own a man or woman—if he wanted work done on his property, he'd hire people, and pay them. Quakers abhorred the practice of slavery. Patrick, a man who'd made his fortune with his own two hands, understood the value of working for a day's pay and more, he'd do whatever his beloved wife wanted.

It was because of her that he said yes when he was asked to return to the river.

It wasn't new to have river pirates terrorizing merchants on the Mississippi. It wasn't new to have them murder the occasional traveler. But a local band of pirates had become too bold, daring onto land. A family a half day north of Ferry was found slaughtered and the only way they learned of their fate was when the fourteen-year-old daughter was found on the shore. She'd been thrown overboard after the pirates had tired of her.

They hadn't realized she could swim.

When a second family was attacked, it was clear that the pirates wouldn't desist.

They would have to be stopped.

Patrick McKay was the man chosen to take charge of the task. Within a year, he and his men had hunted down and executed two separate bands of pirates. They'd then gone on to deal with those who had been terrorizing the merchant crews.

Patrick took his job seriously. He'd been hired to deal with pirates and that was just what he'd done.

But some of those pirates he'd taken out had . . . employers. Wealthy men who'd actually been making money off the merchants and travelers. A great deal of merchandise moved up and down the Mississippi, everything from food to slaves and thanks to McKay, some of those who'd been making money off the wares were now not getting the money they'd come to expect.

It might have all gone away, except McKay was told he'd done well enough and he could go home.

Well enough? There are still people being robbed blind, still people dying, he'd said. *Children being stolen from their homes while their mothers die hearing their cries for help. And ya call this done? It is not done!*

There will always be people being robbed and people will always die. You had a job and you did it. You earned your money. Let others get back to earning theirs.

Foolish words to say to a sharp man.

They'd been said after a few too many drinks and perhaps it was assumed that since McKay had more than bit of whisky himself, he wouldn't think much on it. He'd just been paid, and handsomely, too.

But those words bothered Patrick.

It took months, but he unearthed information that painted an unpleasant picture.

He shared that information with two men, his best friend Jonathan Steele, and then a shrewd Englishman he'd met a few years earlier, a man by the name of George Whitehall. Neither knew that he'd told the other, because while Patrick was a good friend, he trusted very few people.

Because he trusted so few, he left the small, bustling town that was growing around his small, bustling plantation to hand deliver the information into the hands of the people he felt could best pursue it.

Before he left, he kissed his wife and his two sons. He told Madeleine that the youngest would be the girl she'd so hoped for and Madeleine had laughed. "It is you that hopes for a daughter to dote on. I only pray the child is healthy, Paddy."

He'd laughed and turned to go.

The next time she saw him, he was behind bars.

She was given the chance to kiss him good-bye and only that. If she fought, she was told she'd hang along beside him.

Tragedy struck Ferry that time because a man tried to do the right thing and wouldn't lie when he was faced with the choice to lie and live.

George, the man who'd claimed to be his friend, had strutted up to knock on the door of Patrick's widow, already planning what he'd do with this land. Patrick McKay had actually *paid* colored people to work. He'd had the best property around and he'd wasted resources. He'd had a beautiful wife and he'd let her lead him around by the nose.

He'd knocked on the door, tapping his thumb against the written *confession* he would show to the world. He'd written the confession, of course, just as he'd forged Paddy's signature. He'd always been good at that, copying another man's signature.

The world would see Patrick as a thief.

Madeleine McKay could convince him otherwise, of course.

It wasn't Madeleine who answered.

It was a big, hulking brute with fists like iron—George never even got a word out before Jonathon Steele dragged him inside and threw him across the foyer.

George had played his game well, but he hadn't

counted on Jonathon also knowing the truth. Jonathon, sadly, had been called out of town the very night he'd heard the story and he hadn't returned in time to save his friend.

He could save his friend's family, though.

George was in a fine mess. While he could do away with a Scot, Jonathon Steele was more of a problem and George knew it. He'd had enough trouble buying and blackmailing the people he'd needed to get McKay thrown in jail and his neck stretched without much more than a hurried, laughable mockery of a trial.

His wife had but one chance to see him and she'd cried, sobbed, and begged.

There was no way he could play such games with Jonathon. The man's uncle was the governor. His mother's family was one of the richest in the country.

George was staring into the eyes of death and he knew it.

Save for Madeleine.

She intervened. She abhorred violence, even in the name of vengeance. But Jonathon found a way to get a bit of it anyway. George didn't even recall leaving the McKay house—everything just went black and he found himself on a miserable excuse of a ship, bound for England. All he had with him was his valise, packed with his journal and pitiful few clothes.

He took ill on the journey and although he recovered, he was never quite the man he'd been.

He married and he made the woman quite miserable.

When he died four years later, leaving behind two heirs, nobody truly missed him.

Jonathan Steele, the man who'd uncovered the truth after months and months, had married Madeleine and raised Paddy McKay's children as if they were his own, and indeed, they'd been the only children he *would* have, because Madeleine was never able to conceive after the birth of the third child . . . a girl, as Paddy had hoped. The Steele family lived on through his brothers and he was quite happy to raise the children of his best friend, but he would have no children of his own.

Now, as Moira stood in the museum, studying the paintings of Patrick McKay, Madeleine McKay Steele, and Jonathon Steele, she rubbed her thumb across her locket.

She rarely wore it.

The chain had been replaced a hundred times—well, maybe not *that* often.

The locket itself had been carefully repaired several times over, although it looked the same as it had when Patrick McKay had given it to his beloved Maddy.

"How did you do it?" she asked the silent portrait of her many-times great-grandmother.

There was no answer, but Moira couldn't stop herself from moving a step closer and asking again. "When it was so dark and awful, Paddy gone and Jonathon out there running down the men who'd taken him from you, how did you handle everything? Raising your children, dealing with everything? How do you deal with it when things seem like they'd never be happy again?"

The sound of the door opening had her spinning around and she pressed a hand to her chest, willing it to calm.

Brannon stood there, Hannah at his side.

Hannah wore a simple dress of deep blue, the sleeves short, the hemline coming just to her knee. Moira could just barely make out the swell of her belly.

A baby.

Longing swam through her and she had to force it aside. Once upon a time, she'd dreamed of a family.

Once.

But she'd come to accept it wouldn't happen. Not for her.

So she'd lavish all the love she had on her brother's baby . . . and probably her sister's, in another year or so.

"Are you ready?" Brannon asked, his expression unreadable.

He'd been guarded and tense for days, ever since the body—

No. Alison. Her name was Alison.

And somebody had killed her.

Guilt haunted her and she looked away, swallowing the knot that rose in her throat. "Yes," she said, her voice husky.

They were having a memorial service out at the winery. It had been Alison's favorite place. Not many people had gotten to know her in the short time she'd been here, but it hadn't seemed right to not do anything.

A few minutes later, they were seated in Moira's car, pulling out down Main and heading out of town. They weren't the only car heading east down the highway and Moira suspected more than a few were going to show up just to gawk, get free food and wine, and gossip.

Such was life in small-town America.

Funerals and the like made for great small talk.

"Have the cops found anything?" she asked softly.

"No." Brannon's voice was grim. After a moment, he slid her a look. "They think it was a professional hit."

"The senator, then."

"That's my guess." From where she sat in the backseat, she could see his hands tighten on the steering wheel. She'd had to argue to make Hannah take the front seat and in the end, she'd said if she didn't take the front seat, she'd insist on driving and Hannah would be sorry, because Moira was a lousy driver.

She'd lied. Moira actually preferred *her* driving over

her brother's but she wasn't about to have her brother's
pregnant . . . girlfriend? What was she? But regardless,
Hannah was family now and she was pregnant. Moira
could damn well sit in the back.

"Has Gideon talked to Roberts?"

Brannon's eyes came to meet hers. "I was actually
going to see if you'd talk to Gideon, ask him that very
question."

"I . . ." She paused and then looked away. "Why don't
you ask him?"

Brannon snorted. "Because he's more likely to tell
you. Don't pretend you don't know that."

She bristled but remained quiet. She was well aware
of what people in town said. She was also well aware that
it was bullshit. There was nothing left between her and
Gideon. Even if part of her still wished there was. Even
if she still dreamed about him.

"I'll ask him but don't expect him to tell me anything,"
she said.

"I can't tell you."

Moira stared into the soft red wine and snorted. "Of
course you can't."

Looking up, she gave Gideon what she knew was a
lousy attempt at a smile. Too bad. She was in a bitch of
a mood and manners could, for once, take a flying leap.
"Thank you, Chief. You have a nice day now, ya hear?"

With that parting comment, she turned on her heel.

She didn't even manage two steps before he caught
her arm.

"Why don't you say what you really mean, Moira?"

She took a long, deep drink of the wine instead, staring out at the crowd that had gathered on her brother's
property. Had any of them even known Alison?

Moira had, casually.

She'd liked her.

But she'd be willing to bet a case of her brother's best wine—not that it was costing *her* anything, but that wasn't the point—that most of these people hadn't known Alison.

Maybe they were just here to show support.

Maybe they were just here because, like her, they were frustrated with all the bad things happening in Treasure lately.

She didn't know.

When Gideon's fingers didn't fall away from her arm, she dropped a look at his hand. "Care to let go, Chief?"

"Care to tell me what's eating you, Mac?"

The nickname from long ago, another time, another *life*, made an ache rip through her.

Carefully, she put her wine glass down.

"Don't call me that," she said quietly.

Twisting out of his reach, she walked away, quickly.

He called her name, but she didn't dare stop.

A few months ago, Neve had told her that she didn't think Moira had ever gotten over Gideon.

The bitch of it was, Neve had been right.

She sniffed. Reaching inside her purse, she drew out a handkerchief.

She was going to find one of the benches in the private area back behind the winery and sit down. In a while, she'd leave and . . .

"Oh. Hello, Marc."

Marc lifted his face from his hands and blinked at her.

Tears streamed unceasingly down his face and Moira looked at the handkerchief she held and then, without thinking, held it out. "It's clean," she said.

He eyed it for a moment and then took it. "Thank you."

"Would you like me to leave?"

"Yeah . . . . no." He shrugged. "The hell if I know."

Slowly, she sat on the surface of the table next to him. "I'm really sorry about Alison. Brannon told me you were . . . close."

A heavy silence fell and then he looked over at her. "I think I was falling in love with her."

Oh . . .

Uncertain what to say, she reached out and wrapped an arm around his shoulders. He started to cry, soft, quiet sobs that tore at her heart.

"I'm so sorry, Marc."

He could handle her walking away from him.

Gideon was used to that after all this time.

He handled standing at the corner, unseen by either of them, as she comforted a grieving Marc. His Moira had always had a soft heart, hidden under a prickly exterior and lots of steel.

It got harder later, though.

She'd moved out of the public area into the areas marked *private*, taking one of the paths that led out behind the big building made of reclaimed timbers into the trees.

Gideon wouldn't have followed if he hadn't seen Charles Hurst separate himself from the trees and go after her.

He shouldn't have followed even then, but everything about Hurst got his back up.

From the fact that Moira had actually *accepted* his love to the fact that . . . well, she'd accepted his love.

While she'd rejected Gideon's.

After so many years, you'd think he would have resigned himself to it.

But after so many years, it still hurt as much now as it did then and he knew, as sure as he stood there, that he'd never get over her.

He should just stop trying.

The path led deep into the dark, heavy growth of trees and when he heard their voices, he paused to listen.

"I'm *fine*, Charles. I just wanted to be alone."

"Is now really the best time to be alone, darling? So many strange things are happening . . ."

"Yes, well, I'm quite capable of taking care of myself."

There was a pause and Gideon moved in closer.

The next murmurs were harder to hear.

". . . miss you . . ."

"Odd that you didn't think about that when you were busy *shagging* my admin, huh?"

Gideon grinned at the blade that edged Moira's words as he rounded the last curve in the trail. He watched where he stepped, automatically falling back on the lessons he'd learned both as a youth hunting these woods and when he'd hunted a different kind of prey back when he'd served in the Army.

"It was a mistake. I'm sorry for it . . . Moira. I *miss* you. I miss *us*."

Hot male jealousy burst through him as he stepped into the small clearing by the banks of the river. Moira stood on the old wooden dock and Charles held her by the arms, caught up against him, his mouth on hers.

It lasted for just a second and then Moira jerked away. "I *don't* miss us, Charles. We're . . ."

Her gaze slid away.

Gideon arched a brow as she caught sight of him.

"Spying on me now, Gideon?"

"Just out taking a walk," he said, lifting a shoulder.

As Charles' gaze came his way, he gave the other man a sharp smile. "Charles, I think your attentions are unwelcome."

"Gideon, I think your assistance is unnecessary." But Charles pulled back and smoothed his tie down. He gave

Moira a terse nod and left, striding past Gideon without another word.

"Looking to rekindle an old flame?" Gideon said easily.

"Go fuck yourself, Marshall," she snapped.

There were easily a hundred people back at the memorial who would have been shocked to hear Moira McKay speak that way.

But Gideon wasn't one of them.

He moved toward her. The boat dock butted up against an old shed and he leaned up against it as he studied Moira. She gave him a withering look before turning her attention back out over the river.

"Has he been bothering you much?"

"No." She kept her response terse. "I can handle Charles."

Oh, he was sure she could. One of the things he'd always loved about her was her ability to slice a man off at the balls. Not the knees—the balls. The balls were so much more effective when it came to dealing with men.

"Okay." He nodded. "I was just wondering."

"You have an answer. Stop wondering."

Behind her back, he rolled his eyes at her pithy response. "You're certainly feeling bitchy today, Mac."

She spun on her heel and stormed toward him, a diminutive goddess clad in jade green. She jammed her index finger into his chest. "Stop calling me that," she said, punctuating every other word with another hard poke in his chest. "You hear me?"

He caught her wrist. "Unless you're trying to shove your finger through my chest, stop," he warned.

She jerked, trying to free herself.

Reckless need had him jerking back.

She crashed into him, a startled noise escaping her.

He reached up with his free hand and cupped her hip, holding her against him.

For the longest moment, they just stared at each other.

"Let me go," she whispered, the hoarse murmur shattering the silence.

"I did that. Once. I've regretted it and been miserable ever since."

Moira's lashes fluttered down over her eyes. Leaning down, he pressed a kiss to first one eye, then the other. When her mouth fell open on a gasp, he leaned down and licked at her lower lip. "Do you know how hard it is to go through life holding onto memories . . . Mac?"

She made a low noise in her throat.

It could have been protest.

It could have been assent.

He didn't know.

He prepared himself to pull away.

What he didn't prepare himself for was for her to curl her right arm around his neck and tug him in closer.

Her tongue slid out to meet his.

It was a nervous, almost shy kiss—so much like their first one.

He could remember it, clear as day.

That first kiss had shaken the very bedrock of his world.

This one threatened to end it.

Fisting his hand in the material at the small of her back, he brought her in closer.

She came willingly and when she arched against him, he slid that same hand down her hip, toying with the hem of her skirt.

She rolled her hips against him and Gideon swore, tearing his mouth away.

"You're supposed to be the smart one, Mac. So show it. Pull away and walk up that path, get away from me now."

She licked her lips, her tongue lingering on the upper bow. Then she curled her hands into his shoulders and rose up onto her toes. Softly, she whispered, "I'm tired of being the smart one, Gideon."

She told herself she was ready.

She told herself she'd been waiting for this for too many years.

But when he spun her around, shoving her up against the rough side of the boathouse, Moira knew she'd lied.

She wasn't ready.

Even when he hiked her up, shoving her skirt up in the same motion, she knew she wasn't ready.

Her panties disappeared in a jerk and a tear and then he was between her thighs.

She still wasn't ready and she didn't care.

"You're wet," Gideon rasped against her ear.

Yes, she was wet and getting wetter as he stroked two fingers down her slit, opening her.

She gasped when he slowly screwed those same two fingers inside her. Clamping down tight around him, she arched up and rocked, trying to take him deeper.

But Gideon wasn't in the mood for slow and teasing foreplay.

She'd barely had time to feel him stretching her before his hand was gone, replaced by the blunt, probing head of his cock.

She whimpered at the feel of him as he moved in closer, hooking her knees over his elbows to open her fully. A moan rose in her throat but lodged there as he started to forge his way deep, deep inside her.

She was stretched tight around him, her flesh hot and slick, straining to accommodate him.

Gideon knew exactly when he'd felt like this—the last

day he'd made love to her—only a few short minutes before she'd told him good-bye for the final time.

He banished that memory to the very depths of his consciousness and focused on the here and the now, staring at the sight of his cockhead, slowly disappearing inside the satin wet depths of her pussy.

Moira keened out his name, her voice strangled and broken.

Her nails bit into his shoulders, short, neat half moons that he'd carry with bittersweet, vivid memories until they healed.

Her hips twisted in his hands and he shuddered as that action drove her more completely down on him.

Retreating, he started to ride her, sinking a little deeper, a little faster each time.

Moira responded with a shattering sob, shaking in his hands and quivering as though with a fever.

His own climax was already rushing on him hard and fast.

It wouldn't be enough.

Nothing with her would ever be enough.

Nothing.

Judging by the angle of the light, Moira knew they had to have spent well over an hour inside the boathouse.

Her clothes might not be totally beyond salvaging, but she probably was.

She went to stand up, but before she could, Gideon kissed her back. "Leaving already?" he asked.

"It's a memorial service. I'm supposed to be out there for my brother."

"Yeah. We should be out there." He pulled her onto her knees and moved between them. "But I'd rather be in here."

She gasped as he came inside her.

She was swollen and sore and she didn't know how to handle telling him she'd stopped taking the pill a few months after she'd divorced Charles.

But in that moment, nothing mattered but feeling him inside her.

Unlike the others, this climax was slow and sweet and lazy.

When it ended, she let him pull her back into his arms and she cuddled up against him.

I miss you, she thought, half desperately.

She did miss him.

But how did one reach across a void of so many years and tell the man she'd always loved that she was sorry?

That she'd made a terrible mistake?

Hannah studied the picture of Alison, trying to ignore the creeping dread that crawled up her spine. Absently, she reached down to rub her belly. She wanted the next few months gone. Wanted her baby to come and wanted to forget about every bad thing that had happened lately—

"Don't think that," she muttered. "You've forgotten enough, haven't you?"

Something bumped against her hand.

She jumped.

The sensation was so startling, so unexpected, she looked down, staring at the spot where she'd felt it.

It happened again.

"Oh, my goodness," she whispered, the words hardly more than a breath of sound as she realized what had just happened.

The baby had just moved!

The dread, the uneasiness that had chased her much of the day fell away and she turned, ready to rush and find Brannon.

She almost crashed right into Lloyd Hanson. At the sight of the smirk that curled his thin lips, she balled one hand into a fist. Immediately, she backed away, automatically bracing both feet wide and turning her body slightly to the side.

She knew for a fact that dealing with him could end badly. Her experiences with him brought about that instinctive *fight or flight* response and when it came to scum like him, the response was *fight*. He was a coward, a wife beater, and trash—in that order.

She didn't like Lloyd, not at all. She hadn't liked him even before she'd shown up on the scene when he'd been beating his wife senseless.

Hannah hadn't been on the clock when she'd heard the screams coming from inside the little house where Joanie had lived with Lloyd since their marriage four years earlier. That hadn't kept Hannah's bosses from tearing into her when she'd used a rock to break the window and let herself inside. She'd called the cops first—she wasn't stupid. She'd then used that same rock on Lloyd's head.

He'd wanted to press charges but it was found there were no grounds.

So then he'd tried to claim she'd caused him physical and mental trauma.

But that hadn't gone over very well because when his lawyer had even *attempted* to give Hannah grief, Hannah had handed him his ignorant ass. She hadn't even needed her lawyer—and the woman had practically applauded by the time Hannah was done.

Then she had looked at her counterpart and asked, "You really want to put her on the stand? Your client is a *known* abuser. My client's mother lived with an abuser for years. You'll never win because my first witness is going to be Hannah and you've already gotten a glimpse of what runs through her mind when she sees a woman being beaten."

The lawyer had told Lloyd he'd never win.

Joanie had even left Lloyd . . . for a while.

She'd gone back but even now, people liked to ask him how he was doing with his *mental trauma*.

All of that might add up to why Lloyd was staring at her with complete and utter hatred in his eyes. Some of the people around them glanced their way. Hannah braced herself. This just might get ugly.

"Gonna be nice, being a babymaker for the richest fuck in town. How long did it take you to sleaze your way into his bed, huh?"

"Kiss ass, Lloyd," she advised him, shoving past him—or trying.

He caught her arm, his fingers digging in.

She jerked away. Knowing him—and knowing he wouldn't let go—she didn't just pull away, though. She swung out, jabbing him in the throat with a stiffened hand.

He fell back, gasping and rubbing at it.

"You . . . fuckin . . ." He sucked in a wheezing breath and waited a few seconds before he tried again.

She debated about walking on, or nodding at one of the men who were clearly looking in her direction with silent offers of help.

But no.

She was tired of this.

This wasn't the first time Lloyd had hassled her and Gideon had already told her if he kept it up, they'd have enough to slap a restraining order against him. Unlike Joanie, Hannah wasn't scared of her own shadow and *she* wouldn't drop the order.

If the son of a bitch violated it, she'd have his ass in jail.

Hannah set her jaw, glaring at him.

"One of these days, you fat cunt, a man's going to teach you a lesson," he said, leaning in so that nobody around them caught the low threat. He was so close, she could catch the garlic off his breath. "It might even be me."

"Nah, Lloyd." She moved back and smiled at him. "You see, that can't happen. *You* would actually have to *be* a man for it to be you."

He snarled and made to reach for her again. "You watch how to talk to me, you whore!"

The shadow that fell across him was the only warning he had.

Hannah caught a glass from a passing server, lifting it in a salute to Brannon as he closed his hand over Lloyd's skinny shoulder. Brannon's hand tightened. She watched as his knuckles went white and bloodless and Lloyd winced, trying to jerk away but he couldn't manage it.

Brannon dipped his head low and said softly, "You want to say that again, Lloyd?"

"I . . ." Lloyd jerked his head. "You don't want to do this here, Brannon. The sheriff is here. Gideon Marshall's around somewhere." He sucked in a breath and whimpered as Brannon's grip tightened. "You stupid fuck. If you don't let me go right now, I'll fucking sue your stupid ass."

"Sure, Lloyd." Brannon gave him a calm smile. "I'll let you go."

He did—with a hard shove that sent him stumbling into the dirt.

A low laugh broke out into the crowd and when Lloyd came up, he came up swinging.

Hannah winced as she watched Brannon take a punch—and that's all there was to it.

He *took* the punch.

Then, when Lloyd went to slug him again, Brannon blocked it. "I'm going to give you the same advice you gave me. You don't want to do this here," Brannon said. "My property and I'm warning you. If you lift your hand to me again, I'll defend myself."

"Suck my dick, you uppity, rich son of a bitch," Lloyd said, panting. A grin spread across his face.

He'd gotten a taste of blood, Hannah thought. It had made him stupid.

Otherwise, he would have realized that Brannon wasn't even breathing hard.

Brannon took one more punch.

The next one, he caught and trapped.

Hannah gagged when she heard the bone break. It was a sickening sort of sound, a cracking wet one, followed immediately by Lloyd's shriek.

Tank Granger chose that moment to emerge from the crowd, swearing a blue streak. He stopped at the sight of Hannah and the other women and instead started to mutter under his breath. That lasted precisely ten seconds. She could count on Tank to keep things routine. He gave himself a specific amount of time to indulge his temper before he became all business. Slapping his hands on his hips, he looked at the writhing, whimpering form of Lloyd Hansen before shifting his attention to Hannah and Brannon. "Please tell me there's a damn good reason you snapped his arm like a twig, Brannon McKay."

"Self defense," Brannon said, jerking a big shoulder in a shrug.

Tank ran his tongue across his teeth and then looked at the skinny, lanky form of Lloyd Hansen. For a moment, he almost looked like he wanted to laugh and then he dragged a hand down his face. Hannah thought maybe he was wiping the smile away. He called out into the crowd. "Devin! Levon! I need you boys! Hope you're sober."

Two men separated themselves from the crowd—they were in civilian clothes—and sober as far as Hannah could tell.

As they came closer, Tank made a quick call into dispatch for an ambulance and then he focused a pair of hard hazel eyes on Brannon. "Explain this to me, son. Just how did you break his arm defending yourself? If I recall correctly—"

A high-pitched wail came from Lloyd as Levon and Devin hauled him to his feet. Levon had stabilized Lloyd's arm—he'd been a field medic in the army up until two years ago. Hannah couldn't fault how efficiently he'd done it.

Tank cocked a brow and then looked back at Brannon. "As I was saying, if I—"

Lloyd wailed again.

"For the love of Mary, boy, have some dignity and quit your caterwauling!" Tank bellowed.

"It fucking hurts!" Lloyd sobbed, leaning heavily against Devon. He shot Levon a dirty look. "That idiot you got there got no idea how much it hurt when he . . ." He fumbled to a stop as he looked at his stabilized arm.

Levon folded his hands behind his back. "I apologize, Mr. Hansen. When I broke my leg during my last tour, I discovered it was a lot more painful to leave the broken limb *unstabilized*, but if you'd like me to unwrap it, I can do that." He gave Lloyd a placid, unperturbed smile.

Lloyd muttered something uncomplimentary under his breath.

"In my day, when somebody did something to help a man out, he said *thank you*," Tank said. Then he looked back at Brannon. "One more time."

Brannon looked at Hannah. "He called her a whore."

Then he looked back at Tank. "He was in her face and he called her a whore. So I got in his face and asked him if he'd like to repeat that. I had my hand on his shoulder and he told me to stop touching him." A smirk of a smile lit Brannon's features.

It was terrible and primeval and juvenile, but that gleam that came into his eyes made Hannah's heart race. She rested a hand on her belly and tried to think calming, soothing thoughts.

It wasn't working.

Brannon, totally unaware of how off-topic her thoughts were getting, shrugged. "I stopped touching him." He shrugged. "I might have pushed him . . . hard. He went down and got up, punched me. Twice. I told him each time he needed to stop and get off my property. I didn't strike back or attempt to defend myself until he went at me a third time."

"That's a bunch of *bullshit*," Lloyd snapped.

"No. It's not." Hannah rubbed her hand over her belly, then gasped as the baby kicked in response.

Brannon's eyes flew to her.

"It's okay." She fought not to smile at him. It so didn't seem to be the time. Shifting her gaze over to Tank, she gestured to Lloyd. "It's no secret there's no love lost between Lloyd and me. He's been getting in my face off and on ever since that incident with Joanie. Last week, I had to call Gideon after Lloyd threw something on my car when I was driving—"

"You can't prove I did that!" Lloyd protested.

Hannah ignored him. "There's a police report about it and I've talked to Gideon about Lloyd and his hassling twice. I'm about to file a restraining order." Curling her lip at the man in question, she added, "As a matter of fact, I think Gideon's office is my next stop when I leave here."

"You ain't got cause, bitch!" Lloyd jerked away from

Devin and then went an ugly shade of pasty white as he fell, off-balance, into Levon.

"You called me a whore," Hannah said. "You accused me of sleazing my way into Brannon's bed just to con him out of child support. You *repeatedly* get into my face and invade my personal space and put your hands on me. You grabbed me not even five minutes ago and called me a fat cunt, told me that some man—maybe even *you*— would teach me a lesson. I think I've got cause."

The pasty white had long since gone red.

Hannah toasted him. "I told you to stay out of my way, Lloyd."

He roared. Forgetting his arm, forgetting the sheriff and his deputies, he lunged in her direction. In the process, he rammed into Tank who had moved to block him.

Five seconds later, he was on his ass, screaming in agony.

"Well, I think you'll be spending some time in lock-up, Lloyd." Tank's ruddy face was bland as he shook his head at the wailing man. "You need to cool off, son."

Hannah studied him over the rim of her glass.

She wondered if she had an icicle's chance in hell of talking Joanie into leaving while her darling husband was taking his time out.

"The baby kicked."

It was nearly four hours later.

The memorial was supposed to have ended nearly two hours ago, but it ended up dragging on longer than planned, and not just because of Lloyd Hansen's melt-down.

Nearly forty-five minutes after the sheriff and his men had followed the ambulance and its furious patient off the winery grounds, a decidedly disheveled Moira McKay had emerged from the trees.

They wouldn't have thought much of it.

Except Gideon Marshall came from that same area ten minutes later.

Nobody said much of anything at first—and they definitely said nothing within earshot of Moira, but they did say plenty after the general surprise died down.

Brannon wasn't sure he could handle one more question that had to do with his sister and Gideon.

He really couldn't.

He had desperately needed a reprieve. This . . . well, hell. It was definitely something to distract him. Feeling like *he* had been kicked, he stared at Hannah.

She looked serene, unfazed.

Swiping the back of his hand over his mouth, he tried to form some sort of a response. "I . . . you . . . what?"

She smiled at him. She'd pulled out the two long, skinny sticks that had held her hair in some sort of complicated twists and now her golden brown hair fell in gleaming skeins to twine around her shoulders and breasts. The sun caressed those golden strands and her skin, making Brannon jealous. He'd do anything to play across her hair and skin the way the sunlight did, caressing her at will.

That smile . . . it was mysterious and female and as old as time. She brought a hand to the ripe swell of her belly and rubbed it. She'd done that today, often.

"The baby kicked." Then the smile faded and she looked away. "It was right before Lloyd decided to make an ass of himself again."

"If he touches you again, I'm going to break more than his arm."

Hannah arched a brow. "Caveman."

Shoving off the railing, Brannon came to her. "Absolutely." Then he reached out, letting his hand hover above her belly. "Can I . . . ?"

She responded by reaching out and taking his hand, guiding it to her belly. "She kicks there," she murmured, holding his palm in a spot just to the left her navel. "Right there."

"She." He swallowed the knot in his throat. "You always say she."

Hannah just shrugged. "Yeah . . . I just . . . I don't mean to. I don't really care if it's a boy or a girl. I just want a healthy baby. But I have a feeling she's a girl."

He rubbed his hand in a circle around her belly.

Then, staring into her eyes, he dragged his hand, cupping one of her breasts through the dress. "I want you," he said bluntly.

Hannah slicked her tongue across her lips. "It's . . . um . . ." She looked around.

"There's nobody here. I had everybody take the rest of the day off." Staring into her eyes, he moved his fingers to the buttons of her dress and started to free them, one by one.

Her breasts rose and fell, her breaths ragged, and in moments, her dress hung open, framing the lush, ripe curves of her body. Rose lace cupped her breasts and he freed the front catch, watching as her breasts swung free. "You're getting bigger," he said, his voice hoarse.

She made a face. "I know. Half my bras don't fit. I have to go . . ." Her voice hitched as he cupped her breasts and squeezed her nipples slowly. "Shopping."

"Let me take you."

Her gaze flew to his.

"I've had a hundred fantasies about the kind of silk and lace I'd like to see you in. And even more about the kind of silk and lace I'd like to peel you out of." He tugged on her nipples and watched as her lashes fluttered and fell low, shielding her eyes.

A flush started low on her breasts, spreading upward

and he dipped his head, pressing his mouth to the center of her breastbone, right where that pretty pink blush began.

She reached up, cupping the back of his head.

Brannon caught her hips and slid his hands inside her panties. They were cut low, the waistband going under the faint swell of her belly. He pushed them down and when they hit her knees, she wiggled until she could step out of them.

She was all but naked now and he still wore the clothing he'd donned that morning for the memorial.

Hannah slid one hand down the front of his shirt and Brannon felt his muscles jump in response.

His cock pulsed and when that hand slid down, down, down, he could feel his balls drawing tight against him in anticipation.

Before she could start to stroke him through his trousers, he pulled back.

Catching her hands, he guided them back to the smooth wood that formed the railing around the deck. "Don't move," he said, his voice low and guttural.

She watched him as he undid his belt and button to his trousers, then freed himself. He removed nothing else. He didn't have the patience. Going back to her, he cupped her face while she lifted her hands to his shirt.

As he stroked his tongue along the curve of her lower lip, Hannah loosened and tugged his tie free.

He had no idea what she did with it.

He could feel the tips of her fingers brushing against his chest as she unbuttoned his shirt and he decided, yeah, maybe getting some of his clothes out of the way wasn't a bad idea . . . not if it involved her touching him.

Then she pushed his shirt open and dragged her nails down the simple white undershirt he'd pulled on hours earlier.

He hissed out a breath.

She bit his lip.

Grabbing her hips, he boosted her up onto the wide, fat lip of the railing.

She gasped and caught onto his shoulders.

"I've got you," he promised, moving to stand between her thighs.

She shot a nervous look over her shoulder.

He curled an arm around her waist, staring into her eyes.

"I won't let you fall."

Bit by bit, she relaxed and when he nudged against her, she shuddered and widened her thighs, gripping his hips with her knees.

The wet heat of her pussy kissed the head of his cock and Brannon gritted his teeth against the urge to thrust, deep, hard, fast.

Instead, he watched her as he filled her, slow and sweet and easy. She stretched around him and he watched her head fall back, gritted his teeth as she whimpered and wiggled and rolled her hips forward to take more of him.

Her lashes drooped low.

"Look at me."

But she didn't.

Tightening the steadying arm he had around her waist, Brannon slid his free hand up to cup her jaw, splaying his fingers into her hair. "Look at me," he demanded, his voice rougher now, hunger making him half wild.

Hannah's lids lifted.

Need made her eyes almost black.

He swiveled his hips in the cradle of hers and she cried out.

Her muscles clamped down on him and he arched his hips, slamming harder into her. At the same time, he tugged her closer, angling her hips. She tightened the grip she had on his knees.

He swore.

Couldn't get deep enough, couldn't get close enough.

Pulling her up against him, he turned.

Hannah cried out and wrapped her arms around his neck. Her weight drove her down on his cock. It took less than three seconds to get to the picnic table, roughly the same amount of time to lay her down and then he drove deeper, harder inside her.

She cried out.

It still wasn't enough.

Catching her legs behind the knees, he surged within her.

"Brannon!"

Hannah reached up, fisting her hands in the lapels of his shirt, hanging loose off his shoulders.

She tried to arch up, to rub herself against him—she was so close. Her orgasm was just a whisper away. One flex of his hips and she'd—

She keened out his name as he withdrew. She gulped air, staring up at him.

The table beneath her was hard, flat, warmed by the sun. Brannon's body was just as hard, even warmer. She felt caught, trapped, surrounded.

He came down on her and moved up.

It shifted his body's angle, had him rubbing against her clit and she whimpered.

Sunlight shone down, forming a nimbus around him that made him almost painful to look at.

Tugging him closer, she pressed her mouth to his.

He kissed her, his tongue demanding entrance even as his cock took it.

She opened for him—in every way. So close . . . so . . .

"Say you want me," Brannon muttered against her mouth.

"I . . ." She panted, hardly able to breathe now.

"Say it." His voice was insistent, impatient.

"I want you."

"Say you . . ."

But the words faded away and he shifted, burying his face in her hair. "Hannah."

That was it. Simply her name.

His cock pulsed, jerked—and she lost it, shattering beneath him and coming hard.

Say you want me . . . Hannah squeezed her eyes shut tightly as the bits and pieces of a fragmented memory tried to break free.

Say you want me.

She sucked in a breath and as she did so, she caught the scent of Brannon. It was in the air, on her skin. Everywhere. Surrounding her.

Like she'd gotten caught in a riptide, Hannah's mind jerked away from her and she found herself caught and tumbling in the current of memory streaming free.

"I want you. Say you want me." Brannon rasped the words against her lips before he lifted his head up to stare at her, the demand on his face clear.

"Want . . . I guess that's one way to phrase it." I want chocolate three times a day. I want to sleep until noon and stay up to watch the sunset over the river. But I don't always get what I want. *She didn't tell him that, though. Instead, she guided his mouth back to hers.*

She groaned when she felt him tearing at the button on his jeans, fumbling with the zipper and then she tensed in anticipation when he rocked back and forth against her mound. She was already wet and the sensations had her crying out, arching closer.

He came inside her in one hard, driving thrust and her whimper of shock was smothered by his kiss.

It was bliss and it was hell and it ended far too soon.

Wet trickled down her thighs as he lowered her feet to the ground.

Hannah's legs wobbled and she clutched at his shoulders, trying to steady herself.

He'd come inside her.

No rubber.

She mentally groaned, even as she thanked the irregular periods that had eventually forced her to start taking the pill. That much, at least, should be okay.

Brannon stroked his hand down her back, easing in closer, his breathing still heavy and fast.

"We didn't use a rubber."

Hannah was still and quiet.

He wanted to hear her say it.

He had no right to expect it of her.

But he wanted to hear her say it.

Eyes closed, he stood in the main area of the winery, listening to the water running in the bathroom as she cleaned up.

Neither of them had spoken.

Hannah had lapsed into a taut silence and he recognized that look in her eyes by now. She was remembering something. Or trying to. And there he was, struggling with the guilt that still choked him over the things he hadn't shared with her.

He was falling in love with her, so hard and so fast. He needed to fix the mess he'd made of things, but he didn't know how.

She'd told him she loved him, but she didn't remember it.

She'd told him she loved him and he'd thrown it back at her.

The water came to a stop and he pushed off the counter, trying to force some sort of coherent thought into his head.

The door opened and he turned to look at Hannah.

She was fiddling with the buttons on her dress, smoothing her hair down, making it clear she would look at anything and anybody but him.

He cleared his throat.

She darted a look at him.

He took a step toward her.

She headed for the door. "I need to get going," she said, her voice overly bright. "I'm barely going to have time to shower and change before I'm due in my shift this evening."

Brannon opened his mouth. *Say something, dumb ass.*

"I love you."

Hannah crashed into a wire rack of cards.

They were all done by local artists, everything from Americana to medieval, mythical looking fairy creatures. She tried to catch the rack, keep it from falling, but it slid out of her fingers and toppled, sending colorful bits of paper flying.

Surrounded by hand-drawn steamers and lovely inked fairies, she just stared.

Hearing the scuff of a shoe on wood, she slowly looked up and found herself staring at Brannon.

He was moving closer.

She backed away, one hand coming up.

Her blood roared in her ears and her heart pounded like thunder.

And beneath all of that, she heard a vaguely familiar voice. *Her* voice . . . maybe.

I've been in love with you since I was in high school.

She had loved Brannon since high school—almost half her life, she thought.

But he'd never . . .

He cupped her face and his hands were rough, yet so gentle. He used his thumbs to tilt her gaze to meet his. Hannah swallowed, the knot in her throat large, all but choking her. "I love you," he said again. "It could have happened yesterday. Maybe it happened a year ago—five years ago. It could have happened in the past five minutes. I don't know. I just know I love you."

She thought maybe her heart had stopped, wondered if she should be worried about that.

But then he kissed her and the only thing she could think about was that—Brannon was kissing her and he'd just told her he loved her.

Did anything else even matter?

CHAPTER FIFTEEN

"I say we bring the senator in and sweat him."

Gideon looked over at Tank, a headache pulsing at the base of his skull. His eyes felt like sand-covered golfballs—inflamed sand-covered golfballs—and they were burning holes in his sockets. He hadn't slept worth shit. He rarely did, but the past few days had been particularly lousy. "We bring him on what evidence?"

"Two deaths." Tank shrugged. "Loosely connected to him, but there is a connection."

Gideon rubbed the back of his neck and went back to staring at the murder board. "Well . . . . I got some money in the bank. House is paid off now. If I end up out on my ass, I'll be okay for a while. You got two ex-wives and a kid, though."

Tank snorted.

"Yeah, laugh it off, you jackass."

"This isn't anything to laugh off." Tank shrugged and settled down on the chair in front of Gideon's desk. "Look, we can connect him to Shayla. So what if he was flat on his back in the hospital? I don't think he killed her, either, but he doesn't have to know that. But you and I *both* know he's involved in the death of Alison

Maxwell. You can take it to the bank. We'll bring him in, sweat him, and see what happens." Now Tank's smile turned cagey. "The man's spine is made up of wax and straw. He'll melt. All we have to do is put a little heat on him. Do it the right way and even his lawyer won't shut him up in time."

"The lawyer will fuck us if we aren't careful." Gideon curled his lip.

"The way I see it, we're fucked now. At least this way, we have a chance." He shrugged with practiced casualness as he added, "All we need is one decent lead and we can push for a warrant—climb all over his bank records, phone records. The son of a bitch is arrogant. There's a trail somewhere."

Gideon had to agree, but his thoughts drifted back to Shayla. "He won't lead us to her," he murmured. "I know he won't."

Tank didn't speak, but Gideon suspected they were both thinking the same thing. Sometimes you just had to take what you get and right now, Alison Maxwell's killer might be the easier one to pin down. It was a sad fucking state, because pinning a crime on a politician was always a pain in the ass. Their money and position made it a dance of politics and eggshells.

"It's not making sense," Gideon said, his hands going to his hips. So far, they'd talked to almost everybody on their list, and of those people, the few they could see with the capacity or *ability* to strangle a woman, neither Tank nor Gideon could see them killing Shayla in cold blood.

The one woman who might have been able to do it just out of sheer meanness was Tessie Foreman, and that old bat was seventy if she was a day and didn't weigh more than a hundred pounds. She also liked to do inappropriate things with her farm animals and she had more cash hidden away on her farm than Croseus. She wasn't quite up there with the McKays, but she wasn't hurting for money.

But she'd bluntly told Gideon, *If I was going to kill that bitch, I'd have done it in town—right on Main in front of everybody.*

Gideon could believe it.

"What's not making sense?" Tank asked.

He gestured to the board. "The people who had the most reason to kill her? They are the ones we can't see doing it." Moving to the list, he skimmed the notes he'd made.

Most of them had to do with affairs and while the people involved thought they were being discreet, half the people in town knew. Shayla was just the one greedy enough to cash in and the people with their pants down were foolish enough to think they were still fooling everybody else.

"I can see Jimmy Bradshaw killing over this."

Gideon looked over at Tank. "Then you haven't ever been in the pub on a Friday or Saturday night. That man has been known to pass out at the sight of blood."

"Shayla didn't bleed."

Gideon rolled his eyes. "Splitting hairs. He's big and loud and has a temper, likes to get in your face." Shrugging, he went on to the next name. "But I've seen kids half his age back him down. He just can't handle fights or confrontation."

They brooded over the list for another fifteen minutes before Gideon turned to Tank. "Know what bothers me about this list? If it was somebody on here, they did it out of rage or desperation, wouldn't you think?"

"Stands to reason."

Gideon moved to the folder that held the autopsy photos of Shayla Hardee. "She wasn't killed with any rage. There was no desperation. She was just . . . disposed of."

He looked up to meet Tank's eyes but the other man was studying the images.

Gideon passed them over, already knowing what Tank would see. A body, pale, waxen and bruised from the quick, brutal death. Mouth slack and eyes closed. Nothing had been done to her before or after death, other than the injury that had ended her life.

"She was in the way," Gideon murmured, more to himself than anything else.

Tank glanced up. "Pardon?"

He went to shake his head and then stopped. "He disposed of her. It wasn't about any of this . . . or if it was, it was just a nuisance. She was a nuisance, so he just eliminated her."

Gideon thought back to the body. "She was just disposed of," he murmured. "Done away with. This was cold-blooded, planned."

"What makes you think that?" Tank asked.

Gideon suspected their minds were in sync but he understood how important a sounding board was. "Gut instinct. She never went out to the park. I've talked to a dozen people, more, who hang there, run there, fish . . . some of them have a houseboat out there like Hannah does. None of them ever saw Shayla. She was lured out there or she asked him to meet her there. Privacy."

The picture came together in his head. Tank was nodding and Gideon knew he could see it, too. "A new mark, maybe?"

"Fuck." It felt right. Gideon went back to staring at his list. He blew out a breath between his teeth.

Tank made a low grunt, echoing Gideon's frustration. "You know . . . I still say we bring the senator in, sweat him. See what happens." Then he smiled thinly. "If nothing else, it will make me happy. The guy's an asshole and we have a motive."

Gideon's response was cut short when he caught sight of a sleek, silver convertible just as it turned onto the road. His heart slammed against his ribs. Moira.

She climbed out and although it was quick, he saw her dart a glance toward the police department. Did she see him?

Judging by the way her steps faltered, he thought maybe she did.

His hands flexed and although it was just sensory memory, he found himself thinking of how smooth her skin had felt. How soft. Just as smooth, just as soft as she'd been all those years ago.

And more, she still responded the same.

She responded like she was still his.

But she didn't want to be his. She couldn't have made that any more clear if she tried.

And he needed to yank his head out of his ass.

"Alright. Let's do it. Let's bring him in." He gave the sheriff a thin smile. "Since the murder happened out on your turf, you get the honors. I hope you'll give me the courtesy of sitting in."

"I hope you have a good reason for this." The lawyer Crooks gave Tank a bland look before shifting his attention to Gideon. "Well, hello, Chief Marshall. I didn't realize this was an interdepartmental exercise."

"I'm just observing," Gideon said easily, glancing toward the silent man walking alongside Crooks. "Naturally you can understand how concerned the people in my town are. I'm just looking to provide them with answers."

"Then maybe you should be out looking for the real killer instead of hassling an innocent man." Crooks said nothing else, just stepped aside as they came to the door so the senator could enter.

They'd wasted three hours already, first hunting the man down and then convincing him that it really was in his best interest to come down to the station. After all, if they went for a warrant, it would become public knowledge that much quicker.

Crooks had tried to insist they take that route.

But Roberts had seen something in Gideon's face and had smiled that genial politician's smile. "Now, now," he'd said. "I do like to cooperate with officers of the law."

How kind of him. Gideon wondered what he was up to, but now that they had him in the station, he realized that Roberts was *nervous*. Crazy nervous, a shiny film of sweat dotted his upper lip and his eyes kept bouncing around.

If somebody leaped out and shouted *boo* at the man, Gideon might be putting his first responder skills to the test. He really didn't want to have to perform CPR on this old goat. As Tank shut the door behind him, he glanced over at the sheriff, arched a brow.

The corner of Tank's mouth twitched. That was the only reaction, but Gideon knew the man. He'd picked up on the senator's jumpiness as well.

Something was eating at the man.

"Let's get started," Tank said, moving to sit at the table. "We just have some things we'd like to clear up."

The senator had the hands of a working man, which was odd because he'd been born with a silver spoon in his mouth, and if he ever had to do something so menial as changing a tire or raking the leaves in his yard, Gideon thought he might break out in hives. As Tank took a chair, Henry Roberts put those big, workingman hands on the surface of the table and smiled his big, easy politician's smile.

"I think I can clear all of this up." The senator was known for his powerful, persuasive speeches, his voice warm and soothing, echoing with the warmth of his southern upbringing, but not overpowered by it. He was what probably would have passed for nobility in America's Deep South, had such a thing existed, and Gideon was in no way fooled by the affable manner or the smile.

The senator was playing a game, of that he had no doubt.

In the plain white room with bright lights reflecting harshly back at them, there was barely room for the four of them and Roberts took the time to look at Tank and Gideon in kind. It was so quiet, Gideon could hear the faint ticking of his watch.

When Roberts took a deep breath, Gideon narrowed his eyes.

The man's shoulders stiffened slightly under his expensive suit.

Instinctively, Gideon pushed off the wall.

He knew the look of a man when he was bracing himself.

Tank was doing the same thing.

Crooks caught sight of them and glanced over at his partner. The lawyer was clearly no fool.

But all the senator did was clench his hands into fists and then open them.

In that brief moment, Gideon had a look at the table. Damp marks in the shape of a man's hands lingered on the surface. The senator was sweating like a pig in the brisk, artificially cooled air.

"I did it."

Tank stiffened.

Gideon felt like somebody had just jabbed him in the ass with a hot poker.

The lawyer clamped a hand on his client's shoulder.

"I need a mom—"

"Be quiet, no. Better yet, leave." Senator Henry

Roberts looked over at his lawyer and said quietly, "You're fired."

Then without waiting another moment, he looked back, his attention clearly split between the both of them. "I'm going to make a confession. I suggest you read me my rights."

"What the hell . . . ?"

The two of them stood in the hall, looking in on their lone prisoner via the security feed. The small city prison was equipped to hold several guests but they rarely had more than one or two people locked up at a time. More often than not, these bars slammed shut behind the idiots who were stupid enough to get behind the wheel after a few too many at the pub or stupid enough to pick a fight with a man after he found you in bed with his wife. Of course, in most cases, both men would find themselves locked up. Or as it sometimes happened, both *women*.

On one memorable occasion, it had been a man and *two* women . . . and one of the women was the aggrieved spouse. She'd walked in to find her husband of less than six months having a happy little party with his ex-girlfriend and her new boyfriend.

She'd gone after the girlfriend with a wine bottle and ended up smashing her husband in the face with it. The ex-girlfriend had pounced, and it had all gone downhill from there.

To Gideon's knowledge, this might be the first time they'd had a politician behind bars here in McKay's Treasure.

As he rubbed a hand across his mouth, he let everything settle inside his head. Or he tried to let it settle. Some of the pieces fit, but the rest didn't.

"He's not telling us everything," Tank said, echoing what Gideon was thinking, down to the letter.

Gideon nodded. Of course, the question was figuring out how to get the truth out of him. It might be almost impossible to sift through the carefully explained story and separate the fact from fiction.

They'd spent three hours with the senator after he'd dismissed his lawyer. He'd waived his right to counsel, explained that he did indeed understand just what that meant, and then he'd proceeded to explain how he'd killed Alison Maxwell.

On his own.

That part, at least, Gideon didn't have to wonder about—he was lying. But he knew details that they hadn't released, and he had explained why she was dead, and he was waiting even now to sign a confession, waiving away his right to trial.

"It makes no fucking sense." Gideon didn't like it when things didn't make sense. It pissed him off.

Blowing out a breath, he nodded to their man and then looked at Tank. "I'm going to talk to him."

"We spent three hours talking to him," Tank said sourly. "But have at it."

Tank left him alone and as the door behind him shut quietly, Gideon moved toward the cell. He leaned against it, meeting the reddened eyes of Senator Henry Roberts.

The FBI had called.

They had questions for the senator.

Gideon and Tank would be lucky if they had this man anywhere near Treasure within twenty-four hours. Gideon wasn't particularly territorial. He was more about locking up the criminals and keeping his city safe. He didn't have anything to prove.

But he didn't want to let this man go until he had answers to certain questions.

"What aren't you telling us?" he asked, staring at Roberts.

It had been less than twenty minutes since they'd concluded their interview—or rather, since Tank had concluded his. Gideon hadn't been involved officially.

In those twenty minutes, Senator Henry Roberts had disappeared and the man now before Gideon was older, more tired, and clearly scared. He'd seen the fear in the senator's eyes earlier, but this terror was blind, so pure and sharp, Gideon had to fight the urge to check behind him and all the dark corners as well.

The senator rallied at the sound of Gideon's voice, giving him a polite smile. "I'm sorry?"

"You're lying about something." Bracing his elbows on the horizontal bar of the cell, Gideon leaned forward. "I want to know what it is."

"I assure you—"

There was a clattering crack from out in the hall and the senator jumped up off the bed where he had been sitting, eyes wide, face going pale. His breath came in hard, hitching starts and stops as he stared toward that noise.

"Hinges are messed up on the maintenance door," Gideon said, suspicion forming inside. "If you don't close the door by hand, it bangs shut."

The senator's laugh was calm. "Forgive an old man. I'm very tired after the day I've had."

"Sure. Confessing to a murder. Has to be tiring."

Henry Roberts stared at him with chilly eyes. "Extremely."

"Know what else is tiring? Covering up for somebody. Taking the heat." When something flashed in the man's gaze, Gideon knew he was right. "Of course, when you do something, you go all in. You're going to jail. No passing go, no collecting two hundred dollars."

"I already explained that I'm aware of what my confession means." With a dismissive wave, the senator sat down, his hands folded in his lap. They might have been conducting some sort of promotional interview, the way he acted.

"Who's worth going to jail for?" Gideon asked. "I mean, I look at you and see a guy who'd kill over his own damn pride. So who are you willing to go to jail for? To *lie* for?"

To his surprise, the senator's proud shoulders slumped. "Surely, Chief Marshall, there are people in your life that you would lie for, die for. Can't you imagine that most people, selfish or otherwise, can say the same?"

The realization hit hard and fast. "You're being threatened."

"No." The denial came too hard, too fast.

Gideon knew. He just knew.

"Who is—"

"Nobody!" Senator Henry Roberts drew back his shoulders, practically sneering the word. "You're looking for shadows where there isn't even any sun. I've explained what I did and why."

As Chief Gideon Marshall walked away, Henry Roberts fought the urge to curl his hands into fists.

He was having a hard time holding it together and it had been even harder with that cop in there, watching him with calm, knowing eyes.

He didn't know shit.

Once he was alone, Henry dragged a shaking hand through his hair and closed his eyes. His mother, bless her soul, had told him more than once that the things he did in life would come back on him, good or bad.

Mama always did know best.

She'd been gone thirty-two years now. He missed her still, but she wasn't here to see him and he was thankful for that. It was enough that he was leaving behind his wife, his kids.

Closing his eyes, he rested his head against the concrete and pondered all the decisions and choices that had led him here, all the wrong turns.

It had started with a stripper, one who had teased him with a taste of her . . . and cocaine.

When she'd pushed for more, a man on his staff had told him that he could get in contact with somebody who could eliminate certain problems from a man's life.

Henry no longer dealt with that particular *problem solver*. He'd turned out to be a problem himself. He should have remembered what his current troubleshooter had told him when they'd started working together.

Don't fuck with me and I won't fuck with you. It's that simple, Senator.

But Senator Henry Roberts had let his own arrogance blind him and he had indeed tried to fuck with the assassin he knew only as Joseph. Infuriated by everything that had gone wrong since the McKays had come into his life, he'd contacted Joseph and demanded another hit—this time on all three McKays.

Joseph had told him that he was going into retirement and would be unable to complete that job. Would he like a recommendation for another troubleshooter?

Henry had ranted, raged . . . then threatened.

Perhaps if he'd let it go at that, he might not be here now.

But he hadn't. Henry was used to taking out the trash and Joseph had crossed him, thereby crossing the line that made him trash. So he'd reached out to another acquaintance but he hadn't been as subtle as he thought and just that morning, he'd woken up to find himself gagged and tied to a chair.

His wife had been sleeping peacefully while Joseph lay next to her, a gun to her temple.

"She'll go first," he'd said. "Then I'll go after each one

of your children. I might leave their little ones alone, because they aren't to blame for you being a fucking asshole, but then again, you've made me very angry."

The senator knew how to read people and as Joseph lay stroking the hair of Henry's beloved wife, he knew he was staring into the eyes of a man who could and would kill without a blink. They'd discussed how Henry could fix this.

Then Joseph had left and Henry had laid down to hold his wife for the last time. It took three hours for the drugs Joseph had pumped into her system to wear off.

When she woke up, he kissed her and told her that he loved her.

Then, rising, he showered and made calls to each of his children, telling them the very same thing.

It was fortuitous that the county sheriff had called when he did.

Of course, Joseph expected him to go to jail and rot there, but Henry wasn't that self-sacrificing. He'd pay, certainly. But in his own way.

The door creaked open a short time later and he pasted a bland smile on his face as a uniformed officer stopped in front of his cell. "I'm supposed to ask you if you need anything to eat or drink while you wait."

"Yes." Henry folded his hands. "I've heard great things about the pub across the way. Treasure Island? I've been having some issues with my blood sugar and I need to get some food in me soon."

"Sure thing." The officer gave a professional nod. "What would you like?"

"Fish and chips, please. If you could, try to be quick. I'm not feeling very well."

"I'm telling you. He's covering for somebody." It had been almost an hour since he'd left the senator alone and between Tank and him, they'd fielded three calls from the feds. They couldn't put them off forever, but an afternoon of being out of the office or unavailable wasn't going to do them irreparable harm.

From the corner of his eye, he saw Teddy passing by, plodding along in his solid cop's shoes as he headed for the back where the cells were. He had a bag of takeout in his hands and two drinks balanced in a tray. Trust Teddy to never pass up a chance to grab a bite to eat.

"He's eating damn fine for a man who just confessed to murder," Tank grumbled, not even looking at the remains of the peanut butter and jelly he'd put together in the break room.

Gideon pinched the bridge of his nose. "The last meal of a condemned man."

He drew a deep breath, irritated and on edge. There were a million things that could be getting to him, a million things that were getting to him. The senator had confessed to murder and he had all the details right. Maybe he didn't have the muscle, but maybe he did. He was pushing up on his late sixties, but he was fit and strong, played golf, and enjoyed walking and fishing. Alison had been a tiny bit of a thing, not much bigger than—

He cut the thought off before it could go there.

The scent of food hung in the air, compliments of the bag Teddy had carried over from the pub. Gideon would recognize the scent from anywhere and it had his mouth practically watering, but he wasn't about to let his stomach distract him.

As Teddy slipped out of the back, he shot the officer a look. "Problem with the food?"

"No, sir." Lifting a big shoulder, Teddy glanced back and then looked at Gideon and Tank. "Guy's weird. Says he doesn't like to eat around others. Called it a personality quirk."

"He should have thought twice before confessing to murder then," Tank said, grumbling.

"Think I should go back in there?" Teddy asked.

On the far side of the bullpen, there was a long narrow strip set up with monitors, feeding them video from various parts of the station, including the back room where Senator Roberts was laying out the flatware for his meal.

"We can watch him from here." He lifted the headphones back to his ear and nodded at Tank.

Tank pressed play and once more, they listened.

"*. . . in the tub, her back to me and the door. She had her head on the lip of the tub, her eyes closed. There was a glass of wine, white wine, half empty . . .*"

They listened as Roberts recounted the moments before Alison had died—before he had supposedly killed her.

Gideon glanced at the clock, his belly rumbling again, pretty much a demand this time. If he didn't get some fish and chips of his own—

He dropped the headphones, shooting upright to stare at the monitor.

Henry Roberts was lying with his back to the camera, facing the wall.

Most of his meal was on the floor in front of his bunk. It looked like there was only one thing missing.

The entrée.

"Teddy!"

As he called for the officer, he was already running for the back. The sheriff, his deputies, and Gideon's own men were staring at him, but he only had eyes for that door.

"Yes, sir?"

"Tell me you didn't get fish," he demanded.

"The senator asked—what?"

Without answering, he wrenched open the door.

It took only seconds to get to the cell, even less time to get inside.

It took about the same amount of time to realize he'd wasted those seconds, because Senator Henry Roberts was dead. Because he had to do his job, he checked for a pulse while Tank put in a call to EMS.

Teddy and Gideon hefted the man from the bunk and moved him to the floor to attempt CPR and a moment later, Levon was in there, barking out orders.

They were emptying out pockets, searching for an EpiPen, the adrenaline that would save a person suffering from anaphylaxis. Of course, there was no EpiPen. They'd taken the senator's personal effects.

The metallic scent of blood filled the air and feeling as though he were watching a movie, Gideon watched as Levon, the former military field medic, threw down the knife he'd just drawn across the senator's throat.

"What the fuck are you doing?" Teddy demanded.

"Wasting my time. Man's gone," Levon said. Then he added, "Tracheotomy. Airway's closed off. But I'm trying."

The paramedics showed up before he was able to get the hollowed out pen he'd planned to use as an artificial airway. Gideon caught sight of Hannah, the professional mask set firmly in place as he pulled his officer back. They stood there watching.

When the medics went to lift the senator, two things fell to the floor, one from each hand.

A piece of fish fell from his right.

A piece of paper fell from his left.

Gideon stared at the half-eaten chunk of fish, oddly mesmerized.

"What the fuck?" Tank said as they watched Hannah and her partner hustle the still body out of there. Every single one of them knew it was a wasted effort. They knew too much about what dead people looked like, but they also knew the paramedics had a job to do.

Gideon continued to stare at the food. He didn't want fish now, that was for damn sure. "The senator had an allergy to shrimp. Probably was allergic to fish, too."

Teddy swore. "Sir, he fucking *told* me to get him the fish. I didn't know, I swear!"

Gideon lifted a hand, but it took his officer several minutes to calm down. Tugging a pair of gloves out of his pocket, he drew them on and knelt down, poking at the food. It had indeed turned out to be the condemned man's final meal.

He hadn't even brought his damn EpiPen.

He picked up the note and it wasn't any surprise to find that it was written to his wife and kids.

He'd killed himself.

He'd come in here, scared to death, confessed to a crime, and then he'd killed himself.

CHAPTER SIXTEEN

Hannah had worked a double. She hadn't planned on it, especially not after the punch in the throat she'd gotten when she realized she was trying to save the life of one Senator Henry Roberts—the man who'd probably been behind Alison's death.

The operative word, of course, would be *trying*.

His allergy to seafood must have been pretty damn awful. They hadn't been able to establish an airway and even if they had, he'd been without oxygen for so long by the time they got him to the hospital, the amount of brain damage he probably would have had . . .

She didn't want to think about that mess. By the time her night had ended, all she'd wanted was sleep but only one person from the crew to relieve her and J.P. had showed up. Another person from one of the other teams had ended up calling in sick.

So she and J.P. had volunteered to cover. She wouldn't be able to work doubles much longer. Already she was dead on her feet and she had to wonder at all of the women who did this sort of thing day in and day out *and* went home and took care of kids for years. She just couldn't fathom it.

As tired as she was, she'd been almost grateful for the work, though. Not that she'd tell anybody. She was trying not to think, trying very, very hard. She'd collapsed into bed without eating and gone straight to sleep, desperate to escape the silence of her head . . . and the loudness of the memories she could feel churning closer and closer to the surface.

I love you . . . .

In her sleep, Hannah rolled over and pressed her face into the pillow. It still smelled of Brannon—his soap, his shampoo . . . *him*. She clung to it and snuggled deeper into a sweet, wonderful dream.

Love you . . .

Brannon's voice echoed all around her and in her sleep, she smiled.

She reached for him.

But he faded away before she could touch him.

Turning her head, she searched for him.

"Brannon?" Even to her own ears, her voice sounded uncertain. "Brannon?"

She took a step and the apartment around her re-formed. Confused, she looked around and realized she wasn't in her place. It was Brannon's. His loft across the street, so much bigger than her place, wide, open, airy, and elegant. It had money stamped all over it, but at the same time, it was welcoming. Or she thought it was.

The door to the bedroom opened and Brannon stood there.

She smiled at him, her hand outstretched.

He stared at it for a long moment.

Her smile faltered. "Brannon?"

He just shook his head.

"I love you," she said softly. "I've been in love with you since high school."

In the bed, Hannah started to cry.

Brannon frowned at her. Finally, he folded his arms over his chest. "This isn't going to work. Look, Hannah. I've known you too long. In my head, I've had you about a hundred ways to Sunday and every time I see you, I want to try at least one of those ways out. But sex is all I really want."

Staring at him, she fell back against the wall and then, slowly, she slid to the floor. "What are you saying? I thought . . . you told me you loved me."

"Please." Brannon snorted, the derision in his voice thick and mocking. "Honey, you should know better. I'm not looking for any sort of relationship. Sex is all well and good, but I don't want anything else. That's not . . . I just don't want it. Especially not now. I've got too much going on as it is and somehow, I get the feeling casual sex isn't really your speed."

"But I love you." The words sounded hollow, even to her own ears. "I've always loved you."

"So you've said ." Now Brannon smiled. It was a sad, bitter smile. "You've loved me since high school. But it was a dream, sugar. Just a high school girl's dream . . . haven't you figured that out yet?"

The ringing of the phone jerked her awake.

Hannah jolted up in the bed, her face wet with tears, the dream shattering and falling into sharp, painful shards around her before fading. It still stung, though, still pricked at her.

Swallowing, she dashed the tears away with one hand as she reached for her phone with the other.

She took one look at the number and laid her phone back down flat.

She couldn't handle talking to him just then.

He'd hear something in her voice and Hannah could just imagine trying to explain why she was a sobbing, shaking mess at . . . she caught sight of the clock on the wall and swore.

It was two o'clock.

Sorry, Brannon. I know we were supposed to have lunch, but I overslept and now I'm crying and shaky because I dreamt you told me that you didn't really love me. Hold me!

Jumping out of bed, she rushed into the bathroom.

She figured she might have ten minutes before he showed up knocking on her door wondering why she wasn't over at the pub. They were supposed to have lunch.

Ten minutes. Maybe.

She rushed her way through the shower, finished up in five minutes, didn't bother shaving her legs. She could always do that later, because she really doubted she'd have time for any nookie. Brannon was only in town because he had a meeting with a local brewer who wanted him to try out some new ale at the pub.

He'd mentioned he had his hands full out at the winery and she could only imagine. That and the stress of having Alison . . .

Her throat choked up.

Alison.

Fear tried to edge in but she pushed it back.

She was getting really good at that. Considering that missing week of her life, Hannah suspected if she didn't keep a chokehold on fear, she'd probably lose her mind.

After wrapping a towel around her dripping hair, she reached for her robe. She thought she was down to maybe four minutes. She needed to go ahead and just text Brannon.

Her robe . . .

She looked over.

Her robe wasn't there.

Scowling, she stared at the painted door.

The robe was always there.

Jerking open the closet where she kept her dirty clothes, she checked inside. Nope. Aggravated, she just grabbed another towel and wrapped it around herself. Water dripped down her body and she left the bathroom.

She'd worry about the damn robe later.

She grabbed her phone and texted Brannon.

Overslept. Be there in about fifteen minutes.

That done, she tossed her phone onto the bed and headed over to her closet. Pulling the towel from her hair, she started to rub at her still wet hair, mentally going through what she needed to do.

She had to dry her hair, get dressed—

Her robe was hanging in the closet.

The towel fell from numb fingers.

A shiver raced down her spine.

Slowly, she reached out and tugged it from the hanger. It was hard to miss, as it had been hung up almost as if on display, facing her—not *on* the rack, but hooked with the curve of the hanger looped over the outer part of the rack. The way a fancy dress might have been hung to keep it from being wrinkled.

Not the typical way anybody would treat a worn cotton robe that was easily five years old.

And not the way Hannah had hung it up after her shower not even five hours ago.

Her fingers shook as she carried it over to the bed and laid it down.

She stepped back and stared at it. Maybe because she was staring at it so hard, it made it easy to notice the odd little lump in the pocket.

Her breathing hitched in her throat as she pushed her fingers inside the pocket.

The rock was smooth and worn. The way the rocks

were after they'd spent some time in the river. She had a collection of them, out in the bowl on her coffee table . . . at the houseboat.

The houseboat.

Those dark and hiding secrets shoved against her conscience and she dropped the rock, backing away.

The small stone lay on the floor, practically mocking her.

Seated at a table near the window, he saw the police cruiser pull up.

He wasn't surprised when Gideon Marshall climbed out.

He couldn't even claim to be irritated.

That fucker was always nosing around in things. Even in a small town like this, one might think the chief of police could learn how to delegate, but then again, some men just had the sort of complex where they felt they had to take care of everybody and everything.

Perhaps, though, he could understand.

He was a man who believed in handling his own problems as well.

Absently, he reached into his bag and pulled out a journal. It was filled with scraps and notes and copies. He flipped through them, taking time here and there to pause and read a note or study a sketch. He'd long since committed everything inside these worn pages to memory.

Whitehall had kept thorough records, but sadly, he couldn't have recorded what he didn't know, what he hadn't observed.

Solving a mystery that was well over a century old was proving to be quite . . . intriguing.

"Oi! Brannon!"

The sound of Ian Campbell's booming voice had him looking up, watching as the big, red-haired McKay emerged from the back of the pub. Without making it obvious, he watched as Ian and Brannon spoke quietly. He wasn't surprised when Ian jerked a thumb over his shoulder toward the window, or when Brannon practically ran from the pub.

The dumb bastard had been all but tripping over himself over Hannah Parker for years. Men often made fools of themselves over women, though. He'd been seeing it happen for years.

For a few more moments, he watched Brannon. The man tore across the road and disappeared inside the building where Hannah lived.

He'd wondered if she'd think much of his . . . visit. She'd lain sleeping on the bed, undisturbed when he let himself inside. He'd lingered in the hallway, watching her sleep like the dead and debating. He could kill her so easily. She hadn't stirred when he'd let himself in, hadn't made a sound when he plucked her keys from the counter and used the keyfob to disarm the system intended to keep men like him out.

Handy things, security systems.

He'd taken the time to reset it when he left, leaving Hannah sleeping soundly.

The last thing he needed to do was kill her. That was a last resort. Hannah meant nothing to him and if he had to kill her, he would, but he'd prefer to avoid it. The more lives he took, the more trouble he'd find himself embroiled in, and the more complicated things would become. He had every intention of *avoiding* complication, not twisting himself up in it.

Another police car came wailing down the street and he bent back over his coffee, smiling to himself. What could the cops really do? All he'd done was move her robe around.

This time.

"You gotta be kidding me." Officer Beau Shaw, still baring some faded scars from his bout with chicken pox a few months earlier, rubbed a hand up and down his face before he shot a look at his boss.

Said boss stared at him, his face impassive, but the eyes were hard as granite.

"Is there a problem, Officer?" Chief Gideon Marshall asked politely.

Beau looked at the bagged rock, robe, and hanger. Then, choosing his words carefully, he said, "Chief, you want me to dust for prints because Ms. Parker doesn't remember hanging the robe in her closet?"

"No. You're dusting for prints because a woman who is possibly a witness to an unsolved murder knows she didn't hang that robe in her closet."

Beau tugged at his ear, debating. Then he decided, *in for a penny* . . . "My dad was in 'Nam. Had himself a head injury. Ended up with memory problems for pretty much the rest of his life. He didn't remember hardly anything about the war and when he came back home, for a long time, he didn't remember my mother . . . or me. Bits and pieces came back, but not everything. And he'd forget things. All the time. Our house almost burnt down because he started a fire in the fireplace and then up and walked out of the house. Wasn't nobody else there. Once, I found his gun in the freezer. I saw him put it in there, though he swears he didn't. Mama had to take the bullets and everybody in town knew not to sell him any. He had problems with the drink, too."

Gideon listened. Beau wasn't from Treasure, hadn't

moved here until he'd accepted the position with the force ten years earlier. He didn't often talk about his dad—not because he was ashamed, but because . . . well, Beau just didn't care to talk unless he had to.

"He came after me for putting the gun in there," Beau said, looking away. "Mama made him stop. She could always get him to stop. Right up until the end—she wasn't there that day. When he finally realized what he was doing . . . well." Beau stopped and shrugged. "The thing is, Chief, with head injuries and amnesia, people do things and don't always remember doing them. Especially when there's trauma involved. I know. I seen it, grew up around it."

Gideon rubbed at his jaw and like Beau, seemed to take time, thinking through his answer. "Beau, I'm sorry about your dad. That said . . . we're talking about two very different people. If you knew Hannah, you'd probably see that. Anybody who works with her, or talks to her . . . well, they can tell you that. This isn't a woman who's going to stick a gun in the freezer or leave a fire unattended."

Beau studied his boss for a moment and then looked down at the rock and the robe.

"Okay, then." Maybe he didn't know Hannah well, but he knew the chief. Besides, some crazy shit was going on. Shayla Hardee, then that Maxwell woman.

So Beau would do his job.

He didn't know whether he was hoping that she'd done something weird with her robe and the smooth little rock . . . or wishing that she hadn't.

Which was the better alternative, he wondered.

"A rock? Really?" His wife laughed softly as they sat down to dinner.

Beau glanced up at Ellison and shrugged. For once,

his beautiful wife wasn't on call. He had plans that involved getting her naked and maybe bringing out his handcuffs.

She really did enjoy that.

"A rock. Her robe." He shook his head. "I wouldn't think much of it, but the chief says she's not the forgetful type. I mean, with her amnesia and all . . ."

Ellison reached out and touched his hand. "Everybody is different, love. You know that."

He nodded, averting his eyes. He did know that. He'd come to accept—and even forgive—his father to some extent. It had been years since he'd thought about the old man with any kind of bitterness. But . . . sighing, he pushed those thoughts out of his head. He had other things in mind tonight that were much better than the past anyway.

"So . . ." He drew the word out, keeping his tone casual. "What do you think? Is she . . ." He hesitated, because this was dodgy ground.

"Damn it, Beau." She slammed her glass of wine down, rising from the couch to pace. "I don't know why you keep doing this. Patient confidentiality is patient confidentiality."

She swung back around to face him, her full lips compressed, color riding high on her cheekbones. She folded her arms under her breasts and he had to remind himself not to stare.

If he got distracted, she'd get distracted and then she'd get pissed and accuse him of using sex to distract her.

The bottom line, though . . . with Ellison, she could get sidetracked with anything as simple as a lotion commercial—the kind where it showed a woman slicking up her legs with lotion before she went out for a night on the town with her man. He both loved and hated how easily she embraced her sexuality. Loved it, because he benefited from it. Hated it, because once upon a time, other men had, too.

Clearing his throat, he eased himself to the edge of the couch and braced his elbows on his knees, staring at the aquarium that graced the far side of the wall. It took up almost a quarter of it, built into the wall and catching the light of the sun as it came through the windows in the morning. He found it soothing. Ellison found it sexy. Go figure.

"Ellie . . . it's not so much me wanting to invade privacy," he said diplomatically. "You have to look at this from my point of a view."

"*My* point of view is a doctor's," she snapped.

He surged upright, his temper snapping. He got damn tired of keeping the peace when she jumped boots first down his throat over the smallest damn thing. "And mine's a cop's, Ellie!"

Her eyes widened at the bite in his voice. Something sparked in her eyes and she licked her lips.

He held up a hand. "Don't," he said quietly.

Her lids drooped.

He wanted to swear. Then he did. "Son of a bitch. Would you listen to me? Ellie, if she's stable and her head isn't . . . if she's not like my dad, then maybe she *didn't* put that damn robe in her closet and that rock in the pocket."

"It's just a robe," Ellison said softly.

"But that don't matter." He moved toward her and caught her hand.

She squeezed back and he knew the storm was over, but he still needed her to understand. Tugging her with him, they moved down the hall. The master bedroom had a big, elaborate bathroom, but he'd decided when they moved in that he'd just leave that bathroom to Ellison. Every damn thing in there had a place.

They stopped in the doorway and he flicked on the light.

After seven years of living here, he did know that certain things belonged in certain places. Ellison even had a list for when a replacement had to come in for their cleaning lady. There were two robes, one for spring and summer, one for fall and winter. The robes were washed, like clockwork, on Saturday mornings and then went back into place on the hook beside the shower. Two towels were precisely folded on the heated rod next to the robe, while another was on the rod inside the shower.

"If we came home from work, the two of us together at the same time one day . . . for once . . ." He caught sight of her rolling her eyes and he grinned at her. "Humor me, okay? Say it was Tuesday and you knew you'd left everything in its place and the cleaning lady hadn't been in . . . now."

He stepped around her and took the robe, carried it out of the bedroom and laid it on the bed, arms open wide, as though a person had gone to lay down in it and simply . . . faded away while the robe remained. "Say we came in and found the robe like that. Would you be spooked?"

Ellison swallowed, staring at the robe. Then she lifted her eyes and stared at Beau. "Yeah." She nodded.

"So that's my thing. I don't know Hannah."

"I do," she whispered. "Not as well as some, but . . . yeah."

She licked her lips and nodded again, slower, more thoughtful. "She's a paramedic, baby. She's a paramedic and she wouldn't have gotten the go-ahead to come back to work if the state of Mississippi thought she wasn't mentally sound."

Beau went back to staring at the robe. Passing his hand over his neatly trimmed beard, he heaved out a hard sigh. "So the chief has a reason to be concerned. But why would somebody break into her apartment—and how *could* somebody break into her apartment so easily—just to rearrange some of her clothes?"

There was only one reason, though.

Somebody had wanted to scare her.

I've loved you since high school . . .

Hannah brooded over the decaffeinated sweet tea she'd been given along with her dinner.

She'd drunk half of the tea and had pushed her food around enough so that it looked like she'd eaten more than four bites.

She kept remembering bits and pieces of a dream and she kept thinking about a river rock, shoved into the pocket of her robe.

She hadn't been back inside her apartment all day but she'd have to soon.

It was almost dusk and she was so tired, she was dragging.

Yeah, she'd gotten up at two o'clock, but she didn't care. Night shifts had never been her favorite and between that and the pregnancy, her mental clock was so off-kilter, it was pathetic.

"Hey."

She glanced up at the familiar voice and smiled at Neve. Nodding to the wide, mostly vacant booth, she said, "Please. Join me. Save me from myself."

"But you look like you're having so much fun . . ." Neve teased as she dropped into the booth. It was a big U, and she scooted around so that she and Hannah were side by side.

A big green utility-styled bag hung from her side and Neve slid the strap from her shoulder, letting it fall to the seat. She wore it with a silk shirt, a pair of slouchy, loose khakis, and sandals that looked like they cost the sun. Only on Neve could such a mix of styles look so coolly, casually perfect.

Dangles of gold and gems fell from Neve's earlobes, catching in the dim light as she brought her hands up and folded them on the table in front of her.

"So." Neve said the simple word with an air of finality.

"So." Hannah echoed, drawing it out into a question.

Neve canted her chin up and arched a brow. "Seems like my bad luck fell into your lap."

Hannah snorted. "Nah. I didn't have some nutbag come into my kitchen and try to drag me back to Scotland."

The skin around Neve's eyes tightened.

"Ah, hell." Hannah blew out a breath. "I'm sorry, honey."

"Why? It's nothing but the truth." Neve leaned an elbow on the table, shifting her body to face Hannah. "You got a different, special flavor of nutbag . . . into rocks and robes. Now *that* is fancy crazy, Hannah."

Hannah couldn't suppress a shiver.

Neve's eyes softened. "Are you okay?"

"It was just a rock. He moved my robe. Why be so freaked out?" she murmured.

"Because you don't know who he is?" Neve offered helpfully. "Because there's no idea how he got inside your place? Because he came into your place while you were sleeping?"

"Yeah." Hannah reached up and worried the neckline of her shirt, staring off into the distance, but seeing nothing.

"I don't . . ." She started to say, only to realize she didn't know what she'd planned to say from the get-go. She passed a shaking hand through her hair and then lowered it, staring at the faint tremor of her fingers.

"Sitting here is making me nuts. I need to get out of here for a while."

"But—"

Hannah shook her head. She pulled out the money she'd readied for the bill and dropped it on the table.

She hurried out the door, leaving Neve behind her.

Ian joined her a moment later.

"Brannon's going to kill us," she said quietly.

"We only promised we'd keep an eye on her while she was here, love," Ian said, a grim look in his dark eyes. He skimmed a hand down her back, staring through the window at the bent head of Hannah Parker as she crossed the street. "We can't exactly wrap her up and put her in a box, now can we?"

"Brannon would prefer it."

"Well." Ian seemed to ponder the idea before he met her eyes. "There was a time when I might have preferred it for you. But ya would have thrashed me, wouldn't you?"

Hannah climbed into her car and drove.

She had no destination and nothing in mind, other than the plain and simple fact that she had to *move*.

Had to get out and had to breathe.

She felt like a million people were staring at her.

She felt like a million people wanted to ask her questions.

Questions . . . she had a million of them herself and she was almost certain there were answers locked up inside her head, but they were going to stay there, obscured behind a fog so thick, nothing could penetrate it.

You were down at the river, Hannah. Do you remember?

She thought about what Gideon had told her months ago.

Rubbing her belly with one hand, she pulled to a stop

at the four-way at the edge of town. She had three choices. She could turn left and make a slow, meandering circle that would take her back through town. She could go straight and eventually find her way to the highway and that would put her on the interstate. Maybe she could just disappear for a few days. Not too many. Her savings would only last so long and she might be able to beg a few days of personal time, but eventually, she'd have to come back.

Or she could turn right.

That would lead her to the river.

To her houseboat.

To the running paths.

Do you have any idea what you were doing down there, Hannah? Have you ever seen Shayla Hardee there?

You saw something.

You called 9-1-1. Think, Hannah. Think. You need to remember.

Her head pounded hard, so hard, she felt herself getting nauseated.

But she turned right.

"She left?" Brannon pinched the bridge of his nose as he listened to Neve's apologetic voice, coming soft over the phone line. His instinct was to snarl—that was almost the norm for him lately. He bit it back. "Neve, stop. It's not . . . look, it's not like you could sit on her, right?"

Neve's laugh was weak. "Well, I could have tried. She would have shrugged me off like I was nothing."

"Exactly."

Both of them were close to equal in height but while Neve might have fit the image that society had in mind for their idea of beautiful—slim and lithe—Hannah looked more like a starlet from the golden age of

Hollywood, a delightful powerhouse of curves. And he knew for a fact just how much strength those curves hid. Yeah, she could have picked up his baby sister and probably carried her across a football field if she had to.

"Any idea where she went?" he asked, gesturing to Marc to shut it down for the night. "She head home?"

His gut wrenched at the idea of her being in her apartment alone. He'd told her to hang out and wait for him at the pub. He'd been planning on asking her to . . . well, not move *in* with him, but maybe . . . well. Stay with him. For a while.

And now she was out there without him. While some freaky fuck broke into her house and shoved rocks into her clothes. What the hell was that?

"She took her car. I don't know where she was going, but I saw her pulling out from behind her apartment."

Brannon's gut wrenched.

Leaning against the stoplight, he watched as Hannah Parker drove out of town. He considered where she might go, then he considered whether he should follow.

He still had no idea if she remembered anything.

She'd spent most of the day sitting around the pub or wandering the sidewalk back and forth in front of the building where she lived, her expression tight and drawn, eyes dark.

He'd passed her by once, said hello, and she'd barely glanced at him.

Nobody was saying much of anything, so if she'd done any talking, there wasn't any news to be had. Plenty of people had heard that she'd had some excitement at her place, but very few were talking in detail. It was all speculation. As a matter of fact, speculation was about all anybody had about Hannah. She rarely spoke of anything concrete.

Abruptly, he made up his mind and pulled his keys from his pocket.

He had an idea where she might be going.

As he moved at a quick clip to his car, he pulled out his phone to see if he'd heard back from the delightful doctor. Her husband had been in Hannah's apartment today, but the phone calls had gone unanswered and he imagined she either wasn't on call or she was deliberately ignoring him. She was on rotation with several other OBs in the area, so she did get her share of evenings away from the hospital, and the beautiful bitch did enjoy teasing him.

He'd once taunted her back by stretching himself out and wrapping a hand around his cock, stroking himself and capturing an image of it. Careful to make sure anything that could identify himself was cropped out, he'd sent her the picture, along with the words, *I was thinking of you.*

She had him listed simply as *F* in her contacts.

When he'd asked her about that, she'd giggled and gone down on him, wrapping her lips around his cock and sucking until he thought she might suck him dry. *Fuck . . . as in my fuck, as in fuck me, as in please fuck me now . . . fuck, lover.*

He asked her how she kept all her *fucks* straight and she'd beamed at him. *You're my only fuck, darling. There is a cock, there is a dick, there is one pussy . . . but you're my only fuck.*

And what do you call your cop?

Her eyes had gone dim.

He'd never asked her about her cop again.

He decided he pitied her. Love, as he'd always believed, made a fool out of anybody.

It had certainly made a fool of Dr. Ellison Shaw.

He'd worry about Ellison later, though. Right now,

he needed to focus on Hannah and see if his hunch played out.

A year ago, if somebody had asked him how well he knew Hannah Parker, Brannon would have scowled and said, "I don't."

But he would have been lying and now, he knew it.

He knew a dozen things about her—no.

More.

He knew that she loved soft, almost spring-like colors and he knew she also loved battered jeans and motorcycle books and black t-shirts. She had a leather jacket she wore in the fall and he'd actually bought himself a motorcycle without realizing that the reason was because of some subconscious fantasy to feel her tucked up against his back as they tore up and down the roads that twined through southern Mississippi.

He knew that she hated beer but loved cider and he knew that she'd drink almost any kind of cocktail that tasted sweet, but she could also throw back bourbon. She hated vodka and she loved tequila.

She loved to read, but you couldn't catch her with a western.

She loved TV, but if you tried to talk to her about reality TV, she'd laugh in your face.

She loved children and she hated bigots.

More than once, he'd seen her get in the face of any man who was giving his girlfriend a hard time and more than once, he or Ian had thought they'd have to intervene . . . only to see Hannah set the son of a bitch on his ass.

Gideon had once commented that at some point, he expected he'd have to arrest her, but the whole damn town would pitch in for her bail.

He knew that every Sunday she visited her mother's grave.

He knew that at least two weekends a month, she went down to the houseboat. He knew that because he'd find himself looking for her car as he sped past the dock as he drove into town and more than once, he'd find himself letting up on the gas so he'd have a chance to maybe see her up on the deck, or maybe even jogging along the path before she disappeared into the woods.

That path connected the docks to the town, a good five mile stretch. It was that path where Hannah had been running when she came across Shayla's murdered body.

Did he know her?

Yeah.

He knew her.

He knew her better than he knew just about anybody and looking back, he realized he was the biggest idiot in town. Half the town had probably seen the truth long before he had.

But that was fine.

Brannon could live with being an idiot.

As long as he had her.

He slowed as he drew near to the turnoff for the dock where several people kept their houseboats, Hannah included.

His headlights fell across the bumpers of two cars. One was Hannah's. He hit his turn signal and pulled into the parking lot just as another car drove past him. Absently, he glanced over and saw the long, sleek lines, his brain mentally cataloging the car, then filing it away.

He had other things on his mind.

He had Hannah on his mind.

In his head.

In his heart.

Down in his gut and in his soul where he didn't think he'd ever be free of her.

Bent over the table, Neve focused on the genealogy records she'd printed out from Ancestry.com. She wasn't being very green and she felt kind of guilty about it—but hey, it was all recycled paper, so that was good, right?

But she thought better when everything was printed out.

"What's all this?"

Ian sat down next to her and she looked up at him with a smile. The smile turned greedy when she saw the pints he put down in front of them.

"Ohhhhh . . ."

"It's new," he said. "Some cider from a local brewer we're thinkin' of usin'." Ian brought it to his lips and grimaced, then shrugged. "Not bad if ya want your drink to taste like you're eatin' an apple."

"I do." Neve lifted her pilsner to her lips and took one small sip, then a bigger one as Ian plucked a page up and studied it.

"Neve, love . . . if this is your birth certificate, I'm afraid we'll have to rethink this relationship." Ian gave her a sober look.

"Ha, ha." She smacked him and snatched the copied document back. "Yes, honey. I was born in 1912."

"Weeeelllll . . ." He leaned back and tugged at his beard. After a thorough study, one that ended in a lascivious wink, he leaned in and whispered, "You're holding up well for somebody who's seen a century come to pass. Maybe I'll keep you."

She shivered at the feel of his beard tickling her skin and then she wiggled away.

The noise from the bar was at a muted roar, but it was still busy.

She glanced up. Sure enough, a few people were looking their way and grinning. She'd already been asked
when the wedding would be. Ian hadn't so much as said
a thing about it. But she was kind of thinking . . .

"How far have you gone?"

"Huh?" Startled, she bobbled her cider and some of it
splashed onto the table. Swearing, she put the drink down
and in the process, sent some of her papers flying.

Documents scattered and she groaned.

Ian chuckled and leaned over, kissed her temple.

Then, the two of them slid off the bench and started
picking up the pages. "You've been through all of these
already?" he asked, glancing at a few of them as he
stacked them.

"No." She grimaced and eyed the motley assortment
of information she now had. "I've just been filing things
in my shoebox and . . ."

Ian cocked a brow. "Your shoebox."

"It's like a . . . file. Just for random things." She waved
a hand at him. "Don't ask, okay? Some of the stuff is
connected to my family, some might be, some isn't. But
I get too distracted when I'm just staring at things on the
screen."

She glanced at a sheet and then froze.

"What are *you* doing in here?" she muttered.

She crushed it in her hand and looked over to see Ian
studying her with an arched brow.

"What was that all about?" he asked, voice mild.

"Nothing." She made herself smile as she shoved the
crumpled up piece of paper containing information on
George Whitehall into her bag. He wasn't worth getting
mad over—history had turned him into nothing.

CHAPTER SEVENTEEN

A cold wind came in off the Mississippi.

Fall was winding down and the bite in the air no longer promised a chill—it delivered one, cutting through to the bone and bringing to mind images of a roaring fire.

Hannah wasn't thinking of a fire, though, even as she shivered on the deck of the houseboat, wrapped in a thick blanket. The wind was damn cold, yes, but she didn't retreat inside. She sat and she stared into the woods while a voice echoed inside her head.

You need to remember.

Had she been in the woods?

I've loved you since high school.

She groaned as her own voice seemed to echo with threads of Gideon's as he pushed her about the hours lost from those days, particularly that night, all of it tangling into a twisted skein. One single tug and it would all unravel, she thought. But the threads were all connected to those missing days. Missing nights.

I found this . . . .

Her breath abruptly caught and she closed her eyes, seeing herself, staring in the doorway.

No.

It wasn't her*self* she saw.

It was Brannon.

He was in front of her.

Bare chested.

Sweating.

She'd . . . she'd been sweating, too.

"I'd been out running," she whispered.

Do you remember . . .

Closing her eyes, she focused on that image—no, that specific set of images. Her, standing in front of Brannon. Holding his wallet.

"Is there a reason you're always such an ass to me, Brannon McKay? Did I piss in your Cheerios or something?"

"Maybe I don't like being your morning entertainment."

"My . . ." Arrogant ass! Staring at him, she smiled and let her eyes roam over his hot, entirely too sexy body.

"Honey," she drawled. "I wouldn't call that entertainment. Scenery, maybe, but it takes more than a good-looking guy in the buff to . . . entertain me. Now, if you want to entertain me, I can give you a suggestion."

Eyes locked on hers, he dipped his head.

"Well?" She swayed so close, she could have kissed him.

He said nothing.

Sighing, she murmured, "Too bad. Here."

He didn't even look down.

Nipples tight, aching, she went to slam the wallet down.

"Oh for crying out loud. You have a ni—"

He kissed her.

A car engine rumbled, close by, and the memory fell apart like it was made of gossamer.

Hannah jumped, startled by the sound.

Heart racing, she turned her head and stared at the car that pulled into the parking lot.

It slowed to a stop right in front of her houseboat and she stood up, watching as Brannon McKay climbed out of the car and looked up at her, his eyes unerringly seeking her out in the dark.

For the millionth time in her life, her heart gave a little leap at the sight of him.

For the first time in weeks, some other part of her whispered . . . *this might not be a good idea.*

But as he started toward the narrow walk that led to the houseboat, Hannah knew one thing for certain.

She wouldn't turn him away.

It was Brannon, after all, and she'd loved him half her life.

It was more than a little disappointing to recognize Brannon's car on the stretch of highway near the docks.

That overly phallic, ridiculously tawdry Bugatti was good for one thing, though. Nobody else in the damn county had one and once you saw it, you couldn't mistake it for anything else.

He'd seen it coming and he'd known he wouldn't be visiting Hannah tonight.

But he had other things he could do.

He'd made her uneasy and for the first time, he was seeing shadows in her eyes.

Maybe it was time to up the stakes a little more. After he made certain they weren't planning on leaving, of course. He didn't want to be interrupted.

Hannah had a pale, bruised look to her.

Brannon wanted to find whatever had hurt her and tear it apart.

She stood in the doorway, staring at him and he reached up, cupped her face in his hands.

Slowly, he brushed his thumb across her lower lip.

A slow shudder wracked her body.

"What's happened?" he asked. "What's hurt you?"

Clouds entered her eyes. "Nothing," she said, shaking her head. "I'm just . . ."

She backed up and turned. "Come on in, Brannon."

Outside, the wind started to howl and she moved over to the window, staring outside. "Rain's coming."

After closing and locking the door behind him, he crossed the floor to her.

He had the oddest feeling he was walking on eggshells.

"Unless you're upset over the weather report, then I don't care." He curved his hands over her shoulders and pulled her back against him. "Now if you are upset by the weather . . . well, I can't do anything about it. I can't beat up the meteorologists and Mother Nature never returns my calls."

"She's a bitch, isn't she?" Hannah laughed weakly. Then she dropped her head back against his chest. "Don't . . . it's nothing, Brannon."

He rubbed his cheek against hers. "That look on your face isn't nothing."

"Maybe. But there's nothing you can do about it." She turned and slid her arms around his waist. "How is Marc doing?"

He wanted to push it, but figured now wasn't the time. "Okay. I guess." Tucking her up snug against him, he rubbed his cheek against her hair. "He's busying himself with some blends for next year and going crazy about a fungus that he thinks *could* hit our crops."

"A fungus." Hannah wrinkled her nose as she looked up at him. "What, like a grape fungus?"

Brannon flashed her a grin. "The exciting life of a vintner, Hannah."

"Hmmm. I bet." She reached up, almost absently, and scraped her fingers against his jaw. "Neve was telling me something about how she's getting schooled in winemaking—you roped her into helping write copy for the brochures." A faint grin came and went. "I've got to admit, I like my wine, but my eyes glazed over after she started explaining there are like five hundred chemical compounds—"

"Fifteen hundred."

Hannah blinked and then her eyes *really* started to glaze. "Ah . . . whoa. Are you serious?"

"Yeah." Grinning, he hugged her. "But don't worry. I won't bore you with the details and specifics, or tell you why you only find wines like muscadines down south."

"Gee. Thanks." She rubbed the mound of her belly and went back to staring outside. Rain was starting to come down. It was those hard, slow drops that were a prelude to a heavy storm. "I really don't want to talk about muscadine wine anyway. Seeing as how I can't have any for a few more months."

A heavy sigh escaped her. "I could really use a glass of wine, too."

"Why don't you talk to me instead?"

For a moment, he thought she would.

But then she turned to him and placed her hands on his chest.

His heart made a hard leap when she covered it with her palm. "I've got a better idea. Why don't you distract me?"

Brannon suspected it wasn't smart.

Whatever was bothering her, she really did need to talk about it. And he needed to be the guy she was able to talk to. He needed to be *the* guy period, because he was shit-faced in love with her and had been for . . . hell. He didn't even know when it had started.

But then she trailed that hand down lower and cupped him through his jeans.

His eyes started to roll back in his head as she freed him from his jeans and briefs in short order. She closed her hand around him, moving with quick, rough strokes that would have had him coming all over her if she wasn't careful.

He caught her wrist.

"Stop," he rasped, backing her up against the window.

"I don't want to." She lifted her face to his, staring into his eyes. "I don't want to stop. I don't want to think. I just . . . *want*."

"Hannah . . ." His heart broke a little.

"Make love to me, Brannon." There was both plea and demand in her voice.

He was completely her slave, because he couldn't deny her.

"I will." He went to strip her shirt away, but she shoved him back and yanked it off.

"I don't want slow." She stared at him, a challenge in her eyes. "I don't want *sweet* and I don't want you to stroke me and pat me and try to make me feel better."

She caught the lapels of his shirt and jerked him back to her.

"Then what do you want?"

"I want you to fuck me." She stared at him, her gaze unapologetic. "I want you to make me forget all the things I'm starting to remember . . . and all the things I can't."

There, he realized.

That's where the hurt was. Right there. But he couldn't fix it. All he could do was be there . . . and this. He could do exactly what she'd just asked and he'd enjoy it. He'd enjoy it and pretend the twist and rub of guilt didn't exist. He could ignore the guilt.

Staring into her eyes, he freed the front clasp of her bra and watched as her breasts swung free. They were big and full—she'd always had the most amazing breasts, but now they were enough to make his mouth water.

"I want to bite and suck on your nipples every time I see you," he said.

Her eyes went dark and opaque.

"I'm fine with that idea."

He braced his hands on the window by her head and said, "This is your show, Hannah. If that's what you want . . . then show me."

"My show?" She licked her lips and then a slow smile curled her lips and she reached up, curled her hands around the back of his head. "Come here, then. I want to feel your mouth on me."

Her nipples were already swollen and when he sucked on one, she gasped, arching closer, her fingers tightening in his hair.

Brannon slid one hand down between her thighs, stroking his thumb against the crease there. Her breath caught—he heard it and sensed the anticipation building in her. But he didn't do anything.

Yet.

"Your show, Hannah."

She caught his wrist and guided it between her thighs. "Touch me."

Touch her . . . it was like being given the keys to the kingdom . . . or a sweet car that had been specially designed just for him. There was a faint tremor to his limbs as he pressed the heel of his hand lightly against her mound and rubbed.

Hannah's head fell back, a low humming sound of a moan building in her throat.

Her cheeks were flushed, her lashes lying low over her eyes.

She rocked against him.

He pressed harder.

She moved with more determination, riding his hand and as he bent over her, her lashes lifting until she was staring into his eyes with burning intensity.

"I want you naked," he said.

"Okay." Her lips bowed up in a smile.

He eased back. Eyes still on her face, he went to his knees in front of her, but after a moment, he looked down, gaze locking on the faint swell of her waist.

Her belly was getting thicker and the sight of it, the knowledge that his baby grew within her filled him with a crazy, burning need. He leaned forward and pressed his lips to her navel.

"I want to see you holding our baby," he whispered against her skin. "I want to watch her sleeping in your arms."

A soft, shaking little moan escaped her and he looked up in time to see the glint of something bright in her eyes. But then that familiar, cocky smile returned and she said, "What . . . you think she's a girl now, too?"

"Girl. Boy." He rubbed his cheek against her belly. "It doesn't matter. I just want her healthy . . . and I want to hold both of you."

Her hands came up and cradled the back of his head. "Damn it, Brannon. I'm wanting hot and crazy monkey sex and you're making me weepy."

He chuckled and slid his hands up, cupping the ripe curve of her ass. "Can't have that."

Through her thin cotton pants, he nuzzled her. She was already wet. He could feel it and the thought of stripping her bare, taking her here, like this, was now a pulse in her brain.

But he forced himself to move slow, to tease and stroke.

But she wasn't feeling that—she twisted her fingers in his hair and hooked one leg over his shoulders. "Stop *teasing*," she bit off.

"Is this teasing?" He ran his thumb over her and he'd swear her body temperature shot up five degrees. Even through the yoga pants and panties, he could feel her getting wetter and his cock gave a demanding jerk as he thought about sinking inside her.

Right here.

With her back against the wide, dark pane of glass as the rain pounded down outside . . .

Thunder boomed and it was like it started to pulse inside him as well, adding to the frenzy of the moment.

He swore and stood up, impatient now. Shoving his hands inside her pants, he cupped her ass, pulled her close. He could feel the wet warmth of her clear through his jeans and he moved deliberately against her, watching her eyes widen, as her throat worked.

A moan shuddered out of her and he did it again, circling his hips in the cradle of hers as he kissed her mouth, licking at her parted lips, feeling her hungry moan.

Again and again, he moved, feeling how close she was to coming, just from that lazy, teasing movement, his cock abrading her through their clothes.

He didn't want that, though. He wanted to feel her coming around him, hot and wet.

But when he went to pull away, she clung to him, whimpering low in her throat and bringing one knee up, opening herself more fully.

Brannon shuddered.

"Please . . ."

Swearing, he spun her around and began to pump his hips against her ass. She whimpered and then cried out as he shoved one hand down the front of her pants, seeking out the honeyed depths between her thighs. Slick heat greeted him and the moment he touched her, she started to ride his hand.

He screwed two fingers inside her pussy and bit her ear.

She came—hard and fast. She clung to the arm he'd wrapped around her waist as she rode the hand between her thighs.

When she turned her head around and up, he pressed his lips to hers, desperate and hungry for more. He pushed his tongue into her mouth.

She bit, then sucked on him and his cock gave a hard, hungry jerk, practically yowling at him.

Impatient now, he shoved her pants down. They tangled around her ankles and she kicked them out of the way before he had a chance to deal with them.

He tried to crowd her up against the window sill, but she wiggled free and braced her hands against his chest, staring boldly up at him. "My game, remember?"

"You're trying to kill me." Bending his head to hers, he scraped his teeth down her neck.

She reached for the buttons on his shirt. "You spent half your life completely oblivious to the fact that I wanted you . . . needed you. You can suffer a little now."

She stared at him through her lashes as she slowly freed each button. "Off."

He shrugged out of it.

But she wasn't done.

She scraped her nails down his chest, circled them around his nipples.

He swore and moved against her, rocking his cock against her thigh.

"That's not going to help you."

"I don't care." He bit her ear, tangling her hair in his

fist. Anything to distract himself—oh, *fuck*—she cupped his balls and tugged.

Dragging air in, he shoved his weight up, looking down at her as she wrapped cool fingers around the base of his cock, working him free of his shorts and jeans. When she was done, she slid her hand down, all the way down to the base and then back up.

Then down.

Back.

He covered her hand with his and started to pump.

"Hey!"

He silenced her protect with a desperate kiss. "You're taunting a desperate man, Hannah," he warned.

She laughed, the sound low and husky and then, under his grasp, squeezing him, dragging the milking sensation out.

He swore.

Hannah could have done it forever, stroking him and watching his eyes glaze with potent mix of desperation and desire. Caressing him and feeling that long, hard body shake. Touching him and watching his normally impassive eyes go foggy with need.

She would have laughed when he started to curse, a litany of noises that made little sense, but then he boosted her up and braced her against the window. She yelped as she came in contact with the cold, then reached for him, wrapping her arms around wide shoulders.

He came inside her in the next breath and she cried out, throwing her head back against the pane of glass. Thunder crashed and she clamped down tighter.

Lightning flared and her normally dim room went bright as day for a split second.

She could see nothing beyond him. She could *feel* nothing that wasn't him.

He stretched her and filled her and surrounded her and cradled her . . . .

Her eyes started to sting when he slowed his thrusts and bent his head, running his lips over hers. "Hannah . . ." he murmured, his voice a low rumble in his throat. "My Hannah."

She clung to him, and desperately wanted to believe that.

CHAPTER EIGHTEEN

It took little to ascertain that Hannah was still at her houseboat.

It took even less to ascertain that she and Brannon wouldn't be going anywhere. Not for a while, at least.

After all, he only had to look up from the rain-drenched parking lot and use his eyes.

Out there, this late at night, nobody was likely to see them.

Except him. Now that he knew, he could go about his job and get things dealt with. That was, after all, what he did best. Unlike the rest of his family, unlike half the people in this pathetic town, *he* dealt with problems. Fate continued to conspire against him, but he wasn't going to sit around and moan like some miserable old fool.

He was going to deal with it, as a man should.

He made the drive back to town in the rain. The down-pour made for pathetic visibility but he welcomed it. It meant fewer people would wander out and that lessened the chance that anybody would see him.

He parked behind Hannah's apartment building and used the key he'd had copied. It had been pathetically easy to do that. Just get the master, drive into Louisiana and make the copy. Return the master. Nobody was the wiser.

He let himself in and used the spare keyfob he'd stolen from the drawer on his first trip here. Truly, people were idiots. If they were going to have spare fobs for the security system lying around the house . . . well, they shouldn't be surprised if they ended up being used against them.

He left a note on the table.

> *What did you see?*
> *What did you hear?*

That was all.

He just needed to know if she knew anything and if she did, he had to take care of her.

If she didn't, well, then he had his hands full enough as it was.

Then he went to take care of the bedroom. He'd do a quick job there and deal with the rest of the place before he left. In and out in under ten minutes, he'd bet.

It took ten minutes and then he was out the door. When he left, he peeled off the gloves and slid them into his pocket before heading on to his next stop.

He'd thought he was done with one particular annoying bit of baggage, but perhaps not.

He had more questions to ask and since there were only so many people who could answer them, he was going to the source. He'd heard something rather troublesome at the pub, one thread of truth in all the rumors that were slung about Shayla Hardee and if that thread of truth *was* real, he had to know.

It wasn't like he could just walk into the county courthouse and ask for a copy of the report or anything. If he'd developed any skills at hacking, he would have most definitely put those to use, but while he was more than adequate at picking locks and other slightly shady skills, his electronic know-how was just average. He could cover his trails when he was trolling about online and he knew how to find people, but any idiot with half a brain could do that these days.

Having some affinity with Google wasn't going to help him anonymously access the police report for Shayla Hardee's death. So he'd go to the one person who would know more than anybody, next to the cops.

The drunken fool her husband had become wasn't even a shadow of himself these days. He was lucky that he'd been well off before all of this, otherwise, he might be on the streets already. His manager at the car dealership was running the show now and the last he'd heard, Roger wasn't even keeping up the pretense of coming in.

It would make it easier, what he was going to do.

When a man spent seventy or eighty percent of his time drunk, he wasn't going to think clearly and chances were, he wouldn't remember very well either.

He banged on the front door after parking his car some distance away and taking his time to walk to the house, arriving at the Hardee residence soaking wet. When Roger finally stumbled to the door, he flashed the man a half desperate smile. "Let me in, would you? I'm soaking wet and my car's stopped running. The motor club is giving me the runaround, too."

Roger stared at him blearily.

To sweeten the deal, he held up a paper-wrapped bottle. "I'd picked up something for me to while away the night. Want to have a drink with me while I sort out the mess with my motor club?"

Roger nodded, rubbed at his bloodshot eyes, and stepped out of the way.

Thirty minutes later, his gaze foggy, Roger stared into his glass while the man silently worked the computer next to him.

Roger was so drunk, he hadn't even questioned the thin, blue gloves he'd donned.

He might not even notice.

"Alright, man. That's not working, either. Got any other ideas for passwords?" He gave Roger a charming smile. "You never know. She could have more information in her online video storage that could lead to her killer."

It was nothing more than garbage, but the bereaved man didn't have to know that. Roger's eyes lit with hope and he rubbed at his heavily stubbled cheeks. "Cat. She had one, as a girl. Name." He yawned and looked away, head slumping.

He waited patiently, but Roger didn't say anything else.

"What was the fucking cat's name?"

Roger jerked his head up and some of the clouds cleared from his eyes.

Calm the fuck down, he told himself. With an easy smile, he nudged the bottle closer. He hadn't had any himself, nor would he. He'd doctored the thing, spiking it with the same white powder he used with Ellison. "Want more?"

Roger stared at the bottle, his thick tongue coming out to wet his lips. Then he nodded.

Pouring more into the glass, he shoved it over and then leaned back to wait until the man had taken the first drink. He was taking a risk being here, but he had to take it.

Out of all those rumors, all of those twisted tales, two things had struck him. Somebody had mentioned that Hannah had actually made the *9-1-1* call from *Shayla's* phone. He hadn't even seen Shayla's phone.

Then there was the other concerning fact.

Shayla's camera was missing.

She'd been looking to blackmail him. He'd known it then, hadn't had any doubt. What he hadn't known was that she had all but made herself a career of doing it. He'd found her camera—it hadn't even been hidden.

But apparently it hadn't been the *only* camera. Or maybe it wasn't. He couldn't be sure. There was a camera, though. One that was missing. The police knew the make of the camera, they knew the model. They had countless videos that had been shot using it.

What they didn't have was that particular camera.

Where the hell was it and what had she captured on it? Was *he* on it?

"Come on, Roger." He couldn't even pretend to be helpful anymore. He was just too pissed. Logically, he realized that if there was anything on this computer, the cops would know—they and would have searched it, taken it. But it was still here. And that fear was a gnawing little demon in his belly. "Roger!"

But Roger wasn't looking at him anymore. He was fumbling with the phone in his hand, hands clumsy, swiping at the screen.

Swearing, he lunged for him and knocked it out of the man's hands.

Roger made a startled grunt as the phone was ripped away. Swinging his head up, he stared at the phone, now out of reach.

Out of reach . . . and talking.

"Hello . . . ? Roger, is . . . Roger, is everything alright?"

Roger's face crumpled. And then he started to cry. "Ellie. Ellie, he took my phone."

Fuck.

He left.

There was no other choice.

He did pour the rest of the bourbon in the glass down Roger's throat and watched as his eyes went more and more glassy. By the time he'd washed out the glass he hadn't even used and put it away—couldn't have anybody thinking Roger'd had company—Roger was nodding off on the couch.

He tossed the phone down next to the man and left.

He'd like to take the computer with him, but it wasn't an option now.

He barely had the time to get out of there and move his car, because he knew exactly who *Ellie* was.

Ellison. One of Ellison Shaw's other lovers was Roger Hardee . . . and if he knew anything about the good doctor, she'd be on her way to check on him.

He was in such a hurry, so pissed off, that he left behind one crucial thing . . . all without realizing it.

The bottle of bourbon remained sitting on the table in front of Roger and when the door slammed resoundingly, it jerked the man out of the drugged, drunken daze and he leaned forward, grabbing the bottle. He miscalculated and half of it spilled.

It didn't matter, though.

There was still enough inside the damn thing that he could pour more down his throat . . . and just forget.

"He's dead, alright."

Gideon looked at Griffin, his eyes gritty, head pounding. He'd stayed up a little too late, drank a little too much whiskey and the last thing he wanted to be doing tonight was standing over a dead body.

But here he was.

The dead body also stank of whiskey, piss, and shit.

And misery.

Looking into Roger Hardee's death stare, Gideon dragged a hand down his face and then looked around.

Everything looked too pat.

The man had sat down for a drink and then just kept on drinking. There was a mostly empty bottle of Jack Daniels, which was Roger's poison of choice.

Then there was the other bottle. It was a better brand of bourbon, the small batch craft kind that had been popping up more and more. It lay on the floor by Roger's bare, mottled feet, just a few drops left inside.

Could have seen he was running out, Gideon supposed.

Gotten up and gone to crack out the good stuff, sat down and just drank himself to death. He sure as hell smelled bad enough—like a day-old vat of clothes that had been soaked in pure alcohol and piss, then left out in the sun.

But Gideon wasn't buying it.

Something was off.

For one thing, Roger Hardee just didn't have the stomach to drink himself to death. Not that he thought Roger was a complete and utter *no* when it came to suicide. To be honest, Gideon wouldn't have been surprised to get that very call, had half expected that to be the case today. But it wasn't.

Roger half-sat, half-lay on his couch, face slack and vomit dried on his mouth and chin. Had likely choked on it and never even realized. This was just all wrong.

Gideon crouched down in front of the bottle, careful to avoid touching the carpet, stinking of puke and piss and alcohol. The smell would permeate the room for a long, long time. "There's a little bit left in the bottle," he said to Griffin, one of the other cops who'd shown up to answer the call. "Make sure they sample it."

Griffin nodded and moved away, leaving Gideon there with Outridge.

A woman's sob caught his attention and he looked up.

Dr. Ellison Shaw was sitting on the couch, arms wrapped around herself.

Her husband, Officer Beau Shaw, stood behind her. The expression on his face was a terrible one.

Nobody had yet mentioned just why Ellison had come over here.

It was pretty obvious, given the way she was dressed.

Beau had been out riding patrol tonight and Gideon wished to hell the man had been off . . . at *home*.

Beau's eyes met his and then bounced away.

Ellison sniffled again and she looked up at Gideon blearily.

Averting his gaze, he said to Outridge, "Why don't you go talk to her? Send Beau over here, if you think he can handle it."

"This is going to do them in, you know that."

Gideon shook his head. "They were already done. Beau just hadn't figured it out."

He felt for the man. He knew what it was like to put his heart into a woman's hand and watch her crush it. But unlike Ellison, Moira hadn't done it out of any selfish needs. She'd done it because she'd been focused on those around her, those who needed her. Focused on everybody but him.

It still didn't make it hurt any less. Especially now, twenty years later when he'd had his hands on her— *again*—and then just hours after it happened, she saw him, colored, and then walked away.

Beau joined him at the circle of whiskey, vomit, and urine.

Gideon asked quietly, "Can you be a cop here or should I just send you home?"

"It ain't his fault Ellison is how she is," Beau said tiredly. "Maybe if he was alive, I could hate him for it. But he ain't. And I'm a cop. Always."

"Good." He pulled out the gloves he'd jammed into his pockets. "You're assisting while Outridge tries to calm her down."

Some bitterness worked its way in Beau's voice. "He'll be lucky if she don't climb into his pants."

"It won't happen." Gideon gave him a steady look. "The man is in love with his wife and even if he wasn't, Outridge respects you."

"Don't see why." Beau shook his head. "I stopped respecting myself a long time ago."

Then he shook his head and methodically pulled on gloves of his own. "Let's do this, Chief. You thinking suicide?"

"No. I'm thinking somebody fucked up."

And he was right.

Gideon wanted a tox screen and any other damn thing the medical examiner could find. His team was looking for trace evidence. He wanted *something*—skin under nails, a stray hair, anything that would prove this wasn't an accident. Too much alcohol in his system, not enough . . . *something*. "I want the best," he ordered as Hardee was loaded up onto the gurney. "I don't want some new kid doing this and I don't want some hack. I want the best fucking body they can find. I'm tired of this shit and I want answers. I want everything, no matter how trivial."

He was a man who was considered to be calm and

collected under most circumstances and that response had more than a few giving him the side eye, but he received several solemn nods. When he turned back to the house, he found a uniform from the county in front of him.

He'd called for help and he'd gotten it. One thing about playing nice with the rest of the boys, it meant he usually had extra hands when needed.

"Chief." The woman's eyes gleamed. "I got something for you."

She indicated he should follow with a jerk of her chin and he fell into step behind her, his tennis shoes soaked through with rain, his hair dripping. *All* of him was dripping.

"What the hell could you have that survived this?" he demanded.

"You'll see." The deputy smiled, a wide, brilliant smile. "Trust me. You'll like it. You might even want to kiss me when you see it."

He cocked a brow. "Then why don't you show me?"

Thunder boomed in the middle of his sentence and he had to raise his voice to be heard.

She grinned and led him over to the far side of the porch. Rain still reached there but with less force, although the rain was slowly encroaching on what remained of the dryness.

"Here," the deputy said, crouching down.

He glanced at her nameplate, saw that it read *Cordell*.

Lights had already been strung up, but the house was painted white and that tiny bit of paper was plastered against the house, making it hard to pick up with just an ordinary glance.

He frowned, watching as she used tweezers to carefully peel it away and place it in an evidence bag.

It was hard to make out the print, half smudged away from the rain, but he saw enough.

A receipt.

Dated today from a liquor store . . . in Baton Rouge. Refusing to get excited, he looked up at her. "This could belong to anybody," he said. "Hell, Roger could have been out there."

"No." She smiled slowly. "He couldn't have. It's dated for 3:23 p.m. At 3:48, I was pulling Roger over. He was veering and I had to give him a sobriety test. He was most definitely *not* in Baton Rouge today at 3:23."

Hot satisfaction ripped through him. "You fucked up, you son of a bitch."

Cordell's smile wobbled before it firmed. "It's . . . well, Chief. It's just a receipt. Might not be anything."

"True." He lifted it to the light and eyed the area where rain had ruined half of the paper. What had been sold was illegible, but he could see the cost. Seventy-six dollars and change. Close, he thought, to what some of those small batch bourbons ran.

"It's something, though. I can feel it in my gut. Good job, Cordell." Then, because he was still bruised over Moira, he grabbed her by the back of the neck. "You asked for it."

He planted a quick kiss on her mouth, loud and smacking.

As he strode away, Cordell pressed her fingers to her mouth. A little dazed, she murmured, "Wow."

The word was lost to the rain and to the chief's booming voice as he shouted for the crew to get their asses over there—*now*.

Dreams chased her. Mocked her. Tormented her.

Struggling to get away, she twisted in her sleep, grabbing the blanket and wrenching at it as she curled into a tight, tiny ball. Or tried.

Something stopped her.

Or somebody.

It was a big somebody and in the small bed, as he shifted around, he caught her in the back.

She muttered, grumbled in her sleep. His low, muttered apology only vaguely came to her ears. *Sorry, Hannah.*

Her subconscious recognized that it was Brannon.

And that made her shiver even more.

Sorry . . .

The dreams were back.

Darker.

Angrier.

"I'm sorry I hurt you. I just . . ."

Hurt me? "I'm fine, Brannon."

"Then what's wrong? You haven't . . . how insane will you think I sound if I tell you I've kinda missed seeing you on your balcony?"

"What? You miss me playing peeping Tom? Although, FYI, you could always just close your damn curtains."

"Then I wouldn't see you."

Don't touch me, don't touch . . . "I find it hard to believe that it would bother you much. You go out of your way to avoid me."

"Because I didn't want . . . this."

"This." He wouldn't even look at her.

"I . . . look, Hannah. I've known you too long. In my head, I've had you about a hundred ways to Sunday and every time I see you, I want to try at least one of those ways out. But I . . ."

"You what?" It hurt already. Why did it hurt?

"I'm not looking for any sort of relationship. Sex is all well and good, but I don't want anything else. That's not . . . I just don't want it. Especially not now. I've got too much going on as it is and somehow, I get the feeling casual sex isn't really your speed."

Hannah understood agony then. This was what they meant when they talked about having your heart shattered. Not just broken, but shattered. She went to turn away, but stopped. "I've been in love with you since I was in high school."

He stared. She should be humiliated. Should hide. But she just looked at him, numb, cold. "No, Brannon. Casual sex isn't my speed."

"Hannah, I . . ."

"You don't need to say anything." Now she knew how it felt to die inside. She didn't want to hope anymore. "You just need to leave."

"Hannah, wait . . ."

"No! Go away, Brannon."

"Hannah, come on."

"Are you fucking deaf? I want you gone!"

Then he was gone.

She was in the forest. Running. Running from him. Running from the pain.

Both. Maybe. She didn't know.

She was running.

And then, she stumbled.

Confused, Hannah looked down.

A scream tore out of her.

It was a hand.

Outstretched.

Following the hand, she found herself staring at Shayla.

Shayla was dead.

Dead—

Hannah blinked and all over again, she found herself in the forest and she knew.

She knew—she was remembering.

It might be a dream, but it was more than that. Like she was standing outside herself, she stared at everything all around her. She'd shoved her fist into her mouth in an effort not to scream.

Shayla had been jerked up against somebody. A man.

Hannah hadn't seen much. He'd worn something over his face.

Not a mask, but . . . a hood? Glasses?

In the dark, all she could see were shadows.

Feet kicked, jerked.

And Hannah just sat there, struggling not to make a sound.

Terrified.

He dumped Shayla.

And Hannah ran.

She ran and she ran, chased by the choking, gagging noises Shayla made as she died.

And by Brannon's voice, those words.

His cool, dispassionate voice.

I don't want anything else. I just don't want it.

She came awake hearing that echo in her voice. Lying on her side, she fought not to sob.

The man behind her would hear.

He would wake up.

Then he would tell her more lies.

She was tired of lies.

Shaking, she drew her knees to her chest and shivered.

The thin blanket that was usually perfectly adequate for her—in the summer—was doing a piss poor job of covering both her and Brannon.

Unable to keep lying there, she slid out of the bed.

He didn't stir.

She left the small bedroom and grabbed the throw off the back of the chair near the window, wrapping it around herself.

I don't want anything else.

Those were the words he'd said to her. He'd *said* them to her.

Hours ago, he'd called her his.

Days ago, he'd told her he loved her.

She'd *believed* him.

She was a fool. A fool. Misery wrenched at her gut and she brought her hands to her face, tempted to give into the misery and cry, wail . . . scream. Instead, she sucked in a few deep breaths, smashing her pain down and bottling it up.

She'd deal with all of the hurt later.

There was something more awful to deal with. Shayla's death. Because she'd remembered that, too.

She hadn't seen anything that would help identify Shayla's killer.

She had her memory back, or most of it. She could tell Gideon a few details.

She'd do that.

Then she'd . . .

She didn't know what, but whatever it was, it wouldn't include Brannon McKay. Whatever the past few months had been about, one thing was clear.

It had all been a lie.

She'd been out running that night to clear her head and make herself accept the truth.

She and Brannon were nothing but a kid's dreams.

He hadn't been in love with her, the way she'd wanted to think.

The way he'd *made* her think.

Slowly, she slipped inside the bedroom and gathered up her clothes. He was still sleeping.

She swallowed back tears as she moved back into the tiny box of a living room and dressed. She had two hours to kill before her work shift started. She'd push herself through work and later, when it hurt a little less, she'd figure out what to do.

Oh, and at some point, she'd call Gideon. Give him an update.

The one thing she *wasn't* going to do was think about Brannon.

Not right now.

Not yet.

Maybe not ever.

CHAPTER NINETEEN

"Did you hear?"

Hannah looked up from the decaf coffee J.P. had given her.

Decaf. Who the hell thought *decaf* was anything worth drinking? She didn't know. Although she'd already had one cup of *real* coffee. She had one every day. Just the one. She'd drink more but she'd feel too guilty. Her mother drank three cups of coffee every day from the time she'd been sixteen and Hannah was fairly certain the caffeine hadn't destroyed her brain.

Still, she stuck to the one cup.

But she really needed a hit of the real stuff. Cradling a protective hand over the swollen curve of her belly, she looked over at J.P. "Hear what?"

He jerked his knee back and forth, his gaze nervous, locked on the knee of his uniform, which was faded and worn. Finally, after a moment, he put his coffee down and opened the door of the ambulance, hopping out.

She followed, moving around the front of the truck and leaning against the front next to him.

"You need to move in with Brannon or something, Hannah."

She laughed, tipping her head back up to stare at the sky. "Ah, yeah. That ain't happening."

"Look, I don't care if you think you're rushing it. Just make it clear it's temporary or some shit—"

"I'm not going to be seeing Brannon anymore." She shoved away from the truck and paced over to stare down the river. An early morning mist clung to it. The long, pounding rain had passed and it was warmer than it had been in a few days. The sun would burn the mist away soon enough but for now, that mist gave the river, and the surrounding area, a surreal look.

Gravel crunched behind her and she turned to look at J.P.

"What happened?" he asked.

"Reality." She shrugged and tried to give him a casual smile. It wobbled and fell. "I . . ."

Tears burned her eyes and she lifted her face to the sky. "Hell. I remembered what happened, okay? All of it. The past few months, they've all been a lie. I thought he was . . . I thought he cared. He doesn't. He just feels guilty."

She went to go around him, but J.P. caught her arm. "That's bullshit, Hannah," he said brusquely. "Anybody with eyes can see that he's tied up in knots about you."

"Yeah. It's called *guilt*."

"No." J.P. shook his head. "Men don't get that hook in their mouth look over *guilt*."

Bitter laughter filled the air. "Maybe you should explain to him that he's *hooked* then. Because he outright *told* me that he's not in the mood for a relationship. Sadly, I ended up pregnant, hurt, and you know Brannon. He's everybody's hero. Had to step up and save the day." She shrugged and gave her partner a bitter smile. "But I don't need a *hero*. I can take of myself just fine. When the baby gets here . . ."

She hesitated and then cleared her throat. "When the baby gets here, he can be involved in her life. But I don't need him in mine."

She strode to the waiting ambulance, almost desperate for a call.

But the radio stayed silent.

She was opening the door when J.P. said, "Roger Hardee is dead, Hannah."

"Daddy Warbucks is here."

Brannon eyed J.P. narrowly, saw the man give him a *kiss-ass* look, followed closely by a *what did you do, you dumb schmuck* look.

Erring on the side of caution, he tucked his hands into his pockets and said nothing.

It had already been a lousy fucking day, starting with the fact that he'd woken alone when he'd hoped to wake up wrapped around Hannah.

He couldn't even rectify the problem and make love to her because she wasn't anywhere on the houseboat. She hadn't answered her phone earlier. Before he'd even tracked her down, he'd gotten two panicked calls—one from Marc and another from two of the guys who helped Marc out.

One of his damn crops was probably ruined—he'd been planning to try his hand at Chardonnay, but Marc and his crew had found an infection, probably Pierce's Disease. It would kill the whole damn crop—Marc had been panicking over the fungus thing for a reason after all.

But just then Brannon didn't give a flying fuck.

He would. Later.

Right then, though, he wanted to talk to Hannah.

He *needed* to talk to Hannah.

Roger Hardee had been found murdered that morning.

Okay, it hadn't been confirmed as murder, but Gideon had called him, barked out a demand to know where he'd been last night, so if the jackass was barking demands, then that must mean he had a reason.

Hannah slid out of the ambulance and gave him a cool look.

He resisted the urge to cuss a blue streak, but just barely. Sometime in the past twelve hours, the world had gone straight to hell. It had only been twelve hours, too. It was noon and at midnight, he'd been buried balls-deep inside the woman now staring at him like he was something she'd scraped off the bottom of her boots.

"You weren't there when I woke up," he said, uncertain what else to say, uncertain just what had caused the drastic change in her attitude.

She was dressed in the serviceable blue uniform the county paramedics wore. It shouldn't look sexy as hell on her, but just about anything she wore struck him as crazy sexy, so he was okay with it. She could make sackcloth and tar sexy.

Even the distant, cold look on her face was sexy.

But it also scared him.

"I had to work," she said, nodding her head to the ambulance at her back. Her partner ducked behind her and climbed inside, handing her a clipboard.

From inside, he started calling things off and Brannon stood there as she checked things off and fired questions back.

When there was a lull, he went to ask her a question.

But she just started talking to J.P. again.

It was like he didn't exist in her world anymore.

He didn't know what to make of it and it pissed him off. That also scared him. Scared him and made him want to grab her and haul her against him.

He cleared his throat and managed a tight smile. "I was up pretty early."

"Not as early as I was. I needed to shower, get some breakfast." She shrugged and flipped her long braid over her shoulder. "Not everybody lives in the lap of luxury, Brannon. Some of us work. That means we take our jobs seriously. I had to shower and get ready, get to work on time."

He took each pointed jab in silence and when she was done, he asked, "Maybe we can get together for lunch."

"I already ate."

"Dinner?" Dread was now twisting him into knots.

"I don't think so." She turned back to the ambulance and he watched as she checked something else off on the clipboard. "Anything else we need to check, J.P.?"

You're dismissed.

Everything about her posture screamed it.

I don't think so.

He caught her arm. "Fine," he bit off. "We'll talk now."

She jerked away. "I don't care to be manhandled, Brannon McKay."

"And I don't care to be totally shoved out without you telling me what the hell the problem is!" he shouted.

"Shoved out?" She stared at him and then, she started to laugh. It was a cold, brittle sound and it hurt his ears, his heart, to hear it. "Shoved *out*? Oh, *honey*. But that gives the implication you *even wanted in*."

Time slowed to a pause as she leaned in. She pressed her lips closed to his ear. *"I'm not looking for any sort of relationship. Sex is all well and good, but I don't want anything else."* She settled back in front of him, one brow cocked. "Those words sound familiar, Brannon?"

Fuck.

"Hannah—"

"Hey." She held up her hands, palm out. "It's all cool,

Brannon. I told you that last day, I'd find a way to stop loving you. I guess I should thank you. Lying to me the way you've done? You helped me figure it out—I think I can stop loving you now, Brannon."

"I didn't lie to you!"

"Didn't you?"

She stared at him, her eyes empty.

He swore and shoved a hand through his hair.

"Look, Hannah—"

The radio on her collar squawked.

She jumped, the sound startling them both.

J.P. hopped out of the back. "Gotta roll, sweets!" he called.

He gave Brannon a grim look as Hannah ran around to the front. "You better fix this, you dumb shit," J.P. said in a low voice.

Fix it?

He was still standing there in dull, dazed shock as the ambulance screeched away, sirens wailing.

"Any chance you're being too hard on the guy?" J.P. asked.

It was nearly three hours later and both of them were exhausted.

Of course, anybody would be exhausted.

They'd been called out to Doris Waverly's house and although they'd hoped that it would just be another false alarm, it had been an empty hope.

Doris Waverly was one of the sweetest ladies in town, with a heart the size of the entire state of Mississippi. Sadly, her body seemed to think it was supposed to keep up. She weighed nearly four hundred pounds and that great, massive heart of hers had given out.

She'd called in numerous times, claiming she was having a heart attack and this time, she'd been right.

They'd been able to get her heart started and now it was up to the doctors to keep her alive—and Doris herself, of course. If she didn't get her weight under control, sooner or later, the heart attacks would kill her.

Hannah's back was killing her.

Her thighs were killing her.

Everything seemed to be killing her.

Giving J.P. a baleful look, she warned, "Don't."

"I can't help it." He shook his head. "Hannah, look . . . I can't claim to know the guy well, but I know what a dumbass in love looks like. And he's got all the symptoms."

It was elbow to elbow inside Treasure Island and he all but had to shove his way through to get a seat by the window.

A couple of people hailed him.

One woman slid her hand along his back and smiled at him.

His ex-wife nodded at him and went back to her discussion with several other women.

He'd planned to be here to keep an eye on Hannah's place. He knew she was working today and he'd wanted to see what she thought of what he'd left for her, but that was no longer his primary concern.

"Did you hear the news?" He glanced up to see Toot Fink look at him expectantly.

"The news?" He shrugged. "Hard not to hear it. Unless you're in a coma."

He was most certainly *not* in a coma.

Roger Hardee was dead.

Roger wasn't *supposed* to be dead.

He certainly hadn't *left* him dead.

Toot leaned in and whispered, "Doc Shaw found him. You know about her and her . . . problems, right?"

Because it was considered polite, he waited a moment before he nodded.

Toot gravely nodded back.

"She was over there. Had probably gone over for . . ." Toot shrugged in lieu of saying anything. "Then she found him. Called Beau. Man, that had to get him in the gut, his wife calling him from where she'd been planning to screw some other guy and then she finds him dead."

Toot's watery blue eyes narrowed and he added, "Some people are saying it's a conspiracy. That Beau actually killed him and they fixed this all up so Beau would look innocent, because who'd believe she'd actually *call* him like that."

"Officer Shaw didn't kill him," a man next to him said with a snort.

He flagged down the bartender, a solid-looking black man with an easy, affable smile. "Glenlivet." He paused, then said, "A double. Neat."

A smile creased the man's dark face. "Been a lot of that goin' around today. Now the man who could really use a drink can't really have one, though."

"I'm sorry?"

The bartender's brows shot up. "Roger Hardee, man. He's dead."

"Dead." He said it slowly and then shook his head before looking over at Toot. The old man grimaced.

"You heard me." Nodding, the bartender set him up with his scotch and after he put the whiskey down, he braced his elbows on the counter. "It's why we're so crazy busy in here. Everybody's here to speculate, make no mistake."

"Poor bastard." He lifted his glass to his lips and took a slow drink, even as he fumed inside. Miserable bastard was more like it. "What happened? He didn't . . ." He grimaced and then added, "Well . . ."

"Wasn't suicide, I don't think." The bartender shook his head and then looked up as a big, bearded man shouted from the other end.

"Chap!"

The black man grimaced and shoved away from the bar. "Gotta move. You running a tab?"

He nodded and turned his attention back out the window.

Hannah's lights were still out.

It was a mild irritation, but only a mild one. He'd put a great deal of thought into that but now, he had other concerns.

What had gone wrong?

"Well, I heard it was his heart."

Tensing, he shifted his attention to the mirror that ran the length of the bar, following the voice, waiting until he could assign it to an owner.

The old bat who let her dog shit everywhere. Mouton. She had her hand pressed to her chest as she leaned in, talking to the stooped old figure that was Janet Stafford. Her daughter-in-law, Jennie Hayes Stafford, now owned the bookstore that had been a fixture in town for years. Janet and Mrs. Mouton were fixtures themselves, gossips. Fountains of information, really.

Janet Stafford nodded, her frail hand gripping a glass similar to the one the man at the bar held. There would be no fine Scotch in it, though. She preferred her whiskey cheap, akin to paint thinner. Claimed it kept her young and her mind sharp.

Nobody would argue with her, either. She was ninety-five years old and sharp was just the tip of the iceberg.

"His heart, alright," she said, sipping her whiskey and shaking her head. "In more ways than one. His daddy died of a heart attack. Wasn't even sixty. Should have tried having two fingers of whiskey a day instead of the crap red wine everybody talks about these days."

Mrs. Mouton leaned closer, looking around. Secrets, of course.

But then her voice carried.

Everybody sitting within ten feet made a show of doing something else, talking to their neighbor, checking the time.

As soon as she looked back at Janet, the matron said, her voice strong and clear, "My granddaughter was getting some bloodwork done a few months ago when he had to get one of them stress tests. His ticker was shot. He didn't do it here, though. Went into Baton Rouge. She had to—her insurance and all . . ."

She waved a hand, dismissing her granddaughter's reasons for not getting whatever she needed done here, although everybody knew the likely reason.

Bethany Mouton was five months pregnant.

Nobody cared about that.

They all latched onto the other key bit of information.

A stress test.

Blindly, he stared into the amber liquid in his glass. The surface trembled slightly and he lowered it, then pressed his hand to the surface of the bar.

His hands were shaking.

It was a fine tremor, likely unnoticed by anybody.

He'd noticed though.

Roger Hardee's heart had been bad.

That was why he'd died.

It wasn't that much of an issue, not really.

But it was a fact he should have known.

He'd missed it.

He'd messed *up*.

CHAPTER TWENTY

Hannah pressed her back against the door and closed her eyes. She stood inside her dark, quiet apartment and took a moment to just breathe. That was all she wanted.

A few moments of quiet.

She had had days from hell but nothing like this.

Brannon . . .

Her heart ached, like a gaping, open wound and there was no emergency medical treatment in the world that could provide any relief for this pain.

More and more memories were slowly churning their way free, like she'd dragged a rake through the soil of her brain and now all those little rocks were stabbing tiny holes into her heart.

But he'd looked at her like *he* was the one who'd been torn open. Like *he* was the one who'd had his chest cavity pried open, his heart ripped out and stepped on.

He'd been doing that to her for years. Then he'd *lied* to her.

All of these months. Coming over here.

Making her think he cared. Like they had a chance.

She swallowed and dashed at the tears that had started to fall.

Screw that.

Screw the tears.

Hadn't she hurt enough over him already? All her damn *life*?

All he had to do was be honest. Tell her they'd slept together and if he wanted to be part of the baby's life, she would have let him. Why did he have to mislead her like that? And he'd told her he loved her.

But all he'd been doing was making himself feel better or some shit like that. Assuaging his guilt, maybe. It wasn't like she'd *blamed* him. He wasn't at fault for what had happened.

Groaning, she dragged her hands up and down her face. Now she was thinking about Roger, too. And how *he* had looked at her. Her stomach twisted violently and she swallowed back the bile that had been threatening to rise all afternoon. She was well past the morning sickness stage, but her stomach had never exactly returned to normal and this was a little more than she could take.

That poor bastard.

She'd never really cared for Roger Hardee, but she knew he'd loved his wife. Now Shayla had annoyed Hannah something awful, had pushed all her buttons in the worst way, but Roger had just been a nuisance.

Then he'd been pitiful, and pitiable.

He'd loved his wife. Roger had loved Shayla and grieved for her and pushed to find who had killed her. Now he was gone, too.

He'd come to Hannah, all but begging her to help, to remember.

There was still a pit in her mind, a few holes left to be filled. The amnesia was nothing she could control and she knew it, but it didn't help the knot of guilt she felt inside.

Tears burned her eyes while a headache pounded inside her skull and her muscles knotted with fatigue.

As a day, today had been a complete and total pain in the ass. Of course, it had been worse for others. Gideon had to have his hands full, dealing with everything going on from Roger's death, not to mention still trying to tie up everything from Senator Robert's strange suicide. The cops around the small town needed a bonus—and lots of chocolate.

She still needed to call the chief and update him, but she'd do it later, when she wasn't so exhausted.

She couldn't even find it in herself to shove away from the door or turn on the lights.

She was so tired. Resting a hand on her belly, she said, "It has to get better. Right?"

She laughed and the cynical sound of it bounced off the walls, came back to her.

For some reason, it sounded . . . wrong.

Slowly, she reached out a hand and flipped the switch for the lights but nothing happened.

At the same time, she took a step forward, bracing her body. For what, she didn't know.

Something crunched under her work boot. Something fine and brittle. Like a light bulb.

The lights didn't come on.

She pulled the pen light she used for work from the pocket on her cargos and flipped it on.

She sucked in a breath through her teeth.

Simultaneously, she jerked open the door behind her, letting light shine in as she grabbed her phone from her pocket. But she didn't dial. She just stood there, fear a scream in her brain.

Hannah didn't handle blind terror well.

She didn't handle terror well *period*.

Most of it had been burned out of her as a child, at the hands of her stepfather, then it had been choked out of her as she'd watched him brutalize her mother even as Hannah begged the small, terrified woman to leave, to run away.

Years of watching that kind of abuse had strengthened Hannah's core to one of tempered steel.

But she could still feel fear.

What she saw in the wedge of light shining in from the hallway behind her left her frozen with the soul-stealing numbness of terror.

She was staring at a threat.

Possibly more, but absolutely nothing less.

Nor was it an empty threat.

Her mind flashed back to the robe, to the rock that had been left in the robe's pocket.

Such an innocuous thing, that rock. She had seen hundreds of them. Thousands. When she ran along the path by the river, especially down there by the house boat, she saw them all the time. How could she have forgotten something so simple as that?

He had been warning her. Perhaps even mocking her.

And now he was doing it again.

Hannah gripped the penlight tighter as the fear slowly gave way to another emotion. It started out as an ember and she fanned it, nursed it until it was a raging inferno, one born of fury.

Anger was better than fear any day.

The fear didn't die and she was fine with that because Hannah understood the value of fear, just as she understood the value of anger.

Fear wasn't a bad thing in and of itself.

Fear could be healthy. Fear could keep you alive.

But she needed the anger.

Slowly, she pushed away from the doorframe and used her penlight to stare into the apartment. First, she checked the floor. It had been a lightbulb, the one from the lamp by the door most likely.

Clothes, movies, books, knickknacks and pictures were thrown across the floor, like an isolated tornado had been set loose in her home and been given free reign.

Her gaze landed on the picture of her and her mother. The last one that had been taken of them before her mother died.

The frame lay shattered on the floor and a knife had been driven through the picture and backing. One of her steak knives. Something, probably that knife, had been used to jab ugly gouges into the picture, ruining it forever.

"You son of a bitch," she said softly.

Her voice echoed in the confined space, the way it does when you're alone.

And she knew.

Whoever he was, he was gone.

She lifted her phone and dialed *9-1-1* as she strode into the kitchen and pulled out the Maglite she kept for emergencies. Then she flipped it on and moved back to the door, refusing to risk being caught in a small, dark space, even though all her instincts screamed that who-ever had done this was gone.

She used the beam of the light to sweep the room and it landed on a phone sitting on her coffee table. She rec-ognized the model immediately. It was just like Shayla's had been. She saw the note and felt a smile twisting her lips.

"You *evil* son of a bitch," she said again.

A voice came across her phone just as she had said it.

"*Nine one . . .*" There a pause as the woman on the other end of the line processed what Hannah had been saying and then she continued. "*One. Please state the na-ture of your emergency.*"

Hannah gave her name and address, then said "Some-body's broken into my apartment. I'm pretty sure he's gone now but he's totally trashed my place. And he left a message for me. Call Chief Gideon Marshall and tell him to get his ass over here."

"Is anybody in the apartment with you now?"

"I don't think so. But I can't be sure."

"You need to vacate the premises."

Hannah stared hard at the message that had been left for her. "No. I'm not vacating the premises. Get Chief Marshall. I want him here. Now."

"Ma'am, I'm advising you to get out of the apartment—"

"Look, the longer you argue with me, the longer I'm in this apartment alone."

The call-taker paused and Hannah heard the resignation in her voice. "I'm contacting the police. Please stay on the line."

Bet your ass I'll stay on the line.

Gideon punched in a number. It rang. And rang. And rang. When it finally went to voice mail, he left a short, pissed-off message. "Something's going on with your woman, Brannon. Get your ass to town."

Then he hung up and swung through the door that led up to Hannah's apartment.

He should have sent Deatrick over, but he felt responsible for Hannah and not just because she was a citizen of the town he'd sworn to protect. She was a friend of Neve's. She was involved with Brannon. Gideon was so tangled up with the McKay family, he knew he'd never be free of them, even if he ever did find a way to sever the ties that held him to Moira.

He thought of the pretty deputy with the sheriff's department and told himself he should ask her out.

He'd refrained from getting involved with anybody— physical relationships weren't the same thing as getting involved, but even his physical encounters were limited to when the need just became too strong.

But he was tired of fooling himself, tired of waiting, tired of hurting. Deputy Maris Cordell would never be Moira, but he was starting to realize he and Moira were just never going to happen.

Yeah, it had taken twenty years, but Gideon hadn't ever claimed to be a quick study. Especially not when it came to matters of the heart.

What he needed was somebody who *wasn't* Moira. Somebody who wouldn't cut him to ribbons every time he thought of her. Every time he saw her. Every time she looked away and pretended she didn't feel exactly what he felt.

Of course, what he needed right now was five more uniformed officers and a couple more detectives. A double of himself wouldn't be a bad thing.

But since none of that was possible, he'd focus on what was.

Gideon was a man who believed in priorities.

Right now, he needed to find a man who had probably killed at least two people and just might be involved in whatever was going on with Hannah Parker. One of his uniformed officers met him at the top of the steps, eyes bright, almost viciously so. "Her place is trashed, Chief. Seriously trashed."

"Where's Hannah?" he asked.

Officer Stanton grimaced. "Ah. Inside her apartment. She won't leave. Hasn't touched anything, she says, but she won't leave."

"Son of a bitch," Gideon muttered, shaking his head. He grabbed his phone, checked it. Brannon still hadn't called.

Then he strode down the short, wide hallway. The building boasted four units. The upper two units were for residential apartments and the lower two were business units. The apartment on the left only had a sporadic occupant—a professor from the nearby college campus. She spent most of her nights with a boyfriend, but liked to have her own space. It was an arrangement that had been going on for quite some time. Gideon didn't even have to check with the woman to know she wouldn't have seen anything. She only came into Treasure on the weekends, and that was just once or twice a month.

They weren't likely to have any witnesses. But because he was thorough, he nodded at the other door. "Track down Dr. Huxly out at the campus. See if she was here at any time over the past forty-eight hours."

Stanton pulled out his notebook. "Already did. She was here last weekend, but not since. Didn't notice anybody suspicious—unless you count Barney and Bert."

Cocking a brow, Gideon waited.

"They were having a row." Stanton shrugged.

"That's normal, not suspicious. I'd want to know if they weren't having a row." Gideon ducked into Hannah's place and found himself staring at what looked like the remnants of passing tornado.

"Damn."

Hannah was standing at the window.

She turned her head and stared at him over her shoulder, then nodded slowly. "That about sums it up, Chief."

He pinched the bridge of his noise and then looked back at Stanton. "Get Lloyd . . ." Then he stopped, shook his head. Lloyd Hansen was back in prison, serving out the rest of his sentence. And his wife had left the state, moving up to Wisconsin, living with a cousin. Couldn't be Lloyd. "Okay. Okay."

Hannah turned and pointed to the coffee table.

His eyes narrowed on it and he saw the phone lying there.

"That's not yours, is it?"

"No." Her voice was faint, but steady as she said, "Shayla had one just like it. I don't think it's hers, but the message is pretty clear."

What did you see?
What did you hear?

Gideon stared at the words, printed out in block print on plain, ordinary white paper.

He imagined it was the kind of paper anybody could buy in reams of five hundred at just about any office supply or discount story anywhere in America.

The block print was simple, the kind of font that could come off just about any computer, found in just about any house anywhere in America.

He wouldn't find shit from it.

But at the same time, he felt a slow, satisfied smile spread across his face.

"Well, Chief," Hannah drawled. "I've lost a great deal of my personal possessions. He trashed a lot of my clothes, cut into them and dumped bleach on what was left. He ruined the last picture I ever had taken with my mother. But it appears this sick fuck has amused you. I'm so pleased."

Hannah's eyes were hot with fury when he looked into them.

"He fucked up, Hannah," Gideon said, turning his head and taking a good long look around her apartment. "All of this? He's pissed off and he's scared. I'm sorry for what he did here, but this means he's scared. That's a damn good thing."

He took another thorough look around the place as he drew out a pair of gloves, unease starting to burn inside him. One thing wasn't adding up for him.

It had nothing to do with the trashed apartment and everything to do with the watchful woman.

"You heard from Brannon?"

When things were bad, you went home.

As far as Brannon was concerned, they were pretty miserable.

He stood out on the dock that faced out over the slowly rolling river and he brooded.

He had to fix things with Hannah, but the problem was, he just didn't know how.

A wind kicked up, blowing his hair back from his face and the scent of rain danced in the air, but he didn't notice.

He was thinking about Hannah.

Only about her.

When the old boards of the dock creaked behind him, he didn't bother looking back.

Neve was in town.

So was Moira, working.

Not too many people would follow him when he was clearly in a temper. It took him a while to get to one, but once he did, most people steered clear.

Ella Sue had never been one to steer clear of anything, though.

She came to stand next to him, neat and tidy in a pair of pressed khakis and a shirt the color of roses. She was sixty-five if she was a day, but if he didn't know her, he wouldn't have thought she had even seen the first blush of forty. She had that ageless quality about her and a serenity that rarely failed to give him some measure of peace and comfort.

But it failed him now.

He jammed his hands into his pockets.

"I fucked up, Ella Sue."

She lowered herself to sit on the edge of the dock,

staring out into the water. "You know, my daddy used to take me fishing out here on the river. All the time. Wasn't far from here. Your grandfather was alive then. He'd sometimes join us. I was terrible at fishing then. Didn't know how to be quiet for anything."

Brannon sat down next to her, knees drawn up to his chest.

She turned her head and looked up at him. "Out of all of the McKays I've known—and honey, I've known a lot—I'd have to say you are the most like him. Your grandfather. He was determined to protect every single person he knew. When my daddy died, he showed up on Mama's door and offered her a job."

She sighed and looked up. "My mama, God love her. She didn't want to work." Ella Sue laughed. "Not for anybody, but definitely not for some rich white man. Do you know what she did?"

Brannon flicked her a glance.

Ella Sue was still staring up at the sky. "My mother, while I was in my bedroom, crying into the doll Daddy had given me for my birthday, told your grandfather that she'd be just happy to take his money. What did he have in mind? And he said that he knew they needed a typist or two at one of his businesses. You people." She shook her head. "You already owned so much of the town. He talked about the little local airline they owned— your daddy sold it when you was just a baby, but your grandpa, he asked Mama what she'd think of being a stewardess. She said, no. She didn't think she'd like that. Or being a typist. None of that would really work, because she had a little girl, didn't he see? So he asked her just what she thought would work."

Ella Sue sighed. "She told him she'd be happy to go to bed with him. Thought maybe once a week, for a thousand dollars. Your grandma didn't never have to know."

"Ella Sue." Brannon swore and went to stand, blushing now, all the way down the collar of his shirt. This woman who was like a mother to him. He didn't want to hear this.

She laid a hand on his arm. "How do you think I felt? I was ten years old. He told her no. She left town three weeks later, left me with my aunt and I never saw her again. I don't know where she went and I can't even claim to understand why she did what she did."

Brannon stared at her hand on his arm, watched as she patted it and then she stood. "My mama died a couple of years later. She wrote me, you know. A letter, every week. But she never sent them. She was embarrassed. After she'd died, when my aunt had to go and identify her body, she was given the letters and she brought them back. I was twenty before she gave them to me. I'd been angry at your grandfather for a long while."

"At . . ." Brannon stopped, scowled.

"Oh, baby." She brushed his hair back from his face. "I didn't understand what I overhead that night. I just heard this rich white man telling my mama he'd help her, and then he said he wouldn't. A few weeks later, she left me. I was alone. I spent a lot of time angry over the wrong things. Then I read the letters. If she'd sent them . . ." Ella Sue stopped. "But she didn't. She was too embarrassed over the mistake she'd made. Over *her* fuck up."

Brannon felt his shoulders tightening.

Shrewd eyes bore into his and she lifted a brow. "Now . . . why don't you tell me about whatever it is that has so you sad, boy? And don't you be lying to me. Whatever it is, you can fix it. But not if you run from it. Not if you stay down here at the river and hide."

"Fix it." Brannon tipped his head back and stared up at the leafy green canopy overhead. "How do I fix it? She's loved me most of her life, she told me."

"Boy, I know that." Ella Sue gave him a look like she was talking to an idiot. Then her face softened and she reached up, cupped his cheek the way she had when he was a child. "She loved you and she waited. Because I think some part of *her* knew just what I've always known—that you loved her, too."

Brannon shook his head. "No. I—"

"Don't you give me that. You were too old for her, the first time you really noticed her." She arched a brow at him when he would have interrupted. "You're my boy— maybe I didn't give birth to you, but you're my son all the same and I see exactly what a mother is going to see. She'd been coming here for years, but then you started to really *see* her. She was too young, so you did the only thing a good man could. You stayed the hell away. But she hasn't been a girl for a long time, Brannon. She's not seventeen anymore. Although sometimes, I think *you* just might be. You are *still* running away." She moved away, huffing out a sigh. "You run away from your feelings because it's easier for you to not feel anything. Both you and Moira—the two of you decided it was just easier to never feel anything. And Neve, she couldn't stop herself from feeling everything."

Brannon snapped his jaw shut.

Ella Sue's eyes narrowed as she turned back to face him. "You want to argue? You want to tell me *one* time when you didn't push somebody away? Everybody?" One hand went to her hip while she gestured grandly with the other. "If you have a for-instance, Brannon, I'm listening."

Because he didn't, he stayed quiet. Arms crossed over his chest, he glared at her.

"Now . . . just what is going on, Brannon?"

"I . . ." *lied.* He hesitated. This soul-baring shit sucked. Only Ella Sue could pull it out of him, too.

She arched her brows. "You *what*? Did she tell you about the baby and you freaked?"

"Hell, no! I didn't know about the baby until after the accident." He wasn't *that* much of an asshole. Turning away from her incisive stare, he started to pace. He couldn't stand there and look in her eyes and not talk. She was like a living, breathing lie detector.

He paced to the end of the dock where it gave way to the path. The cool wind kicked up and he slid his eyes upward, peering through the branches to find the skies dark and leaden. A storm was rolling in again, another soaker, bringing with it the bite of cold air and the promise of thunder. Even as he thought it, the distant rumble of it echoed off in the distance.

"We should head back," he murmured.

"Ain't like I've never been rained on before. You get back to the house and you're going to dodge me again."

He flicked a glance back at her and then looked back toward the skies. "I lied to her, Ella Sue. We—no—*she* had decided she was done. She realized I was more trouble than I was worth."

"Smart girl," Ella Sue muttered, moving to stand beside him. But she wasn't looking at him.

She was studying the sky.

He glared at her.

"She told me how she felt—said she'd loved me. Then she said she'd do her best to stop loving me," he said, and a familiar ache settled in his chest. It was an ache he knew well. It came back every time he thought of that day. "That was in the afternoon. That night . . . she had the car wreck."

"Oh, honey." She turned, the storm forgotten.

He backed up before she could touch him. "Don't," he said gruffly, catching her hands. "I lied, Ella Sue. When she woke up, I had every chance to tell her the truth, every chance to apologize and tell her that I'd figured out what a fool I was. But I didn't. I told her we'd fought . . . but that day, I went to her because . . ."

Ella Sue filled in the blanks on her own and the look she gave him was one of pity and aggravation. "Boy, you *did* fuck up."

Before she could say anything else, a voice rang out through the woods. Somebody was calling them.

Hers—then his.

Neve's voice, clear and loud, carried easier on the wind.

But it was Ian who got there first, his legs longer, more powerful.

He gave Brannon a dark look. "You bloody arse. We've been looking for ya all day!"

"I've only been here a couple hours," he said.

"Well, a couple hours then." His face was ruddy from the run, his accent thick. "You left your fuckin' phone. We been tryin' to call. Somebody broke into Hannah's place. It's been trashed."

Brannon stared at him for one second as the words came together.

Then he lunged.

Ian caught him, huge, powerful arms stopping him from tearing off down the path.

"Hold up, hold up, man!"

"Let me go, you son of a bitch!"

"She's not there!" Neve shouted.

Slowly, Brannon relaxed but Ian didn't let him go, not right away. While Brannon stared at his sister, Ian strained to hold him. "You going to listen there, mate?" he asked softly. "For a minute, yeah?"

"A minute." His blood was roaring. His heart felt like it had lodged in his throat—or maybe down near his ankles. He wasn't sure. "You've got one minute."

CHAPTER TWENTY-ONE

Hannah braced her elbow against the car door.

The wind raced in, blowing her hair back and chilling her flesh.

She was shivering, but she needed the air, both to calm her nerves and to keep the cop next to her from trying to talk to her.

She'd been given two choices.

Well, three, really, but one of them hadn't really been a choice. She was exhausted and there was no way she was going to try to curl up in the hallway while the cops went over her apartment with a fine-toothed comb. That was the non-choice.

The other choice, another non-choice as far as she was concerned, had been to let one of the uniformed officers take her to the police department and sit on her—as Gideon had phrased it—so she could rest there.

She'd told him to go fuck himself.

So he'd suggested Brannon's.

She'd flipped the chief of police off and he shrugged. "Those are your choices. He's got a security system, and if I tell him to lock you down, he will."

"Fine." She'd bared her teeth at him and told him to

call Brannon. Once he got there, she could punch him in the teeth and then fine, he could *lock her down* and she'd brood and steam until she figured out another option besides staying with a man who'd lied to her.

Except Brannon wasn't answering his phone.

Gideon had gotten more and more frustrated, she'd gotten more and more tired, so Beau had volunteered to drive her out to the sprawling house where Brannon lived. He'd stay there with her, too.

Gideon had grunted his assent, but as they left, he was already putting in another call—this one to McKay's Ferry. Moira, Neve, or Ella Sue would be able to track Brannon down. She knew it without a doubt and glumly, she had to acknowledge that she'd be dealing with the bastard sooner than she'd wanted—she'd been planning on not dealing with him *period*.

She shivered as another gust of wind blew in and the windows went up—not all the way. Wrapping her arms around herself, she rubbed at her arms and sighed.

"Thanks."

"If you were cold, you just had to ask," Beau said amicably.

She smiled weakly. Not like she was about to tell him she'd rather freeze just so they didn't have to talk, now was she?

They sped on in silence a few more miles and she breathed out a sigh of relief.

But she breathed easy way too soon.

"You're mad at Brannon."

Frustrated, she closed her eyes. "Anybody ever tell you it's dangerous to piss off a pregnant woman?"

Beau chuckled. "Well, I'm an officer of the law. I think I'm safe."

She made a face.

A few more moments of silence and then he asked, "Want to talk about it?"

"Don't you have enough problems going on, Beau?" she asked tiredly.

"There is that." He blew out a breath. "I got problems all the way up my ass. Excuse my language, Hannah. I just . . ."

She slid him a look. "Why do you stay?"

"Love makes fools of us all." He shrugged as though that explained everything. Then he glanced over at her. It was a quick look then he went back to focusing on the road in the driving rain. "So what happened between you and Brannon? Seemed it was going rather well."

"Yeah." She curled her lip. "Then I went and remembered a few details."

From the corner of her eye, she saw how Beau's hands tightened on the steering wheel. It was only for a moment. But his grip was so intense, his knuckles stood out in stark relief against his skin. "Your memory is coming back."

Hannah pushed a hand through her hair and looked down.

The thick, dense strands fell to shield her face, giving her a veil of sorts. It wasn't perfect, but it let her see somewhat, without letting *him* see her.

He'd relaxed his grip on the steering wheel. And he seemed to be looking outside.

"Not everything," she said, struggling to keep her voice casual. "Just a few more bits and pieces. About him, is all."

"Has to be frustrating." Beau sighed. "I can't imagine missing a week of your life, Hannah."

"Yeah."

He lowered a hand, drumming out a beat on his leg.

Hannah lowered hers, too, casually resting hers on her thigh. The pocket a few inches away held her utility scissors. They had a blunt edge but could cut through just about anything. A hell of a tool. Not much of a weapon.

"You don't need to be so nervous."

She looked up at Beau.

He was still staring at the road.

"We'll take care of you, Hannah. That's a promise."

Slowly, she shifted her attention to the bend in the road, watching, waiting. The car was slowing down.

Thunder boomed overhead.

Lightning split the sky, casting its brilliant, searing light for a fraction of a second and blinding her.

The car came around the curve, Brannon's massive home was visible for just a moment as another jagged spear of lightning bloomed.

"Won't be long now."

Another hair pin curve. She said, "I need air, Beau."

He sighed and put the window down. It wasn't all the way down but it would work.

Please, God. Don't let me hurt my baby.

She glanced at Beau. "Hey, Beau?"

When he looked at her, she grabbed the wheel.

And wrenched.

"You sent her . . ." Brannon shoved the heel of his hand against his eye socket and then swore. "I'm not *at* my place."

Across the line, Gideon muttered under his breath.

Brannon thought he heard something along the lines of *Stupid, asinine, idiot McKays.* He was almost certain most of it was directed at him—and maybe Moira. Gideon adored Neve. The kid could do no wrong in Gideon's eyes. Just then, Brannon was inclined to agree, because both he and Moira were idiots lately.

And none of it mattered.

"Maybe," Gideon said slowly. "You could *get* to your place. It's not like it's far from Ferry."

Then he disconnected the phone.

Brannon lowered his cell, stared at it, then jammed it into his pocket. He was already almost back to the house, but soaked to the bone now, thanks to the deluge that had started less than five minutes ago. While Neve started asking questions, he cut into the house and pulled open the cabinet that held keys to the cars out in the garage. He studied them, then selected a set for the Jeep.

"I'm heading out to my place," he said.

"I'll come."

He shot Ian a look and shook his head. "No."

"I'm coming wi' you," Ian said flatly.

"No." Brannon jerked his head toward Ella Sue and Neve. "Something's not right. Hell, something's been messed up since the day Hannah wrecked. Yeah, so William's gone, but somebody broke into Hannah's apartment, and not just today, either. I want somebody here with Neve and Ella Sue."

He turned to go out the door and then stopped, looked back at Ian. "And call that prick, Charles. Tell him to hang around Moira until she gets here."

Ian's mouth twisted in a grimace. "I'd rather shove my hand in a meat grinder."

But he pulled his phone out and dialed.

"Charlie! Hello, mate, it's Ian . . ."

Brannon, despite his worry, managed to smile a little.

Hannah cut through the seatbelt.

Beau had hit his head the window and he was unconscious, although she didn't know how long that would last.

She had to get out first.

That was all that mattered.

No reason to be so nervous, huh?

Then why were you gripping the steering wheel hard enough to rip it off? A hysterical bubble of laughter welled up in her but she swallowed it down, barely.

Between Beau assuring her she didn't need to be nervous and him about to pull a Hulk in the car, she was pretty certain she'd never been more *nervous* in her life.

But she'd cut through the seat belt and—

"Hannah . . ."

Beau's voice was slurred.

She didn't look at him as she tried to force the door open.

It wasn't budging. Okay.

She hauled herself up and twisted.

He was staring at her blearily and then made a lunge for her. "You . . ."

"Don't!" She reversed her sheers in her hand and went to stab at him.

"Can't go . . ." He shook his head, trying to clear it. "What . . ."

She shoved herself through the window, shoulders first.

"What you—" He swore.

She screamed when he caught her ankle.

"You remember!"

She didn't waste her breath talking to him. She just jerked away, kicking at him when he tried to stop her.

She got out and pressed low, staying near to the car and using it as a defense in case he tried to shoot. Then she started to crawl. Up ahead, she saw the closest structure—one of the barns.

She was no more than ten feet away when lightning struck again and the stink of ozone filled the air.

She'd been staring at the lights, using them as a beacon.

But in the blink of an eye, that beacon was gone. Drenched, covered in mud, and shuddering with cold, Hannah watched as the lights winked out and everything around her went dark.

She might have stood there, frozen with indecision as a hundred aches began to make themselves known. But two things forced her to move. Car lights swept across the grounds. And she heard somebody shout her name.

She lurched over into the pouring, driving rain.

Brannon whipped the Jeep off the road and slammed on the brakes.

If he was honest, really honest, and if he was trapped in a shrink's chair, the shrink might make some connection between Brannon's recklessness behind the wheel and the way he'd lost his parents.

He had a fierce love of the automobile.

He had also a fierce fear of losing somebody in another wreck.

So when he saw that twisted mess of metal just around the final bend before his house, his heart jumped up into his throat and then sank to somewhere down around his feet.

"Hannah!"

He threw himself toward the vehicle and came up short when he saw it.

Nobody inside.

The radio squawked, but his mind was already racing ahead to what could have happened. He couldn't reach in to grab it—the hand piece was on the floor and his arms were long, but not that fucking long. Swearing, he shoved off the vehicle and turned around, staring off into the empty night.

He didn't even stand there a minute before he spun around and ran back toward the Jeep. The tires sent mud spinning and flying up into the air, flinging it across the road.

It splattered across a man's face, crouched down, hiding in the grass.

He was unseen by Brannon as he remained there, hiding . . . and waiting.

"Hannah!"

She heard a man's voice, muffled by the downpour as she moved through the barn. The smell of wine was thick in her nose and the thud of her heart seemed to drown out everything thing else.

"Hannah! Come out! We need to get you safe before he finds us." He was closer now.

He . . .

She swallowed. Shoving her back against the wall, she closed her eyes and rested a hand over her belly. A sharp pain twisted her and she barely managed to bite back a moan.

She flinched and her foot bashed up against something—it was small. It went skidding and flying and each echo was progressively louder. Biting her lip, she started to work herself farther away from the noise. Away from where she'd heard his voice—but then she saw his shadow.

Damn it.

Desperate, she began to inch the other way, even as she saw his head craning this way and that.

He was following the sound of whatever it was she'd kicked.

Her foot brushed against something again. It didn't move this time. She was moving slower, testing each area with her foot.

She bent down and scooped it up.

Rubbing her thumb over it, she tried to identify whatever it was. Metal. That was all she could tell. A nut? A bolt? She couldn't tell a wrench from pliers on the best of days. She didn't know what she was holding, but it was heavy. Eyes on the shadow, she threw the bit of metal in her hand. She threw it hard and high, straight over his head and as the noise clattered and echoed back to them, she looked around. She had a split second to make a decision. She had two directions she could follow—left or right. To the right, lay the light and the promise of safety. A security light shown down in a pool of yellow light, revealing the way to the house, and hopefully, Brannon.

To the left, lay darkness.

She ran to the left, away from that glare shining like a spotlight—like a trap.

Behind her, the nameless man said her name again and it floated to her in the darkness. "Hannah, he was able to get into your apartment. Who but a cop could do that? He's been talking to his wife . . . his wife who is your *doctor*. Who else would know what is going on with your memories?"

She's my OB, Hannah thought.

But then she started to think.

This wasn't making sense. She had a man behind her who was trying to convince her of . . .

Fuck.

She spun around a corner and then shrieked as she crashed headfirst into Beau.

Blood ran down his face in a pink, watery trail, the rain mixing with it as it trickled from the cut on his brow. She opened her mouth.

He clamped a hand down on her mouth before she could speak—or scream.

"I heard," he said, his voice grim and quiet. His left

arm came around her upper body, holding her arms pinned down and against her right bicep, she could feel the hard, unyielding weight of his weapon.

She went to jerk away again, panic and confusion tearing her up inside. But then that other voice rang out again. Louder. Closer.

"Hannah, you need to trust me. I just want to get you to Brannon. He *told* me to get out here and find you. He couldn't get here in time. He was in town, with Moira. I was closer."

Another pain tore at her belly and she couldn't bite back her moan this time.

As she stumbled, Beau caught her and he watched as her hand went to her belly. "Aw, shit, sweetheart," he mumbled. Then he caught her with one arm around her waist, easing her further into the darkness of the barn. "First things first—you are *not* listening to whoever that son of a bitch is. Brannon hasn't been in touch—you know that. Now, come on. Let's get you somewhere safe."

Safe.

She wanted to laugh.

But she was too busy trying to concentrate on breathing.

He didn't go straight up to the house.

Brannon was following his gut and his gut told him that whoever was in that car would have taken the straightest route to safety. Why? Because they hadn't stayed in the car.

It was a cop and a trained paramedic, two people who knew all about what to do when there was a wreck. You stayed with the wreck unless you had no other choice.

So they would have gone for his property and the nearest building—the barns. The lights were off so he had to assume that the storm had kicked them out. Good.

That was just fine with him because he knew every inch of this place inside and out. He could find his way around blindfolded.

And he also knew that the door shouldn't be open.

His gut wrenched and he moved quicker, while every beat of his heart urged him to move even *faster*.

Hannah.

She was in there.

Hannah.

He slid inside and listened.

The echoes in here were crazy and when they came back magnified, it confused the hell out anybody who wasn't used to the acoustics in the old, remodeled barn.

But he was used to it.

And when the faint voice echoed ahead of him, he knew it wasn't because somebody was far away.

"I just want to get you to Brannon. He told me to get out here and find you. He couldn't get here in time. He was in town, with Moira. I was closer."

A silent snarl on his face, he moved through the barn, following the hall that had been constructed when they'd converted the wide open space into what he'd needed for the winery.

Lightning flashed through one of the windows and he saw a man's shadow.

Tall.

Lean.

Did he know the man?

The voice was familiar, but he couldn't place it. That didn't mean much, though. Put Brannon in a garage, blindfolded, and he could tell you what kind of engine a car had just by the sound of the engine. But he was shit when it came to voices, unless the person was somebody he loved.

So that just meant he didn't love this guy.

Great. It ain't Ian and it ain't Gideon. Nice to narrow the field, he thought sourly.

He edged closer, his back to the wall. He was coming up on the area where they barreled the Chambourcin. Loose boards, all the way around. Had to be careful.

"Hannah!"

When there wasn't any response, the man started to mutter, low, ugly noises.

That's right, you prick. My girl ain't an idiot.

The shadow shifted, spun back.

Brannon saw the shape in the man's hand just as he lifted it and he swore, realized he was fucked.

The asshole had a flashlight, a thin, narrowing stream of light shone on him in the darkness.

Fight or flight—

Brannon lunged, flinging himself toward the bright light. It was a beacon, the way he saw it. Of course, somebody who didn't know the twisting turns here would be lost without one.

"Surprise, you dumb fuck. I ain't in town."

The flashlight went flying as they tumbled to the ground and the bright beam flickered, then went off. Brannon caught a handful of hair as he drove somebody's skull into the rough brick ground. Some part of him was calm, rational, able to file away a few details. The man *had* hair and it was pretty damn attached. The man was *strong* and it was the wiry strength of a man in his prime. He filed that away even as a fist drove into his gut.

"What are you wanting Hannah for?" He drove a knee into somebody's balls, heard a groan.

It wasn't enough.

"Was it you?" he demanded.

No answer, save for an elbow right into his mouth. He spat blood and kept going.

"Are you the fucker who killed Shayla? Were you down there that night?"

"Get . . . off . . ."

The first words that had been spoken and it had Brannon snarling. "It was *you*." He slammed his forearm against a vulnerable throat, shoved.

The man started to pummel his ribs, but Brannon held tight.

"Let . . . me . . . up!"

"Ain't happening," Brannon said, grinning like a lunatic as he slowly choked the air out of the man beneath him. "You been chasing after my woman, you dumb shit. You messed with Hannah. I could kill you for that alone."

The struggles were getting weaker and weaker.

Off behind him, he heard a noise, but he ignored it.

"Get . . ."

The blackness had a different feel this time.

Desperation swam through him and flooded him with one final burst of strength.

Shoving a hand down, he clawed in his pocket.

He hadn't wanted to hurt her but he'd been prepared to do it. It would have bothered him, but he would do what must be done.

Duty dictated it.

Hurting Brannon wouldn't bother him.

He swung, the movement awkward and slow.

But Brannon was on top of him, practically laughing, gloating already.

The McKays had always been arrogant peacocks.

The knife went in like butter.

Brannon tensed, and then slumped.

He didn't fall off, not immediately.

But as the pressure on his throat lessened, he was able to shove Brannon's weight off and clamber to his feet.

He stumbled as his head cleared. Each second made it easier to see, to think.

Hand at his throat, he looked back, staring at the fucker on the floor. Blood spilled out of him. He could smell it. Smiling, he took a step—

"Freeze! Don't move!"

There was a loud, cracking noise—it echoed endlessly.

He dove to the side, tensed for the pain.

There was nothing.

Swearing, he began to back away, crabwalking on his feet and hands, eyes on the gloom in front of him. His hand smacked into the flashlight and he grabbed it, clutching it in a death grip and concentrated on putting as much distance between him and the people who could ruin everything.

Had they seen him?

He kept listening.

Kept waiting.

The only name he heard, though, was Brannon's.

"Brannon? Oh, shit, *Brannon*!"

The dim light made it almost impossible to see, but Hannah's eyes had adjusted somewhat and she sought out the solid figure that was Beau Shaw. "Call *9-1-1*."

"Already done it." He kept his weapon up in a two-fisted grip, sweeping the room.

"I need light!"

He didn't say anything, didn't give her a light.

She could have screamed as she covered the wound in Brannon's side. With nothing else to staunch the flow, she tore off her shirt and bound it to him. It was near the kidney. How close, she couldn't say without at least seeing him. But close. She sought out the notch of his hip, moved up, felt a sob burning in her, but she swallowed it down.

Another pain twisted her own belly.

No . . . I can't lose you. Can't lose either of you . . .

"I need a fucking light, Beau!" she shouted and the snarl in her voice got his attention. "That son of a bitch is gone. Whoever it was, he doesn't want us to see him and with three of us here, it's too hard to make sure that *none* of us—"

A wail of sirens cut through the air and she let herself hope.

"There. Back-up. Now give me a light." She shot him a look, hoped he could see better than her. "If he dies because you won't shine me a damn light . . ."

The cop gave a tired laugh as he came to stand at her back, eyes on the doorway. "Don't hurt me, Parker. Just doing my job." But he shone the light on Brannon.

She was hampered by the pain inside, hampered by the lack of equipment. The blood continued to pump. Beau's radio squawked. "Negative . . . can't come out to meet. Injured civilian . . . inside the southernmost barn. Be advised, at least one armed individual in the area."

She pressed her hands harder against the wound. It was already soaked through with blood. "Beau, I can't put enough pressure . . ." she gasped, swallowed the pain that seized her. "Can you please . . ."

Brannon made a low noise, then whispered her name.

"Hush," she said.

"Hannah," he muttered again.

She ignored him and snapped, "Beau, please!"

Two officers appeared in the doorway, their lights blinding them. Beau hunkered down beside her, his big hands covering hers. "Let me do it now. You just sit."

She sagged, cupping her belly.

"Hannah . . ."

"Talk to him," Beau said, his voice firm. "He needs it. You know that."

She nodded and reached for Brannon's hand.

"I wasn't . . . lyin'," he mumbled. "I . . ."

A huge breath shuddered out of him.

Paramedics came rushing in.

"Wasn't lying. Love . . . love you. Always did."

His head went slack, and fell to the side.

She screamed.

CHAPTER TWENTY-TWO

Brannon.

Brannon bleeding.

Brannon whispering that he loved her . . . then *dying* . . . .

She jerked upright and then moaned, cradling her belly.

"Easy there."

She rolled her head on the pillow and saw Ella Sue sitting in a chair next to her bed. Memory swarmed back and Hannah blinked back the tears. "The baby. Did I . . . I lost the baby, didn't I?"

"Oh, honey."

She started to sob.

"It's my fault. I was in the car, and Beau . . . he was saying stuff and he freaked me out . . ."

"Hush."

But she couldn't. She was crying, all but choking on the tears.

"Hannah, give me your hand."

Unable to fight, she let Ella Sue take her hand. But the woman wasn't in a coaxing, comforting mood. She guided Hannah's hand right to her belly. "Sweetheart, you haven't lost your baby."

Hannah's eyes flew wide and she turned her head, staring in stunned shock into the dark, calm eyes of the woman at the bedside. "But . . ."

"You were trying to go into labor," Ella Sue said calmly. "The paramedics got you here in time and Dr. Shaw stopped it. Beau told her what had happened and . . . goodness, honey. He feels terrible."

Tears stung her eyes and she looked away. "It wasn't his fault. I started remembering. And then somebody broke in and—hell, Ella Sue. I think I'm going crazy."

"You're not." Ella Sue's hand rested on Hannah's belly. "You're not going crazy. But you are going to have to take it easy."

The door swung open and Hannah turned her head, watched as Dr. Ellison Shaw came in.

The woman looked tired and strained and even her smile looked frayed around the edges, but when she saw that Hannah was awake, some of the tension in her shoulders eased. "Well, I thought I heard talking. I came up to check on you."

Hannah managed a weak smile. "I don't know why. I sort of made your husband wreck his car."

"Yeah." Ellison looked away. "He . . . well. He told me. I think he understands, Hannah. It's not like you haven't been through one hell of a time lately."

"Am I under arrest?" she asked.

Ellison laughed, but it was a weak echo of what it would have been. "I don't think so." She put her stethoscope on and listened to Hannah's chest and Hannah lapsed into silence for the exam.

"How is the baby?" She was almost afraid to ask, but she had to know.

There was another question she was afraid to ask . . . but that one, if she asked and . . .

She blinked back the tears and focused on the doctor's face, even as she tightened her grip on Ella Sue's hand. She hadn't even realized she was still holding it until that moment.

"Right now, she's holding her own." Then Ellison squeezed her mouth shut. "Shit, Hannah. I . . ."

Hannah started to laugh, the sound edging near desperate. "Dr. Shaw. Right now, the last thing I care about is you letting *he* or *she* slip. She's . . ." Hannah licked her lips. "She's okay?"

"Yes." The doctor gestured to the monitors that Hannah hadn't even noticed. "Look."

She fiddled with the monitors and a moment later, a quick, rapid sound filled the room.

A heartbeat.

A *baby*'s heartbeat.

"She's too little to have a good chance if she comes now," Ellison said, staring at the monitors. "So we stopped the labor. I'm going to keep you here for several days and when you're released, you will be on bedrest for a few weeks. If everything goes well . . ." She looked back at Hannah and smiled. "We'll reevaluate. You're just coming up on twenty-four weeks. The big thing now is to keep that baby inside you for as long as possible. If we can manage another six weeks, I'd be happy. Hell, I'm shooting for full-term, but you know how important it is from here on out. Every extra day helps. So . . . bedrest."

Hannah nodded. She cradled her belly and thought to the little girl inside. *I'm sorry . . . I'm so sorry . . .*

And when the doctor left, she turned her eyes toward Ella Sue.

Tears blurred her vision.

"Where's Brannon?" she asked.

* * *

"He died on the table." The surgeon met Gideon Marshall's eyes with a grim look of his own as he scrubbed off. "We brought him back, but do us both a favor and don't get in my face and demand to know when you can see him and interrogate him."

Died on the table—for a moment, Gideon heard nothing else. Then his brain clicked on and he was able to speak. "Okay, fuck the interrogation. Tell me how my friend is."

Neve and Moira were sitting in the family lounge, half-shell shocked and the surgeon hadn't yet talked to them.

He was on the way, but Gideon had badgered his way in because he'd seen the stark expressions on the faces of the nurses.

"He pulled through, okay?" Dr. Gil Barrett tugged off his cap and tossed it aside. He blew out a breath and lifted his face to the sky. "He lost so much blood and it was touch and go. Whoever stabbed him wanted him dead, there's no doubt of that."

Gideon just waited.

"But he's a stubborn bastard and he's always been healthy. Doesn't smoke, doesn't drink much. We stopped the bleeding, pumped him full of fluids. I think we salvaged the kidney. He *should* be okay." He stopped then. "He should. Now we just wait and see. Let me go talk to his sisters, okay? You can get out there and hold their hands."

He managed a tired smile. "Come to think of it, that's probably just as much why you're here as anything, isn't it?"

Gideon followed the doctor and waited by the door.

Revered Pratchett from First Methodist was sitting next to Moira, holding her small hand in his. Orville Pratchett was a big, rotund man, his beard snow white, his dark skin shiny and smooth, voice was gentle and soothing as he spoke to Moira. He looked every inch the man of the cloth, from his high clerical collar to the tips of his shiny black shoes, his Bible held in one hand. "In times like these, it's sometimes hard not to ask why . . ."

Pratchett lapsed into silence, a weary smile on his lips as he saw the doctor.

"Moira . . . Neve . . ."

Hannah stared at the blood pressure monitor, checked her pulse, everything.

Then she nodded at J.P. "Disconnect me."

He gave her a pained look.

"I have to see him."

It had been twenty-four hours since she'd been brought into the hospital.

She'd been given a detailed report of his surgery—including how he'd flatlined on the table—but she hadn't seen Brannon.

Nor would she, unless she took the initiative on her own.

They didn't want to move her because of her bedrest orders.

He couldn't be moved, because the hard-ass wouldn't wake up.

J.P. squinted at her and then just nodded. "Okay. But if you cost me my license, you're conning him into giving me some job on easy street. I can taste all the wines at his place for a thousand a week."

"Sure. I'll have him make sure some lush, leggy brunette brings you all the booze you could ask for, too."

"Now we're talking." J.P. shot a look at the door and went about setting her up for transport. He eyed the numbers as he worked. "Blood pressure is good. Pulse is fine. They said the baby looked good this morning, right?"

"Yes. I wouldn't be doing this otherwise."

He nodded, a quick, jerky move of his head and then he moved to the door, glanced out. "You're in luck. Two moms came in, both of them are about ready to pop, sounds like."

"That's such a professional description."

He grinned over his shoulder at her as he opened the door. He put the *no visitors please* sign up and then came for her. J.P. helped her into a wheelchair and they were out the door in ten seconds, pausing just long enough for him to shut the door. Luckily, Hannah's room was positioned just at the bend in the hall, so once they were around the corner, the nurses wouldn't see them. They just had to get—

"Made it," J.P. said, blowing out a breath as he hit the elevator button.

"Not this elevator." She pointed, glaring at him. "Go down the next hall and go left. Med-Surg unit. If anybody comes around . . ."

"Hannah . . ." He sounded pained. But he started pushing her chair.

It was fifteen minutes before he had her to Brannon's unit.

Hannah was already tired, but she was determined.

When Neve saw her, her eyes flew wide.

When the nurses at the station saw her, they came up as a unit.

"Get lost," she said to J.P. out of the corner of her mouth. Then she focused on Neve. "Get me in there. Please. Five minutes."

Neve glanced over at the nurses, already moving toward them.

Then she nodded.

The nurses—two of them—didn't move quite fast enough and Neve already had Hannah at Brannon's bedside.

"Family only, Hannah."

Hannah glanced at the nurse who'd spoken—she looked familiar, but she knew so many people from the hospital, she couldn't keep names straight. Hand on her belly, she stared at Brannon's lax face. "He is family. This little girl inside me proves that."

The two nurses exchanged a look. "Ah, well, it's not . . ."

Neve nudged her closer and murmured, "Talk to him. I'll deal with this."

"Don't cause too much trouble."

"Would I ever do that?"

Hannah laughed and reached out, resting her hand on Brannon's. Just that effort made her tremble.

"She can't be in here, Neve," The nurse's voice was sympathetic but firm. "You have to understand—"

"Here's the thing—I can think of two very good reasons why she belongs in here," Neve said pleasantly. "She's pregnant. Almost lost the baby—it's *Brannon's* baby. My brother hasn't woken up in more than twenty-four hours. She's his best bet. If anybody can get through to him? It's going to be her. So how about we just chill on the damn *family* bit and give her five minutes?"

"It's *policy*—"

"Five minutes," the other nurse said.

Hannah closed her eyes and squeezed Brannon's hand.

"Okay, pal. Positions are reversed. How did you wake me up last time?"

Neve bent over her and hugged her gently. Then she whispered, "He read you romance books."

Hannah laughed. It turned into a sob as the other woman left, giving them five minutes.

She came back the next day.

This time, it wasn't as easy to get out of her room

and J.P. wasn't there. But Ian and Neve came to spring her and when the nurses *loudly* advised against it, Ian flashed him his wicked grin and then gestured at the monitors. "She's supposed to stay calm and relaxed. If you really want her to be calm and relaxed, the best thing you could do would be to just let me wheel her bed *down* to him."

The doctor appeared in the doorway at that moment and studied them all. Then she sighed and called for a gurney.

So Hannah spent her five minutes talking to Brannon on a gurney.

"I don't have a romance book to read to you, dumb ass. Why can't you just wake up and tell me what it is you want me to read?" She waited and stared, watched his face as his eyelids flickered. "Come on, Brannon. I love you. Don't do this to me . . . to us . . ."

"Time's up, Hannah."

Dr. Shaw stood in the doorway. She was dressed sedately, in black slacks and a gray sweater, her eyes sad.

"But . . ."

Then she sighed and nodded.

When she went to pull her hand away, Brannon's fingers tightened on hers.

"'Nother minute," he mumbled.

Ellison straightened, her brows arching.

"Brannon," Hannah whispered.

"Stay." He rolled his head toward her and lifted his lids. But they drifted down again, almost immediately, like it was too much of an effort to hold them open. "Stay with me, Hannah."

"I don't see why we can't share a damn room."

Brannon was sitting in a wheelchair next to her bed, staring at the monitors.

It had been fifteen hours since he had opened his eyes.

He was weak.

He was pale.

He'd almost puked when they had moved him, but he had told the nursing staff they could either get him to Hannah or he'd fall on his face when he tried to crawl to her.

They took him at his word and contacted his surgeon.

The surgeon agreed. Brannon McKay would definitely fall on his face and try to crawl to Hannah, so it was best if they just took him to see her in a wheelchair.

Drained by the stress of the past few days, Hannah closed her eyes. "Because it's not the policy."

"It's stupid."

He was smirking. She could hear it in his voice.

"Maybe I should buy the hospital. Then do I get to write policy?"

"Not if it's stupid and ineffective. Your policy doesn't improve patient care, Brannon."

His hand squeezed her thigh. "Wrong. I can name five reasons why this would help. I'd feel better. You'd feel better. We'd leave the staff alone. They'd be happier. You'd be happier. I'd be happier."

"That's six." She rubbed her belly. "You better learn to count before your daughter gets here."

"My daughter . . ."

His hand joined hers.

"Yeah." She cracked open one eye and stared at him. "Your daughter."

Then she laced their fingers and murmured, "I'm tired."

"Rest, then." Brannon rubbed at her belly. "I'm here. You can rest."

CHAPTER TWENTY-THREE

Gideon went over the statement carefully and then passed it to Hannah.

She read it, feeling more than a little nauseated now.

Beau was in the room with her, along with Deatrick, one of the detectives. He'd been handling Shayla's murder.

Brannon was also in the room and he'd just heard how she'd intentionally wrecked the car, intentionally put her baby—their daughter—at risk.

She hadn't looked at him since she'd finished talking. She was afraid to.

Deathly afraid. But she couldn't put it off forever.

Tomorrow, both of them were being released from the hospital and the plan had been for them to go to McKay's Ferry and stay there for a few weeks, until Hannah was off bedrest and then they'd decide.

She thought maybe he'd ask her to move in with him.

She thought maybe she'd say yes.

But would he change his mind now?

"You're certain you have no idea who it was you saw in the woods?" Gideon asked softly.

"No." She looked down at her belly. It seemed to get bigger and bigger each day and she was very happy with that fact. Bigger meant the baby was still growing. Bigger was *good*. It had been four days since the events out at Brannon's and every day put their daughter closer to survival.

She thought back to the shadow she'd seen inside the dark, dreary halls of the converted barn, tried to recall the voice. "I've heard him," she said softly. "I know I've seen him, talked to him. But I don't know who he is."

"Okay." Gideon blew out a sigh and then met Beau's gaze. They shared a look and then Deatrick took a step forward.

"I have a source—works for the paper in Baton Rouge. I'm going to let some information slip. We need the killer to know you don't know who he is, Hannah, or you're not going to be safe. But we can't exactly have you on the evening news." He shrugged, a wry smile lighting his narrow, dark features. "People would all assume you were just saying that. I would. You probably would. A source makes it a little different. I'll spin it, make sure my man knows how frustrated we are by your returned memory and how little it helps us."

He paused, giving her a minute to process. "Do you understand what we're talking about?"

"Yeah." She nodded. "It may not work, though. He might assume you all are lying, trying to flush him out."

"True." Deatrick shrugged. "But then again, if it's somebody you know, somebody you've seen, once he realizes you *have* remembered and that we haven't come looking for him, he'll figure it out. This man isn't an idiot. He waited, bided his time. That's why when I plant my story, I'm going to make sure there are some details from your statement."

She sucked in a breath. "Oh. Oh, I see."

"Everything is accurate, correct?"

"Yeah." She gave him a feeble smile. "I was out running,

trying to convince myself how easy it would be to stop
thinking about Brannon, to just . . . forget about him."

He stroked his hand down her hair.

That light touch made her relax.

"Well, you did forget," he murmured, picking up her
hand and bringing it to his lips.

She laughed.

Then she started to cry.

She was still crying several minutes later when she realized everybody had left but Brannon.

He lowered the bedrail, easing as close as he could
without climbing onto the bed with her and then he said,
"Hannah, baby, you're killing me and I can't come up
there. Please stop."

"I could have killed our baby," she said, sobbing.

"You thought you were in danger—both of you."

She just shook her head. "I was stupid."

"No." Brannon cupped her cheek. "Look at me . . .
come on, Hannah. Look at me."

She sniffed. Swallowed. Blinked at him as he reached
up to brush her hair back from her face.

"Hannah, honey." He stood up, wincing, grimacing as
he pivoted his weight around. He was in a pair of sweats
and a t-shirt. He wouldn't wear the t-shirt if he didn't
have to but she'd seen too many eyes sliding over his bare
chest and she'd told him to stop distracting the nurses.
So he wore the t-shirt.

She was wearing a blue silk nightgown he'd told
Moira to find for her. It was slippery and smooth and
beautiful, out of place in the hospital room, but his
eyes had lit up when he'd seen it on her, so she wore it.
Tomorrow, she'd wear the green. No, tomorrow, she was
going home. Maybe tomorrow night, she'd wear the
green.

He eased his weight down on the bed. She squirmed a little.

"Be still." He tapped her nose. "Bedrest."

"I can move," she muttered, sulking.

"Be still." Then he leaned in and pressed his brow to hers. "The day you came over to our house, the first day I really noticed you. Your knuckles were busted and bruised. Neve asked you why. You remember?"

She swallowed.

"Your stepdad had been drunk again. Knocking your mother around. You made him mad and when he tried to hit you, he didn't move fast enough. Then you hit him. You told Neve it was the most fun you'd had all day."

She managed to smile a little. "It was fun. All I did was pop him in the nose. He fell and passed out. Too much whiskey. He had one hell of a black eye that next day though."

"Everybody else in town just ignored what he did to your mother. You stood up, right in his face. He could have hurt you so bad, but you never backed down."

"He was a coward," she said, her throat tight. Then she curled an arm around his neck.

"I started to fall in love with you a little that day. Tough, strong Hannah . . . my Hannah." He rested a hand on her belly. "You did what you did to save yourself. Save her. No, it wasn't Beau. But it could have been. I'm not angry that you followed your instincts. Because what if it *had* been him . . . and you had done nothing?"

Tears burned her eyes.

"I thought you'd hate me."

"I never could." He hooked an arm around her neck and pressed a kiss to her neck. "I love you, Hannah. I just took a damn long time to figure it out."

"Too long," she said, her voice watery.

"Too long."

He stood in the trees, staring up at the house.

The falling twilight painted it in shades of gold and orange, reflected off the windows. The water of the pool danced, cerulean in the darkening light.

It was a place of legend, a place of beauty.

And it should be *his*.

Hand fisted, he fought the rage that threatened to overwhelm him.

The fucking McKays.

He had tried to play nice, but he was rather done with that now.

The door opened, a final ray of sunlight falling on the gleaming red hair of the eldest McKay as she walked onto the deck and stood there, staring out over the expanse of green that rolled around her.

Studying her domain.

Her shoulders slumped and he watched as she lifted her hands to her face and began to cry.

Poor little princess, he thought, disgusted.

Life is hard on you now, is it?

A brother in the hospital. How stressful that must be.

He could teach her a thing or two about stress.

Poor, poor little Moira.

Something moved behind him and he stiffened, looked up. He wasn't alone in these woods. Slowly, he shifted into the trees and lost himself into the shadows.

It wouldn't do to be seen skulking about, he supposed. He wouldn't hide much longer though.

Moira looked up, startled, as Charles settled into the chair across from her.

He held out a white handkerchief.

"What are you doing here?"

He gave her a sad smile.

"Waiting for you, love." He nodded toward the path. "I was out walking. Nobody answered the door when I first arrived, so I parked near the garage and just wandered around. Ella Sue at the hospital?"

"No." Moira shrugged. Dabbing at her eyes, she wiped the tears away. "She was. We rode into together. She dropped me off. Guess that's why I didn't see your car. Neve's with Ian."

He nodded. "I . . ." Charles stopped and slumped in his chair, staring up at the star-studded sky. "I've well and truly messed things up with you, Moira. Not just you, but with your family. You almost died. Your sister almost died. And now Brannon and his lady. And I haven't been there for you."

"We're not together anymore, Charles." She swallowed the knot in her throat. She didn't *have* a together. How many times had she wanted to reach out, to call somebody? To have a man's arms around her in the night? But it wasn't Charles' arms she wanted. It wasn't him she longed to have holding her. She managed a smile. "You don't have to be there for me."

"But I want to be."

He stared at her, his blue eyes penetrating, deep. Searching.

When he stood and came to sit beside her, she looked away. "Moira, I miss you."

She said nothing.

Shoulder braced against a tree, Gideon remained where he was.

He'd been prowling around, trying to work up the nerve to go to the house. To Moira.

Actually, that was wrong.

What he was trying to do was go to her and tell her good-bye.

That he was done.

That he couldn't love her anymore only to have her push him away, hold him at arm's length.

He'd heard trees rustling, thought maybe somebody else had been out there. He'd debated on taking a look, finding out. Almost did just that, but then he saw Moira. And when she started to cry, he had been frozen.

If he went to her now, he'd lose his resolve, all over again.

The love he had for her was like a cancer, tearing away at him and destroying him. If she'd just let herself love him back, it would be the cure—the cure they *both* needed.

He turned to go.

Even managed to take a step.

But because he was always weakest when it came to her, he turned back.

That was when he saw Charles moving toward her.

Charles.

Lip curled, Gideon watched him. Wondered for a split second if it had been Charles out lurking in the trees, but then he brushed the possibility off. The man was like a toddler in the trees, thrashing about and crashing into everything.

Besides, he didn't have any reason to skulk in the dark to moon on Moira. He'd always done that right in the open.

"Unlike me," Gideon muttered, disgusted.

He turned on his heel and strode off.

As he did, he punched in a number.

He had reports to write. He had a murder to solve.

But damn it, he was going to have a drink.

And tonight, he was going to have a drink with a beautiful woman.

"Hello?"

"May I speak to Maris Cordell?"

"Speaking." There was a faint pause and then she said softly, "Would this be the chief of police by any chance?"

"It would."

"Hmmm . . . you know, I have my cell phone down for official communications," she said lightly. "So why are you calling me at home?"

"Because I'm calling to see if you'd like to have a drink with me sometime."

Maris laughed. It was a pretty laugh, light and free and easy. Not the low and sexy purr of Moira, but still pretty. *Don't*, he told himself. *Don't hold her up to Moira. Let her be Maris.*

"I'd love to have a drink with you, chief. When were you thinking?"

"Tonight. You free?"

"I can carry you in." Ian's face was straight, eyes serious. "I can, really. You sure you should walk?"

Hannah glared at him.

Ian rubbed the flat of his hand along his scalp and looked over at Neve. "I'm just tryin' to help. Babies make me nervous."

"Hannah's fine," Neve said, patting his arm. "I'm more worried about Brannon."

Brannon was pale, sweat beading on his brow and upper lip. He looked at the sidewalk that stretched out like a river between him and the front door then he scowled at Gideon. "You could have parked closer."

"Unless you wanted me to park on your porch, I wasn't getting closer. Quit your bitching and move." Gideon gave him a lazy, relaxed smile.

That lazy, relaxed smile made Brannon want to punch him.

Grimacing, he took a few steps toward the house and stopped.

Hannah was already up the stairs and waiting for him. "Need a wheelchair?" She smiled at him, eyes dancing with laughter.

"Smart ass. Keep it up and I won't let you have your present."

She rolled her eyes. "You won't do that. You like giving me presents. I think you're addicted."

"Damn straight." He moved a few more feet, mostly because the railing that led up the rest of the way was a few feet away and it looked like heaven. Felt like it too, having something take his weight.

"Maybe I should have volunteered to carry *you*," Ian said, laughter lurking in his voice as he jogged up the steps, arms laden with bags.

Most of them were shopping bags, full of the new clothes Brannon had asked Neve and Moira to get for Hannah.

He was just being helpful, the way he saw it. Gideon had said most of her wardrobe had been trashed.

Grim purpose gripped him as he eyed the back of Hannah's head. Trashed and ruined, along with a message.

The story about how she'd regained her memory, about how she'd seen a murder but had no idea who she'd seen kill Shayla Hardee, that was the big story hitting the regional media today. They'd held it until she could be discharged.

Hopefully, she'd be safe now.

But Brannon was going to make damn sure they found whoever had tried to hurt her in that barn.

Who'd tried to gut him like a fish.

"Come on, Bran," Neve said. "A few more steps."

"I can walk, you morons," he muttered. He could also

puke, and he thought he might. Why the hell was he so weak?

It took a ridiculous ten minutes to shuffle into the living room and he would have fallen into the chair, but Gideon and Ian caught his arms, helped him ease his weight down. "No flopping around for a while, Bran," Gideon said, rapping him on the head with his knuckles.

Brannon flipped him off.

Casually, Gideon looked around. "Where's Moira?"

"Getting stuff for dinner tonight with Ella Sue." Neve hovered over Hannah, who was already glowering. "You sure you're comfortable on the couch?"

"Give me a pillow," Hannah said after a moment of quiet.

Neve did. Then she dodged as Hannah threw it at her.

"I'm fine," she said. Then she scowled. "Although you're awful far away, Brannon."

He grunted. "Get me an hour to recover, then I'll move."

He breathed in. Then out. Gave himself three minutes while they all chatted and then heaved himself up. He really was too far away.

Hannah shook her head as he sank down next to her on the couch. She'd taken the end with the reclining chair and had her feet up. He stretched out and put his head in her lap. That felt just about perfect. Especially once she started stroking his hair. Breathing out a sight of satisfaction, he smiled up at her. "Now I'm fine."

"So glad to know."

Gideon's voice caught his attention and he slanted his gaze toward the man standing near the door.

"How was your date?" he asked.

It must have been the pain pills. Brannon wouldn't have asked that in a thousand years if he hadn't been strung out on pain and still loopy from the meds they'd given him before he left. Granted, when the nurse had mentioned it, he'd been damn well aggravated, but he hadn't meant to *say* anything.

The room went quiet.

Slowly, Gideon shifted his gaze to him.

Neve blinked. "What date?"

Ian was staring intently at the bags he'd lined up along the wall. "Neve, why don't you help with these, darlin'? Show me where they go?"

"What date?" Neve asked, mystified. "You weren't out with Moira. She was . . . oh."

She turned to the bags, grabbed some blindly. "Come on, Ian. I'll show you where these two lovebirds are staying."

When she went to shove past Gideon, he caught her arm. "Neve, sweetheart . . ."

"Don't." Her voice was hoarse. She shook her head. "I get it, okay? You deserve to be happy and I know that and all she does is push people away. But . . ." She sniffled. "Moira should be happy, too, shouldn't she?"

"If she'd let me make her happy, Trouble, I'd do it in a heartbeat." Gideon sighed and looked away. "But she doesn't want to be happy. Not with me anyway."

Moira stood in the hall.

Eyes closed, tears burning, she regulated her breathing and didn't let herself move.

They'd made it back quicker than they'd planned but Ella Sue had rushed back out because she'd forgotten something.

Something important, she'd claimed.

So she'd left Moira there to put up the groceries.

If Moira had just moved her ass when she heard Gideon's voice, she could have avoided this.

But no . . .

Slowly, she moved back into the kitchen, swiped at the tears on her face.

So he'd gone on a date.

He was done waiting.

She understood.

She'd been waiting for that, really.

But still . . . it hurt.

A sob welled up in her throat, tried to choke her, but she wouldn't let it. She forced herself under control and then grabbed her iPhone, a pair of earbuds, jammed them in. She dribbled water on a paper towel to dab at her eyes.

She waited another moment and then moved out into the hallway, smiling when she saw Ian.

"You're back. Ella Sue?" Ian's teeth flashed white in his beard.

Moira shook her head. "She had to run back out. Are they already here?"

Ian nodded, although his eyes were . . . sad. When she passed by him, he caught her in a quick hug. He said nothing and she forced herself to give him a curious look.

For a moment, she thought he'd say something. But then he just shook his head. "Come on, then. Ready to hassle your brother?"

"It's a sister's job." They walked together into the large, cheerful room where everybody waited. Light shown in brilliantly, but for her, everything seemed dull, dark, and lifeless.

Her gaze landed on Gideon. He gave her a short nod, but that was it. Unlike the way he'd always looked at her, the way she'd always *expected* him to look at her, she realized.

She gave him a casual smile as she told herself, *Show time*.

CHAPTER TWENTY-FOUR

To a McKay, family is all.

Family is everything.

Brannon sat with Hannah at his side and his family around them. Moira was at the head and he wondered what she thought it meant that Ella Sue continued to seat Gideon at the foot, across from her.

Of course, if Moira—or Ella Sue—knew that Gideon had spent the better part of last night traipsing around town with Deputy Maris Cordell, then Moira would shut down and Ella Sue just might upend the soup tureen over the man's head.

He then wondered if that might count as assaulting a police officer. Not that Gideon would ever charge Ella Sue for attacking him with a big bucket of soup. He loved the woman too much.

Distracted, he glanced around the table.

Everybody was there.

But not everybody was sitting.

Ella Sue was still bustling around and he tried to catch her eye.

He was already worn out. Not that it took much. He

eased a little higher in the chair and slid Hannah what he hoped was a casual glance. She had her glass of water in her hand and smiled at him as she took a sip.

He wished they could do champagne. But it wasn't fair to her, so he wasn't having any if she couldn't.

After. Once the baby was born.

If she said—

"I was going to wait for this," Ian said abruptly, standing up from his chair.

Ella Sue appeared in the doorway, her brows arching high over her eyes.

Everybody else was looking at Ian.

And then grinning as Ian went to one knee in front of Neve.

"Hey!" Brannon snapped. Then he had to stop.

Ella Sue clapped a hand over her mouth, a laugh escaping.

Ian glared at him. "Do you mind?"

"Actually, I do." He would have slumped in his chair or gotten up to kick Ian's ass, if he could have.

But he didn't have the energy, or even the strength, for that, so he sat and brooded.

When Hannah glanced at him, he managed a weak smile.

Ella Sue continued to laugh.

"Neve." Ian stared at her as though she had hung the stars in his universe, teeth flashing in his beard.

She had a hand pressed to her lips. Her right hand, because Ian had her left hand.

"You're my heart, Neve," he said simply. "Say you'll be my wife."

Her response was to fling her arms around his neck and start kissing him.

"Is that a yes?" Gideon asked.

"It better be," Brannon muttered.

Hannah smacked at his knee. "Oh, hush. Quit being so grumpy."

"I got good reason."

Ella Sue had finally stopped laughing, leaning against the door. "Hannah, honey, give the man a break."

Then she slid her eyes over to Brannon expectantly.

"I shouldn't do this now," he said sourly. "He ruined it."

All of a sudden, every eye in the place, Neve's and Ian's included, were on him.

Hannah looked startled as he shifted around and caught her hand. "I can't get down on bended knee," he said softly. "If I do, they'll have to pick me back up. But I've got this . . . and unlike that ass, I *was* planning to do this. Here's my proof."

He flipped open a box.

The box, other than a quick check that afternoon—from him and from Ella Sue—had remained closed for twenty years, closed, and sealed, tucked away in a vault inside the bank in town.

Hannah sucked in a breath, startled.

"This was my mother's," he said softly. "My father gave it to her. And before that, my grandfather gave it to my grandmother. The diamond has been in the family for generations . . . since Patrick McKay had it set in a ring and gave it to his bride Madeleine and brought her here from New York."

Hannah slowly lifted her eyes to his. "Brannon . . ."

"It always goes to the oldest son, for him to give to his wife. As the only son . . ." He cleared his throat. "Hannah, will you marry me?"

He couldn't go to his knees. So Hannah climbed into his lap, gingerly, taking care not to bump into him as she wrapped her arms around him. "That better be a yes," he said into her ear.

"Yes, you big idiot," she said, a husky sob tripping her up halfway through. "It's a yes."

"Then let me put on the ring."

She clung to him another moment and then straightened up, watching as he slid the old, elegant band into place. The diamond, almost as large as her pinkie nail, gleamed up at her, set in a band of platinum. It was elegant and genteel and beautiful.

"You can get a new setting. My mom did. That's—"

"I love it." She leaned in and kissed him. "I absolutely love it."

He buried his face in her hair.

She laughed, a shaky, nervous sound. "This is seriously as old as the town?"

"Yes." The answer came from Moira and Hannah looked up, saw the woman she would soon be able to call sister.

Moira pulled something out from under her shirt. "We all have something—by tradition. The locket goes to the oldest daughter. Neve has a ring. That goes to the youngest child. If there are middle children there are other pieces, too. They stay in the vault otherwise, although any of us can use them. But these pieces are the main ones, the wedding ring, the locket, and the emerald that Neve has."

"I don't wear mine," Neve said, her voice husky. She smiled a little. "I'll wear it at my wedding. But that one *is* still in the original setting and it's pretty delicate."

Hannah rested her brow against Brannon's. "Wow. We're really doing this."

"Damn straight. You said yes. You can't back out now."

She laughed and then, grinning, she shot Neve a look. "Maybe we should have a double wedding."

"Ohhhh . . ." Neve started to grin.

"Hell, no," Brannon said. He glared at Ian. "The man already stole my thunder, popping the question when I had everything planned for this."

"Nobody could ever steal your thunder, baby." Hannah curled an arm around his neck and relaxed against his chest.

Around them, conversation started to rise and fall, but they were caught up in their own little world.

Brannon placed his hand on her belly just as the baby kicked.

He jumped, looking up at her.

She guided his hand back, held it in place.

"I think she approves," Hannah said softly.

"That's good. Because I don't plan on going anywhere."

Read on for an excerpt from the next book by
SHILOH WALKER

The Right Kind of Trouble

Coming soon from St. Martin's Paperbacks

Gideon cupped her chin, lifting her face to his.

She swallowed and the pull of his eyes was so intoxicating, she almost forgot to notice the pain in her throat.

"Don't cry." He moved in closer, hips angling in slightly, shoulders rounding as he drew nearer to her. She felt surrounded by him, but it wasn't enough. "Please don't cry. You gut me when you do. You know that."

Shaking her head, she reached for his waist, kneading the taut muscle there. She didn't know if she was telling him she wasn't going to cry or what. But the tears continued to burn and she wanted nothing more than to curl herself around him and cling tight.

If she clung to him tight enough, he could never leave. The scent of him started to go to her head, the rasp of his fingers sending shivers through her as he slid one hand around her neck to stroke her skin.

She caught one wrist in her hand, bringing his hand to her cheek.

Gideon had gone rigid and he didn't move at all when she pressed her mouth to his palm.

She didn't let it stop her.

She'd known he hadn't brought her up here with any

intention other than to make her rest. Gideon, ever her protector.

She didn't want *protection*, though. She just wanted him. She wanted what she'd been throwing away all these years and she wanted him back for always. After she'd pressed a kiss to his palm, she nudged him back. His eyes glittered, his cheekbones standing out in stark relief against his deeply tanned skin. He was all hollows and angles and long lean lines. He'd always been able to stop her breath and the rugged masculinity of him had become even more refined over the past few years.

She caught his face and tugged.

He resisted for a minute and she was almost certain he'd pulled away.

So she rose onto her toes and pressed her lips to his chin, slid them down. When she got to his neck, his head fell to the side—slightly. It was enough. His skin was salty and warm and she could have happily spent the next few hours doing nothing but learning the taste of him all over again. She found the rapid beat of his pulse with her tongue—then her teeth.

"*Fuck!*" Gideon's snarl was vicious and he tangled his hand in her hair.

She found herself trapped in the next moment, between his long, rangy body and nearest column of her poster bed. Her breath stuttered out of her as he boosted her up, shoving his hips into the cradle of hers. "Don't," he said, his breath coming out in ragged pants. His eyes burned as he stared at her. "You aren't jerking me around like this again, Moira. If you don't mean this . . . if you . . ."

He stopped and looked away and she saw his jaw clenching, his Adam's apple bobbing. The emotion coming out of him battered at her and she wanted to draw him close, stroke away all the misery. But she'd caused this. She'd done this. Could she even *begin* to fix all the pain she'd brought him?

"If you're just going to walk away again, Moira . . . don't."

He put her down and started to pace. Moira wanted to go to him, but what was she supposed to do? Pantomime what she was feeling? She'd already tried to *show* him and that wasn't working.

A muttered curse caught her ears and she looked up just as he spun to face her, rage written all over his normally calm features. "You're killing me inside, okay? You're . . ."

Then he stopped, his cheeks puffing out as he blew out a slow breath. He drew in a deeper, slower one, holding it for a few seconds. She opened her mouth, but he lifted a hand.

He wasn't asking her, though. The question was directed inward.

"Look, you can't even talk," he said, still not facing her. "You can't explain what's going on and I can't see inside your head. I don't know what you want—"

She reached for the buttons on her shirt. He'd never leave without looking back at her one last time.

She didn't think.

But then again, she'd messed up something awful.

Maybe this wasn't the right way to tell him, but there were a hundred *wrong* ways to let him leave. And that was without trying again. Without reaching out, the way he'd done a hundred times.

She shrugged out of her shirt while he was still standing there. Her bra fell away next.

"When you're feeling better, we'll have to talk any . . . Moira."

She looked at him through the fringe of her hair. He'd turned around.

She found no pleasure in knowing she'd been right. She was manipulating him and she hated herself, but if this would keep him here, with her, a little longer, until she could convince him she was tired of running, tired of pushing him away?

Then she was going for it.

When she reached for the button of her jeans, her fingers shook.

Gideon was staring at her, his chest rising and falling in a harsh rhythm. She thought maybe that if she reached out just then, he might have turned and walked out. So she just pushed her jeans down her thighs, along with her panties.

Naked now, she stood there waiting. She figured this was best. If he turned around rejected her while she was naked, vulnerable, maybe it would even the scales.

The old wooden boards of the floor creaked a little as he took one step, then another toward her. She licked her lips, hardly daring to breathe.

"And what about tomorrow, Mac?" he asked. "You going to push me away . . . *again*?"

She saw the answer he thought to be true in his eyes.

Slowly, she shook her head.

"Mac?"

She held out her hand.

For the longest time, he didn't move.

Then he did—toward her.

In the time it took for her to take a deep breath—whether it was to blow out in relief or to brace herself, she didn't know—Gideon had hauled her up against him and she found herself pressed against the wall.

She went to kiss his neck, but he tangled a hand in her hair and yanked, forcing her gaze to meet his. So she stood there, trembling and barely able to think past the want while he tore at the zipper of his jeans.

He let go of her hair but only so he could pick her up and brace her against the wall at her back. A moment later, he came inside her, hard and forceful and the screams trapped inside her lungs seemed to explode throughout her entire body instead. She could *feel* that scream—it had a taste, a rhythm, a need all its own and it belonged solely to the man who held her pinned to the wall.